The Education of Kia Greer

Alanna Bennett

The Education of Kia Greer

ALFRED A. KNOPF · NEW YORK

A Borzoi Book published by Alfred A. Knopf
An imprint of Random House Children's Books
A division of Penguin Random House LLC
1745 Broadway, New York, NY 10019
penguinrandomhouse.com
rhcbooks.com

Editor: Katherine Harrison
Cover Designer: Liz Dresner
Interior Designer: Cathy Bobak
Production Editor: Melinda Ackell
Managing Editor: Jake Eldred
Production Manager: Liz Sutton

Library of Congress Cataloging-in-Publication Data
Names: Bennett, Alanna, author.
Title: The education of Kia Greer / Alanna Bennett.
Description: First edition. | New York : Alfred A. Knopf, 2025. | Audience: Ages 14 and up. |
Summary: Sixteen-year-old Kia, the teenage daughter of a reality TV family, struggles to
experience normal teenage life, and when a fake PR relationship begins to turn real, she
must confront who she truly is and what she wants for herself.
Identifiers: LCCN 2024049015 (print) | LCCN 2024049016 (ebook) |
ISBN 978-0-593-80610-4 (hardcover) | ISBN 978-0-593-80612-8 (ebook)
Subjects: CYAC: Fame—Fiction. | Family life—Fiction. | Self-actualization—Fiction. |
Romance stories. | LCGFT: Romance fiction. | Novels.
Classification: LCC PZ7.1.B45374 Ed 2025 (print) | LCC PZ7.1.B45374 (ebook) |
DDC [Fic]—dc23

The text of this book is set in 10.8-point Warnock Pro Regular.

Manufactured in the United States of America
10 9 8 7 6 5 4 3 2 1

The authorized representative in the EU for product safety and compliance is
Penguin Random House Ireland, Morrison Chambers, 32 Nassau Street,
Dublin D02 YH68, Ireland, https://eu-contact.penguin.ie.

Every reasonable effort has been made to supply complete and correct credits; if there are
errors or omissions, please contact Penguin Random House so that corrections can be
addressed in any subsequent printings.

Random House Children's Books supports the First Amendment
and celebrates the right to read.

For Justin Casselle, who gave me orange blossoms.
But mostly for my seventeen-year-old self, who was
so afraid but so excited for the life ahead.
I think you did good, kid.

There are many Beths in the world, shy and quiet,
sitting in corners till needed,
and living for others so cheerfully
that no one sees the sacrifices
till the little cricket on the hearth stops chirping,
and the sweet, sunshiny presence vanishes,
leaving silence and shadow behind.

—Louisa May Alcott, *Little Women*

PROLOGUE

On the morning of my sixteenth birthday, I woke with one singular purpose in mind. It was still dark when I wiped the crust from my eyes, tiptoed down the cold stone hallway, and shook my little sister in her bed. Her eyes shot open like she'd woken from a nightmare, but they softened when they saw me. Then they rolled.

"You are so corny," Lark said. But she was smiling as she threw the covers back and joined me, just like I knew she would.

The halls were lined with flowers and gifts from corporate partners, friends, and family. Birthday offerings that were less about me and more about the ever-growing number of people who wanted a piece of our family's growing empire. But this morning was not about them.

This was our time, these hours before the noise.

I spread my arms and walked backward, waggling my eyebrows at Lark like, *See? We're getting away with it.*

"Stop!" she said. "You look like Dad when you do that."

I promptly tripped on a stray gift, landing with a *thud* on the ground. Lifting myself from the floor, I saw a new gaming console wrapped in a giant pink bow. Lark grabbed my arm and pulled me out of the living room before the sound stirred anyone awake. Her eyes were alight.

The gifts were well and good, but they didn't really feel like mine. This, though. This did.

Our mother's spare keys were easy to find, stashed in a back corner cabinet of the garage. They hung with all the keys to the family fleet, easily accessible to any assistant tasked with a monthly detailing or with making sure the AC sat *just right* when my mother slid in on a hot day.

Mom had forgotten about the variable of teenage mischief. Why wouldn't she? Lark and I were subdued little dweebs compared to her other children. We were the ones in bed by ten of our own volition. We thought a Friday night mainlining old movies with Dad was the height of luxury. My older sisters, the grown ones, Sola and Destiny, had fueled ten seasons of a reality show with wild fights, bared bodies, and unexpected tears. They'd been the ones to make off with her keys, to drive our mother's fleet of expensive vehicles to parties in the sketchy part of the Valley, to be arrested for indecent exposure, get DUIs, and come back with infected belly button piercings, tattoos on their lower back, a surprise new husband (Sola), or a baby (Destiny).

Lark and I, though, were not to be counted out. What my mother hadn't taken into account was *the itch*. I hadn't slept well through most of fifteen, and my last night of it had been no different. I'd tossed and turned, restless, my covers winding round my feet until in my dreams I was a creature of the ocean gasping against the air, suffocating, caught in a fishing net.

Finally dawn hit. Orange light had crept through my window, and I'd thrown the sheets aside. The chilled air of a California morning hit my skin, and for once in my life I knew exactly what I wanted to happen.

There was none of the waffling that usually held me up. No

knot in my chest or foreboding roil in my stomach. I was steady, strong. Bold. I did what I needed to do.

Now I walked up and down the aisles, scanning the thick vehicle covers and shined rims peeking out beneath. I wasn't in search of just any car. Only one would do. It had been in one of the old movies both Dad and Mom loved dearly, the one in which two women drove off in this car, desperately needing a break from their dreary lives. In that movie this car was air, this car was freedom, this car was the place where two women could choose who they most wanted to be. It's why my mother had wanted it so badly.

It's also why I needed it on this early, clandestine morning.

And there it was. Tucked in a far-back corner, behind the trio of Mokes reserved for hot summer days. The one I wanted was covered by a light layer of customized cream fleece. With one pull it fluttered off like a breeze, and she was in front of me: a 1966 Thunderbird, robin's-egg blue and gleaming. Our father'd bought it at auction for Mom's fortieth, the exact one from the movie. Neither Lark nor I had ever been allowed to touch it without her there.

My hands shook as I fumbled with the key. It hit me just then: My first time breaking the rules would be grand theft auto.

"Damn, Kee, get on with it," Lark breathed from the passenger seat. My driver's test was still weeks away, but I'd been practicing enough with our nanny, Miss Carol, that I knew I could get us to our destination safely. I just had to keep my wits together.

Lark's nerves egged me on. A huff of hysterical giggle escaped me, but finally the car let out a mighty groan. It ignited, and something within me did, too.

As the rubber of old tires hit the freeway, Lark and I whooped and hollered. The clear spring sky felt brand-new. We were *gone.*

We breezed through the winding Santa Monica Mountains, hands outstretched as if to touch all the brush and boulders and valleys of unspoiled green. As I navigated the car around curve after curve, my nerves melted away. We kept driving. Past Carbon, past Zuma, past everywhere we'd been a thousand times, past everywhere we knew there'd be eyes on us. We didn't stop until empty road gave way to a beach we'd never heard of.

This place had the aura of a glitch. A stretch of sand and dune and rolling rock tucked away from the highway, it felt like the kind of place that might disappear the second we turned away. It was perfect for us.

Hours passed, somehow. That was the best part. We'd left our phones at home, afraid we'd be too easily tracked. Lark had scrawled a note to our parents and nanny on a grocery receipt: *No, we haven't been kidnapped. Yes, we'll be back and dressed in time for the party. Yes, we know we're grounded, but also you should be nice to Kia—it's her birthday!*

We were unreachable in our own pocket universe. There's a kind of scream only possible when you're entirely alone, unencumbered by societal expectations of propriety. The ocean pulled echoing cackles and cascading howls from us that day, the weight of its waves tossing us in every direction. By hour two, the only other person we'd seen was an elderly man sitting at the far south side of the cove with a fishing pole and a book. He rarely looked in our direction. I wasn't worried even when he did; he didn't seem like our family's key demographic. Like he'd rat us out to the paparazzi. Besides, I liked his wrinkles. They were set deep into his skin like etchings in a cave. They made me want to hear his stories. My mind flooded with questions: What had this man seen? Who had he loved? What did he do with his days when he wasn't fishing? Did he struggle paying rent, or did he own a two-bedroom ranch house that was his pride and joy? Was he far from where he'd grown up? Or, like me, did he always feel, on this stretch of California coast, like he was just down the street?

But Lark and I kept to ourselves. Much as he intrigued me, I didn't want to be proven wrong. Too many people already felt ownership over my sisters and me. Now, especially as we got older, that translated into prying eyes, too-familiar hands, and probing questions about whether we'd yet kissed our first boys. This was not the day for that. I would let nothing spoil this day.

We'd packed tote bags full of sunscreen and contraband snacks. Mostly we danced across the sand, grunting and making faces, laughing while we acted out a fight Sola and Destiny had gotten into the night before. Cameras had been rolling, and Destiny was sure Sola had gone behind her back to steal a cover story from her. Our imitations were weak, but we laughed through them, exaggerating huffs and kicking up sand.

We splashed into the waves, past the invisible line where the adults in charge usually stopped us from venturing. Lark did handstands in the water, feet flailing in the air with such abandon, I had to dodge her halos of salt water. I caught her as she tumbled back down, waves unseating her balance. In turn, she stopped me going too far into the rocky areas, from being swept onto jagged edges as I craned to get a good look at the anemones and starfish nestled into tide pools.

"That's their house!" Lark shrieked, laughing, tugging me back to sand. "You don't like it when people peer into your windows uninvited—why would they?"

"But is it their home, do you think?" I asked, taking in the crest of a wave in the distance. "Or did the water just wash them here one day, and they can't get back?"

"Jeez. Why are you so dramatic?"

5

I kicked salt water and sand and seaweed at her. "Think about it! How would you feel if one day you're a Catalina starfish, and then suddenly there's a storm, and a wave almost blows you into the mouth of a passing shark! You black out with fear, but you survive, and next thing you know, you're lost. You're a Malibu starfish now."

"Sounds like a good deal to me, missing them shark teeth."

"You're missing my point."

Lark was done with me. She sprinted into the surf, scream-singing "Part of Your World" from *The Little Mermaid* at the top of her lungs, and the conversation was over.

We went on like this. Minutes, hours. The old fishing guy left. We watched as the sand absorbed the waves: gallons of water gone just before our eyes, sucked beneath by some hidden force field, some trick of chemistry and physics that I couldn't quite grasp. We lay in the sun, wet with salt, sand in every crevice, until our stomachs hurt from laughing. We became so soaked in *outside,* it crept up our nostrils and curved around our brains, squeezing until all we could smell or see or feel was sun and salt.

The sun peaked. We ran back into the ocean for one last hurrah. We ducked our heads underwater, and when we emerged, we role-played Jenny Han characters. Lark was Belly Conklin from *The Summer I Turned Pretty,* and I was Lara Jean Song Covey from *To All the Boys I've Loved Before.* We loved those books, and when we were alone, we loved to pretend to be in them. To be normal girls whose biggest immediate problems were the lies they'd told to the boys they liked.

Sure, there was the occasional dead parent, but we ignored the sad parts. We weren't being tested on reading comprehension. In these moments I was sixteen going on eight, Lark fourteen going on six. These were normal girls finding themselves, finding their power, finding their drives and their desires. They were girls who went to high school and had normal problems. They meant so much more to us than any Disney princess. They were free in a way they'd never even realize. A thousand days like this would pass and girls like this would never know how special they were.

It was a perfect day. Gleaming and salty, etched in something that would stay inside me forever. A core memory right until we turned the Thunderbird back onto the Pacific Coast Highway headed north.

$$\sim$$

On the way home, at a café off the highway, someone snapped our picture. We were waiting in line for smoothies, babbling to each other. I was probably going on about the fuzzy taste I got on the roof of my mouth when I drank the ones with bananas or kiwis. I should have known what was happening. We weren't new to being famous—far from it. I was relying on the fact that the public was more interested in our older, hotter sisters than in the two spare Greers with acne and adolescent-stretched limbs.

Still, we were usually hyperaware of our surroundings; grow up in a family like mine and you develop eyes in the back of your head as a basic survival mechanism. But we slipped. Forgot, just for a moment. Our minds were still on that beach, still whipped up in a frenzy of sand, sun, salt, and serenity. We never saw the gaggle of grown men watching us.

The photographers must've been parked at the gas station across the street. They were probably trying to catch Lady Gaga or Jennifer Aniston filling their tanks. Instead, they stumbled on a jackpot. We were background characters—the sweet, funny kid sisters no one usually cared about, only now we were *growing.* The next morning *The Daily Find* plastered their site with pictures of Lark and Kiara Greer "daring to flash it all" in bikinis and "barely there" cutoffs. I hadn't even realized there was much to show, but the pictures were all belly and thigh. Lark and I were sloppy—free, in our own worlds—with tongues out, lapping up our melting smoothies. Zoomed in, the photos looked . . . suggestive. Seeing them, even now, makes me nauseous.

I'd had those shorts since I was twelve. I don't even remember when they'd turned into cutoffs. They'd been in the bottom of my drawer for years, a laundry-day staple and not much more. Too tight for everyday use. That day at the smoothie stand, after a morning gorging on SunChips and Twizzlers, my stomach hung over the edges even with the shorts unbuttoned, my bikini bottom exposed. I wasn't thinking about it. I was focused on getting my fourteen-year-old sister home before our mom got too mad or Miss Carol got worried. I was thinking about whether we'd brought enough towels to prevent damage to the interior of the Thunderbird, and how to sneak inside for a vacuum before my mom caught us. I didn't want some member of the house staff to be left cleaning up sand that had snuck into the seams.

The telephoto lens caught curves on my and Lark's bodies I didn't know we had. By noon the next day, there were men on obscure Reddit threads counting down the four years until Lark turned eighteen. One said I already looked thirty-five, which I didn't think was true.

Eventually we were a meme. To this day, if a stranger eats too much of their meal, there's a nonzero chance they'll pull up that picture of me in those shorts. I'd been happy, babbling away, but in some of the photos my mouth is paused in a grotesquely wide gape, my eyes half closed. Without thinking much about it, they'll attach that photo to some social media missive—usually about their stomach bloat, or waking up with a fresh hangover and rolling into an eight a.m. meeting. It's even been used as a "caption this" on a late-night show.

I still think about that man on the beach sometimes, the one with the etchings of his history all down his face. I wonder what his days look like. If he's okay in his old age, if he has family that cares for him. I wonder if he still wakes at the crack of dawn to catch and release halibut along the California coastline. And sometimes, when I can't help myself, I wonder if he, like literally a billion other people, saw those photos.

If he did, he surely didn't register it as the same girl he'd seen that morning. The one who'd crashed her body with abandon through the waves. The one who'd coughed up seawater and laughed while doing it. The one who, when he'd packed up his gear and made way back to his truck, had raised one hand and flashed a shy smile before turning back to her little sister and tackling her into the sand.

PART ONE

Just a Discombobulated Nepo Baby in an Overwhelming World

(One Year and Four Months Later, as Summer Ends)

Growin' Up Greer Renewed for Season 12—but Is This the End of the Road for Our Favorite Guilty Pleasure?

Litty.com | Top Stories | Celebrity Vertical

By Alexis Borges

We have good news and bad. The good: After months of limbo, wigs, nude photos, breakup songs, and public scandal, Ignite Network has *finally, finally* announced they are renewing everyone's favorite guilty pleasure, *GROWIN' UP GREER*. Season 12, here we come! Can you believe we've been with the Greers this long? We've even watched some of them grow up before our eyes! The snobs among us may decry reality TV, but the Greers' star power is undeniable—and we can't wait to see what they cook up next. What psychological torture will Mama Melora inflict on her gaggle of daughters in the name of ratings? Whose faces will have been pumped full of filler between seasons, and which Greer will throw a fit in the season finale? We can't wait to find out.

Next season's news isn't all sunshine and roses, though: After spending six of the past 11 seasons as both our favorite comic relief *and* the show's hunkiest leading man, Levi Ellis will officially NOT appear in this new season. Not unexpected, given the messy public divorce unfolding between Ellis and soon-to-be-ex Sola Greer. Some of us were still hoping they could work it out, but it's fast becoming clear there's just too much bad blood between these two. In case you missed it, catch our detailed timeline of their love story here.

What's worrying audiences now is where the show goes with Ellis out of the picture. "That bitch threw 6 seasons of love story out the window!!!!!! I'll never forgive Sola," @BBSnakeQueen tweeted after the news dropped. User @StepOnMeSola seemed to agree, responding with "Why would I even keep watching???" Then there was the TikTok by influencer @TurnUp2Turn, who went on a three-minute tirade about the shifts that *GROWIN' UP* has experienced in recent years. "Is this the end of the road?!" @TurnUp2Turn screeched in a viral video that's racked up over a million views. "What are they gonna do now, give a storyline to snoozefest Kiara?! KILL ME NOW." @Baddestbeeeee responded to @TurnUp2Turn's comment on the second-youngest Greer sib in the comments: "Can't wait to watch Kiara quietly reading a book in the corner for 30 minutes. At least make Papa Ray get on camera!"

Only time will tell how Ignite Network reignites viewer interest in the aging franchise. But let's be honest: Just like always, we'll all be tuning in to find out.

CHAPTER ONE

I drew in a shaky breath and tried not to slip away. If I moved my foot an inch in either direction, an inky abyss would swallow me up. I would topple, knees slipping out from under me, and land with a splash and a *thunk* beneath the water.

I planted my feet and told my body it was being ridiculous: Everything was fine. I was not running from a bear, I was not inches from plunging into the sea. I was in Brooklyn, in a man-made tank filled with frigid water. With fourteen people staring at me. In $200,000 worth of borrowed designer clothing. Trying to smile and look like the stylish sea witch the editors of this magazine had envisioned. It was just another Friday morning. I was just doing my job.

I was great. I was living the dream.

Some Cassius Campbell song was playing as I posed. "Luxury," I think. I settled into the sultry beat and refocused on making sure my eyes emoted but my lips didn't. Fashion people didn't like when my smile spread to my cheeks. It made my face look "bulky," apparently. They wanted a jaw that was relaxed but not drooping, a chin jutted out and angled down. This was surprisingly hard to do at the same time.

"Up!" barked Laurent, the photographer assigned to this

shoot. "Look at me. Up toward the heavens." He sat above me on a metal rig, pointy face obscured behind a large camera. The lights shone into my eyes, but there were no heavens visible here. Only scaffolding and concrete.

This editorial spread would go in whatever C-list magazine this was—I told myself to look it up later—alongside a joint interview with me and Lark. Some journalist had spent twenty minutes with us on the phone and was writing an article about how the power duo of youngest Greer girls was "poised to take the world by storm."

Taking the world by storm sounded hard. I focused on not falling down. If I did my job right, we'd be done soon.

I hadn't slept well the previous night or the night before, and getting out of bed that morning felt like pulling teeth. All I had in my stomach was a protein smoothie from hours ago, and a dense fog had settled over my brain. If I did a good enough job, I could climb back into my sweats and, in a few hours, back into my Netflix queue. I could go home, to my own bed.

"*Kee-aaahhh!*" Lark sang from somewhere beyond. I strained to see her but was met only with the oppressive bright of the lights. "Look alive, boo," she persisted anyway, and I could hear a playful smile in that floaty Disney princess voice of hers. She snapped her perfectly neutral manicure. The editors had decided she'd be a Glinda type, and I'd be the Wicked Witch. I tried not to take that personally. "This pout is not cutting it. I'm sleepy—hurry uuup."

A huff escaped my nostrils, a laugh stifled, and my smile spread my face twice as wide.

"Get off my dick—I'm trying!" I hollered back. The photographer grunted, dismayed by the interruption. Lark giggled.

"Girls, settle," came a familiar deadpan from somewhere center left of the light void. Greta. My mother's right-hand woman, and our boss on shoots like these when Mom couldn't attend. I knew she was texting our dear momager between every look change, keeping her up to speed in case one little thing upset the perfectly planned itinerary that ruled our lives. Even when Melora Greer was not around, she was still calling the shots.

I forced my face back to what Lark and I called "sleek 'n' slack," concentrating on pushing every ounce of emotion into my eyes and eyebrows and relaxing the lower half of my face. I pinched my shoulder blades together, a trick Sola had taught me that's supposed to perk your whole body up in photos. It was possible I'd been drooping.

"Finally we get somewhere," Laurent mumbled.

I blocked out the reality of the ten-by-ten water box, the dozen assistants, hairstylists, makeup artists, and brand reps staring like I was some confined, gleaming betta fish. I blocked out my own lagging brain. I posed like my Netflix queue depended on it.

"Perfect," Laurent barked, his voice a punctuation mark.

"*Yes*, honey!" Lark hollered.

Soon bright lights gave way to reality, metal scaffolding, and then our assistant Maxine's gleaming apple cheeks. I was glad she was here. She'd been best friends with my big sister Sola for ages and was always a comforting presence on our travels. Max grasped my hands, helping to hoist me as I made my way up rickety steps, and didn't let go until my feet were firmly on dry land.

"Grateful for you," I whispered.

Max draped a robe over my shoulders and marched me toward the greenroom, past monitors where Greta, Laurent, and the editor lady milled, inspecting the fruits of the day's labor: photos of me and Lark splayed out like mythical creatures lost in an ethereal swamp.

"Beautiful, beautiful," the editor lady mumbled.

"Yes, these'll do," Greta asserted, hands on the hips of Brunello Cucinelli trousers. They were gray, of course; one of the many unspoken rules of Greta's life was that she only dressed in aggressive neutrals. "Melora will be pleased."

"Hmmph," Laurent huffed. There was a quiet disdain to the noise. "The taller one. I tried to cover her weaknesses, but that jaw . . . it's doughy. Soft. We'll have to edit it."

I tried not to move a muscle in case they realized I was there. I felt Max's hands gently tugging me forward, but my feet stayed planted where they were.

"Ignore them," Max whispered. But my stomach twisted, like I was seeing something I shouldn't . . . even though they were talking about me. About *my* body. There's a thrill to hearing people talk about you without knowing you can hear them. But there's this gross feeling that comes with it. Like something's crawling under your skin.

"We're aware," Greta said, curt. "There've been discussions about . . . addressing the issue. In the meantime, just do your damn job."

What did that mean? Would I need to lose more weight? This diet was already making me woozy. Or would this be like what Sola and Destiny did sometimes? Mysterious appointments with surgeons and dermatologists, lasers and needles with long names I could never remember? Max squeezed my arm as we reached the door to the greenroom. Lark was already somewhere inside, getting ready for the next slot on our agenda.

"You know how these fashion photographers are. Bitches, every one of 'em."

"I know," I said on autopilot. I tried to smile to make her feel better, but my attempt was weak. It didn't reach my eyes, so I rolled them to cover my tracks. "Bitches every one."

I slipped away before she could press the issue further.

CHAPTER TWO

Comments sections had called me the ugly duckling of the Greer girls since I was eight, but most days I was in firm disagreement. I thought I was cute enough. I loved the color of my skin, a shade of brown the Lark & Kiara–branded makeup kit called Warm Deep. I liked my nose, its straight jut forward, the curved spread of my nostrils. Unlike so many people in Hollywood, I would never have to pay someone to inject a false fullness into my lips. I had it naturally.

I didn't quite love my "baby fat"—the stubborn circle of flesh around my middle that never seemed to go away, the moon shape my cheeks gave my face. But I didn't hate it, either. At least most days. It was just a fact of my body, and not a defining one.

When it got to me the most was when Lark and I were photographed next to each other, which was a lot. We did the majority of our brand collabs and press as a pair. I had four inches on my little sister in height and waist circumference, and there seemed to be a consensus from the public that Lark was prettier. I couldn't argue that she was beautiful. But why did it have to be a comparison? Why did her beauty have to mean that I was somehow less than?

Part of what felt icky about the way people talked was the fact that Lark was lighter than me. Our dad was Black and our mom white, and the four Greer sisters had come out all over the melanin spectrum. I loved my skin. Miss Carol had made sure I knew all about how colorism functioned in the world. It helped to know the context, that there was something insidious and much bigger than Lark or me at work. But that didn't stop people's comments from stinging.

On the whole, I felt pretty okay about myself. But there were so many ways, every single day, that I wasn't quite . . . enough.

I buried these thoughts deep and quick. I peeled off the wavy wig they'd had me in and turned the water in the greenroom shower as hot as my skin could handle. I let it hammer my chest and loosen whatever tendons and muscles had been holding tension. The shoot's makeup artists had applied camera-ready makeup in layers, and it had caked deep into my pores. I peeled off fake lashes and doused my whole body in coconut oil. Dark metallics ran down my neck, and I scrubbed until the water at my feet ran all the way clear. I scrubbed until *We're aware* stopped blaring like a siren in my brain. Until Laurent and his comments swirled out of my head and down the drain along with all the other detritus of the day.

I didn't wipe the steam off the mirror as I slicked my hair into a bun, taking extra care around my edges. Being a Black girl in the public eye came with its own set of rules, and stepping outside with my hair a mess would bring on way more trouble than it was worth. Gabby Douglas had made Olympic history, and all the while the media still questioned her about her hair. When Simone Biles got married, the headlines focused on the *audacity* of letting her edges sweat out in the Cabo heat. They were world-class athletes who performed feats most of the world would die trying, and they still got flack. I just did my best to stay out of the fray.

I checked my email while I waited for my skincare to soak in. There was something from my tutor, Mr. Hillis. The message was brief, but it made my breath hitch as I read.

Monday 11 a.m. work for you? Amanda's down if you are. She'll be discreet.

The Amanda in question was Amanda Roth. She was an author of historical romance, the kind that took what could have been very dreary topics like the Spanish flu pandemic of 1918 and added twisted, gripping love stories that kept you on the edge of your seat, unsure if they had any chance at ending happily. She was also an alum of Vassar College.

Mr. Hillis had been pushing me to meet with her. "I think you'd be happy at a place like Vassar," he'd insisted. "It's beautiful, and it really is this wonderful liberal arts bubble of a place."

"Am I putting out liberal-arts-bubble vibes?" I'd asked.

"I can't tell you what you want," he said with a laugh. "What I can say is there are benefits to a campus that acts as its own miniature world. Kids from all over disappear into them, and it can give them the space they need to find themselves."

Mr. Hillis said that kind of school was built to teach its students how to think, instead of what to think. I really liked the idea of an entire place designed to make you more yourself, not just turning you into another cog in a machine. But Mr. Hillis was delusional if he thought it was possible for me to disappear anywhere. It sounded like a dream, in theory. But being closed in with 2,500 students who'd all come of age watching *Growin' Up Greer*? That was a nightmare. Getting any kind of regular college experience was already a reach for me.

Still, I'd consider Vassar for him, even though it was a complete pipe dream. Mr. Hillis knew me better than almost anyone besides Miss Carol and my immediate family. Plus, he'd already gone to the trouble of making sure this Amanda Roth lady wouldn't leak the details of our meeting to anyone outside the Vassar admissions office.

I'd be turning eighteen in eight months whether I liked it or not. Growing up for real. So I figured I owed it to myself to explore my options. Everyone around me had such big dreams—and then there I was, a blobby jawline, floating in a sea of insecurities and indecision.

⌒⌒

I was in better spirits when I left the greenroom. Lark was waiting in the hall, reclined on a chair, bobbing her head cheerfully to a beat. Tiny daisies dotted her tank top and matching jeans slung low on her hips. My eyes hit her feet and I stopped short. She was in a pair of vintage Air Jordans—taken directly from *my* goddamn closet.

"Um, excuse me. Are those my shoes?" They were. I just had to hear her say it.

"Oh." She looked down with innocent brown eyes. She'd gotten Dad's eyes, which he in turn had gotten from our grandma Millie. They were so round and expressive, it was no wonder they'd won Dad an Oscar. "I thought Daddy said these were a present we could share?"

The gall. "No, he did not, and you know he did not," I volleyed. "Thief!"

"C'mon, Kee," she whined, "we're going to the same place. I'll give 'em back at home."

"We're not even the same size!" I protested, bewildered.

She shrugged. "I wore thick socks."

A squeak of outrage escaped me. I wound myself up to go full violent big sister on her ass—but the door slid open, light breaking in as if to illuminate the indignity. Greta's stern figure appeared. She waved us forward, and there was no more time.

We stepped out to a wall of sound. Fans gathered in masses crowded around the door, screaming our names—Lark's the most, as expected, but mine, too. They even screamed for Max and Greta. The supporting cast of my family had grown to a size that rivaled that of *Game of Thrones.* One of the more prolific Instagrams following our comings and goings dubbed the staff and friends seen on the show the "Greer family court." After the noble courts of old. Because that went so well for the Tudors.

This was what it meant to know a Greer.

It was nothing compared to what it meant to be one.

I tried to ignore the knot in my chest. Meanwhile, a natural billion-watt smile spread across Lark's face. I shot a look to Joe, our burly bodyguard, to make sure he was in place. If anyone has eyes in the back of his head, it's that bear of a man. A teddy bear, with a penchant for gardening—but with several weapons I'd rather not think about stored under his black blazer.

I snapped to Lark's side and told myself to smile. These people had come here to see us, and we had the power to make or break their day.

If this were one of the more trafficked studios in Manhattan, the fans would have been corralled behind portable metal railings. Bushwick ain't that. Instead they'd bunched them around the sidewalk, nothing but air and goodwill between them and us. I locked eyes with a young girl about my age with bubble-gum-pink hair, and she thrust her phone out with a wordless smile.

Her face was so wide-open, the knot unclenched just the tiniest bit, for just a moment. I wondered what her life looked like, what she'd be off to after a morning camping out to meet the Greers. Did she have a summer job, too? Did she have sisters who stole her shoes and a mom whose presence was somehow always felt, even when she wasn't around? Did she go to school?

Lark and I leaned forward in unison, framing ourselves into the tiny boxed world of the girl's iPhone. This was a practiced dance for us by now. If the U.S. Olympic team had medals for best three-second group selfies, my sisters and I would have taken the gold every time.

Pink Hair Girl snapped her pic with a grateful smile.

"Thank you! Lark, I can't wait for your song with Cassius Campbell! What did he smell like?" she gushed rapid-fire at my sister, who smiled serenely.

"He smelled like citrus and kindness." Lark giggled as she drifted down to the next person. Pink Hair squealed and turned to me.

"Thank you *so* much, Kiara," she said, breathless.

"You're welcome," I responded, trying not to sound as shy as I felt. I'd been doing this most of my life, but of all of us, I was still the worst at it by far. I was missing some crucial Greer gene. I stepped to walk away but turned back at the last second. "What's your name?"

"Raquel!" she exclaimed, visibly thrilled to be asked. "I looove Sola's designs! Destiny's my favorite on the show, though—she's so tough and awesome." She caught herself: "You're really cool, too!"

I laughed, and it reached my eyes with no effort this time. We made our way down, down, down the line, greeting the rest who'd come out in the humid New York summer to meet us. I took a selfie with a mother-daughter pair holding signs that said HI FROM STATEN ISLAND! As I stepped away, I felt the mother's hand on my arm.

"Levi always seemed so lovely," she said almost conspiratorially. "I can't believe your sister did that to him—it's just rotten. Are you still in touch? How's he doing?"

I froze. *What?* I knew social media was still salivating over Sola's divorce, but this was a new take—not to mention one that was gallingly incorrect. Still, engaging wasn't a good call.

"The girls have to get to their next engagement," Joe said, gruff, finally yanking open the door to the Escalade.

The door closed and my eyes adjusted to take in the unmistakable loom of my mother. I got this sudden, unexplainable rush of feeling like I'd disappointed her.

Melora Greer, queen of us all, the reason anyone cared to sweat through hours waiting to see the lot of us. She took off her sunglasses and greeted us with a wry smile that revealed perfectly spaced, gleaming teeth. Then her perfectly angled jaw cocked, transforming into the faux exasperation she'd become famous for on the show, the kind frequently brought out by her four daughters. Her eyes were on my sweats.

"Really?" she groaned. "Baby, why? There'll be photos."

"Sorry, Mom." I ran my hands down the thighs of the old sweats I'd put on after my shower. My comfy sweats, my cozy sweats. Sweats that sagged just a little bit in the butt and had pilled all down the crotch. They were so soft I didn't care. My edges were for the public; the sweats were for me. "You're not winning this one."

I fought back so infrequently that sometimes she just let me win. I suspected this was because I'd never asked for anything that truly rocked the boat.

Her eyes turned to Lark, but my darling baby sis just shrugged and slouched down in her seat, gluing her eyes to her phone. Mom sighed and knocked the roof of the car, signaling the driver.

Mom's wry smile didn't return. She tapped wildly at her phone, typing something with fervor. After a minute she heaved another sigh and massaged her temples. Maybe the exasperation wasn't so faux after all. If I hadn't known any better, I'd have said she looked worried.

"Bad day?" Lark asked, tilting her head in concern, her big, round puppy-dog eyes wide.

"It's not the best time to be caught off our game," Mom said. There was real irritation in her voice. I shifted in my seat, a bad feeling creeping in.

"Some lady just said something weird to me about Levi," I said, just in case my inkling was right. "Is this about him again?"

Mom huffed a bitter laugh and looked out the window. "You'll find out soon enough, I guess. Why don't you give your sister and her rat ex a Google."

Lark and I exchanged a look, but we obeyed. My page was still loading when I heard Lark suck in a sharp breath.

The Track List for Levi Ellis's "Maneater" Album Is Out, and It's Full of Draaamaaa

Did Levi Ellis Just Hint That Sola Greer Is a Serial Cheater?

How Many Times Did Sola Greer Cheat on Levi Ellis?

Levi Ellis Just Called Ex Sola Greer a "Master Manipulator" on Instagram

Could Levi Ellis's New Album Be the Death Knell of the Greer Empire?

There were dozens of headlines just like that. I speed-read one about Levi's new album, which he'd had the audacity to call *Maneater*. He'd apparently dropped the track list today, and it featured such subtle song titles as "Mourning the Sun (Sol)," "Split in Two," "The Devil Has Curves," and "Cheater." Whoever wrote this article had remarked that "*Maneater* is shaping up to be a banger of a breakup album."

I wanted to vomit. I looked over at Lark, and there were tears shining in her eyes. When I looked at our mother, she was practically vibrating with anger.

It was all lies. When Sola and Levi had broken up eight months ago—a good six months before the news went public—it was because she'd found out Levi had been cheating *on her* for years. She'd suspect something, and he'd lie to her face—over and over again, until she stopped believing herself altogether. Then one day Sola was in line for the bathroom at a club in Milan, and a model burst into tears at the sight of her. The woman told her everything.

The rest was a hidden history: not public, thanks to ironclad NDAs, but one that blindsided all of us.

I'd been twelve when she married Levi, and before long he was basically a big brother. He was this curly-haired white boy from Indiana, and he'd grown up shy and a bit nerdy like me. That first year he convinced Miss Carol to join a D&D campaign so he could teach Lark and me how to play. Levi would rock out onstage at Coachella and then come home to dungeon-master two middle schoolers and a middle-aged nanny in LA.

At events and parties I was a wallflower; I'd take a while to work up the nerve to join some intimidating circle of talkers. Levi would rescue me, sweeping over to ask me about what strange history fact I'd learned that week or what old TV show I was watching.

For weeks after the split, I'd walk past rooms in our house and hear my mother raging into the phone. Sola wasn't the only heartbroken one—the breakup broke all of us. Lark slept in my bed for a month after, head tucked into the soft hook of my shoulder, her tears pooling on my skin. Losing Levi felt like someone had died.

We'd thought we'd known him. That's what hurt the most. When you think someone is kind and they turn out to be the opposite, it shatters something inside of you.

"How can he do this?" Lark asked, looking up from her phone and breaking the long silence in the car. "Just lie so blatantly?" Her eyes were rimmed with tears, which told me she was feeling about the same as I was.

"Is it even legal for him to spread lies like this?" I asked. "Isn't that libel or something?"

"So far it's all anonymous sources and vague insinuations," Mom said. "He's not breaking his NDA, but if we were to say anything, we *would* be breaking ours."

She cleared her throat and turned her gaze to the Brooklyn streets out the window.

"The Ignite execs were on a tear today," she continued, not looking at us. "They've been worried about the ratings since the split was announced. I had to talk Lucas Williams off a cliff—he was threatening to rescind our renewal."

"Can they do that?" Lark asked, dumbfounded. Lark and I exchanged another look. Our mother didn't often look worried. When she did, it meant she'd lost control—and that was a rare enough sight to shake us. She always emphasized that we were a united front: a ride-or-die family whose destinies were irrevocably linked together. The public saw us as one. According to her, that's what made us strong. So why did she look so defeated, almost scared?

"Don't worry too much, my babies," Mom said, sniffing. Her tone had shifted to something stronger, with more conviction. I couldn't tell if she was trying to convince herself or us. Her thumbs hovered over her phone, clearly itching to get back to her endless pile of emails. "I'll right the ship. We're in this together and we're not going anywhere."

"This is all so *fucked*," Lark said, and Mom and I both turned toward her. Lark never cursed, especially not in front of our parents. I wasn't convinced she even did it with her friends. Mom blinked, nonplussed and amused.

"It is. But enough about Levi. We focus on *us*." She tapped each of our knees with her talons. "This may be the end of a Greer era, but it's also the beginning. I need each of you to step into your own this season. We've got a legacy to build."

She looked between us, but then her gaze landed solely on me. I shrank into my seat.

Lark was already in the midst of launching a music career, and she'd just finished four seasons on a hit kids' show. She'd already stepped into her own. I was the only person in my family with no accomplishments to my name, no clear talents to speak of. Mom stared hard at me, clearly wanting assurance that I was listening. I nodded.

"My little stars, this is your time," she continued, satisfied. "We'll give 'em plenty else to talk about, and they'll move on. They always do. Even if we have to give them a little push."

CHAPTER THREE

My mother *looms*. There's no other way to put it. Melora Greer, born Melissa Anne Giordano, was and is and always will be a force to be reckoned with. Even when the time comes that she is no longer on this earth, Melora Greer will find a way to be remembered, to be seen, to be known. It's why my dad fell in love with her. He's said it in countless interviews and to his own daughters as a bedtime story, and he told it the same every time: She was always undeniable.

He'd even said it on the Oscars stage, accepting his statue: "I thought if I teamed with her, maybe I could be undeniable, too. I was right."

That had proven true for all of us, really. Because there was something unspoken in that speech, something only visible to those who knew Melora and Raymond Greer: To know Melora was to do everything in your power not to disappoint her. You either rose to the occasion or got out of her way.

My parents met in December 1990, at two a.m. at a combination Thai food spot and dive bar in Atwater Village. My mother was nineteen and my father twenty-one. In old pictures my mother looked like Julia Roberts in her *Mystic Pizza* era: hair wild, eyebrows thick, face round with youth. My dad was doing his best refined Sidney Poitier drag because his agent had told him that's how he'd get roles, but it never quite fit him. Raymond Greer looked best when he ditched the pretense and put on the oversized leather jacket my mom thrifted for him; when he finally grew his hair long enough for the locs that eventually became his trademark. Mom was the first to spot that. She became his manager, and Ray Greer's career changed practically overnight.

The line between then and now—from broke kids hustling Hollywood Boulevard in the early nineties to, well, *this*—feels inconceivable but also somehow totally inevitable.

Because of course my mother ended up in an Escalade with tinted windows, pulling onto the tarmac with her own cavalcade, on the way to her private jet. She extended her arms upward as the car pulled to a stop, turned left and right to stretch her back and neck. I joined in, cracking the day out of my shoulders. That shower had done wonders, sure, but I'd still spent the morning with every muscle clenched, posing while trying not to fall on my ass.

"Yo, oldies," Lark teased, smile big and silly so she wouldn't get smacked. "We haven't even boarded the flight yet—you can't be that stiff."

The glare my mother shot back looked exactly like Destiny's, moody and intense, and the contrasting smirk on her face was the mirror image of Lark's smile. The combo made Mom come off playful but dangerous—captivating. Which she was. She had the Nielsen ratings to prove it.

"Sweets, let's talk tomorrow, *after* the sweet sixteen," Mom purred. "See what those bones have to say with a few more years in 'em."

"It's called preventative measures," I said, rolling my neck. "You don't want to seize up when you hit seventy."

"You're not already seventy?" Lark asked, weaponizing those big eyes by widening them innocently. "Had me fooled."

I lunged forward, grabbing at her right foot until I'd worked off my stolen sneaker.

"Hey!" she protested, kicking back at me.

"This is stolen property—what did you expect?" I retorted.

"Moooommm," Lark whined, but Mom literally waved it away with her perfect cream manicure. I stuck my tongue out at Lark.

"Deal with this amongst yourselves, please," Mom said. Her head was already bent once more to her cell phone, no doubt still navigating this latest PR crisis.

Joe opened the door and Mom slid out, backlit against the afternoon glare and then enveloped by it, gone. Somehow she was cinematic even when the cameras weren't around. A lot had changed since that night she'd met my father: three and a half decades, four kids, straighter hair, straighter nose, new teeth, and a new name that no one would ever forget. But from what Dad told me, she'd always been that way. Like she'd just been waiting for the cameras to turn on.

That was something you either had or you didn't. Lark had it. Sola was the oldest and acted like she invented it. Destiny . . . well, it depended on the day, on if she wanted to commit to the bit. Me? I was born without that gene. I was just along for the ride.

Mom strutted forward toward the jet, red-bottomed heels *click-clack*ing on asphalt. The message was clear: We had places to be, an itinerary to complete. I threw the shoe back at Lark.

"You're welcome," I said, so she'd be aware this was an act of generosity. "I'd never let your feet get all ashy out there. I'm good-natured like that."

Lark was lunging back my way when—

"Children," Greta said. Her voice was a period, end of sentence, no room for questions. She was standing on the tarmac with her arms crossed, having exited the other car.

"Sorry," I said. I tumbled out, Lark following, still poking at me but trying to be more low-key about it. Max exited the other vehicle like an adult, and Greta walked the tarmac like she was filming her big entrance on *Selling Sunset*. Ahead of us my mother was already ascending the stairs to her most prized possession.

Mom had reason for wanting our family equipped with a private jet—safety, first and foremost. There'd been a few stalking incidents over the years that taught us not to take any moment of security for granted. But really, Mom had been waiting for an excuse to buy one. This wasn't just practical, a way to sidestep the paparazzi who hounded commercial airports or to keep us out of snatching range from our fan base's reserve of creeps.

No, deep down inside, Melora Greer was always *striving*. I saw it in her eyes every time she stepped out in front of her biggest, most expensive baby—that glint of vindication. She was no longer the Valley girl from the broke, broken family, the one who'd spent her childhood living out of cars and motels. She was free from all that haunted her, the stuff she didn't tell us much about except to weave her past into some cloudy cautionary tale. Melora Greer crafted her own destiny with grit, hair spray, and a new family raised up in her image. The glint in her eye said: *My children will never share my traumas.* It also said: *I'm playing with the big boys now.*

My mother lived her life with a crystalline-clear drive I couldn't help but envy. She knew exactly what she stood for and what she'd do to protect it. I'd never had that kind of clarity, not even for a second. Melora Greer knew exactly what she wanted. She always got it, too.

It made me terrified of disappointing her. It also made me desperate to harness what she had. Those genes had to be in me somewhere.

She'd take care of this Levi thing somehow. Because as Melora willed it, now there that plane sat—gassed up and ready to take us back to the other coast. GREER AIR was painted across its side in purple cursive that popped against the sunny gray of a Connecticut day. It wasn't stopping for nobody. She was never going back.

COLLEGE ESSAY DRAFT 1
By Kiara Greer
September 5, 2024

PROMPT: *Some students have a background, identity, interest, or talent so meaningful, they want to be sure we know about it. If this sounds like you, then please share your story.*

NOTES FOR MR. HILLIS: *This is still too long and rambly, and IDK how to cut it down to fit the word limit??? Ugh, IDK if this one's any good. It just kinda poured outta me on the flight home yesterday. Let me know what you think!*

My favorite part of home is the smell. Eucalyptus and pine, chaparral and night-blooming jasmine. The Santa Monica Mountains feel like a living contradiction: brush and trail dust mixed with green and oak and salted air. Is this place desert? ocean? or a tree-lined mountain town? It's wild that so many seemingly opposing elements can exist in one place at the same time. All those varying vibes come together in a sniff. My home is perched atop an olfactory wonderland.

There's so much I missed about the old house, the big green one off Larchmont my sister Lark and I were born into. The noise of the city had been right there, but as you turned onto our street, it all drifted away. Grandma Millie, our dad's mom, said it was the palm trees and oaks that blocked out the noise like a sonic buffer.

My grandmother had dark brown skin that hadn't wrinkled but had instead spent its last act drifting slowly down her face. That face had an intimate relationship with the forces of gravity. Like she knew its secrets. Like she was connected to so much more than we were.

Grandma Millie made wrinkles and sags seem aspirational. A badge of honor, the mark of a life lived, a world seen. Her parents had moved to Los Angeles in the 1940s and worked as household staff for a pair of movie stars. Grandma Millie wanted to be the Black girl Shirley Temple, so she spent her childhood on studio lots as a bit player. She told stories about being dressed in burlap, her clothes torn on her body by dead-eyed costumers. She played enslaved children in the backgrounds of seven movies before she tired of her childhood dream.

By the time I knew her, she had a hip that gave her trouble. On the days that hip allowed her to move around freely, Grandma Millie would holler up the stairs for Lark and me to put down our tablets. Her gait was stiff but swift, and she would lead us from our manicured street to Koreatown a few blocks over.

The avenues were wide in this part of town, built at a time when the city promised to sprawl on forever. We'd go into every shop and restaurant. Grandma would make friends with every shop owner and shopper who'd humor her comments on the heat, lines of questioning about their days, and probes as to how long they'd lived in Los Angeles, what they thought of it, if it was home yet. Lark would clutch Grandma Millie's right hand and smile serenely. I'd mutter complaints that these strangers didn't want to stop and talk to an old lady and a pair of little girls.

"Everyone has a story," she'd lecture me when we got home. "No matter how big or small their role in your life, everyone is coming from somewhere and going someplace. Don't you want to see the wide array of people who exist out there?" It was important to her that we be curious about where people came from, what they might be battling that wasn't visible on the surface, the kinds of lives they might be going home to. It would help us understand our own place in the world—main characters in our lives, but tiny specks in the grand scheme of the universe.

I was ten when she died. My parents started looking for a new house that same year. Mom said it was only practical. The show was in its second season; it had been two years since my parents or older sisters could walk Larchmont without being stopped by fans. They were starting to stop Lark and me, too. We needed space where the family could breathe without the probing questions of strangers. At least that's what I thought.

That was the same year my family started traveling a lot. Between my dad taking jobs far away and the family TV show succeeding, we were never all in the same place at the same time. That turned out to be lucky, though, because I wasn't there when a man snuck into my family's house and fell asleep in my bed. When they told me about the break-ins, it made even more sense why we'd left the noise. We headed to the hills west of the city, behind towering gates that kept out prying eyes. "They won't be able to touch us here," Mom announced. "And those who doubt us will be able to see just how much we're worth." I didn't know there was anything to doubt.

Our new home was beautiful. *The Architectural Digest* cover broke records.

But also: With Grandma Millie gone, I'd lost the person who forced me to talk to strangers.

This place on the hill is an oasis tucked away from chaos.

My parents filled our garden with native plants: pink muhly grass, California poppies, desert willow, jacaranda. Sitting out there feels like you're on the edge of the world. You can look out over the mountains and see forever.

You can't touch that other world from here, but the gates aren't so bad. They're a protection of sorts, after all. A declaration of success, sure. A brag, definitely. A privilege, certainly. A place explicitly designed to make all our dreams come true.

Maybe dreams are like a love story: It's better to have a dream and leave it behind, like Grandma Millie did, than to never have one at all.

I'm thinking about this a lot because I am eight months from eighteen. By all accounts, I am just getting started. Only I have no idea where to begin. Life behind the gates is so quiet, and I've grown quieter with it.

I need to find the noise again. That's my dream.

I've been away for a few days. Tonight, as we pulled back through the gates, I rolled down the window and inhaled deep. There was still one jacaranda in bloom.

Grandma Millie would walk us through town and recite stories and words she knew and loved. Lines from a poem she quoted often were stuck in my head like a song: on repeat, like a bug in your ear.

"Doesn't everything die at last, and too soon?" Mary Oliver wrote. She was right. It does.

"Tell me," the poem continued, echoing through my mind, "what is it you plan to do with your one wild and precious life?"

CHAPTER FOUR

Amanda Roth had to postpone. She was there, and then she was gone.

> Please send Kiara my regrets. I'm being pulled away by a sudden deadline, but I hope to be able to talk to her soon. I don't know when I'll next be in Los Angeles, however, so if you need to find a different interviewer, I very much understand.

The email buzzed in the back of my head all day. Through a personal training session, breakfast, a dress fitting, an hour spent playing *Mario Kart* with Lark to calm her nerves, four spent in glam with Lark napping through hers in the chair next to me, and the beginning of our car ride to her party.

I had to remind myself this reaction was ridiculous. If I could pull off college at all, it would probably be part-time, in LA or New York to be close to work. I might not be the most popular Greer, but I had contracts to honor with all kinds of brands. I already saw too little of my family, and Lark would need me more than ever when her album was released next year.

And yet that knot in my chest still hadn't unclenched.

Of course Lark had chosen a *prom* theme for her birthday party. We'd taken to life in such different ways. My little sister was sunshine, all energy—always charging forward, with a smirk or a smile at the strange lot she'd been dealt. This world was a wonderland to Lark Greer. I admired that. I envied it. Hadn't we been handed the same basic raw materials? Shouldn't I be the one to help guide *her*, instead of the other way around?

"Hey!"

I needed to take a page from Lark's playbook. Spend less time inside my head.

"Hey!" Destiny barked again, snapping goldenrod manicured fingers inches from my eye.

I did a double take, snapping back to reality and gently guiding my sister's spiky nails out of dangerous proximity to my face.

"You could put an eye out," I whined.

"And whose fault is that? What's up with you?" Destiny retorted. "You're supposed to defend me from these jackals."

Sola sat across from Destiny in the limo taking us to the party. She tsked, rolling heavily lined hazel eyes.

"Pleeeeaaase," she teased. "Dress like Big Bird and you're gonna hear about it. Are you new?"

Lark snarfled a laugh next to me. I knit my lips together to keep my vocal cords from echoing hers. In an oversized suit the same color as her nails, Destiny didn't *not* look like a big yellow bird. But I feared for my eyeballs if I were to voice that opinion.

"It's not that you don't look good," Lark argued, touching up her lip gloss. "It's just that, if *Sesame Street* was looking to do a gritty, heauxy reboot, you'd be their lady."

"Like *Joker*, but with Big Bird? That could be a hit," I offered, helpful. Destiny smacked my knee.

"Exactly," Lark said sweetly, her voice as gentle as if she was singing to a bluebird in a goddamn meadow—and that's what made me lose it. A rogue puff of air cracked up my nasal cavity. Trying to keep it in only caused it to exit my nose as some kind of demented ogre snort. Sola cackled at the noise, and I couldn't help but join in, the snort warping into a wheeze. Hey, at least my mind was off Amanda Roth and my flailing college prospects.

"I can't believe you," Destiny growled. "You're supposed to be the nice one."

"The tailoring is impeccable!" I offered. And it was. Destiny's outfit was oversized and bold, the love child of Katharine Hepburn's style from the forties and the zoot suits I'd fixated on in Dad's favorite movie, *Malcolm X*. It was kind of iconic, really.

Destiny sighed, accepting my uselessness. She turned back to Sola, eyes flashing. "What about you?"

"What about me?" Sola asked with her usual air of haughty arrogance.

"You know this is a child's birthday party, right?"

"Hey!" Lark protested. "How'd I catch a stray?"

Destiny slid Lark a look that basically called her a tiny baby.

"And what of it?" Sola shot at Dest.

"Your tit's gonna fall out and bop a Disney Channel kid in the face, Sol."

The image knocked me out. I wheezed laughing. Sola had dressed in a classic three-piece tuxedo, her own twist on the theme. Only under her crisp white waistcoat was . . . nothing. Just smooth, glimmering brown skin, her breasts taped back behind the tailored black jacket—extensively, I had to assume, if she wanted to avoid public indecency charges.

"Since when are you a prude?" Sola shot back.

"Just didn't know being a sex offender was on your list of ambitions."

The two of them erupted into argument. Lark sighed and pulled out her phone. She knew as well as I did they'd carry on like this for the rest of the ride. Sola and Destiny's squabbles were a looping soundtrack of our childhoods, as comforting as Miss Carol's chicken soup on a cold day. I leaned back and closed my eyes, letting their voices crowd out my own thoughts.

It could have been two minutes or ten before the car slowed. Destiny squeezed my hand. When I opened my eyes, she cocked a brow at me, a glint in her eyes.

"Let's face the wolves." Her lip was curled up, her eyes sharp and ready. Sola straightened her spine and checked that the lapels on her suit were still firmly in place. A night like this was *play* to both my big sisters, at the same time as being work. It was a game to them. One they took pride in winning. I inhaled a deep breath and steadied myself.

The door opened, and Sola slid out, Louboutins-first. Lights flashed a thousand times within a second, layered voices shouting her name.

The plan was for Lark to go last, since it was her night. None of us wanted to steal her thunder, and Sola was a professional thunder stealer. So she went first, and Destiny counted to thirty before nudging me forward. She kept hold of my hand, which I thought was nice. Dest had always been kind, but she'd become less of a bruiser since she'd had her kid. Back then, now, and always, she'd never let me fall on my face.

"See you out there," Lark trilled.

Destiny held on tight as I found my footing in heels on the concrete. The crowd outside was half legit photographers—the ones Ignite hired to cover the red carpet—and half rabid paparazzi. We had to pass through the paps before we could get to the carpet.

"SOLA! LEVI SAYS YOU SLEPT WITH TWENTY-THREE MEN WHILE YOU WERE STILL MARRIED."

"KIARA! LARK! YOU GONNA GROW UP A WHORE LIKE YOUR SISTER?"

"SOLA! HOW'D YOU BREAK THE HEART OF THE NICEST GUY IN TOWN?"

I froze. Destiny did, too, but for so short a time, you wouldn't notice if you didn't know her like I did. I could see her fight-or-flight activate—but Destiny's mode was always fight. She clenched her jaw and pulled me forward, pushing us through the line of paps, but I could still hear their shouts as I took my place in the photo line.

Weight on back foot, I recited in my head. *Turn body forty-five degrees, chin forward but also down, big eyes but not bug eyes, relax your jaw, give 'em angles.*

"SOLA! SOLA! WHO WERE THE OTHER GUYS?"

"IS IT ALWAYS THE SWIRL, OR'D YA GO FOR CHOCOLATE WHEN YOU WERE MAKING YOUR ROUNDS?"

"SOLA! IS IT TRUE YOU GAVE CHANNING TATUM CHLAMYDIA?"

Dest nudged me forward, and I rearranged my dress on the carpet. I could see the rage in her eyes, but I could also see that she was channeling it to absolutely slay the camera. My only relief at that moment was that we were on a break from filming the new season.

"Don't slump," Sola said through her teeth a few feet down the line, her smile megabright, as if none of this was happening.

I rolled my shoulders and realized that I had, indeed, been slouching. Unlike Sola, I was having a hard time tuning out the men yelling lies ten feet from us. Lies about *her*. My blood boiled.

I clung to Destiny's hand, relying on her to guide me down the short carpet. The three of us were supposed to be done with photos by the time Lark stepped out of the limo, but we hadn't expected the deluge of misogynoir garbage flying our way.

Right on cue, the car door opened again and Lark practically levitated onto the carpet. She was a goddamn vision. Draped in the chiffon of her Valentino gown, she looked like the heir apparent to some sort of mythical kingdom. The kind where people floated instead of walked and ate their food off four-leaf clovers. She had the smile to match—well, until . . .

"LARK! DON'T YOU MISS YOUR BROTHER-IN-LAW?"

"LARK! YOU'RE SIXTEEN NOW. YOU GONNA GET FAKE TITS, TOO?"

Lark's face fell. I felt a jolt of Destiny run through me: I wanted to rip off my earrings and tackle these men into the street.

"Motherfuckers," the actual Destiny mumbled next to me. If Sola was mad, she didn't show it. She remained untouchable.

"THINK YOU GOT THE RIGHT SIB IN THE SPLIT?" one man hollered.

"DO YOU APPROVE OF YOUR SISTER'S EXTRAMARITAL ACTIVITIES?"

"DOES SOLA HAVE A SEX ADDICTION?"

Lark recovered quickly, sliding that smile back onto her face. I could practically see her building an invisible wall between them and her. Destiny's hand was still squeezing mine tight. The only thing stopping us from storming those men and smashing every one of their cameras was that we both knew the consequences.

Starlets were always punished for standing up for themselves, but it was ten times worse for the Black girls.

I wanted to scream the truth in their faces. That Levi was the villain, not my sister. That he'd made us all believe in him. Levi Ellis had changed the very set of my eldest, strongest sister's shoulders. He'd dimmed the light in her eyes. I wanted to tell them that by shouting these accusations, these lies, at his soon-to-be ex-wife, it was like all these men were working *for* him, doing his bidding.

But I couldn't say any of that. And so, utterly helpless, I let Destiny guide us through the doors, away from one wall of noise and into another.

CHAPTER FIVE

Vodka slid down my throat like paint thinner. At least this was what I imagined paint thinner would taste like: rancid and sharp, with edges that scratched their way down my esophagus. The liquid landed in my stomach with a sickeningly warm *thunk*.

"Aw, hun. It takes a bit to get used to."

I must have pulled a face. The bartender's brow knit sympathetically. She was pretty, with a big-sister energy I appreciated, but I didn't like being pitied.

I'd copied Sola's go-to drink, an extra dry vodka martini with a twist. I should have known better. Nothing about Sola was for the faint of heart. She was beautiful and daring in a way most people on earth could never touch. Her whole life, people were always trying to emulate her—then getting mad when they couldn't come close.

At that very moment some conservative group called All-American Moms was protesting her, enraged by a billboard featuring Sola's naked body wrapped around a phallic, drippingly cold bottle of liquor. Never mind that everyone in the Western world had already seen my sister naked. Or that the most salacious bits were covered. The moms were *pissed*.

No doubt they were having a field day with this Levi firestorm.

Maybe it was the vodka in my own stomach, or the image of the billboard seared in my mind, but a deranged little giggle escaped my mouth. *If they could see us now.* That same liquor brand was a cosponsor of my little sister's sweet sixteen. I'd just witnessed Jonny Hall, the star of the hit kids' show Lark was on, down a shot two people over. If there was one thing the echelon of rich, powerful Hollywood adults were *not*, it was precious about teen drinking. Still, it was *my* first time.

I turned to watch the party, taking ginger sips as I looked around. Mom and Greta had rented out a club and dressed it to look like the climax of every teen movie turned up to eleven. The room was all black atmosphere, with twinkling lights, LED balloons, and constellations projected on the ceiling. Pink roses were everywhere, picked to perfectly match Lark's dress.

I gagged over a sip. I couldn't keep drinking this. I pulled out my phone and did a quick Google, but all the names of cocktails seemed vague and complicated. Until—

"Can I try a Roman Holiday?" I squeaked out.

My hands went to the waist of the over-the-top dress Lark had put me in. It was a mottled blush number from Paolo Sebastian's Wild Swans collection, with embroidered swans flying across the chest, sleeves, and skirt. A literal castle and a blue, stormy sea were depicted at the bottom. Our hairstylist had clipped in long, kinky bundles that matched and extended my natural hair, then plaited it into a cascading braid. Mom had made sure I was corseted in tight.

"I want you to look like a fairy tale," Lark had said.

"Is this not a bit on the nose?" I'd asked. I usually defaulted to looks more subtle than this, but it was her birthday. I had to do what she said.

"I don't know why you dress like you don't love clothes," she'd said. "I've seen your collection of fashion biographies."

"I like art," I said. "It's different."

I wasn't one of those people who knew how to "express herself" with clothes, so I shied away from trying. I loved learning about the history of things, though. I liked the way you could track shifts in culture through the raising of hemlines, the tightening of bodices. It was a reminder that big changes came with ripple effects that touched everything, even the things you thought weren't connected at all. That was cool to think about.

In practice, on myself? This dress made me feel conspicuous. Like there was a spotlight I couldn't duck out of.

I realized with a start that the cocktail I'd just ordered had *coffee* in it. Ten p.m. coffee. Sure, that would help me act cool and chill and normal. The bartender gathered bottles, pouring liquids of various shades of gold and amber from long metal spouts.

I tried to treat this as a moment of quiet. Lark was where I'd left her, hamming it up with her costars from *Nick of Time*. Jonny Hall—who played the titular Nick—had finished downing another shot and brought two more with him as he cantered back over to them. Austin Hsu took one and Jonny the other, and I watched as they both joined Lark and Reina Hila, her best friend from the show, who were doing a choreographed dance for a videographer.

I'd hovered on the fringes of their group when we'd arrived, but I'd excused myself when Jonny started talking about the Ari Aster movie he'd landed. I was welcome over there—Lark made sure of that. But I'd been the quiet girl in the corner too many times. And I was still stewing about what had happened outside.

If I was this tired of myself, I could only imagine what the rest of those kids would think of me.

"Hey," a soft voice said beside me. I moved to the side so they could get past. I hoped the bartender would be done soon. I hated being in the way.

Everyone in this place was hobnobbing. A thousand conversations yammered around me. "Cuff It" transitioned to another of Lark's favorites, "All for You" by Janet Jackson. I loved this song, too, but I wished I could turn the volume down on the rest of it. Finally my drink landed before me. I braced myself and took a big pull. Better. The cocktail was sickly sweet, like drinking iced syrup. Luckily I had a sweet tooth.

"Hey," that same voice said again. Where had the bartender gone? Most of the line was at the other end of the bar, but someone over here was clearly begging for her attention.

I needed to pay attention. I was being too much of a wallflower, I knew it. Ironically it had always been Levi who pulled me out of that mode. He was so good at spotting when I'd burrowed too far into myself and needed poking. So without him here I'd headed for the bar, fatigued after hours feeling like a third wheel to my parents' schmoozing, Destiny's flirting with various Lakers, and Lark's sparkling social skills. Mom was always pushing me to be in the middle of the action, dancing alongside Lark, Jonny, and the rest of the teen dreams. She didn't see the strain around my eyes, the stress of photographers' flashing lights and flying obscenities that still echoed through my body. Nobody saw me here.

"Hi. Sorry to bother—"

I wondered if maybe I should switch to water. I clutched my stomach, and my feet went on autopilot, leading me around the crowd, past the DJ booth, and all the way to the bathroom.

"Oh . . ." the voice said as I passed. Did they sound disappointed?

Only when the door swung shut did I realize they might've been talking to *me.*

I shook my head. Unlikely. Besides, it was too late now.

Peeing was a whole *thing* in this dress. This might be my only reprieve, though, so I hiked the A-line skirt to my waist, careful not to let it dip low enough to touch the toilet.

When I finished, I heard it.

Heavy breaths. Irregular ones, a few stalls away. I flushed and heard a strangled cough, like whoever it was had tried to stop themselves making noise. I left the stall and washed my hands, trying to mind my own damn business. Nothing good came from meddling.

"Kee?"

"Sola?"

The door to the farthest stall swung open, and out stepped my indomitable oldest sister, tears streaking through her eyeliner. I sucked in a breath. I'd never seen her cry in public.

"I saw your shoes," she explained, voice coming out thick.

"What happened?"

"For real?" she said with a teary huff. "You heard those shitdicks."

Oh. At this point that was hours ago. I was still thinking about it, of course, and I'd have cried all night if a bunch of grown men shouted lies like that about me. But this was *Sola.* Sola was stronger than me. Sola was stronger than all of us.

"That was such rancid crap," I said. My eyes searched her face. "I didn't know that stuff still got to you."

Sola crumpled.

"Neither did I!" Her voice broke as a fresh wave of tears came over her. I pulled her toward me, and she buried herself in my shoulder. Sola was taller than me, but somehow with my heels it worked. Her sniffles were so pitiful, and suddenly I felt massively ill-equipped.

I walked down the line of stalls, banging each door open to check they were empty. Then I locked the outer door, and we sat on a velvet chaise the party planners had placed in the bathroom, likely to make this feel less like a place where people mainlined coke on weeknights.

"Ugh, I'm a mess," Sola said after a minute. A clump of tearstained toilet paper was falling apart in her hands, breaking into useless bits of matted nothing. This only made her cry harder. I wet a paper towel under the faucet. Tracing around my sister's eyes, I saw for the first time how bloodshot and tired she looked. I realized how hard she must be working every day, keeping up appearances. How many eye masks does it take to cover a broken heart?

"I found one of them going through my *trash* yesterday," she said, sniffing. "They've been bad before, but not like this. I think there's a tracker on my car."

"Jesus."

"They're trying to catch me screwing someone else. As if *I* was the one hooking up with strangers everywhere from Foxborough to Phuket."

"Maybe you really should call Channing Tatum," I said in an attempt to lighten the mood. "He'd be *lucky* to catch chlamydia from you."

Sola's laugh was a snort that matched mine, the one she saved for private moments. She wiped snot from her face with her hand, and I felt a warm rush of satisfaction.

"He really would," she said.

"Is there anything I can do?" I braced for the answer.

"Just be you," she said, forcing a smile. She smushed my cheeks between her fingers until my lips went platypus. "You're all I need, baby girl. Don't you worry 'bout me."

She stared into space for a moment, eyes unfocused. Then she sniffed, sucked her teeth, and turned on a glimmering grin that came off eerie.

"Fuck 'em. We'll give them plenty else to talk about. It's what we do." When she looked into my eyes again, her steely confidence was back in full force. "They'll move on."

Her fingers danced at light speed across her phone, moving on from the moment, no doubt texting Max that there was a 911 in the bathroom. I'd lost her. Like our mom, Sola could slide between versions of herself before you had a chance to blink. She didn't have time now to problem-solve the issues in her love life, so she turned to problem-solving the mess on her face.

Max knocked and Sola shooed me away. The warm drawl of her best friend's *"Oh, baby, nooo"* was the last I heard before the door slammed shut, leaving me on the other side, alone again.

A pair of *Bachelor* contestants jostled me, gushing to each other about having swung an invite. I stood frozen as the din of the party reentered my system, bodies pushing around me. How could a room that was teeming with life feel so airless?

I'd known, on some level, that Sola was falling apart inside. Of course she was.

But it was different, seeing her come undone outside our

tight little circle. In public. That distinction might not matter to a lot of people, but it did to Sola. I'd seen her walk fashion shows with 102-degree fevers. She always had a plan, a next big swing, a dream. The pain had to be unbearable for it to overtake her in a place like this. With photographers and gossip hounds around every corner, people who'd gush to her face but drag her through the mud when she turned her back.

I almost marched back into the bathroom. I wanted to drag Sola into our waiting car and home to the big, weirdly structural house she'd rented after the split. I'd tuck her into bed, crawl under the covers, and queue up season three of *Dawson's Creek*, her favorite. That was my job, wasn't it? I was her sister. We were supposed to take care of each other, always.

But she wouldn't let me. It's just not who she was.

We'll give them plenty else to talk about, Sola'd said in the bathroom. *It's what we do.*

And what was it our mom had said the day before? *I need each of you to step into your own this year. They'll move on. They always do.*

The moving on didn't happen automatically.

Sola had always been the biggest star in the family. The most captivating. Every move of hers seemed to spawn news stories across *People, Us Weekly, Deuxmoi, The Daily Find*, and a thousand other sites.

But we Greers came as a set. When one of us hurt, the others hurt alongside them. When one of us failed, the others felt the ripple effects.

Sola wasn't the only Greer who could launch a thousand headlines, but I was certainly the weakest in that regard. This was a ride-or-die situation, and I hadn't been riding hard enough.

Mom was always pointing out that I needed to participate more. Now here was the proof: There was nothing I could think to do to wipe that look off my sister's face.

I felt like I couldn't breathe.

"Hi! Kiara?" a voice rang in my ear, not more than a foot away. I jumped and took a stumbling step back, bumping into an actress I recognized as the daughter of some big producer.

"Shi—sorry!" That voice from the bar suddenly had a face. One right next to mine, its owner's hand hovering nervously behind my back, as if poised to catch me if I fell. "I tried to introduce myself earlier, but I don't know if you heard me . . ."

The first thing I processed was eyelashes. Long ones, arced up and out in a thick halo around dark brown eyes rimmed with spikes of black eyeliner. People think blue eyes are the most audacious, the only ones that sparkle, but that's so far from the truth. These eyes reflected the ceiling's constellations back at me.

I stepped back, away from the hand. Why was Cassius Campbell talking to me?

"Oooorr you did hear me, and I should go die in a corner now," Cassius Campbell continued, full lips twisting into oblong mortification. In this moment of embarrassment, I finally took him all the way in.

Cassius Campbell, the rising teen sensation. I'd heard this voice through sound systems, on Spotify, on TikTok; seen this face papered on billboards around town and in music videos and interviews splashed absolutely everywhere; but we'd never met. He'd released a hit album last year—*Passions*, a fusion of soul, pop, and glam rock that chronicled (what else?) the roller-coaster haze of parties, hookups, betrayal, and the kind of magnetism that leaves everyone falling at your feet. Now he had the whole town swooning over him.

That face was cut out and taped in lockers all over the world. Tonight he wore a pink suit that looked soft to the touch. Was it satin? Silk? Inexplicably my first instinct was to reach out and caress it, but I managed (barely) to resist the impulse. Cassius Campbell looked like one of the centerpieces sprung to life: a pattern of dark green leaves and magenta flowers vined around his arms, up his chest, down geometrically cut lapels and strong thighs before reaching green crystal-studded boots. The colors glowed against deep brown skin.

He was reading my face, looking for confirmation one way or another on the whole dying-in-a-corner thing. And in return I was just staring at him, my lips parted like a helpless little guppy. How mortifying.

I fixed my face, attempting to appear less stunned by his presence.

"I didn't hear you," I said. "Sorry. Everything's just . . . a lot."

"Tonight, or always?" he asked.

"Always," I admitted, eyes darting around. I was still trying to force my brain out of that bathroom. Cassius Campbell's shoulders relaxed.

"Well—hi," he said, his voice now a strong breeze. "I'm Cass."

"Kia," I said, still on autopilot. I stuck my hand out, and a smile appeared as he shook it. His hand was strong and warm. I felt dizzy. That drink was hitting.

Had his publicist sent him, mandating he hobnob with the host family? That had to be it. I was usually exempt from the big-time schmoozing, though. I wasn't the big deal. No one needed my approval to get in with the Greers. Cassius—or Cass, as he'd just called himself—already knew that. His collab with Lark, a disco-y dance single called "Sweet," was set for release in a matter of weeks. He was already plenty in. He had no use for me.

But oh shit—he was still talking. *Why couldn't I get out of my head?*

"Sorry, can you repeat that?" I said, trying to force myself back to the present. He didn't seem perturbed by my blatant failure to pay attention. Instead his look felt *knowing*, even though this person knew less than nothing about me. The presumption in the look irked me. Still, there was something behind those eyes I couldn't read. Something soft.

"I asked if everything's okay," Cassius Campbell said, leaning forward on the balls of his feet. "You looked a little shell-shocked, coming outta the bathroom."

"Oh. Uh . . ." I glanced instinctively behind me, back toward the shut bathroom door, which was starting to accumulate a line of impatient partygoers. "Yeah, someone left a . . . mess in there."

"Grody." Cass's nose scrunched.

"It was not the best," I confirmed with a grim nod. I was reluctant to plant the image of some toilet-related accident between us, but it felt better than ratting out my sister.

The worry on Cass's face faded and he dropped his chin, shoulders shaking in silent laughter. I couldn't help but join in.

"Well," Cass began again, chewing his bottom lip. "If you've recovered mentally from all *that*, I was wondering . . . well, I was wondering if maybe you'd like to dance with me."

My brain. It took me a horrendous amount of time to squeak out a response.

"*Oh . . .*"

I glanced around in search of my mother, as if this was her

doing. But she was in some far-off corner, happily chatting with my dad and some network bigwigs.

I turned back to Cass, but all that came out was "Why?"

Cassius Campbell rocked back on his heels, bemusement lighting up that face.

"You can say no, of course," he said, leaning forward. "Just shooting a shot."

My hands went to my waist again, to the dress. I was feeling more conspicuous by the moment. I didn't know whether to curse or thank Lark for putting me in this thing.

"I was watching you, at the bar," Cass continued. My gaze shot up to his, and he hurried to correct: "Not like a creep! But . . . I dunno, you looked at your drink in this way that I thought, *I gotta talk to that girl.*" He said this with a soft laugh and a shake of his head, as if helpless in the face of whatever he'd seen in me at that moment. In his eyes was *mirth*—but not the mocking kind. There was a gentleness to this person. I felt clunky, always. Cassius Campbell, though, had this graceful, buoyant way of moving through the world.

"How did I look at my drink?" I asked, equally baffled and curious.

"Like you're looking at me now, actually," Cass said, grinning at my attention. "Like you were suspicious of it. Like it might sprout limbs and do the running man. Discombobulated."

"*Discombobulated,*" I repeated, and I felt my treacherous cheeks lift into a smile. "That's a good word."

"Isn't it?" Cass agreed. He took a half step toward me, and I stiffened automatically. He stepped back into his own space, and I regretted my entire body and my entire brain.

"Discombobulated," I repeated again, rolling the word around my mouth. "It's perfect. It's how I feel at all times. Every hour of every day."

He laughed at this, as if grateful I was finally working with him. "Don't we all?"

"No," I said, finally meeting those eyes. "You don't."

"Wow! How would you know? You don't know me like that."

I stood my ground, tilting my head in exasperation.

"Because," I said, "you came up to a complete stranger at a party. Those of us who truly spend our lives discombobulated would be tortured over that decision until the party had ended and all chances of the shot were lost to the ether."

I couldn't remember the last time I'd spoken so many unnecessary words to a stranger—at least one I wasn't obligated to talk to. How had I gone from my first sip of alcohol to comforting my heartbroken sister all the way to maybe-flirting, maybe-fighting with *People* magazine's "Most Beautiful Man Under 20"? It occurred to me that my life might be very, very strange.

Also: Was I tipsy? Was this what tipsy was? I was feeling less than steady on already wobbly feet. Like my blood was vibrating.

Cassius Campbell looked hard at me for a few seconds. I'd just about decided the corner he'd mentioned dying in earlier was actually meant for me when the tight line of his mouth relaxed. Cass shoved his hands into the pockets of his suit jacket and nodded at the ground.

"*Ether*," Cassius Campbell said under his breath. "Another good word." He cut those eyes to mine, that playful gentleness back in full force.

"Okay, I don't qualify," he conceded. "I'm not exactly shy— a trait that *may* be associated with the discombobulated community. But I do empathize."

I realized then that I'd been holding my breath. But why? I'd met a thousand teen superstars. I'd never been particularly attached to any of them. How had I not already made one of the canned excuses I always had at the ready? I blamed the alcohol. A tingle spread through my fingers, and the room's axis tilted ever so slightly.

It wasn't him. It was the Roman Holiday.

"If not a dance . . . maybe another beverage?" Cass asked now.

"Um . . . okay, sure," I forced out before I could get lost in my own head again. "A drink sounds good."

Cass smiled wide and giddy, gesturing for me to lead the way. We approached the same bartender as before—only this time she lit up at the sight of my companion.

"*Ohmygod!* Hi, I love your album so much," she blurted, significantly more animated than she'd been earlier. "'Burned' got me through a gnarly breakup."

"That means the world to me—thank you," Cass said. I had to give him credit: He looked like he really meant it. "And me too, by the way. I'm glad it resonated."

Cass reached over the bar and clasped her hand, and the bartender glowed so bright I thought she might float to the ceiling.

"What can I get ya?" she asked, beaming between the two of us.

"Another Roman Holiday, please," I squeaked.

"Just a Coca-Cola, please, Rebecca," Cass said, reading her name tag. A huff of laughter caught at my throat. He turned to me. "What? Wrong choice?"

"Who calls it by its full name?" I said. "*Coca-Cola.* Is this a sock hop? Are you preparing to audition for *Grease*?"

Cass's laugh was a hard, joyous bell.

I'd learned it was best to keep a wall up against people I met at places like this, but for a second the wall was gone. Then he leaned in closer. My body freaked out: heart hammering while every other cell tried to stay as still as possible.

"Have you seen this crowd?" Cassius Campbell whispered, conspiratorial. "I didn't want her to slip me actual coke."

I barked a laugh. He had a point. A few of the teen dreams had miniature spoons and vials tucked away for that very purpose. They looked like doll toys to me. It was an unspoken but not uncommon habit among Hollywood types. These were people who worked long hours and went hard in their leisure time. It wasn't just the adults, either. Not everyone partook—I certainly hadn't. Lark had tried it once and hadn't liked the crash that came the morning after. But those who did it regularly always seemed ready to go.

"Yo, these kids are *intense*," Cass continued. Then suddenly he held his hands in the air. "No offense if you're one of them. I ain't narcin'."

"Only literal narcotics officers announce they're not narcs," I said. But there I was, self-conscious about my cocktail. Like some narc. I figured the only way out of the awkwardness gnawing at my stomach was to barrel through it. "Can I admit something?"

Cass nodded, mouth pressed into a tight line like he was taking this very seriously. I took a deep breath.

"Tonight I had my first alcoholic beverage. Ever."

"*Oh my god,*" he said, his own breath a huff as his whole body relaxed. "I was so nervous! I thought you were about to admit you've done three rehab stints and this was you falling off the wagon. I wasn't ready to tackle that drink outta your hand. I woulda, though."

"Damn. You really went through it in those five seconds."

"Kia"—Cass's hand reached out to touch my upper arm—"I was not ready for that kind of responsibility."

We laughed together, swaying so close, I became aware of his smell. It was floral but fresh, sweet and citrusy.

"So, what's the verdict?" he asked.

"Does alcohol always taste kinda gross?" I asked back.

"You know what, I think it might," he said with a sad tsk.

Maybe I wasn't alone at this party after all. The thought came so swift and sure, it took me aback. *What?* I didn't know this person.

We stayed huddled close, and I realized there was this goofy smile on my face. I'd finally recognized his smell: orange blossoms. Like the ones we'd had in our backyard in the city. The trees Dad loved so much, he'd had them transplanted at the new house in the hills.

We hadn't said anything for a few long seconds. I wondered if he was expecting me to talk next. But then a hand grazed my back, and a twirl of pink crowded my field of vision. Lark.

"Two of my favorite people?!" the birthday girl exclaimed. "I love this development."

She was fresh from the dance floor, where a steady R&B beat was *bump-bump*ing. Even as she stopped to talk, she seemed to still be in motion, like she was one with the energy of the room. I could tell from her eyes she was sober; this was just my little sister's normal rhythm. She grasped my hand.

"We're just grabbing a beverage," I intoned, shooting daggers with my eyes, hoping she'd get my telepathic message to *be chill and drop it.* Her brow arched mischievously.

"Whatever, you'll tell me later," she said, waving it off. "Right now: Dance with me. Both of you!"

Cass looked my way, gauging my willingness.

"I don't know . . ." he said, eyes stuck on me. "We're waiting for our drinks."

"It's my birthday—you have to," Lark said, and she was already physically dragging us to the middle of the dance floor. She was more Melora's daughter than I'd ever be.

"I guess we're dancing," I said. The *boom-boom* of one song was winding down.

"Wait here!" Lark exclaimed. She was gone again—rushing the DJ booth. I could tell she was delivering intent, specific orders, the kind she barked at me when she needed the living room clear to practice choreo. She pushed her phone on the guy just as the song ended.

I loved the interim between songs. When the beat died down and bodies kept bopping to the old beat, poised in limbo, waiting eagerly for the next one to drop. Ready and willing.

I wondered if I should say this out loud to Cass, but I worried it would make me sound too pretentious, or too dweeby.

"What's happening?!" he asked directly in my ear. I felt a jolt down my spine. I wasn't used to strangers talking this close. Though I guess he wasn't a stranger anymore. My sister knew him. My sister liked him. Maybe that opened a door for me to like him, too.

"Beats me," I said.

"There," Lark announced, arriving back before us with a little hop.

"There, what?" I asked. An electronic *wooOOoo* slid in over the sound system and answered the question. Crashing drums, the whine of a guitar. It was so familiar, but I couldn't place it . . . until Lark's voice broke through the track, an upbeat, breathy *"Ohhh!"* The Lark in front of me grinned ear to ear.

"Oh damn!" Cass exclaimed, fist to mouth. "Is that allowed?"

"It's my birthday!" Lark shouted over the music.

The lively heartbeat disco rhythm of their single "Sweet" filled the room. I'd heard it only once, just before they'd finalized the track. I'd been doing calculus homework when Lark burst in, unable to wait another second before playing it for me. By the first chorus we were jump-dancing around my room, screaming the lyrics in each other's faces.

"Sweet" was destined to be a radio hit: a beat you felt in your shoulders and simple, lively lyrics about two teens making the most of a Friday night out. Around us the crowd began to realize what was playing. People whooped and hollered. Seemingly disembodied hands appeared, clapping congratulations on Cass's and Lark's shoulders. This song wasn't due out for weeks—everyone knew they were being treated to something shiny, gleaming, and new.

Cass's whole face was wide with awe. He was buffering now, unable to compute the sudden turn the night had taken. He let out a bewildered, gleeful laugh. Lark shook his shoulders.

"This is your moment!" she shouted. "What are you doing?! *DANCE!*"

I threw my head back and laughed into the buzzing air.

"This is amazing!" I shouted in her face. She hugged me tight, and I picked her up and twirled her. My little sister was sixteen! And she knew exactly what to do with it.

Lark had always been a star: a precocious little girl singing for televised dinner parties on *Growin' Up*, then a name every kid in the country knew thanks to *Nick of Time*. She'd had her record deal for over a year, and we'd celebrated plenty. But hearing her song in a room like this was a whole different animal.

"Sweet" was her first big feature, her first big single attached to an already popular artist.

"I finally get to show them what I'm made of," she'd whispered to me one night. This was the first time she'd gotten to share a piece of her talent that really mattered to her.

I gulped down my drink and gave myself over. I screamed into my sister's face. I let the cocktails swivel my hips and shimmy my shoulders with an abandon that felt new to me.

Every cell in my body was hyperaware that Cassius Campbell was dancing right beside me. He was, in fact, dancing *with* me, those eyes on me as we threw our bodies to the beat. Even when I turned away, I could still feel every muscle in his body in relation to mine.

The rest of the teen dreams surrounded us in a tight circle, the glare of camera flashes cutting through the dark of my eyelids. It almost threw me off—but each time my nerves broke through the rhythm, I searched for the transcendent sparkle on my little sister's face. Lark deserved my full presence in this moment. This glorious, gleaming, shiny new moment. She was on the brink of something, and maybe I could be, too.

So I danced. Soon Destiny's arms snaked around my shoulders, and I turned to find her, Sola, and Max screaming alongside us. Sola locked eyes with me and mouthed, *Thank you.* Before I could get sappy or worried, she threw her shoulders back and forth and did her spin on the Roger Rabbit, making it goofier and goofier until I joined in, laughing.

"*This night will never end,*" the song went. "*This time will never die . . . it's just too sweet to leave our bloodstreams . . . just you—and—I . . . dancing through this endless ni-iii-iiight . . .*"

One song faded into another, and into yet another, as I rode this wave of energy, buoyed by the presence of my sisters. I forced myself not to check for Cass as often as I wanted—but he was never more than a few bodies away. And I couldn't tell if it was paranoia, ego, or some sixth sense, but even without looking, I knew those eyes kept coming back to me.

⌒

Eventually the music slowed to a D'Angelo classic, and I slipped away. I snatched a handful of napkins from the bar to wipe my brow and pushed through bodies until I hit door, sucking in a sharp lungful of air as I stepped into the open night.

Out back was a makeshift patio, fenced in to block the photographers. A few people smoked near the door. I drifted to a far corner, where a gaggle of heat lamps leaned against each other, out of commission.

The air inside had been so *full*—of booming music, roaring voices, body heat, liquor, and a heady mix of smells. Outside there was room to breathe. To think, to feel.

It was early September. The beginning of the school year, in some other world far away from mine. I wrapped my arms tight around myself and took in the night sky, so blotted with city lights the constellations couldn't shine through.

Tell me, what is it you plan to do with your one wild and precious life?

Slowly, surely, my heartbeat settled in my chest. The din in my mind settled, too.

"Smoker? Or introvert?"

I jumped out of my skin, losing footing in those goddamn heels and crashing into the gathered heat lamps. The chatter of the smokers quieted as they all turned our way.

"Oh gosh—shit, oh gosh—" Cassius Campbell rushed forward.

He pulled me by the arm until I was back to upright, dazed and avoiding his shocked brown eyes.

"I'm okay," I insisted. "Really, I'm fine."

Cass stepped back. The pure overwhelm on his face amused me, and I smiled through my embarrassment.

"I'm really sucking at this, aren't I?"

"At what?" I tilted my head. Before Cass could answer, the *bzzzt* of a phone vibrated from somewhere within the pink cocoon of his outfit. He leveled a look my way that could only be described as mournful as he fished it out.

"Shoot. It's midnight already?" he mumbled. I furrowed my brows. "My sister. She's picking me up . . . now, apparently."

"Oh," I said, trying to hide my . . . was it disappointment I felt? Or nausea, from the liquor? "Okay. Have a good rest of your night."

Cass blinked, and even barely knowing this person, I got the sense his brain was moving at lightning speed, trying to piece something together. He looked to the street, then back to me.

"Um—do you want to come with?"

"Oh . . . What?"

"With us. We're going to Mel's Drive-In. You're welcome to join if you're done in there."

Now it was my turn to blink. I took an instinctual step back and looked around the patio, as if that would provide an answer. Then it did: The door swung open to our left, and I heard Sola and Max before I saw them.

"That was so much *fun!*" Sola sang, stumbling forward. Her gait took a hard rightward tilt that threatened to collide with the ground, but Max caught her just in time. Sola giggled—and then she saw me, and her whole face burst open in a smile. She lurched out of Max's arms and into mine, smashing my face between her hands again. Her breath—her entire being—smelled like that martini I'd gagged on earlier in the night. She'd clearly had a few.

"Baby girl! You're the best," she slurred. "Such a good sister, such a good *girl*!"

"Thank you, Sol. Should we get you some water?"

It was then that Sola noticed Cass standing next to me. Intrigue, excitement, and anger all flashed across her face.

"*Treat her right,*" she ordered, pointing a finger in Cass's face. A blush shot from my toes to the top of my head. I grabbed her hand away from him, but Cass just gave a somber nod.

"You have my word," he said.

"You def need some water," I whispered, mortified.

"I got her," Max assured me, much steadier in her five-inch stilettos than either Sola or me. She reached for my sister, and Sola melted into the arms of her longest-lasting friendship. "Don't worry. Already got one of those IV nurses meeting us at hers in forty."

"Maxi, *thank you,*" I effused. Sola smiled, suddenly serene, up into Max's face.

"You two really know how to spoil a girl," sang Sola. Her eyes were glassy as she kissed my cheek, her grasp sloppy as she squeezed my hand. "Don't worry about me, babyyyy. It's only up from here!"

I trailed behind as Max guided Sola out of the patio area, back onto the street, and into a waiting Escalade. Photographers milled around the sidewalk waiting for a moment just like this. They sprang into action, cameras flashing as Sola slid into the back of the car. Max hovered over her, ensuring they didn't get any shots that were too vulnerable.

"SOLA! HOW ARE YOU HANDLING THE DIVORCE?"

"SOLA! YOU GOT A NEW MAN YET?"

"SOLA! WHAT'D YOU TAKE TONIGHT?"

"Can I help?"

Cass was a soft voice through the violence. He'd followed me out to the street.

"She's got it." I tilted my head to point toward Max. "It would just draw more attention."

Max gave me a reassuring wink as their driver shut the door behind them. Photogs crowded their windows, salivating over the opportunity to capture America's latest slut-shamed starlet glassy-eyed after a night of partying.

"Fucking vultures," Cass muttered next to me. My head whipped to him.

HHHHNNNNNNNN—a horn cut through the night. Cass turned, agitated, and waved toward the offending old beater of a minivan that idled behind the waiting Escalades and limos.

"Sorry . . . that's my sister," he lamented. I looked between Cass and the van. The sight took a moment to process, it felt so out of sync. The glimmering pop heartthrob was about to be whisked away from the glamorous party in a chariot that was very, well, *beige*. Literally.

I still hadn't answered Cass's previous question. About if I'd be going with him.

But now I was the one buffering. Processing too much information at once. My sister, despondent, trying her best to be okay. Men with cameras swarming, feeding off her misery, hoping to catch her blazer too far open or her mouth slack from drink—some clear sign that she was the overexposed, tawdry mess they needed her to be. The car horn, Cass's sister waiting. This very famously beautiful person always *looking at me,* always with questions I didn't have answers to.

I didn't know exactly what I wanted from life, but I did want this: to dash into the night with a bumbling, charming, interesting person with sparkly dark eyes somehow trained on *me.* To break past the gates, experience the places and people and sensations that were beyond the barriers of my tiny little world and my own mess of a brain.

I'd never met this version of me before.

HHHHHNNNNNNNNNNN, the car horn sounded again. Cameras started flashing our way, and the knot in my chest tightened as I realized that in Sola's absence, they'd turned on me and Cass. Kiara Greer and Cassius Campbell, standing close outside the ball.

Cass was watching me, eyes more urgent now, but still he didn't press his question. He waited patiently for me to tell both of us what would happen next.

We'll give them plenty else to talk about. It's what we do. They'll move on.

Tell me, what is it you plan to do with your one wild and precious life?

Something in Cass's patience unlocked something in me. It gave me permission.

"Okay," I answered, locking my eyes to his.

That eyebrow cocked. "Okay to . . . ?"

"Okay, I'll come with."

Cassius Campbell's smile spread so wide I could see his molars. They were gleaming white, but he had a filling toward the back of his mouth. For some reason I loved that.

I blinked away—more camera flashes. I felt anger in my chest where the knot lived. I looked into the eyes of one of the men holding a camera in our faces. He had silver hair, thick black eyebrows, and Kanye West on his shirt. He circled, unrelenting, getting every angle on us. I hated this man with everything that I had. He was a vulture, and to him I was nothing more than a leftover crumb. I wondered if he was the one who'd put a tracker on Sola's car.

"Hey, dude, back off, please?" Cass said, firm but clearly trying hard to remain polite. He looked at me.

"If you didn't want this, you shouldn't have become famous," the man barked back.

Cass sighed and turned away from him. He stood before me, and his face transformed into something warm and comforting. That face was a reprieve from everything around us.

"No pressure, but she *will* attack if I don't go soon," Cass said, nodding toward the van. The *HHHHNNNNNN* sounded once more. The lights flashed in my eyes, unceasing. Something in me snapped, just a little. If they were going to hound the lot of us, the least I could do was get them off Sola's back. The least I could do was have a good night.

The public needed something else to focus on.

So I grabbed Cass's hand. I made sure they could see it. I squeezed. Cass squeezed back.

We'll give them plenty else to talk about. It's what we do. They'll move on.

Tell me, what is it you plan to do with your one wild and precious life?

More photographers swooped in as we walked to the van. They circled us like rabid coyotes with cameras, shoving Cass and I closer together. I wished I'd called Joe for security—but at the same time it was good he wasn't here. It meant I could run.

Something was boiling inside me. Anger, or fear, or alcohol, or a whole other beast entirely.

When we reached the door of the van, I did something I didn't know I had it in me to do: I leaned forward and kissed Cass's cheek.

"Let's go," I said. Cass's eyes were warm and reassuring. He wrenched the sliding door open and squeezed my hand one more time. I did my best to hide that I was shaking.

CHAPTER SIX

I was a hypocrite. Not as bad as Levi, but bad enough. A teenage dream had whisked me away, and I had sacrificed him on the altar of the gossip-industrial complex. The worst part? He sat on the other side of the table from me in our green vinyl booth, periodically glancing up from his menu and staring me down with wonderful, sparkly, clueless eyes. A happy smile played across his lips—because Cassius Campbell had no idea how treacherous I was.

I had kissed his cheek in front of at least ten paparazzi. That one move guaranteed that gossip hounds scattered across the world were already generating headlines. "BREAKING NEWS: Rising Pop Prince Cassius Campbell May Be Dating Dud Reality Princess Kiara Greer."

I'd let my intrusive thoughts win. Those lights had been flashing in my face, and there'd been a very cute person earnestly awaiting my answer. Even more than that: Sola didn't have time to wait for the next hot story to drop. So I'd grabbed Cass's hand and kissed his cheek.

Now I felt like the grossest little slug.

"Wanna share a root beer float?" Cass's voice cut through my thoughts. "Best drink of all time, in my opinion. Top-tier invention."

I could fucking cry. How was he actually this wonderful?

After my lapse in judgment, Cass had kept his grip on my hand, guiding me as I awkwardly lurched into his family's van. I was greeted by the skeptical glare of his younger sister, Jade. Jade was all slouchy attitude, with an oversized Dick's tee, oversized ripped jeans, and a cavernous orange plaid flannel. She rocked multicolored box braids at least two months grown out, and she hadn't bothered to hide the swath of blemishes dotting her cheeks. I learned on the drive that she was a rising junior, Lark's age, whereas Cass and I were both would-have-been seniors. Cass had been the one to provide that information; Jade was hardly forthcoming.

I, meanwhile, had spent the ride tearing myself up inside while my outsides tried to keep up with Cass's cheerful chatter.

"You're going to see a table of unwashed gremlins, but you do not have to talk to them," he'd said. "That's drama club. Jade will rule them with an iron fist while we do our own thing."

"You were supposed to join us," Jade sneered from the driver's seat. "Remember?"

"Next time," Cass said. Jade scoffed.

"I don't want to get in the way of your plans," I said.

"You're not," Cass insisted. "I know where I want to be."

"You've changed, Campbell," Jade said.

"Change can be good, Campbell," Cass replied.

"Whatever. Just don't act like you don't miss us."

I didn't ask Cass why we weren't joining the other table. A night out with regular kids my age was a constant daydream of mine, but part of me was afraid that if I brought it up, we actually would merge tables, and I'd make a fool of myself. Then I'd know once and for all I could never go back to the real world. I'd spent too much time away, grown too weird inside. Wasn't that a saying, after all? *You can never go home again.*

⌒

Mel's Drive-In was an LA institution with multiple locations. The Campbells had chosen the one on the Sunset Strip, with the lights of West Hollywood's hill houses rising just beyond it. The facade of the diner was all red and blue and white, with a fifties-style angled roof and a big neon sign. A covert Google told me the building had been standing since 1962 and was most famous for its roles in the movies *American Graffiti* and *Guess Who's Coming to Dinner*. In Los Angeles even the buildings were performers. I made a note to ask my dad about this place on one of our thrice-weekly FaceTimes. He'd definitely know something cool about it.

Mel's looked right out of the sock hop I'd accused Cass of attending earlier, only my gown and I were the closest things there to a poodle-skirted teen. The clientele of Mel's just after midnight was more . . . varied. There were local young people clad in Supreme and adults swinging through in mesh and leather 'fits, no doubt lining their stomachs before the club. A few people looked unhoused. Others looked like off-duty porn stars.

Heads swiveled as we walked in, and my hackles went up. There was something about looks like these that made me feel like I was in a zoo. No matter how many years passed, I'd never fully grown used to them.

"See ya." Jade threw a disdainful smirk my way before making a beeline for an overstuffed, rowdy table of kids our age. They were arguing animatedly about some unknown topic I was desperately curious about. As Jade arrived at the table, the whole group erupted in jeers, throwing fries at her. She sat down unfazed. I wondered what it was like to be so part of a group that you take it for granted.

As Cass and I walked by, someone caught my eye. A few seats down from Jade was a young guy who was following Cass around the diner with his eyes. He had floppy straight hair like a nineties heartthrob, dyed green. Those weren't zoo-goer eyes. He knew Cass, I could tell. I caught the guy's eye—mostly by accident—and his expression twisted into something scornful before he looked away.

Cass didn't look his way, either unaware or unbothered. His hand hovered but didn't quite touch my waist as he guided me to a corner booth in the back.

That's where we were now, each scanning menus. I felt like a fraud. I'd never been on anything remotely datelike. The closest I'd come was my brief stint eating cookies with Jonny Hall in Lark's trailer. That didn't count for a million reasons.

Sitting across from Cassius Campbell didn't feel like being out with one of the world's biggest pop stars. It felt like I was out with *Cass*, the cool senior who graduated early. The one whose old friend group clearly still yearned for him, but who'd gone out and made something of himself. This was Americana. The teen experience. Except I knew less about that than I did about virtually anything else. I was thirteen when my mom took Lark and me out of regular school. Ever since then I'd been the weird homeschool girl.

Our server was waiting for our drink order. He was surly and burly, a man in his fifties who couldn't care less that he was waiting on two famous kids. I got the strong impression we were just another hurdle standing between this man and his bed, and I respected it. His name tag read GARY.

"A root beer float to share sounds good," I managed with a small smile.

"Perfect," Cass said. Gary gave a curt nod and disappeared.

Cass leaned back, slinging an arm over his seat. As he scanned my face, I had the uncomfortable sensation that I was being read like a book.

"So you know them, too?" I asked, glancing over at the gremlin table just in time to see a green head swivel away. "You went to school together?"

Cass tugged at his ear as if nervous.

"Yes indeed," he said. "Those used to be my gremlins. Made the mistake of feeding them after midnight one too many times, though. Jade will have to learn that rule for herself."

"I think that's from a movie I've never seen," I said.

"But you still got the reference," Cass said, rapping the table with his knuckles. His nails were painted a glittery black. They looked like a night sky. "My moms made me watch that movie. It was some nostalgia thing for them, like I wouldn't have a real childhood if I missed it."

"Isn't that weird?" I said. "That you can have never seen a movie, or read a book, or had an experience, but you still walk around knowing these important pieces?"

Cass grabbed my gaze with his and held it.

"I've never thought about that," he said, his voice softer now. "But you're right. Like, I've never seen all the *Star Wars* movies, but I could still tell you about the really big plot twists."

"You've never seen *Star Wars*?!" I exclaimed before I could think better of it.

"I've seen bits and pieces over the years, but I've never sat through all of them," he said. "I will one day. I'm considering it delayed gratification. I'll find the right moment in my life to finally do it, and I think I'll like them."

"My dad wants to be Harrison Ford," I said. "So we watch the original trilogy every Christmas, and then he makes us watch the holiday special."

"Do you like them as much as he does?"

"I like them. But I have my *own* Christmas tradition inspired by our rewatch."

Our root beer float arrived. Cass plopped two straws in the glass tumbler and pushed it my way. As I took a sip, a perfect combination of sweet cream and fizz hit my tongue.

"You have to tell me what it is," he said. "This tradition."

The mound of ice cream was melting fast into the soda. Sweet cream foamed up around the glass's edge, and I poked at it with my straw. The cream sank, dancing its way to the bottom.

This thing had a lot of calories. My mom and the very expensive nutritionist she paid to monitor our eating would not want me to drink this.

I took another big slurp anyway. She didn't have to know.

"It's not exciting," I said, embarrassed now that I'd brought this up. "I reread Carrie Fisher's books. She's the coolest part of *Star Wars,* if you ask me."

Cass cocked his head a bit to the side. He was still studying me.

"I didn't even know she was a writer," he said. "That's so cool. Now I'll read her stuff."

"She was *so cool,*" I said. "She wrote a bunch of books, but she was also an uncredited script doctor for a ton of stuff. Her last memoir, *The Princess Diarist,* that's my favorite."

I was talking too much—not my usual problem. But I couldn't help it. We'd tripped into one of my favorite topics.

"Say more," he said when he saw I'd stopped myself from continuing. I smiled shyly.

"She had this affair with Harrison that makes it really juicy, but it's also all when she's still a teenager," I said. "She has no idea she's on the verge of this huge thing, and you get to live in all the mess that was going on in her head. I think I find it comforting she was so publicly messy and unapologetic about it, since I feel like a mess all the time."

Cass didn't say anything. His head had relaxed and was gently bobbing in the air, as if in a perpetual nod. Something soft played around the edges of his features.

"Sorry," I said, "I'm talking too much."

"Don't stop," he said, leaning forward and laying his arms over each other on the table. "I like it. Keep going, please."

I chewed my bottom lip. I still didn't know how far to go with this person. I pushed the root beer float his way.

"I guess I like that she wasn't afraid to share her mess, even though there were always consequences. It affected how people saw her, but her sharing her struggles also helped a lot of people. I wish I could be more like her."

"You seem pretty fearless to me," Cass said. "You're sharing with me right now."

"I'm not like that at all," I said with a laugh. "Everything's a lot, always, and I'm not particularly good at dealing with it."

He nodded, slow and knowingly. Beneath the table I felt his knee graze against mine. I moved mine away, an instinct I regretted instantly. Cass took a big pull of our drink, and I could tell the exact moment it hit his tongue, because he closed his eyes and let out this small groan. That noise did something strange and illicit to my stomach.

I studied the glass, the way the ice cream changed the color and texture of the root beer, and tried not to fixate on the fact that I hadn't felt the knot in my chest since we started talking.

"Are you worried about Sola?" Cass asked, pushing the glass back to me.

I shifted in my seat, even farther from his wayward knee.

"She's a grown-up. Probably gonna be hungover tomorrow, but at least she . . . had fun tonight."

"Fair," Cass said. "I just feel for her, is all. Levi Ellis seems like a real douchenozzle. What he's doing to her isn't right."

I scanned his face, looking for any hint of ulterior motive. But Cass's gaze was steady. Curious but kind. Still, I had to be cautious. There were a lot of liars in this town, people who'd get close to you and then sell the details of your pain to the highest bidder. Too many to count had come before Levi. I cleared my throat.

"What did Lark tell you about all that?" I asked.

"She didn't say anything. But I met Levi last year, at Jingle Ball. That dude's got *bad vibes.*" Cass shook his shoulders out as if the vibes needed to be banished. "And he didn't exactly hide his, uh, *intentions* with the women hanging on his every word."

I chewed my lip. "Yes, well," I said to buy myself time to process. "He does suck."

"I'm sorry about that," Cass said. I could feel in the timbre of his voice that he meant it. "That must be tough, having to put up with that guy in your family for so long. And to have so many people think your sister's the problem? I'd be throwin' hands. Or wishing I could."

I blinked again, this time to ensure there'd be no mist in my eyes.

"We all loved him," I corrected, trying to push down the flood of embarrassment at the fact that my voice cracked. "That's what sucked the most. That was my brother . . . till he wasn't."

What was I doing? I didn't know what he'd do with this information. But there was something about Cassius Campbell that kept me doing and saying the last thing I expected.

"Shit," he said. "That's *so* much worse. I'm so sorry."

I'd brought down the vibe—or whatever puny wisp of one we'd had a chance at. Gary arrived back at our table to save me from myself. Cass ordered a chicken potpie, and I gave in to the rabid part of my heart dying for the bacon cheeseburger. If I was going to rebel, I might as well go all in. Gary muttered something unintelligible as he walked away.

"Is it weird that I want to know absolutely everything about Gary's life?" Cass asked, watching Gary retreat toward the kitchen.

I laughed. "No, because *same*," I assured him. Cass's eyes gleamed at my answer.

You know that thing people say about stars, about how someone like Beyoncé walks into a room and they radiate an energy that makes them shine brighter than everyone else? Cassius Campbell had that. His very being was shiny, attractive, magnetic.

But there was something else about Cass, too. Something beyond that.

My stomach was doing that strange thing again—and the knot in my chest was back, and tightening. Because having crushes that worked out wasn't my reality. It never had been.

I kept trying to convince myself to pull away, call Joe and

hightail it home. It was the kind thing to do, right? I'd used Cass by flaunting our fledgling connection in front of the paps. As a result, hadn't I forfeited all right to the soft edges of the way he was looking at me?

And if that wasn't the case—if he'd approached me at the urging of his publicists, perhaps looking to deepen his association with my family? Well, I wasn't sure if I could handle that. If that was the truth, I had the strong feeling I'd crumble into dust.

Because the reaction I was having to the presence of Cassius Campbell wasn't just about his star power. No, something about sitting across from Cass felt *natural.* Like he was just another teenager, a boy I could've met in second-period bio. Like he could've approached me in the hall by my locker instead of at a star-studded sweet sixteen.

That was so far from the case. We were two famous kids sitting in a diner in very ostentatious outfits. We'd been surrounded by paparazzi a half hour before. There was nothing normal about that. Nothing easy or chill.

But I couldn't pull away. And despite myself I was still smiling.

"What do you think Gary does in his spare time?" I asked Cass, feeling tentatively sick to my stomach. Usually I played this kind of game all by my lonesome. It was scary to invite someone else in.

But a slow smile spread across his face as he prepared to answer.

That night I learned that Cass's laugh came with intoxicating ease. He was a little cocky, but at least that was warranted. He was talented, and he knew that; he was gorgeous, and he clearly knew that, too. Mostly, Cass was a happy-go-lucky person, the kind who loved chitchat but wasn't afraid to dive deep. The longer we talked, the more his smile grew, spreading wider and freer as the night wore on.

The cocktails had worn off, but now I was fully sugar high, snort-laughing into my second root beer float of the night. My burger had been demolished, as had Cass's potpie. I learned that Cass and Jade had older moms, who hadn't had kids until their fifties. One was around and the other was not, though I didn't ask why. He seemed to dodge that information, and I promised myself I wouldn't Google the answer the second I got home, because I hated when people knew things about me before I told them.

What he did tell me was that he grew up in the Valley, way out in Northridge, where the mom who was around, Violet, was a nurse at the VA hospital. This was apparently how Cass became the world's only eighteen-year-old superfan of *Grey's Anatomy*: Violet had put it on one day and Cass and Jade binged twenty seasons in a matter of months. Violet's favorite pastime was pointing out everything that was inaccurate to the medical profession.

I learned that Cass still lived with Violet and Jade, in the same three-bedroom ranch-style house he'd grown up in, even though he was eighteen and had plenty of money to find a place of his own. He didn't even have his own car; he and Jade shared the van, and his record company would send a car service for all his fancy events.

I learned that Cass liked to talk, but he also asked a lot of questions, so many that the ones I levied at him were mostly repeats of what he'd asked me. I wondered if I was doing this whole maybe-date thing right. But each time I answered a question—"What kind of kindergartener were you?" ("The one with her head in the clouds"), "Do you like video games?" ("I like *The Sims* and *Mario*"), "Do you think humans are inherently good or bad?" ("Somewhere in between")—Cass's eyes would light up or one of his dimples would appear, so I was doing something right.

I learned that Cass had *energy*. He was like Lark that way. I had to assume this person was some extreme extrovert, because otherwise I don't know how anybody could have so much life radiating from them at two a.m. He was infectious; somehow his zest for life lit me up, too.

Cassius Campbell made me forget myself. Dangerously so.

Once I let myself really talk to Cass, I didn't want to stop. I knew perfectly well that tonight was way too good to be true. But I couldn't make myself pull away. Not yet.

"All right, brand-new question," I declared, giving in to this new intoxication. He grinned, game, and, goddamn, he really was beautiful. "Why'd you leave school? Why not stay and go to college, do the whole rock star thing later?"

It was the first time we'd broached the fame. Refreshingly— wonderfully—absolutely none of his questions had to do with showbiz.

He thought for a moment, rapping his knuckles against the table.

"That . . . is a complicated one," he said. "Simplest answer? None of the other options really fit who I wanted to be."

He screwed up his face as if worried it was a stupid answer.

"Say more," I said. It was what he'd been saying to me all night. To push me forward, past the media training and to what I was actually thinking. Cass exhaled, chewing his lip. I wondered what was behind this question that made him more skittish than he'd been all night.

"For me, college felt like this conveyor belt kinda thing," he said. "I don't know if that makes sense. What I mean is, it felt like the default, what everyone in my family had done and what everyone around me in school was expected to do. I was going to do it, too—but I don't think it ever really excited me? I spent so many nights blowing off homework to sing into my phone, and then some guy saw my videos and came to one of my shows . . . and he was A&R, and he wanted me. That was Simms. Uh, Simmons Jeffrey?"

"I know who Simms is," I said. Cass had been discovered by the same guy Lark was now spending countless hours a week with in a recording booth.

"Course you do. Anyway, I figured why wait, if I already knew what I liked to do most? They were handing me an adventure, and I took it. I don't think my fam ever really forgave me."

For a moment he was far away, eyes focused just behind me.

I let out a soft "Hmm." I envied his confidence in pursuing something so outside the norms of his world. I wanted to press on the bruises that came with it—the vague reference to trouble with his mom and sister.

"Tsk." Jade had appeared at the table. She shook her head and sighed. "Well. You know my thoughts on the topic."

"Yes, Jade," Cass replied, his voice strained. "I am very aware. Thank you for your input, but let's not do this here, okay?"

I looked between them. Again I promised myself I wouldn't Google "Cassius Campbell + Jade + sibling fight?" when I got home.

It was easier said than done, because suddenly the night was over. Jade was ready for bed, and we were ushered out of the diner and back to the van. Cass mumbled apologies, but I lied and told him we were nearing my curfew.

The truth was, my parents had never bothered to give me one. I never went out late.

Was my life truly pathetic? Maybe. But I had to face reality sooner or later. My grace period was coming to an end: Tomorrow the gossip hounds would have their way with us. I'd no longer be able to evade the consequences of my actions.

Cassius Campbell was a temporary gift from the universe. I'd enjoyed him while I could, but our time was about to expire.

⌒⌒

"So, Kiara," asked Jade as she careened the van around a bend and off the 101, "how do you feel being part of a family who's destroying the soul of our nation?"

"Jade!" Cass shouted. He had one arm thrust out in front of me, as if that would make a difference in the fiery car crash we were all about to die in. Still, I appreciated the sentiment. "Don't be rude—and, dude, *please don't use your new license as a weapon!*" That last part went up a few octaves as we hit a particularly threatening turn and one side of wheels left the ground.

"How new is it?!" I screeched, hands clutching the seat for dear life.

"Three weeks!" Jade chirped as the car landed on all four wheels and entered the Santa Monica Mountains. "Failed three times before I got it, too."

I threw a side-eye at Cass. *"And you let her drive?!"*

"She's persistent," he moaned, seeming to regret this choice now. I, meanwhile, was beginning to regret accepting the ride home.

"Relax," Jade intoned. "Only perilously dark, windy roads from here."

"Thanks," Cass croaked, sarcastic. He turned back to me.

"Don't feel pressured to answer her questions. She learned her conversational skills from Kylo Ren."

"So you're saying teen girls write fanfic about me?" Jade drawled. "I knew it."

This drew a chuckle out of me. The corner of Cass's mouth pulled up, thankful I wasn't pissed. Slowly our ride grew steadier, and I relaxed my grip on the seat.

"It's well documented," Jade continued. "Reality TV presents a certain type of person as the norm, and everyone outside it as not hot enough, thin enough, rich enough, white enough—"

"Bruh, her family is not even white," Cass defended. "Not most of 'em."

"But for real! Reality shows *lit-rally* make people more depressed and anxious about their financial status and body image. There's been studies and shit. People want what they see on these shows, but what those people have isn't even 'real' in the first place. It's scripted, or it's lipo, or filler, or filters. I'd love to hear your take, Kiara, as someone being raised inside the reality TV cult."

"*Jade,*" Cass warned again before glancing back my way. "You don't have to answer."

You'd think I'd be offended, but the truth was, I found Jade's frankness refreshing. I'd read those same studies myself, and not even for an assignment from Mr. Hillis. Being famous can sometimes feel like you're living in an echo chamber, like everyone is your biggest cheerleader until your back is turned. There were literally dozens of people in my family's employ whose job it was to make sure our lives ran smoothly, that we were content—or at least beautiful—at every moment. The dream, right? But not that helpful when you're looking for honest feedback. Or, like, the meaning of life.

There was so much I'd never understand. But I could try. That was part of why I wanted to go to college. I understood where Cass was coming from, why he'd walked away from it. But for me college was a time and place dedicated to filling yourself up. To becoming so much more than you already were. I didn't know what I wanted to major in, or what life looked like after graduation. But I wanted to know *more.* To feel more, to *be* more.

So sometimes I spent my free time using the JSTOR account Mr. Hillis set me up with, reading anthropology journals and the occasional academic article about *Growin' Up Greer.*

"Doesn't talk much, does she?" Jade said, interrupting my thoughts. Cass opened his mouth to object, but I cut him off.

"She talks plenty when she's comfortable with the people around her," I said with a sickly sweet smile.

"Aw, I'm not making you comfy, princess?" I caught her faux pout in the rearview mirror.

"You really are sounding more and more like Draco Malfoy," Cass observed. "And *not* the fanfic version. You sound like J. K. Rowling wrote you."

"How dare you, brother!" Jade gasped, hand flying to her chest. The van jerked.

"Eyes on the road, please!" Cass yelled.

I could, I realized, keep avoiding the question. Clam up, like I did most of the time. Crawl further inside myself, into some nook of me. It was the safest option.

But I had this gut feeling that Jade's snobbery would keep her from leaking stories to the gossip press. I also didn't know when I'd next get the chance to talk to two regular kids my age—or, I guess more accurately, one hostile teen girl and her cheery international pop sensation hottie brother. I found myself not really wanting to disengage. So I braced myself and dove in.

"I don't doubt the studies you're talking about," I said. "But I guess my counter would be: Doesn't all media get a bad rap somehow? Video games make us violent, Marvel movies make guys think they need to have steroid six-packs to matter. Every other TV show is about some rich family. People call them guilty pleasures, but isn't it okay, at the end of a long day, to just put on whatever you want and not always think too much? *Growin' Up Greer* is entertainment. Can't people engage or disengage as they please?"

I paused to catch my breath—and to figure out where the hell I was even going with this.

"You *certainly* glommed on to that *Glee* rewatch," Cass said, yawning in Jade's direction. "It doesn't always have to be that deep."

"We agreed not to speak of that," Jade chastised him. Cass let his head fall back on the headrest. He turned to smile at me with sleepy eyes.

"I've seen a few eps of yours," he admitted, a little shyly. "It's *fun.*"

"Define *fun*," Jade deadpanned. "You're dodging the question." Her eyes cut to me in the rearview again. "You're, like, *of* this weird-ass *thing*. Since you were a little kid, right? It *made* you as a person. What's that like? Like, where does Kiara Greer end and 'my friends call me Kia' begin?"

I blinked rapidly. She was grilling me—but not, it seemed, to make me defend the family biz. The bent of Jade's question was more personal, more *vulnerable,* than I'd realized.

Maybe the Campbell siblings had more personality overlap than I'd thought. They both had this thirst to get to the core of people.

I was quiet for so long it got awkward, but they let me take the time to think. I yawned, suddenly so, so tired. It was contagious, because Jade failed to suppress her own yawn in the driver's seat. I let my head bob on the headrest. Then I let myself tell the truth.

"I was eight," I remembered, voice rounded with nostalgia. "Our grandma took me and my little sister to the zoo, and when we got home, there were cameras in our house. I came home from school the next day and the cameras were there again. And then again." Another big yawn . . . "I didn't choose this."

There was another silence as they took this in. Then Cass emitted a quiet, reflective "Bet." It made me smile. He shifted in his seat so his whole body was facing me, shoulders turned and legs a twisted pretzel. "That had to have been a trip."

I looked out the window, at the bushes and leaves and trees rushing past, a blur of dark, barely readable texture. Jade's face had screwed up like she was thinking, and I expected her to butt back in with something like *Sounds like a pretty great life you're complaining about.*

She didn't. She glanced in the rearview, back at me, and her eyes looked spookily like her brother's, but for real this time: softened by curiosity. Like she wasn't here to attack but actually wanted to understand.

"So how do you sort out what's their creation versus what's the real you?"

One of my eyebrows shot up. The eyes of both Campbell siblings were on me, and I didn't have an answer. Or I did, but I had to give myself permission to say it.

"That's kind of a whole thing I'm working to figure out," I admitted. "Sometimes I wonder . . ." I gulped, then barreled on.

I was already here, already talking, already vomiting my whole heart onto the torn upholstery of this van—I might as well keep going. "I don't know that I'm cut out to be famous. But there's not really any quitting once you're there, right? My family's way past the idea of fifteen minutes of fame. But I've been . . . I've been thinking about college, maybe, if I can manage it. Something that's just for me, that isn't about all the rest of it."

My heart pounded. I couldn't read the back of Jade's head. The corner of Cass's mouth pulled up again, and it felt *knowing*, and that made my heart skitter.

The van wound through the hills as what I said hung in the air.

"I think that's really cool," Cass said finally, meeting my eyes. "I could see that for you. Really easily. Even from a few hours of knowing you."

"You can?" I asked, less to challenge him and more because some part of me really, really needed to hear that. From anybody.

"College would be rad as hell for you," Jade chimed in. A shocked laugh shook outta me. "Kiara, Kia, whoever you are . . . I feel like you're gonna be one to watch."

Whatever the hell that meant. The van fell into comfortable silence, the sleepiness we'd each been fighting taking a stronger hold. We rounded bend after bend, a new moon barely visible through the sunroof. Cass rolled down every window. The cool night air smelled of jasmine and pine, and it brushed my face, lifting strands of hair that floated freely around and above my head, a halo in the night.

I closed my eyes to breathe it in, and when I opened them, Cass's eyes were on me again, and a serene smile lit up his face.

I let myself hold his gaze, bold for just a few seconds. I might lose it all in the morning anyway, so why not? The unasked and unanswered filled the air between us. Some delusional, wistful hope took the place of the knot I was so used to carrying in my chest.

Eventually the van pulled up to the tall iron gates that surrounded the Greer compound. Jade parked, and Cass walked me to the mouth of the barrier. He paused, polite—but raised his arms, and I rushed into them, wrapping my own around his neck.

He squeezed me hard. His head dipped low. His mouth just barely brushed my ear, but I felt like one of those women in Regency romances, lit on fire by just the *thought* of contact.

"Tonight was good," he murmured, his voice coming from somewhere deep. I pulled back, not to get away but so I could look at his face. It was just as devastatingly curious, playful, and *open* as it had been all night.

"It was," I said back. I stayed honest: "I'm not sure what to do with that."

"Personally," he said, grinning, "I think it means we should hang out again."

I nodded at the ground. "If you don't change your mind about me and my soul-ruining family in the morning."

His brows furrowed. "Why would I ever?"

The gates swung slowly open—the guards finally noticing it was me standing there—and I stepped through them. I could only manage three steps before I turned back. I was greeted by the absolute luminosity that was Cassius Campbell in pink vined silk under a eucalyptus moon.

"I hope you sleep well, Cass," I said, and this was my goodbye. "It was nice to meet you."

His mouth was still half open when I turned from him and walked, resolute, not stopping until our big oak door shut behind me and he was out of sight.

CHAPTER SEVEN

Never had I ever had dreams so *full*. My dream world was all pink and enveloping warm browns and yellows and greens, orange blossoms and long slides down mountains and into the sea. I ran wooded trails, and someone was chasing me. My heart quickened until I burst into a space in the clouds, in the sky, exposed yet somehow safe, separate from it all. I teetered on the edge of something unknowable. When I woke, jittery nerves ping-ponged inside my torso.

The night before, I'd checked my Instagram for the first time in weeks. I found a DM from Cass's verified profile offering his phone number. I'd held my phone close to my heart before turning it off and tucking it into my bedside drawer.

I made a choice to let Cass go. It didn't even matter if he'd approached me without ulterior motives: I'd sacrificed anything real with him to distract the press from Sola.

Still, something nagged at me. Cassius Campbell, the It Boy, was everywhere, lighting up screens and inspiring fanfic. Cassius Campbell danced across stages in bell-bottoms and glitter with all the energy of a supernova.

But then there was the Cass with the beater van and the combative sister, the Cass who wouldn't stop checking if I was comfortable, making sure I had the exact food, beverage, and seating arrangement I needed to enjoy myself. Cass felt a universe apart from the crackling heartthrob who graced magazine covers and went viral every time he opened his mouth.

I'd met plenty of supernovas in my life. People like that were always looking for the next places or peers who could hold their shine or amplify it. They had all this electricity living inside them. It's what made them incredible to watch. But that electricity made a lot of superstars volatile—restless, or needy, prone to addictions, breakdowns, exhibitionism. All that pent-up energy had to go somewhere. I didn't know Cass's relationship to that light inside him, but I'd seen it bursting through those bright, inquisitive eyes. It was even there in the quiet intensity with which he'd listened. There was still so much I wanted to know about him. Stuff I couldn't Google even if I tried.

An hour into my morning, I found myself still burrowed in bed and trying to ignore the phone psychically screaming at me from my bedside drawer. I didn't dare turn it back on. Now, in the bright light of morning, that would mean facing the death knell. Photos of us would be everywhere, attached to endless Instas, TikToks, and entertainment "news" posts digging into Cassius Campbell maybe dating the reject Greer.

There was no way he wouldn't spot the truth. My move last night had been so transparent. How could I possibly start anything, with that creepy-crawly sense of everyone looking our way? We'd be zoo animals. Endangered pandas, the wide world discussing whether or not we'd mated.

I had no choice but to ghost his DM.

I buried myself deeper under my duvet. Mom had, blissfully, left us unscheduled for the day after Lark's party. I could do what I wanted in my little corner of the house.

My parents had designed this place within an inch of its

life, but mine and Lark's rooms had been ours to decorate how we pleased. My favorite piece was the rattan chest of drawers Grandma Millie had left behind. I'd refused to let them sand the edge of the chest that had been touchworn over time; it was the spot Grandma would lean on as she laced her shoes. Her palm had pressed into the corner until it eroded, day by day and touch by touch, into something warped but smooth. It was a visual reminder of how much life she'd lived. That her life had impact, that she had changed the things around her.

My room was a rare part of my life that felt like *mine*. My duvet was a sage cloud, the ceiling dotted with fluffy depictions of actual clouds painted by Miss Carol and me over a long weekend during lockdown. Over the years I'd replaced my stuffed animals with stacks of YA books, along with adult novels like *Honey & Spice, Normal People,* and *The Vanishing Half.*

This was the same bed I'd snuck out of at age twelve. I'd tiptoed to the end of the hall and knocked on the door to Miss Carol's suite. I'd silently ushered her back to my room, pulling the covers back to reveal the pool of red-brown blood I'd woken up in. Mom had given me the talk about what would happen to my body, but that night I'd woken surprised at this first occurrence. I'd been desperate for a witness, someone to help me strip and remake the bed, send me back to sleep. My cheeks burned. I hated that something had changed in me that was so out of my control. Miss Carol had promised not to tell anyone else. It wasn't her fault my mom found out the next day and put it on TV. Melora Greer never wasted an opportunity.

I'd transformed within this space. Limbs stretched, nose morphed, pimples dotted across my face, back, and butt with annoying regularity. I was still changing. In one of Mr. Hillis's science lessons, I'd learned my brain was still forming, rapidly trimming away how my child self had processed things. My kid cells were metamorphosing into a neural circuitry that was more malleable, more sensitive, more fearful, and yet somehow more impulsive.

"I don't like that," Lark had said with a scrunched nose when she'd gotten to the same lesson the next year. "It's just another way adults find to tell us we're not 'real' people yet. I'm plenty real, thank you very much."

Lark didn't like the implication that whatever she did now didn't count. It made her feel like the decisions she made belonged less to her and more to her brain and some vague idea of "youth." Our prefrontal cortexes wouldn't be fully formed until our mid- to late twenties. That felt so far-off and unimaginable, it might as well have been sci-fi. Who would she be by then? Who would I?

One of the papers Mr. Hillis had us read was by some professor at Yale who said that the transition from childhood to adulthood is not linear. That made sense to me, at least. I was changing, on an atomic level, every day. Yet I felt, bundled up in my bed, still so very much a little kid. Lark's friends all smoked cigarettes and weed, some did cocaine, and some did other drugs that were even more intense. They slept with each other and talked about investment portfolios and the twenty-seven-year-olds who hit on them at industry parties (gross).

They'd been working on sets since they were small. So had I. Those were places where being a kid was a liability, which meant that by age nine I'd developed a sense of when was *not* the right time to have a meltdown. I'd trained myself to save my feelings for when I could close the door and crawl back into bed. That was some kind of maturity, right? But I was insulated from the world. I was barely a year from eighteen and my heart still skipped a beat thinking about *hugging* a boy. How pathetic.

I felt safe in this quiet little room, away from the choices I made out there. But I was growing restless. So I threw back my covers and moved to the big, cozy barrel chair at my desk. Homework would stop my mind from spinning into the abyss. From fixating on Cassius Campbell, who I couldn't have and didn't deserve.

I picked up the copy of *Cleopatra: A Life* by Stacy Schiff that Mr. Hillis had assigned. And as I read, all the rest disappeared.

The book wrapped me up quick. I decided I'd picture Cleopatra as Black, just because that was more fun for my personal experience of her. Maybe then she'd feel closer to me. She'd also had a girlhood, after all. I wondered how hers felt. I wondered how it felt to leave it behind.

I read until my stomach rumbled and I realized with a start the sun was already high over the courtyard out my window. As I headed toward food, the muffled sounds of soul music floated down the hall, and I knew exactly what I'd see when I pushed through the French doors and into the kitchen.

Sure enough, there was Miss Carol, Mr. Mervyn, and my father milling around the kitchen island, chopping away at meal prep while they chatted and sang. I entered right as my Oscar-winner father did a rendition of Ann Peebles's version of "I Can't Stand the Rain" that was so comical and warbly, I knew it'd be stuck in my head for days.

"Good job, Pops," I said. "Broadway's calling."

"Baby girl!" he exclaimed, the glasses he only wore at home slung low over his nose. "You hungry? We're making brunch."

"Yes, please. How can I help?"

Merv pointed me toward an egg carton, and I got to cracking shells over a big bowl.

Merv was Miss Carol's husband and our family's live-in chef. Their own two kids were long since grown, so they'd moved into the east wing and become part of our family. Lark and I often saw more of Miss Carol than we did our own parents. Dad was always on set; Mom was always in meetings, shepherding Sola or Destiny to engagements, or traveling for her own brand deals.

Lark and I turned into Miss Carol's imprinted little ducklings. These days we no longer needed babysitters, so Miss Carol had transitioned into a house manager role. In her fifties she'd completed a master's degree in early-childhood development; she could have easily moved on, but she chose to stay with us.

It felt weird there was ever talk of her leaving. Unsettling that she technically lived in our home as an "employee," when she meant everything to us.

She loved us. That I knew without a doubt.

"Where you been, Tater Tot?" Miss Carol asked now, pecking the side of my head before returning to the pile of real potatoes in front of her.

"Reading. Didya know in ancient Egypt, they gave teething babies *fried mice* to chew?"

"Revolting," Miss Carol declared with a shiver.

"*Enchanting*," Dad countered. "What's that from? Should I read it?"

"Cleopatra bio, and yes." I made a mental note to lend it to him once I'd finished. "Think about it, though: Will we move back to that, as a society, now that microplastics are sliding out of favor?" Miss Carol pulled a face, which egged me on. "Also! Birth control back then? Fully bonkers. They really were just strapping cat livers to their feet and hoping for the best."

"No cat liver talk near the food!" Merv shouted from behind me.

"They also used spiders' eggs and crocodile dung they shoved *up there*. Be grateful we live in the days of ibuprofen and IUDs."

"The yeast infections back then must have been out of control," Miss Carol muttered, shaken by the knowledge I had so generously gifted her. I giggled.

"Ray, get your daughter in order," Merv barked. He was easily nauseated. I will admit to sometimes saving my grossest fun facts for when he was around.

My dad heaved a sigh. "Let's think about this. I suppose you knowing *too much* about birth control is preferable to . . . not knowing enough?" He glanced across the table. "Am I dadding right?"

"Don't have sex," Miss Carol said, her throaty, honeyed voice firm. Then she winked. "But if you do, no croc poop. And make sure they get you off first."

"Miss Carol!" I exclaimed at the same time Merv turned to his wife and let out an aghast "Carol Ann Binion!" My dad threw his head back and cackled. Miss Carol just shrugged.

This was good. Reading, and spending time with my people. No phones. No reminder of the lies I'd peddled out there.

I loved when my dad was home like this, even for short spurts between long shoots in places like Budapest, London, Vancouver, or Seoul. During some summers Lark and I would go with him.

All us girls had grown up on his film sets, propped in director's chairs with big noise-blocking earmuffs to protect us from the sounds of stunts and controlled explosions. But when he was home, Dad loved to be in his study reading every history book he could find, or right here bugging Merv, cooking something for his family.

His phone buzzed. He pulled it from the pocket of his Nike sweatsuit and sucked his teeth.

"Carter—on a *Sunday*? C'mon, man, I've only got a few days home." Carter was his agent. He listened for a second, then darted an apologetic look my way before sliding out of the room, firing off questions about shoot duration and rehearsal time.

I shot a side-eye to Miss Carol, whose expression was deliberately unreadable. Miss Carol was a consummate professional. She'd never speak poorly about my parents in front of me, but I was always curious what she'd say. My dad left most decisions about parenting to my mom, and Miss Carol didn't always agree. She enjoyed my dad's company, at least—my mom's, less so. I wanted to know everything she thought about . . . well, the whole Greer *thing*. And, really, about everything.

"Must be that Ryan Coogler project," I said to fill the silence blooming in Dad's absence. When he was away, we FaceTimed a few times a week, and on one he'd gushed about some script about the Black Liberation Army. I supposed this is where he'd go once the zombie flick (or alien movie? or were they zombie aliens?) filming in Atlanta wrapped. Rarely was my whole family in the same place at the same time.

"How's Sola doing?" Miss Carol asked, setting her jaw.

Miss Carol, like the rest of us, had fallen for Levi's charms. He and Miss Carol had this inside joke where he'd bring her a bouquet of sharpened pencils on special occasions. I think it was from some movie. I never got it, but it made her giggle like a little girl. The day we found out what was really going on was the first and only time I'd heard Miss Carol curse. Turns out she had quite the mouth on her. But that was also the first day I saw her cry—at least over something happening in real life and not a romance novel.

"She's . . . okay," I started to answer. "Well, no. I found her hyperventilating in a public bathroom last night. So . . . you could say she's suboptimal."

"That an SAT word?" Miss Carol asked with a knowing glance.

"Those aren't actually a thing anymore," I told her.

"I'd be freaking out in a bathroom, too," Lark's voice trilled from behind us. She threw a wink my way as she clattered into the kitchen, a gallon water bottle and the sheen across her forehead signaling she'd just come from a workout. "Maybe Dest's right. What's the point of being rich if we can't just have him assassinated?"

"See, this is the problem with men like that," Miss Carol said as Lark planted a greeting peck on her cheek. "He leaves the kindest among us no choice but to wish violence upon him. A demon." She pointed her knife for emphasis, making this extra menacing.

Lark reached into the fridge and retrieved one of the protein smoothies Merv kept heavily stocked, then perched on one of the island stools.

"Sola's gonna be okay," Lark said, firm. "She has to be. She's Sola!"

"You saw those guys," I countered. "Screaming at her about shit she didn't even do?"

"Language," Merv interjected from where he was now furiously stirring the eggs in the pan. Merv's general rule was to mind his own business. He funneled all his energy into making sure even the most restrictive diets that swept through the house were still delicious, as filling as he could make them, and locally sourced. This imbued him with a haggard air, which was accentuated by the shock of white of his hair and beard. He'd shoo you from his kitchen if you didn't abide by the hard-won dignity with which he governed the space.

"Sorry," I tossed over my shoulder to Merv before turning back to Lark. "But how are you supposed to let that"—I strained not to curse again—"*nonsense* slide off your back? She's only human. It has to be killing her how wrong everyone is."

"But Sis was built for this," Lark reasoned. "She loves being Sola Greer; this is just part of the territory. She's been through stuff like this before."

"Has she? This feels different. It's so, like, *coded.* And the paps have never called *us* whores before—sorry, Unc, that one was just accurate reporting."

Miss Carol gasped, pausing in her chopping. "Those low-life mother— Who do I kill?"

"Yeah, that didn't feel good," Lark said, her voice small. I felt a pang of guilt for bringing it up. But Lark straightened the set of her shoulders. "Whatever. They'll move on by next week."

The twist of my stomach was so audible, it came out as an angry rumble, and Lark handed me the rest of her shake. I took it. Maybe if I drank it fast enough, the brain freeze would block out all memories of Cass. I'd done a pretty good job so far today. Avoidance was working.

"Don't Levi got that album dropping soon?" Miss Carol asked.

"The track list looks brutal," I admitted. "Things will just get worse when it comes out."

Lark shifted uncomfortably. She didn't like thinking about problems unless they had clear solutions. She was a worker bee, game for anything so long as she could practice and practice until it was perfect. She'd done it with acting, music, modeling. The rest of life wasn't so simple.

None of us knew how to solve the Levi problem. Which is probably why Lark turned her attention to me.

"What I'd like to know," she said with an impish smirk, "is how your *big date* went last night."

"Date?" Miss Carol asked, sounding surprised. "You're going on dates?"

"She don't even have friends!" Merv chimed in, deeply unhelpful.

"Hey!" I objected.

"Sisters do not count, and neither does anyone on payroll," Merv asserted, prompting a chastising smack from his wife.

"Damn, Uncle Merv, drag her," Lark giggled.

"Don't listen to him, sweetie—I'll always be your friend," Miss Carol said. Pathetic as it sounded, Miss Carol *was* the best friend I wasn't biologically related to.

"*Bitch, tell me how the date went!*" Lark ordered, pinching my arm.

"*Language!*" Lark said, calling herself out at the same time as Merv did. She pecked him on the cheek with a "Sorry, sir," and Merv softened. Salty Merv was such a sucker for Lark's sweetness.

"Chill, please!" I corrected her. "It was a casual hang with his *little sister* there. And as I'm sure you're aware, sisters are hardly conducive to a romantic atmosphere. Because they're annoying. And nosy. And should shut their assumptive little faces."

"You met through *me*, remember?" she said. "And I'm the one who got y'all on that dance floor, sweat dripping, body parts *grazing*, song after song—"

"Not in front of the food," Merv barked.

"You looked pretty romantic outside the party. Hands clutched, gazing at each other, the titillating shiver of a young crush blooming—"

Well, shit, there it was. If she knew that, then the photos had to be out there for the whole world to see.

Lark saw something in my face, because she stopped talking. "You *have* seen, haven't you?"

She knew I hated shit like this. She just didn't know I'd caused it this time.

Lark unlocked her phone and slid it over, open to a story on an entertainment news site. I could no longer run from the consequences of my actions.

Are Cassius Campbell and Kiara Greer an Item? All About the Budding Romance Between the Teen Stars

Litty.com | Top Stories | Celebrity Vertical

By Alexis Borges

Social media is *lit up* about the possibility that rising pop superstar Cassius Campbell is making moves on *GROWIN' UP GREER* star Kiara Greer. Rumors were sparked by a set of Backgrid photos that hit the internet in the early hours of Sunday morning. In them, the two teen stars could be seen canoodling outside Lark Greer's extravagant sweet sixteen party. They laugh, they look into each other's eyes, they hold hands. There's even a kiss!

Don't you just love young love? But listen. Seriously, lean in closer. We've got scoop that goes even deeper! Sources say they didn't just see Cassius, 18, and Kiara, 17, leaving together from the birthday party—they also saw them getting up close and *personal* on the dance floor and at the bar. Lark and Cassius, coincidentally (or not), have a single, "Sweet," coming out soon, and apparently guests at the party got a sneak peek at the song that night. *Certain* corners of the internet that I'm not allowed to link to *may or may not* have illegal recordings of that very single circulating at this very moment.

ANYWAY! What do you all think of this new celebrity entanglement? Our sources say the two looked besotted as they ran off together into the night. I, for one, am a fan.

The knot in my chest had morphed into a cannonball of dread. I clicked the phone screen dark in disgust. Miss Carol, who'd been reading over my shoulder, stroked my hair consolingly while I stared at the swirling gold and white of the countertops. I had the nonsensical thought that I wished I was a rock, hard and cold and impervious. That I could be truly still, in a world that was anything but. I'd be more useful as a countertop than I was as a girl.

"I thought you knew," Lark whispered, as if afraid to startle me.

"I figured they'd got the pics. I just haven't been online today,"

I explained, monotone. It was a lie of omission. I didn't want her to know I'd done this on purpose.

"Kia . . ." Miss Carol said, her voice warm, her hand firm on the back of my neck.

"No. No" was all I could say. "I'm okay. Really."

Suddenly the room was too bright, too loud, too cold, the eyes of my sister and Miss Carol too pressurized. As I walked out of the room, I heard Merv's confused voice: "What I miss—what happened?"

⌒⁀

I found my mother in her office, in her version of casual Sunday best. She was flawless in a crisp white shirtdress, looking ever the Kennedy and speaking with forceful calm into her phone.

"Listen, Carl, we're almost through this, okay? You gotta hang with me—I'm just looking out for my girl . . . Uh-huh . . . No, no, she needs a rental house, not a hotel . . . Destiny's got a baby, a nanny, and security on-site. Do *you* want to be the one fielding that with the Four Seasons? I didn't think so . . . Yes, she's okay with butt and side boob, but no lingering Michael Bay camera-work . . . also, we've all heard the rumors about this director. So no meetings that just happen to be in his hotel room or you'll be hearing from our— Hmm? No that's not a threat, Carl, just get your guy together. Time's Up, remember?" My mother rolled her eyes as Carl presumably defended his integrity on the other end of the line. She finally registered my presence and shot a wink my way, along with the universal *I'll just be one minute* raised finger. I took a seat in the plush armchair across from her desk to wait it out.

"Yes, I talked to her . . . She'll commit to the twenty-pound weight loss—*as long as* the studio will pay for a trainer and nutritionist *of her choosing.* No studio quacks."

"TELL 'EM THEY'RE ASSHOLES!" Destiny's voice rang from another room. I jumped—I had no idea she was here today; she must be in the rec room with her toddler, Deja.

This was good news. After my chat with Mom, I could drown my sorrows by squishing my face into the baby folds of my niece's perfect arm rolls. She always smelled like Cheerios and fresh human.

Instead of relaying Destiny's message, my mother responded gamely. "She can't wait to work with you. Oh, she's been raving. It's adorable." Carl was seemingly satiated, because she took this as her cue to wrap things up. "All right, talk soon. I've got calls—this distributor fucked up an order for Sola's swim line so royally. My best theory is they want me to have a stroke."

She hung up, letting out a big breath and sinking her head to the tabletop in exasperation. Her desk was white stone, and she always joked she chose that material because its cool surface helped with the headaches that came with managing the lot of us.

She spent a few seconds like that. Then she lifted herself back to perfect posture and fixed me with a warm smile.

"Baby! Hi. You here for Mom or Melora?" she asked. This was her way of sussing out which of her hats to put on—Mom or Momager. I took a cue from her and put my forehead to the stone surface, too. It really was refreshingly cool. A shock of sensation to my confused system. I rolled my forehead back and forth on it.

"Both," I said into the desk. "I need you to tell me if a bad thing I did was worth it."

I sounded so pathetic that she leaned forward. Melora

scanned me up and down . . . and I saw the exact moment she put two and two together. Impressive, given how little I'd given her.

"Oh, honey. You're *not* dating Cassius Campbell?"

"No. Or maybe I could be, but I ruined it." I spoke into the stone, hoping it could muffle my miserable whine. She was quiet a second, and it was like I could *hear* her brain working. Melora Greer had this mental algorithm going at all times: who was where, who'd said what, what trouble there was, what calls to return, what she needed to be ten steps ahead of.

"This is *interesting*," she said, and I looked up. "I expected to have to sit you down, have a real talk. I didn't think you'd do something like this without prompting."

"You were gonna sit me down?"

It was no secret she wished I'd take a more active role in the family biz. Part of me wanted nothing more than to give her that. But I was always hopeless at this stuff. Last night was the proof that that wasn't changing. Still, I'd known this talk was coming.

"Now that you're almost eighteen, it's time we get serious about your future," she said. "The options are really endless, but we gotta get moving." She didn't mean college. She wanted me to find my lane like my sisters had, start some business venture or project that could take the world by storm—a skincare line, CBD supplements, maybe a lit imprint. Whatever it was, in her eyes I definitely wasn't pulling my weight.

This was why I didn't come into her office often; I could already feel myself getting overwhelmed.

"Can we do that part later?" I asked. "I just need to know if last night helped Sola. With the headlines or anything?"

"Oh, baby . . ."

A corner of my mother's mouth lifted as she turned back to

her computer and tapped at her keyboard. She turned her monitor around, pointing my attention to *The Daily Find.*

> **Move Over, Sola: Teen Sister Kiara Greer's the One with the Rocker Romance Now! Kiara Stunned in Fairy-Tale Dress on a Fantasy Date with Musician Cassius Campbell**

"I know they're writing about us," I said. "But was it enough?"

"Look next to it. The trending topics."

To the right of the article lay the day's trending entertainment posts. That first headline I'd read was number one.

2. **"I Just Don't Trust It": Fans Speculate About Britney Spears's Well-Being After She Declares She's Happier Than Ever**

3. **Who Has Cassius Campbell Dated Before? Inside the Crooner's Mysterious Romantic History**

4. **Gwyneth Paltrow Ignites Controversy After Lighting a Loaf of Bread on Fire in Insta Story: "Processed Food Is Toast!"**

5. **"Did Kiara Greer Just Get Interesting?!" and 25 Other Tweets Reacting to the Kiara Greer and Cassius Campbell Dating News**

6. **Common, Pete Davidson, Michael B. Jordan, and More! Every Famous Man the Greer Girls Have Dated**

7. **Did Sola Greer Cheat with 27 Men? Here Are the Rumors Around Levi Ellis's "Maneater" Album**

8. Is Sola Greer Still Yearning for Ex Levi Ellis Despite Her Many Alleged Betrayals?

9. Inside Lark Greer's Epic Prom-Themed Sweet 16: Which Stars Were in Attendance?

10. Eight Easter Eggs We Found in Taylor Swift's Latest Instagram of Her Cat

"Last night that dipshit had four spots in the top ten. You practically pushed him off the map. This is *exactly* what we wanted."

I got a surge of satisfaction that I'd pleased her. But everything inside me was fighting itself. This was the most useful I'd felt to my family maybe ever. Kissing the cheek of one of the world's leading hubba-hubba hunks was a choice I'd made. Still, seeing my name in the press like this made me feel like a target. Like I'd doomed whatever connection Cass and I had before it even started.

Something about the whole situation just felt hopeless.

"Levi's still all over that list," I sighed. "With the album, won't he just dominate every spot in a couple days? This wasn't worth it at all."

A glimmer in her eyes told me Mom had left the building. Momager had taken full control. I shifted in my seat.

"Are you kidding, kid?" Her mischievous smile echoed the one I'd seen on Lark just minutes ago. Genes really are a trip. "This is just the beginning. We can work with this."

She tapped away at her computer again, and I tried to keep up with the light speed at which my mother's brain processed information.

"People will move on from these pics in a couple days," I

argued. "They'll keep caring about Cass, obv, but . . . no one cares about me, not separate from the family or show."

"But they *should*," my mother said with the gusto of, well, a cult leader, just like Jade had said the night before. "And, honey, last night? Being seen with Cassius Campbell *proved* it. Sexist, admittedly, but people are what they are. You know how many meetings I've had with the Ignite execs over what audiences engage with? It's only a handful of stories, really: fights, secrets, makeovers, failures, and which beautiful people are boinking or falling in love. You're right, Cassius is big. You're not, at least comparatively. But that's what hooked 'em." She turned the screen back toward her and read from a post she'd pulled up: "*Though no stranger to the spotlight, Kiara is bookish and shy compared to her older sisters, making her the Greer audiences know the least about. Cassius Campbell, on the other hand, is known for being a gregarious charmer, crushed on by thousands of young people around the world. Maybe that's what makes this romance so interesting: It's the wallflower and the prom king, on display under the Hollywood sign.*"

"That's a great movie," I said. "But it's not my life."

"It could be," she volleyed back.

"I can't believe you said *boinking*," I joked. I was deflecting now. Buying time for my brain to buffer, to make sense of all this.

"Forgive me," Mom chuckled. She had this sly half smile on, like she knew she was onto something. I picked at my cuticles.

"So . . . last night *did* successfully push Levi's smear campaign down the charts?"

"Almost off them completely," she confirmed, batting at my hands to save my manicure.

"But he's not gonna stop."

"Of course not. Little dipshit will ride this as far as he can," my mom acknowledged. "Which is why it's our job to limit the lifespan of this story, however and wherever we can."

"Which I did, for like one night," I supplied, still failing to see where she was going with this. "Now what?"

She responded by zooming in on a picture outside the club. I had just taken Cass's hand, and the photographer had caught his smile just as it began to bloom across his face.

It was surreal, seeing this moment blown up on my mother's work computer. I hadn't held many people's hands in my life, at least not in that way. I'd certainly never had anyone look at me like that. It was a searing moment in time, a split second when something massive shifted between us. A moment like that should have belonged just to us. Instead I was listening to my mom talk about the business ramifications.

"The way he's looking at you, baby . . . that kinda love sells pictures."

"We're not in love," I reminded her.

"He clearly *liiiikes* you." Several organs in my body did little flips. "These things always run smoother when the couple actually enjoy each other's company."

"What things?" I asked. But I already knew. I'd seen this playbook before. "You're saying I should . . . *keep* dating Cassius Campbell? Publicly. To help Sola."

"And to help yourself," my mother offered. "It's as good an excuse as any to reframe your image, kick-start your new era."

"But isn't that so . . . cynical?" I asked.

"People have such misconceptions about PR relationships," she argued. "Most of the time it's just two people taking advantage of a spark that's already there. What's wrong with that?"

I ignored everything after she'd told me I should *fake-date my real crush.*

"He's not gonna go for that," I said. "He wouldn't say yes to some phony PR stunt."

"Pfft." Melora waved this away like a pesky fly. "He did spon-con for Añuli last week. Trust me, Cassius Campbell is not naive to the workings of PR strategy. Plus. he's *cute,* and by all accounts sweet, too. You could do much worse."

"I know," I deadpanned. I felt itchy inside, terrified that whatever I did next would disappoint her. I spun out of my chair, ready to wrap this up. Still, I lingered in the doorway.

"Just think about it," my mother said. "Melora cap off, I'll say this as Mom: I just want you girls to be happy. Whatever path that takes. *That's* my goal."

I looked into her eyes and knew it was the truth. Melora Greer's childhood had been the opposite of mine. She'd grown up in a big family, but there hadn't been a lot of love thrown her way, or a lot of options. My mother had worked hard to put her own misfortunes in the past. To be the person with the power to solve any problem her daughters might encounter. It was her life's mission. It came above the fortune, the fame, the glitz—though she cherished those accessories dearly.

My mother and I were polar opposites in practically every other way. On this, though? Maybe we were the same. We just wanted all the bad parts to go away.

⌒

I really was going to say no. I went and played with Deja for hours, biting at her rolls and stacking foam blocks high until they tumbled down all over us and we screamed. Destiny drove Deja and me to In-N-Out and moaned as she gobbled up her Double-Double, special sauce dripping from the corners of her mouth—my sister's last bites of freedom before a grueling three months of training and dieting in prep for this movie.

There were paps at the In-N-Out. Deja threw a fit; she hated them even more than I did. She called them "pooperazzi" in her little toddler voice.

Back home I retreated to my room and read about Cleopatra until my eyes went crisscross. I tried not to think about any of it. Maybe if I stuck my head in the sand, it would all go away. I could stay this age, behind these gates, bored out of my mind but tucked neatly away. Safe. Unbothered.

But that night Levi's first single dropped. The album's titular song, "Maneater," featured a music video filmed in the house he'd once shared with my sister. In it, Levi is "murdered" in the night, his body found floating in their pool, gardenias surrounding his lifeless body. The woman he'd cast as the murderer bore a striking resemblance to a certain Greer sister.

That night my dreams starred Sola's tear-streaked face. She'd told me someone had put a tracker on her car, and my mind took that and ran with it, stretching the invasion into a three-hour surrealist horror movie. I woke up sweating.

I *wasn't* pulling my weight. I didn't have to keep disappointing my mother—or myself. Not when there was something I could do to help.

"What does it look like?" I asked, lurking at the entrance to my mother's office the next morning. "This whole PR dating thing? *Hypothetically.*"

Melora held my gaze, steady and searching. Satisfied with whatever she saw in my face, she smiled and picked up her phone.

"Greta," she said when the person on the other end picked up. "Get over here."

PART TWO

Take the Excuse and Run with It

(September–November)

Marianne had the sense that her real life was happening somewhere very far away, happening without her, and she didn't know if she would ever find out where it was and become part of it. . . .

But now she has a new life, of which this is the first moment, and even after many years have passed she will still think: Yes, that was it, the beginning of my life.

—Sally Rooney, *Normal People*

The Best Albums of the Year
#2: Passions, Cassius Campbell

Rolling Stone, December 2023 | Music

By Brett Hayes-Ortile

A debut album is an introduction. It tells the world who an artist is and what they might offer, unfair as it may be to pigeonhole someone based on 45 minutes of material. So who is Cassius Campbell, the young man behind the most streamed album of 2023? His debut, *Passions,* made an interesting choice: It left much of that unclear.

Campbell, a 17-year-old from the San Fernando Valley, brought a golden voice and sprawling ambition to the 12 tracks that make up *Passions.* The album spans as many genres as it can hold: soul, funk, indie rock, progressive pop, classic R&B. "Blocking" is a subdued folk ballad tracking the agony of first heartbreak, "Flux" a brash, glimmering summer-sonic waterslide, all horns, guitar, and the tenacity of youth. At times *Passions* evokes Simon & Garfunkel; at others Etta James, David Bowie, or Beyoncé's *Renaissance.* Cassius pulled it off, for the most part, every track bursting with charisma.

Only one thing keeps this album from our top spot—and it's a problem quite befitting its artist's young age. Is Cassius Campbell a musician first, or a pop star?

Fuckboy or loverboy? Masculine or feminine? Sensitive son or cocky international heartthrob? This is an artist worth watching, and *Passions* proved that. Still, the variety of identities on display makes us wonder which version is the truth.

CHAPTER EIGHT

"Yooo, I loved that one!" Lark trilled. "But can we get another take? I want to try something different on the *ooh-oh-ooh*."

"HELL YEAH!" shouted the sound engineer, Tank. He punched a button, and the space filled with the giddy, thumping beat of the track they were working on. In the booth Lark squared her shoulders, a focus in her eyes.

I was struck by how directly it made her look like our mother. Or was it Dad's focus, the look he got reading a script on the couch late at night, scribbling notes in the margins, tracking his character's motivation? It didn't matter. This girl was ready for anything.

I'd have killed for her confidence. When she opened her mouth to meet the beat, Lark's voice came out silky and light as sparkling lemonade as she rattled off fictional doubts.

This song would be a hit, guaranteed.

"Is it you who'll crush me? Is it you who'll love me? Will I crush you back? Will I pen a breakup track?"

"Crushed" was about a couple who started off friends and were afraid of taking the plunge to turn things romantic. Like most tracks on what was to be Lark's debut album, the song was a fusion of Victoria Monét and Taylor Swift, built to announce the arrival of a new pop talent to watch. Half the album was hardcore dance bops, the other dreamy but catchy pop tunes you couldn't help singing along to. "Crushed" was the latter.

One date. That was all I'd agreed to. My people called Cass's people, and . . . he'd said yes. It worried me. What if Cass was the type who surrounded himself with celebs it'd be "beneficial" to be see with? He'd done a remarkably good job of making me *think* I'd gotten to know him, but maybe the diner was just part of the Cassius Campbell playbook. Millions of other girls around the world also felt like they knew him—they'd watched enough interviews, hadn't they, seen enough of his press tour bits, and backstory, and vaguely mysterious family life? They understood him on a deeper level than those who hadn't, right?

Theirs was textbook parasocial behavior. But wasn't mine, too? Wasn't that all the beginning of a crush ever was? I didn't know Cassius Campbell yet, not really.

Both sides agreed to the charade, and a time was set. I hadn't texted the number Cass had DMed me. I just wanted to get this over with.

Given the professional connection between Cass and Lark, our teams suggested he pick me up from their shared recording studio. So, yes, the date was a terrible idea—but at least it had brought me here. Lark's album was almost done, and until now I hadn't been able to bear witness to my little sister *absolutely killing it.*

Before recording started, I used to see her every day; now I was lucky if we spent more than an hour together twice a week. Even that time usually coincided with prescheduled campaign photo shoots, or sitting through long meetings where corporate teams told us about the latest designs for the makeup lines we "ran."

Lark's voice crescendoed as the track went on, showing off the three-octave range that had convinced her label she was more than just another kid actor trying to stay relevant. They were putting real juice behind launching her as a pop star, and Lark took the honor seriously. I wasn't about to complain that her dream was inconvenient to me. But I did miss her.

"So go ahead and crush meeee, oooh-oooh-ah-ha-haaaa," Lark wailed. "Crushed" had a Mariah Carey "We Belong Together" vibe, her voice rising to impressive heights. *"I'm crushed already, can't you see? And you'll be too if you don't beliiieeeeve—"*

Then it was like she came back to earth. Her voice grew more hushed, almost resigned. *"Maybe we'll run away, maybe we'll play the game."* I leaned forward in my seat, marveling at the confidence and skill with which my sister sang, closed-eyed, nose smushed against the mic.

I wondered if this might be the last year Lark and I would live together. Sola and Destiny hadn't lived with us since I was really young, but Lark? She'd always been *there.*

I didn't know where I'd be next year. But whatever changed, it didn't feel possible Lark wouldn't be there, too. Just down the hall like she'd always been. I knew logically that soon she'd join the tour of some more established act and travel the world. But as much as I wanted that for her, I also wished I could keep her forever. Even if only to watch over her.

"Maybe," Lark drawled. *"Maaaaybe. Can't we just . . . try-eyeee-eyeee . . ."*

The beat faded out, and I absolutely exploded. "AYYYYYYYYYY!!!! AHHHHHHH!!!!"

I stood, clapping, whooping, hollering. Lark beamed wide and laughed in the booth, and Tank joined in with a satisfied chuckle. Then he started clapping, too.

"Calm down," Lark said as she exited the booth, but she was struggling to hide her smile.

"Folks, we got a *songbird* on our hands!" I shouted.

Songbird was to be the album's title, a deliberate double reference to Lark's name and her favorite Fleetwood Mac song. Lark rolled her eyes and looked to Tank, her face shifting from amusement at me to something wide-open and hopeful. He gave her what she was looking for.

"That was the one," he confirmed, and her grin burst free, stretching ear to ear. "I'll send to Simms so he can approve."

Simms was the A&R guy tasked with "molding" Lark's image for optimized success. He'd molded many a pop idol—Cassius Campbell included—and Lark trusted him, but there was something about that guy that skeeved me out, so I was glad he wasn't in the studio that day.

Satisfied with a job well done, Lark relaxed into the couch. She kicked off a pair of Chloé sneakers and poked the soft part of my belly with a socked foot.

"Get off me," I laughed, pushing her leg away. "You've been spending too much time here—you smell like unwashed boy band."

"Isn't your *date* getting here soon?" That wiped the smile off my face. "Oh, don't be like that. I told you, Cass is great."

"He said yes to a PR date," I argued. "So maybe he's just great at acting. Or maybe he's for real but he'll hate me by the end of the night. Either way: not great!"

"Girl, get it together!" she said cheerily. "You're just scared something good might actually happen."

Lark was adamant that Cassius Campbell was destined to fall head over heels in love with me. I thought she'd been spending too much time reading romance novels. He was her buddy, not mine, and I was determined to get in and out of this night with as little attachment as possible. I couldn't afford to get caught up the way I had the other night.

"Here," Lark said, scooting closer. Her eyes were fixed above mine as she messed with my hair, rearranging the way my box braids fell across my forehead and over one shoulder. "Even if you're just 'acting,' you should look the part."

"Thanks." Self-conscious, I touched the neckline of the sundress our stylist had put me in. It was white, with tiny strawberries all over it. Completely inoffensive, adorable even. Still, it felt like they'd dressed me as someone else. That wasn't uncommon, but on a night like tonight it left me feeling wobbly in my own skin. The only thing I'd had a say in was my hair.

I chewed my lip. A thought had slowly been forming, and I needed to get it out. "You know . . . it could be you who goes. Instead of me."

Lark scrunched her face up. "What the hell?"

"Think about it. They'd all rather it be you, anyway. He knows you're not some wannabe. It's better for his Q rating *and* a boost for yours. Plus, you and him together would be even better at stealing headlines from . . . you know."

"And then, what, I'm the girl who stole her sister's guy?"

"No! I'd set them straight. Besides, everyone would rather it be you."

"Cass would *not* rather it be me," she deadpanned.

"*Pfft,*" I said, waving a hand dismissively.

Lark scoffed. She was scowling now. She turned to her engineer, who was dutifully ignoring us while devouring leftover Zankou takeout.

"Tank?" Lark's voice was bright but deadly.

"Yes?"

"What's the Tagalog word for chicken?"

"Manok," he recited through a mouthful. He swallowed. "Or if you mean what I think you mean, it's duwag."

"Thank you," she said, then turned back to me. "That's what you are." I did not justify this with a response, so Lark gave up and left the room. I Googled the word, too embarrassed to ask Tank. Duwag meant "coward."

"You eatin' that?" Tank was still looking at me, apparently unfazed by the sister skirmish he'd been pulled into. He nodded to the falafel and hummus left over from my and Lark's lunch hours ago. My plate was empty, but Lark had barely touched hers. Huh.

I shook my head, handing it to him. "All yours."

"What do you know!" Lark exclaimed with pointed cheer as she reentered the room. "Look who I found. I believe this belongs with you." With a serene smile I knew to be duplicitous, Lark shoved Cassius Campbell into the room and disappeared back down the hallway. The rush of movement created a breeze around his entrance that pushed the smell of citrus and shea butter right to me. God damnit. My heart hammered against my will, goose bumps running up my arms.

Cass raised a palm in bashful greeting. "Hi, Kia," he said, soft and sweet, but his eyes bored into me just like they had the other night.

Why did he have to come off so *lovely*? Was he for real? Did he really like me, or was he in this for the press? There was so much to sort out, and my head was a mess on a normal day.

"Hey!" I responded, echoing Lark's pointed cheer.

"Hey, T." Cassius greeted Tank with a nod. "How you doin', man? Been a sec."

I risked a once-over while he waited for Tank to finish chewing. He looked annoyingly good. Of course he did. It was his job to look annoyingly good. If he didn't, how would he get people from LA to Lagos to develop the kind of crush that led them to buy albums, concert tickets, and brand deal exclusives? He wore a lilac-and-green button-down half tucked into black jeans, and his twist-out had his hair flopping just so over his forehead.

He didn't look this good for me. His looks served whatever grand plan came with being Cassius Campbell. I had to remind myself this was business.

I was so busy stewing that I missed Tank's response. The next thing I knew, Cass's fingers were tentatively on my arm, a question mark on parted lips.

"You ready to go?" he asked.

"Sure," I said, as noncommittal as I could bear. I pushed through the door, hoping beyond hope he hadn't felt the treacherous goose bumps crawling up my arms.

Our teams had instructed us to walk the three long city blocks from the recording studio to Craig's, a hot spot guaranteed to be crawling with paparazzi. Greta'd insisted it would make our coupling seem more real if passersby saw us in the flesh. Sightings spread to anonymous gossip accounts like Deuxmoi were just as crucial to legitimacy as getting your photo on Backgrid.

Joe trailed a dozen feet behind, our security shadow. But the walk meant Cassius Campbell and I were at once alone and incredibly exposed. Cass peppered me with questions, but I kept my answers to "Uh-huh," "Yeah," "I think so," and the ever-graceful "Uh . . ." I had no idea *how* to talk to him—not without knowing his intentions. My own were messy enough.

Heads swiveled to follow us as we passed. My pulse quickened. I didn't like the sensation of being *watched* . . . even if that was the point of this whole thing. Phones raised, and while some people pretended to take selfies (with cameras pointed at us . . .), others unabashedly followed us down the block until Joe stepped in to make them turn around. The knot in my chest twisted in on itself with such aggression, I worried I might heave.

Two blocks from Craig's a red double-decker tourist bus pulled up right in front of us. A megaphoned voice boomed from above, and suddenly two dozen people pressed faces against windows and leaned precariously over railings, snapping pics and shouting at us.

"KIARA!"

"CASSIUS CAMPBELL OHMYGOD!"

"IT'S TRUE!"

"WHERE ARE YOU GOING—CAN WE COME?"

Cass laughed and waved. He even posed for the outstretched phone cameras, doing disco moves that made the crowd go wild. Then the light turned green and they were gone. I stood frozen, face burning because I was sure I looked like a freak, freaking out inside over a perfectly fine interaction. Moments like these always made me feel like a broken toy.

"I shoulda mooned 'em," Cass intoned from behind me. I turned, bemused—and though he was shaking his head, those eyes were locked on me, soft with understanding.

"Really, though," he said, keeping in step with me as we resumed walking, "showing them my full butt woulda taken that to a whole new level."

"And what would that have accomplished, exactly?"

"I think it would have established an intimacy," he replied, "but while maintaining a level of high-octane performance. You gotta keep them on their toes. Shock 'em."

"People are used to nudity these days," I said. "What's on that butt they'd find so *shocking*?"

"Wouldn't you like to know." His sloping smirk made my stomach flip.

We continued on in silence for a moment. Then Cass swung around so he was walking backward facing me.

"What do you think—should we give 'em a show?" he asked.

"Aren't we already?" I asked.

"They've seen a thousand people walking before. I think we can really turn the pap walk on its head. Innovate." I did not respond, and Cass barreled on undeterred. "You're skeptical. But the assignment is to make a splash, right? So hear me out. Goofy faces: been done. Giving the finger: so 2019. I saw some old pics of Andrew Garfield and Emma Stone holding up ads for charities. That's good, but again—been done!"

"Then what do you suggest?" I asked, growing impatient.

"I think we have to rob a bank."

This shocked some sort of guffaw out of me, and he smiled, satisfied.

"I didn't take you for someone with a death wish," I said. "Even Oprah gets racially profiled. Two Black kids robbing a bank are getting shot, famous or not."

He pulled a face. "Okay, good point. No robbing. Light vandalism?"

"Remember when Ariana licked those donuts? That sounds more like it."

"YES," he exclaimed. "Now we're talking."

An image of us storming a bank flashed in my mind, and I laughed again. "What would you have done if I'd said yes to bank robbing?"

We paused at a crosswalk. Cass screwed up his face and tilted it skyward, as if thinking real hard.

"I'd've gotten ready to go Bonnie and Clyde," he said. He cracked a smile at the doubtful look on my face. "Or I would have cried and called my mom to take me home."

"Right answer."

The expected paps were gathered outside Craig's, and I made sure to plaster on a smile and look adoringly at my date as we walked torturously slowly to the restaurant's front doors. My shoulders relaxed when the hostess led us to a table all the way in the back. But I'd fallen silent again. I was trying to sort out which version of Cass I'd joked with on the street.

"So, tell me," Cass said after we'd ordered appetizers. "What exactly's happening here?"

I stubbornly refused to look up from the pizza options I was considering. I'd order the margherita one, I decided. No—ugh, I'd get the Tuscan kale salad instead. The family nutritionist could win this round.

"I've never done anything like this before," he continued, and it sounded just the tiniest bit vulnerable. A lump of guilt formed in my throat.

"Anything like what?"

"Anything like a date set up by my publicist?" he continued, his voice lilting at the end like a question. He tapped the table in a nervous, rhythmic pattern. "I've gotta be honest, I didn't see things going this way. But you left all my DMs on read."

I cleared my throat. "I haven't been checking Insta."

"When I got a call from your people instead of you, I thought it might be a real-deal date type thing. Or . . . I hoped."

My stomach flipped again.

"But . . . I can't really tell if you want to be here?" he continued. "So I figured I'd check in, to see if this is real . . . at all."

My head spun. Had I read this whole thing wrong?

"You thought this was a regular date?"

Cass cringed, and I immediately regretted my whole life—but most specifically those last two words.

"Not *regular,* I guess," he said with an embarrassed huff of a laugh. "It was all so . . . orchestrated. But I did kinda hope you wanted to actually hang out?"

"Oh," I said, *"Oh."*

Something rushed through me that was half intense guilt, half overwhelming relief. For the first time all night, I allowed myself to really take in the person in front of me.

In the light of day, with his eyes wide and vulnerable, Cassius Campbell was so *mortal.* He was just Cass, the guy from Northridge who'd made me laugh. Another kid like me. Only somehow I'd already managed to disappoint him.

"I did want to see you again," I admitted. I wrung my napkin in my lap. "If I'm being honest, though . . . it wasn't my main reason for setting this up. And I do feel bad about that."

"Okay . . ." he said, "I'm listening."

I shifted in my seat. I looked to my left and my right, confirming we were still alone in our little corner of the restaurant.

And then I told Cassius Campbell all about Levi Ellis. I'd already hinted at the story, back at the diner, but now I relayed the whole tragic saga. How he'd duped us, betrayed us, and how mad and sad I'd been that night, finding Sola crushed in the bath-room. How I'd run into Cass right after, and how I'd jumped on the opportunity to take the heat off my sister.

"It's not that I didn't want to hold your hand, or kiss your cheek, or whatever," I said. I could feel my cheeks burning. "I just also . . . I guess I used you. I'm really sorry about that."

"Wow." Cass's brow furrowed. I'd delivered most of this speech staring hard at the table setting in front of me, but now I looked at him. He seemed . . . confused? "You've really been beat-ing yourself up, haven't you?"

"It's just not something I'd usually do."

"That's okay. It's okay," he said. I met his eyes, and a reassur-ing smile spread across his face. "You just said it: You *did* want to hold my hand. That's all I need. That's real enough. Besides," Cass continued, "Levi is an epic asshole. So even if you were completely repulsed by me, it's for a good cause, right?"

"Sure." I searched his face. Then I leaned back, crossing my arms over my chest. Something wasn't sitting right, not yet. "Did you really say yes *just* because you wanted to see me again? Or was there something else on your end, too?"

"What do you mean?"

"I've met a lot of people like you before," I said. "We may as well be up front about what's going on here."

"People like me? What does that mean?"

"You know . . ." It felt mortifying to say out loud, but he clearly didn't want to admit he knew what I was talking about. "The pop prince. The teen idol type. The kind everyone falls all over them-selves to be seen with." He looked decidedly lost. I kept going, hoping something sensible would come out of my mouth. "The kind who only hangs around people it's *beneficial* to be seen with."

Cass knit his lips together then, seeming to get it. "And you think that's me?"

"I dunno. You agreed to a whole-ass pap walk. That's a lot of trouble just to hang out with me again. Unless you wanted that to be part of all this."

Cass's face contorted again. His features were like rubber, I was realizing, so many expressions passing over them in such a short amount of time. He looked around the restaurant and rubbed his forearm, as if deliberating how to answer. This sent my defenses right back up.

"I don't know how you're gonna take this, but I don't actually mind the paparazzi," he said slowly. "I like them, even—when they're not acting up. But that's not why I'm here."

I pursed my lips. "You're right, I'm not sure how to take that."

"Even though you're the one who set me up?" He laughed. "Twice?"

"Yeah," I said, curt. "I did. But now you know why I did it."

He nodded and looked sheepish.

"I don't mind attention," he said, playing with a twist at the back of his head. "What can I say? It suits me."

"So you *did* go out with me for the press."

He groaned, sinking down in his seat theatrically. What a drama queen.

"I already told you. Kee—"

"Only my family calls me Kee," I bit. We were going in circles, but I couldn't help it. He righted himself in his seat, raising his hands in the universal sign of surrender.

"Kiara, then. I'm sorry," Cass said, bringing one hand to his chest. "What I meant was: I didn't mind that this was orchestrated, because I am nothing if not an insufferable theater child, and I can get on board with a bit of performance." He spoke with intention, every word coming through crystal clear. "*But.* As I have also expressed, I really did want this to be a real date. I just figured the paps were a necessary part of the Dating a Greer package."

"They are," I admitted. "But it's a shitty package. I don't recommend it."

"I'll take my chances," he said. Then he leaned in, conspiratorial. On instinct I leaned back. "Look, the way I see it, we've already knocked Levi down a few pegs."

Cass had a smile on his face I could only describe as dastardly. "Yeah, we did."

"So why don't we keep doing that?" Cass proposed, and it was so matter-of-fact. "Because I, for one, found that very satisfying."

"So did I," I admitted. Then I narrowed my eyes. "So you want to fake-date me?"

"No," he said patiently. "I want to date-date you—that is, if you'd like to date-date me, too. I think we should take full advantage of what we've got here."

"A chance to build buzz for your next album, you mean?"

"A chance to knock Levi Ellis on his butt, *I mean.* Come on." He nudged his foot against mine. "You know you want to."

The tiniest smirk crossed my face. Cass pointed at it.

"*I knew it,*" he whispered. I laughed.

"I'll think about it," I said.

"Okay, good," he said, and he leaned back, satisfied, roping a lazy arm around his chair. "Then I think we should get out of here."

Huh?

"To . . . where?"

"I think we should get these little piggies and meatballs in a box," he said, gesturing to the appetizers our server had delivered back when I'd been debating pizza versus salad. We hadn't touched them. "Then we should go eat more hot dogs."

Cass held a finger up to catch the server's attention.

"Also burgers, and nachos, and whatever else we want, because I've got a second location planned for us," he said. "The actual-date portion, now that the fake-date appeteaser is out of the way. There will be absolutely zero photographers at this next portion, professional or otherwise, because the only people there will be us. And your bodyguard. Oh, and this one guy, Frankie, who works there but who promised to keep his mouth shut. He signed an NDA."

A strained noise escaped me. But Cass was smiling, completely at ease in his body and in the world, especially now that we'd each aired out the uncertainty between us.

The last thing I'd expected from tonight was that we'd *communicate* my nerves away. Cass's gaze was steady on mine.

"There's no one else at this other place?" I asked. For the first time I was hopeful.

"No public, no press, no pressure," he promised. "Just us."

I couldn't hold back my bewildered smile.

CHAPTER NINE

"C'mon, Greer, you got this!" Cass exclaimed. I was less than convinced.

I focused up, mentally drawing a line from where I stood to the target ahead. I took a few wobbly steps, swung my arm back, and threw with all my might.

I must have miscalculated the geometry of my throw, however, because instead of twirling in a straight line to victory, the big heavy ball hit the lane with a *thud* and bounced left, directly into the gutter.

"*Owowowow!*" Cass howled. "She's got an arm on 'er!"

"She beefed it, though," I deadpanned. "A tragedy. A humiliation."

"I'll show you the proper form. The number of lesbian bowling tournaments I've attended with my moms would astound you."

I felt the shadow of his body behind mine. I froze, unsure if I should look at him or not.

"Can I?" Cass asked. His arm hovered over my hip, seeking permission to touch. I nodded, and his hand pressed into the fleshy area of my lower waist. A rush of breath and nerves shot through me. I tried to bury the worry that my body was not as taut and perfect as the ones Cassius Campbell the supernova was used to.

Be chill, my mind screamed at me.

Also, treacherously: *How can a* hand *feel this good?*

Also, confused: *How the hell did we get* here?!

Cass had snuck us out the back of Craig's and sweet-talked Joe into driving us over the hills to Studio City. He chattered Joe's ear off the whole ride, peppering him with questions just like he'd done with me the week before. It was a sight to behold. Cass uncovered facts about Joseph D'Amiano that *I* hadn't learned in his five years watching over us. Like that Joe grew up in Brooklyn but had followed a girl out to LA twenty years ago.

"Joe!" I gasped when this came up. "You old mush, I didn't know that!"

Joe waved a dismissive hand from the driver's seat. "Didn't last."

"This sounds like a movie—you *have* to tell us more," Cass urged, leaning over the seat.

In the rearview mirror I saw Joe roll his eyes, but he relented.

"She was always living out of hotels. I couldn't hack it," he said. "Proud of her, though. She won an Emmy last year."

Cass and I exchanged a look.

"*WHO?!*" we both screamed.

"Never tellin'. She never did lose her accent, though. Love that for her."

As we exited the highway, Cass instructed me to close my eyes. The car stopped and I let Cass and Joe guide me. When I reopened them, I was standing in an empty bowling alley lit in glowing pinks, purples, and blues. A neon sign on one side of the room announced the place was called Pinz.

"Now *this* is what I call a date," Cass said, walking backward toward the lanes with arms outstretched. "Or a friend thing! I'm cool either way."

This time when my stomach roiled, it was markedly more pleasant than before.

"Let's call it a date," I said. I felt like I might puke, but in a good way.

We ordered nachos and hot dogs from Frankie, a scraggly guy in his early twenties completely unimpressed by the two celebrities who'd rented the place out for the night. He delivered our food and went right back to his paperback Bukowski. Soon enough Joe disappeared, too, and a few minutes later I saw he'd set up his own solo game on the farthest possible lane from us.

I saw the glimmer in his eye. He was doing me a solid, sure— but to him, bowling was a much better Friday night than having to hover over his awkward teen ward.

Cass and I were essentially alone. That left me to completely botch my first turn . . . and *that* left Cass's hand burning into my side. I couldn't catch my breath.

"Teach me by example," I said, chickening out. Cass read the room and stepped away.

"Oh, I will *show you*," he bragged. He waggled his eyebrows as he made his way to the ball return. "My moms would have it no other way."

He examined the balls gathered in the return, touching this one and that, turning them over and testing their fit in his hand. My heart settled in the quiet.

"Sorry I suck at this," I said. "I've never been bowling before."

Cass straightened, eyes wide. "Never? Not even, like, for a birthday party, or forced family bonding?"

I sank into one of the hard plastic chairs and wiggled my toes in my garish rented bowling shoes, wondering how many people had worn them before me. I wished I could watch replays of their nights, the different dynamics and scores and moods that had gone with them.

"I guess it's never been much of a Greer thing?" I tried to explain.

"But *never*?!" he pushed, sliding into the chair next to me. *"Ever?"*

I laughed. I wondered if I should admit this next thing out loud.

"The only bowling alley I've been inside of? Yeah, it was Barbra Streisand's," I said, my face scrunching into a cringe. "And that was only for a second, during an after-dinner tour."

"Barbra Streisand owns a bowling alley?" Cass asked, baffled. The poor kid looked so confused. "Can we go? I'm hoping it's got karaoke and I can wail 'Don't Rain on My Parade' while I slide down the lanes."

"I'd go to that place for sure." I chewed my lip. "But no. It's in her basement. So if you angle for a feature on one of her albums, I'm sure she'd show it to you."

"She has a bowling alley in her basement?!" Cass yelled, jumping up.

I nodded, grim. "And a *mall.*"

"Please tell me what you mean," he said gravely.

"She has all these props and costumes and stuff from, I dunno, *being Barbra Streisand* her whole life. So she used it to build this collection of storefronts in her basement. It's, like, a doll shop, costume shop, even a candy store, frozen yogurt place . . ."

I laughed because Cass's jaw was hanging comically open.

"The frozen yogurt was just aiight," I said.

Cass laughed, then stopped, then laughed again. When he stopped, his eyes were alight.

"I'm still getting used to it, I guess," he said. "All the ways people take the fame, and the money, and . . . get *super weird*."

I nodded. I knew exactly what he was talking about.

"That's, like, the seven-hundredth-weirdest thing I've seen," I told him. "Barbra also cloned her dogs! And speaking of dogs? Reina, from *Nick of Time*? Separate assistants for each of her six dogs."

This sent Cass into hysterics. He was still laughing when he picked up a big glittery ball.

"I'm excited to see the ways I'll get weird," Cass said. "I mean, if my luck keeps going the way it has. I don't think I'd clone, though. Makes me too sad for all the rescue dogs."

It wasn't the right time to tell him the truth: that I hoped he didn't change at all. But money and fame change people, every time. Power and pressure are transformative.

Cass lifted the ball just below his chin and turned back to face me.

"Straighten your wrist and hold it straight as you swing back. Release the ball right as it passes your ankle. Keep that wrist straight and palm up." He demonstrated, arcing the ball beautifully in the air. It rocketed down the lane, toppling every pin. Cass lifted his arms above his head in victory and did a little spin. I was learning that this was a person who enjoyed a twirl. It made me smile.

I got up for my next turn, and for a moment we stood directly face to face, our bodies no more than a foot apart. Cass scanned my expression—and then he sat. I walked to the ball return as if there wasn't this *thing* hanging between us.

"I know it's pathetic," I offered as I browsed the ball selection. "An American kid who doesn't know something so basic. It's the story of my life."

"I don't think it's pathetic at all," Cass said, and he sounded offended on my behalf.

"Why not?" I asked. I laced my fingers into the holes of a green ball. I picked it up to test its weight. Too heavy. "My family's a case study for why they should eat the rich."

I followed his tip to release the ball when it passed my ankle— and was so surprised when I managed to knock something down, I let out an involuntary *"AH!"*

"AYYYYYYY," Cass cheered. He pumped his fist and danced in a circle around me.

"All right, let's not get too excited," I deadpanned. "It was two pins."

"Your *first* two pins," he said, still dancing. "It's a milestone!" He did some corny old dance moves, and I playfully shoved his shoulder, unable to handle the blush now crawling up my entire body.

Eventually Cass stilled and leaned back against the score-keeper.

"You don't have to be embarrassed," he said, his tone gentle. "About any of it."

"I'm not embarrassed," I lied. "Why would I be embarrassed?"

"Everyone has knowledge gaps. Unique things their parents left out. My moms never once allowed us to watch *SpongeBob*. You know how much shit I got at school? I'll never live it down. That's like ninety percent of the world's memes."

"Not the same," I said, rolling my eyes. "You know I've never been inside a high school cafeteria? Been homeschooled since I was thirteen. I get plenty of shit, but it's mostly from strangers online. I don't get out much. Have seen every episode of *Sponge-Bob*, though."

Cass's nod seemed to roll through his whole being. He was so expressive that if one part of his body responded to something, his shoulders, chest, and a knee came along for the ride. This was a person with so *much* inside him, always bursting to get out.

He shrugged his broad shoulders.

"I think it's cool you're *specific*. It's part of what intrigued me about you."

"You're *intrigued*?"

I didn't do it consciously, but I took a small step toward him.

"Yes," he said, matter-of-fact. "I want to get to know you. Because the more I do, the more intrigued I am. From afar, at the party, you seemed like a person who keeps to yourself a lot. But then I saw you with your sisters—and you opened up. Like literally, your whole face changed around them. Like there's a version of you only a few people in the world get the privilege of meeting. I want to be part of that group."

How the hell was a girl supposed to respond to that? The knot in my chest had been replaced by a pleasant buzzing sensation through my whole body.

My eyes went to his lips. They were full and inviting, parted slightly as he waited for me to respond. I made myself look away. If I stared too long, I'd get lost again, and I didn't want to miss a moment of this.

"So you like me?" I blurted. "Was that what 'intrigued' meant?"

"I like you," he chuckled. "You're smart, and you're curious, and neurotic, and you hang around Barbra Streisand's basement like it's no big deal, but you seem to light up around the things everyone else takes for granted, like diners, and root beer floats, and bowling alleys, and buckling into my mom's old van."

"That seat belt's a safety hazard."

"It is," Cass chuckled. "And for the record? I'm nervous, too."

"You really didn't care about the paparazzi thing?" I don't know why, but I needed to hear it again. I needed every obstacle cleared out of the way, all the cobwebs out of my head.

"The hand? The cheek kiss? Nah. Know why?" He tilted his head to my ear again. "You wanted to hold my hand anyway. You just needed an excuse."

If he'd meant to say more, he couldn't—because *suddenly my lips were on his.* My mind swirled with the warmth of him, my nostrils filling with citrus and shea butter and—

I jerked back before I could really feel the kiss—my very first. I sank my head between my knees in abject mortification, hoping the pure force of my humiliation would make me the first person in history able to teleport out of a room.

"*Ohmygod.* Oh no. Oh no, I'm so sorry." I was talking to the floor.

"Why?! Don't be," Cass said, looking equal parts shocked and amused.

"You were talking, and—I don't know what came over me. I believe in consent, I just—"

"I consent!" Cass interjected, waving hands in front of my face. "I retroactively consent."

"That's not how it works! I mauled you!"

"You did not *maul* me."

I sank my head between my knees again so I could hyperventilate in peace. Maybe if I stayed down here long enough, Cass would give up and leave Joe to carry me home.

Joe. Joe had probably seen all that! How mortifying to have humiliating teenage experiences with a middle-aged Italian American bodyguard watching your every move.

Cass's hand grazed my back. He pulled me gently into an upward position, and his eyes were intent on mine.

"Can I kiss you, please?" he asked, and the ghost of amusement flitted across his mouth.

"Okay," I said. It came out a squeak.

He leaned forward and his lips were on mine again, only this time I actually let myself *feel* the warmth of his lips, so smooth and soft and gently commanding. I got to revel in the way his breath mingled with mine, how our mouths played against each other. I was clumsy at first, not sure how much pressure and movement was expected on my end. But then the experience enveloped me. I melted into it, suddenly aware of every atom of my skin, my blood, my brain. Cass's hand on the back of my neck, one of mine clutching the edge of my seat while the other rested on his chest.

Holy shit. *This* was what kissing was like?

"Thank you," Cass said when we pulled apart. He was grinning from ear to ear, his eyes searching my face. He rested his forehead on mine, and now neither of us was hiding our smiles, or our nerves.

THE GROUP CHAT

🎵 SISTA SISTA: Szn 3 Theme Song 👀

DEST: [Link: JustJared.com: Cassius Campbell and Kiara Greer Fuel Romance Rumors with Craig's Date Night]

DEST: Kee. You bangin Cassius Campbell?

KEE: Dee. Must you be so vulgar?

DEST: My bad. You rockin' that rockstar's bell bottoms tho, right?

DEST: Climbing his Billboard chart to the top?

SOL: Only way to stop this is to answer the gdamn question

KEE: I am going to leave this groupchat.

SOL: You can't threaten that every week and have us still believe you

LALA: Just answer the question:)

SOL: Answer the question, Kia

DEST: answerusanswerusanswerusanswerusanswerusanswer-usanswerus

KEE: Jesus! It was just one kiss!

KEE: . . . maybe three

DEST: YESSSSSSSSSSSSSSSSSSSSSSSSSSSSSSSS

LALA: Tell me everything tonight!!!!! U better be awake when I get home

KEE: That is too much to ask, you get home way too late these days

LALA: You're an insomniac. You'll be up sadgirling over Beth March fanvids

KEE: That was one time. I can't tell you anything.

DEST: There's something I've been waiting to give you. An heirloom, passed down from Sola to me years ago. Now, dear sister, I bequeath it to you.

DEST: [Link: YouTube.com: Tutorial: How to Properly Apply a Condom]

—you left the conversation—

Cassius Campbell and Kiara Greer Stepped Out on an Adorable Date to the Pumpkin Patch

Litty.com | Top Stories | Celebrity Vertical

By Sarah Choi

Hollywood's hottest rumored couple ushered in the fall equinox with a trip to a star-studded pumpkin patch. Cassius Campbell and Kiara Greer both looked glam-casual as they browsed, and they even stopped to buy cups of hot cider from a local vendor.

Witnesses say the pair of famous young'uns were clearly on a date. "They were touching each other a lot," one source said. "His hand was always on her back, and she looked at him so sweetly. It seems like they really like each other!"

According to eyewitnesses, Greer suddenly acted shy when an 8-year-old fan asked for a selfie with Campbell. She offered to take the photo for them and was surprised when the little girl wanted her to be in the picture, too. "Cassius pulled Kiara close and asked if she was okay," our eyewitness said. "She said she was and they smiled for a bunch of pictures, even doing goofy poses with the kid and a scarecrow. By the end there was a whole crowd formed around them to watch!"

Could Cassius Campbell and Kiara Greer's Latest Outing Spark a Trend of Bringing Books on Dates?

Vogue.com | Celebrity Style

By Linda Gail

Cassius Campbell and Kiara Greer hit the town for another date night in Los Angeles. The couple held hands as they approached celeb hot spot Sushi Park on Friday. Greer, 17, wore a simple white tee, blue jeans, and a pair of vintage Air Jordans. Campbell, 18, rocked a pair of velvet cargo pants, a crisp white button-down, and Converse. But the statement piece was the copies of the novel *Tomorrow, and Tomorrow, and Tomorrow* by Gabrielle Zevin they both carried.

Witnesses saw Campbell and Greer discussing the book animatedly. That night Campbell posted a photo of the novel to his Insta Stories, with the caption "I don't know if I can keep reading." The next day he followed up with a post to main. "It's beautiful," he said in a video. "But, like, the kind of beautiful that crushes you, you know? Do I really gotta face the fragility of the human life? Man, I thought this was a book about video games!" Greer commented with a black heart emoji, to which Campbell replied: "You did this to me!"

You heard it here first: It's time to start a book club with your next Hinge date. Clearly the results can be memorable.

Cassius Campbell and Kiara Greer Cause Commotion at Lakers Game

Litty.com | Top Stories | Celebrity Vertical

By Alexis Borges

Social media's been abuzz following Cassius Campbell and Kiara Greer's every move, and the same was true at last night's Lakers game. Hundreds of cell phones stayed high in the air throughout the game, craning to get shots of the singer and the rising starlet.

The couple seemed at ease at first, sharing popcorn and making funny faces at the NBA cameras frequently in their faces. "She just seems so relaxed with him," one witness commented. "Less stiff and stick-up-her-butt than she usually is." The crowd was even treated to PDA when Campbell planted a peck on Greer's cheek, causing her to smile wide.

But the night took a turn as Campbell and Greer left the stadium only to be mobbed by fans. They signed autographs and posed for photos, but soon the crowd grew so large and unruly that Crypto security had to put a stop to it for fear someone would be trampled. Reports say a few fans even grabbed at Greer, touching the star without her permission. Click through our gallery below to see a visibly scared Greer as she struggles to find a worried-looking Campbell in the crowd.

CHAPTER TEN

A tiny blond woman named Lara hovered over me, but I couldn't see her. I lay with my eyes closed while Lara slathered chemicals around my eye region. She'd slather, wait, wipe, apply, wait, wipe, slather again, working with such surgical precision that I was convinced this woman could dismantle bombs for a living.

It was my job to stay perfectly still through all of this. Even though my nose itched. And I had to pee. For a natural fidgeter this was very, very difficult. But there was something calming about it, too. I did not have to rush. It was just me and Lara in this room, doing our jobs.

Lara was chatty. She told me her Yorkie-Schnauzer mix, Bruno, had recently made a break for it on an international flight and almost landed her on the no-fly list. I told her about my weekend plans, which consisted of catching up on Spanish homework and conscripting Lark into skipping a movie premiere and joining me and Miss Carol for movie night. It was Gina Prince-Bythewood week.

"Do you have a boyfriend?" Lara asked somewhere around the second wipe.

I stuttered, buffering. Was she playing with me? Had she already seen the buzz around me and Cass and just wanted the tea? Or was she actually curious? I didn't know what to do, so I just told her a truth: that I was seeing someone but we hadn't discussed labels yet. She must have sensed my clam-up, because Lara and I spent the rest of our time in polite silence. She worked, and I wondered if I should have gushed to her what I'd been feeling the last few weeks. I'd been holding all this awe inside me; so much had shifted, and in such a short time.

I was a person who kissed people now.

I was a person who went on dates.

They weren't your usual teen fare, what with the write-ups in *Vogue* and the borderline violent mobs storming our dates. I'd had a few panic attacks after that last one, but I'd be fine. With Cass even the most dystopian moments felt more bearable.

At the end of two hours, Lara told me to open my eyes. She held up a jeweled hand mirror, and I examined the fruits of her labor. My eyebrows were plucked, tinted, and laminated into perfect dark arches, and she'd managed to give me lash extensions that made me look like a Disney princess without turning me into a cartoon. Lara was a pro for the ages.

Then there was another reclined chair, another bright light highlighting one of my flaws, another day. I had sunglasses on, and my lips cracked at the corners as some big machine held them open by force. Heinrich Goldy, a very famous but gruff cosmetic dentist, was working on me. As he moved around the machine, all I could see was the abundance of filler he'd had injected into his cheeks. He looked a bit like he'd eaten shrimp despite having a shellfish allergy.

"Tsk," Dr. Goldy lamented from somewhere above me. He applied something that looked like toothpaste to my gums. It didn't taste or feel like anything, and the lack of taste or feel freaked me out, triggering an uncanny valley reaction in my mouth. I was suddenly desperate to spit. "I see you haven't been wearing your retainer. This lateral incisor is a mess."

"Uh-huh, ssrrry," I said around my mouth restraints.

I thought about my wayward incisor while Dr. Goldy applied hydrogen peroxide to my teeth. My mother had been gently hinting I should get veneers, but after the two years I'd spent in braces, I thought my regular teeth looked fine. I hadn't even noticed the crooked tooth till now.

I lay still for another hour, and this time a powerful blue light whitened my enamel to a perfectly unnatural pearly sheen. That night, though, I felt zings of pain through my mouth. It was like my teeth were in an ice bath I couldn't take them out of. I made two cups of hot tea and left one beside Merv as he caramelized onions for that night's meal. He didn't say anything, but I saw him grab the mug as I left the kitchen, and I smiled to myself.

With every new season of *Growin' Up* came a makeover montage. The Ignite execs expected their Sunday-night lineup to be lined with beautiful people. I just wanted to be mocked as little as possible, and my mother had been extra insistent about the makeover this year.

"Everyone is watching," she'd said proudly. That meant my looks were an open target. Everyone seemed to have an opinion— like the time I'd dared go with Miss Carol to the grocery store. I'd regretted it immediately: Headlines the next day speculated I was weeping and heartbroken because Cass had clearly broken up with me. The reality was that I'd just been makeupless—and if I looked unhappy, it was because we were being followed.

It all made me queasy, but I figured I was in good hands. My mom wanted to protect me. And so I was zipped around to every corner of Beverly Hills, poked, prodded, and exfoliated within an inch of my life. They said beauty was pain—I just thought it was a slog.

Discovered a new type of facial, I texted Cass one day, yawning from the passenger seat of Max's Bronco. They shoot lasers at your face to blast away layers of skin.

I'VE HEARD OF THAT ONE, he replied seconds later. But have you heard of the VAMPIRE FACIAL? They literally suck your own blood out and re-inject it into your face to make you look younger.

That's so goth, I wrote back. Why don't they have stuff like this for our brains yet? Mine could really use a deep cleaning.

The lasers or the blood?

Either/or, I'm not picky, I said. Then I texted again. My fingers flew over my phone screen, and Max smirked knowingly from the seat next to me. Wait, no, I got it. You know that Baby Foot thing that makes all the skin on your feet peel off and leaves them all soft and new? I want that for my brain. And my soul. A chemical peel for the psyche.

I will use my riches to fund this science for you, Cass promised.

Like Dolly Parton with the COVID vaccine, but perhaps a bit less lifesaving, I wrote.

Still, I think the world will thank me.

The next day, my face still swollen and peeling, a medical tech marked my stomach with a pen. She laid me on a table, where they attached some sort of ice gun that I was told would literally freeze my fat cells into oblivion. I breathed in through my nose and out my mouth, using a technique Miss Carol had taught me to keep calm.

"Yoooo, what?" Cass said over FaceTime that night. I was

applying a cold compress to my midsection; he was getting braided for an event. "First off, why you freezin' those off? They're the best part."

I scoffed to hide my blush.

"Tell that to the viewers who take screenshots of my belly rolls," I said. "And yes, before you ask, that's happened. They zoomed in and drew red circles around them."

"Damn," Cass said. "I wanna egg their houses so bad."

"Tell me about it."

"Living in a society, man. What a horror show."

I giggled. "It really isn't. What's up with that?"

"Tell you what, though," Cass said. "All these lasers? That's one thing they don't inform you of till you're in it: Having fame and money can get soooo sci-fi."

"Right?!" I said. "My mom has a cryo stick of frozen stem cells in the freezer. It's not a normal time over here."

"Normal's overrated," Cass said. With him, at least, that was true.

Early the next morning my mother roused me with a protein shake in hand.

"Up and at 'em!" she said, far too cheery. I resented that she was already showered, blow-dried, with a full face of professionally applied makeup, while I felt like a microwaved lab rat. "Jay Dub's waiting."

Jay Dub, also known as Jay West, was an alarmingly muscled middle-aged man from Philly who Lark and I trained with a few times a week. He was friendly in a drill sergeant kinda way, and had a borderline toxic affinity for burpees.

"Wha?" I blinked, trying to force the room into focus.

I was sore and a little itchy from my treatment the day before, still half submerged in the dream I'd been having—one where I was a jelly bean in a giant grocery store, panicking because Destiny had put me on babysitting duty and I'd lost Deja in the cereal aisle.

Muttering to myself that I was not a jelly bean, I threw on biker shorts over the underwear I'd slept in and turned my back as I wriggled a sports bra under my FREE BRITNEY tee.

"Oh, please," my mom chided. "I made those boobs—no need to hide 'em."

"You ever notice how much this family talks about each other's boobs?" I asked. "Because it's a lot."

"Can't say I have." Mom yawned, and this was my only hint that she was the least bit tired under her perfect veneer.

"It's not a bad thing," I said. "Just fodder for the tell-all."

"Come on, now," she said dismissively, "you know you're not doing one of those."

I stretched the sleep out of my shoulders and trailed after her through the quiet halls. Windows across the house were open. It was a crisp morning, the kind when LA actually felt autumnal—at least for the few hours before the heat of the day set in. I inhaled a big breath of it, willing it to wake me the rest of the way up. I felt like this cloud was hovering over my eyeballs.

"Hey," I said as we rounded a corner, my brain jogging to catch up, "I don't see Jay on Tuesdays." Lark had increased her sessions with Jay Dub to six days a week when she'd gotten her record deal. But I only saw him Monday, Wednesday, and Friday.

"Figured you could hop on Lark's schedule. Say bye to the rest of the 'baby fat.'"

I stopped walking.

"Oh, honey," my mom said, turning to look at me. "Don't be sensitive."

"I'm not!" I said sensitively. She walked back to me and stroked my cheek.

"You know I think you're beautiful," she said, like always. "But fame isn't a women's studies class. You're under more scrutiny than ever. I know how to set you up for success. With all these extra eyes on you, you don't want to be, uh . . ."

She stopped there. I thought about turning on my heel and retreating to my room. But standing there in the hallway with my hands on my hips, I was very aware of the softness of my belly under my T-shirt.

I could see Lark in the yard, already stretching. She was putting in long hours in the studio, and when she wasn't there, she was learning choreography, shooting key art, or on her own whirlwind makeover tour in preparation for her very first solo press run. If I didn't join her now, I didn't know the next time we'd get to spend real time together.

Comments sections flooded my head. I usually left my social media to our dedicated socials team, but now sometimes Cass DMed me memes on Instagram. I was checking it more—which meant I saw more posts I was tagged in. In one photo of me and Cass, I was looking down and to the side, every roll of skin and fat around my neck bunched and visible.

"HER?!" one commenter wrote. "Doesn't make sense. He has every beautiful woman in the world at his disposal, and this is who he chooses? Guess you really can't buy taste."

There was no doubt my mom had read that one. She read everything. I sighed.

"I know you know what you're doing," I said. "But do I have to do the ice gun again? I really hated that thing."

158

My mom clapped me on the back with a satisfied smile. "We can revisit the CoolSculpting," she conceded.

I nodded, pretending I'd won. I started walking toward the yard. Then I turned. "Hey. Did Greta ever tell you what the photographer in New York said?"

My mother's face stayed perfectly still, which told me she knew exactly what I was talking about. Of course she did. Greta always told her everything.

"She did," she answered. "And if you say the word, I'll make sure that man never works again."

"You sound like a mob boss when you talk like that."

"I'm serious. I can at least promise he won't be on another Greer shoot."

"There's no need to blacklist him," I said. "I was just . . . Do you think my jaw is doughy?"

My mom shifted on her heels. The knot in my chest clenched.

"You know I think you're beautiful," she repeated, looking me up and down with the surgical precision of a doctor deciding how much truth her patient could handle.

"You didn't answer the question," I pointed out.

She sighed, and it had this flourish like, *Just remember, I'm not the one who brought the conversation here.* I braced myself.

"You know my philosophy," she said. "Insecurities only last as long as you let them. I spent my whole life hating my nose—so I changed it. You don't have to do anything to your body if you don't want to, but there's nothing wrong with a little jawline shaping."

"You think I should get filler?"

"Baby, it's up to you," she said. "You can always get it dissolved if you don't like it."

I nodded, taking that in. Something shifted in my mother's face. Softened. She went from Melora Greer, expert problem

159

solver, right back to the mom who'd sung me to sleep as a baby. The one who'd never steer me wrong. Right?

"Don't let the dickheads get you down, kid. They don't get to decide who you are."

I didn't go back to CoolSculpting. I did go to training with Jay and Lark. And at the end of the week, there was another reclining chair, in another office, under another too-bright light. They stuck me with needles until I looked like someone slightly new.

KEEP IT UP!
FROM: Mom <melora.greer@greer.com>
TO: Kia <keekee@greer.com>

10/03/24 5:23 a.m.

Morning, baby,

I know you hate reading these things, but I figured you'd want to see the progress we're making after only a few weeks. It might be time to start reading more of your own press; studying how the public reacts to our moves will give you thicker skin and better spatial awareness of yourself. Just think of it as cultural anthropology! Don't you love that subject?

The good news is we are ruining Levi's press tour plans! He went on *The Kelly Clarkson Show* this week and she asked him about YOU!

We should set a meeting, talk about capitalizing on this momentum. Maybe we get you a talk show? Shapewear line? Think about it!

Keep up the good work, honey! Links below!

Love you,
Mom(ager)

Cassius Campbell and Kiara Greer Look Cozy at Janelle Monáe Concert

Cassius Campbell and Kiara Greer Make Out at Six Flags—See the Video!

Cassius Campbell Shades Levi Ellis, Says His Music Gives Him "Bad Vibes"

People Are Mad Levi Ellis Dodged a Question About Kiara Greer—
"Boy, Wasn't She Your Sister Five Seconds Ago?"

CHAPTER ELEVEN

Crowds rattled me, every time. No matter how often I experienced arms reaching toward me, grabbing, trying to take a piece of us, I could never get used to it. It always threw me off, even if it only lasted a moment. After the Lakers game Joe pushed through the crowd to get to Cass and me, guiding us between bodies and shoving us into the waiting Escalade. We were out of the woods, but on the ride home Cass got to witness me having a panic attack.

We'd gone on a few outings since then, none with quite as fervent a mob as there'd been at that game. But I think Cass saw the trepidation in my eyes at those next ones.

Okay, so for our next date, Cass texted one day, just as I'd gotten off one of my FaceTimes with my dad, my team suggested we ride the Ferris wheel at the Santa Monica Pier, since it appears in my next music video.

My pulse quickened. Riding a Ferris wheel with Cass did sound tempting, but it would be hard to control the crowds in a place like that. Maybe I'd just have to suck it up; I didn't want to put a stop to our arrangement, not when it was giving me all this time with him. And that was what it meant for a Greer to be out with Cassius Campbell: invasion.

Cass texted again before I could figure out what to say. IDK if that's the right move, tho, he wrote. I think we should do something a little different for our next date.

I cocked an eyebrow, intrigued. What did you have in mind?

Cass and his family lived in a cute yellow house on a wide, sleepy suburban street. The neighborhood was dotted with those little library boxes that offered free books to passersby. It was perfect. Cass's room had walls of dark blue decorated with LPs and posters of James Baldwin, Grace Jones, David Bowie. A keyboard and guitars fought for space in one corner. A notebook-strewn side table sat next to it alongside an old armchair with upholstery so lovingly worn that it had to be where Cass wrote songs. I pictured him there deep in the night, picking gently at his guitar so as not to wake his family.

He'd left me alone in here, so I wandered. I came upon a framed photo of Cass as a toddler. His cheeks were perfect apples, and he was being held by a similarly beaming woman sporting a blond TWA. I wondered if this was Anita, the mom who was gone.

I still hadn't gotten up the nerve to ask what happened to her. Cass mentioned Violet frequently in our conversations, but though every once in a while the conversation danced around what had happened to his other mom, Cass always quickly and smoothly changed the subject. That was a part of him he didn't seem ready to show me, at least not yet.

I took in the woman in the picture, trying to absorb every piece of information possible. Baby Cass was utterly lit up in her presence. However Anita had left their lives—and her own life, I assumed, because he didn't talk like she'd abandoned them—it was a loss that was immeasurable. I'd had people leave, and I'd had people die. Both were awful. But this was different. In Anita's face were echoes of expressions I'd seen on Cass's own a hundred times already. There was a set to her mouth that reminded me of him—a willingness to play, maybe. An awe at the world. I could see that she was a part of him, inexorably and forever.

I looked away, worried I'd invaded a space that wasn't mine. I didn't want to create some version of Cass that only existed in my head. I refused to make him up. I wanted to meet Cassius Campbell on his terms, especially in the rare moments like this, away from cameras and the sidelong looks of strangers. That was what tonight was for. All our other dates since the bowling alley had been public or on FaceTime, and the line between work and our very real crushes had started to blur. I wanted to see past the flashing lights, to where Cass and I could really touch.

I took a step and inhaled deep. The window was open to the backyard, and the room smelled like freshly mown grass and *Cass*. I sat on the corner of the bed.

"I dumped an offensive amount of butter on this," Cass announced, reentering his room with a trough of popcorn. He placed it on the side table and perched next to me on the bed, tapping my shoulder with his. Somehow the gesture already felt familiar. The beginnings of whatever we were had involved so much noise and strangeness, yet through it all we'd managed to build something that at least skirted intimacy.

"Don't be nervous," he said. "Being here, I mean."

I gave him a look. "Have you met me?"

Cass breathed a laugh and kicked a wayward shirt under his bed.

"Fair," he conceded. "Nerves not negotiable. Just know I gotchu. And if Mom comes home, she's gonna love you. You're her favorite type of person."

"Which is?"

"Introverted but interesting," he said. "Polite but inquisitive."

I shoved my hands between clenched knees and hid the obscene smile that was spreading over my face. This was the opposite of our last few dates, in the very best way.

So why was my heart still beating so fast?

"I'm glad we could be alone this time," I said.

"Me too," he said.

"I like your room," I said, bouncing on the bed. I picked up a plushie that lay against his pillows—a little red guy in the anatomical shape of a heart. "What's this thing's story?"

"*That* is Valverie," he said, scooting deeper onto the mattress. I shoved away my barrage of nerves and joined him.

"When I was ten, my mom's hospital invited the kids of employees to come to this day where they 'trained' us as doctors," Cass continued. "They gave us medical gowns and we toured ORs and X-ray rooms. They even showed us how to intubate someone. On a doll, of course. But we got to shove the tube down its throat and everything. And it was *hard*. I can't imagine doing that to an actual body."

"Wait, that sounds *so cool*," I said.

"It *was*," he said, and he was still smiling big. My cheeks flushed, knowing I'd caused that smile. There was something nostalgic in Cass's eyes, like he was accessing a place in the past he hadn't thought about in a long time. He lay down, his movement fluid and casual. "At the end they gave us souvenirs from the gift shop. Thus is the origin story of Valverie. Named after heart valves, of course, but also the Amy Winehouse seminal classic."

I looked down at him, splayed out on the place where he slept every night. There was something about Cass's ability to read my nerves that seemed to strip them of their power. I knew, somehow, that Cass wouldn't judge me even if I fell right on my face. He wanted to know me, and that gave me a confidence I wasn't used to.

"I like picturing you as a kid," I told him, "barreling through the world with all these questions and all these dreams."

I propped myself on my side, and his expressive eyes searched my face. A warm sensation spread through me. I was suddenly intensely aware of my every limb, every eyelash. There was a question in those eyes—a frisson. I realized he might be looking for some kind of signal, some permission, a green light. So I placed my hand on his chest, bold in our privacy. I was pleased to learn that his heart was beating as hard as mine.

My fingers wandered upward to the tendons of his long, graceful neck. I dared to touch his lips, gently tracing the edges of his mouth. His eyes grew more intent, more eager. And then he leaned forward and his mouth enveloped mine.

Cass wound his arm around my waist and pulled me in close, the finely toned muscles of his forearms pressing into my back, and we were in our own world within a world within a world. Our hips made contact, and I was sure of the way he wanted me. I felt it.

His mouth was warm and full. I deepened the kiss, and his teeth playfully dragged across my lower lip. I smiled against it. We could laugh while we kissed, and seconds later we would be sighing or moaning. I loved discovering that. Finding him.

Cass explored my stomach, my waist, my hips. He uttered a soft moan as he felt the softness of my body under his hands.

I felt a rush of relief—he wasn't bothered by all the parts of me other people were trying to fix. Every bit of me tingled, or fluttered, or reached, grasping, desperate to see what might happen next, safe in knowing he was right there with me. Cass may have had more experience, but his heart was beating just as hard as mine.

Cass's hand played at the hem of my T-shirt. I followed his lead and slid my hand up the skin of his back. I felt like I might explode.

"Are we alone?" I asked. Cass's eyes flashed to mine, and they were full of a special kind of hope. I let out a breathless laugh and pulled his mouth back to me before he could answer.

BANGBANGBANG—a knock at the door, jolting us from our reverie. Cass blinked rapidly, eyes glazed.

"Mom?!"

My blood froze. But then there was a loud "HA!" on the other side of the door, followed by another *BANGBANG*. Cass's face fell quickly into annoyance.

"JADE," he yelled, "GIMME A MINUTE." He buried his head in the crook of my shoulder and let out a lamenting groan. I sighed, frustrated.

"FEEL HER UP LATER," Jade yelled back through the door. "I NEED YOU."

"GIVE. ME. A. MINUTE."

"NOPE."

"JADE, I SWEAR TO GOD."

"CASS!" She sounded panicked now. "WE HAVE. A FUCK-ING. *PROBLEM.*"

At first glance you wouldn't be able to tell. As we peeked through the curtains, Citronia Street looked peaceful as ever. But then Cass sucked in a breath. I followed his gaze three houses down, and I spotted it, too.

Two cars, each overflowing with people. Even from almost a block away, I could see the group was *giggling*. They elbowed each other and craned their heads our way. One person, about our age, had glitter on their face and half their body hanging out the back window, phone extended to capture pictures or video. Another looked to be a little girl no older than ten. She stood in the street, shoulders shaking with sobs. On her shirt was Cass's face.

Cass paced, cursing under his breath.

"I came home and it, like, *activated* them," Jade said. She stood with arms crossed, her stern face pinched with worry.

"What did they do?" Cass asked.

"Technically not much?" Jade said. "They thought I was you at first. One of the guys lurched outta the car like, 'Mr. Campbell! Sorry to bother, but would you make my daughter's day?!' As if it's not a bother to literally show up at a stranger's house."

She shrugged, but her trademark nonchalance couldn't hide that she was very clearly wigged out. "They didn't seem violent, but . . . I'm just not sure what to do?" She looked between Cass and me. "I almost called the police, but, y'know, ACAB."

"*Shit*," Cass said in a low hiss. His hands went to his hair. "What the *fuck*! How do they even know where we live?" He sank down on an entryway bench and stared at the floor. "What if they ambush Mom?"

His voice cracked at that last part.

It was a grief I knew intimately: the realization that from this point forward, your life did not entirely belong to you.

Jade sank down beside Cass.

"It'll be okay," she insisted, and now her voice was authoritative. Something passed between them then, that unspoken sibling language. "I feel silly—I'm making too big a deal of it. I'm sure they'll go away."

It broke my heart a little, how vulnerable they both looked. I wanted so desperately to help. Then, just like that, I realized I could.

"Don't," I blurted, the thought still half formed. Their faces swiveled to me in unison, and I blanched. "You don't have to feel silly, I mean. Superfans are practically spies."

I took out my phone and started typing a message, but I kept talking.

"Cass, you've mentioned your neighborhood in interviews, right? They probably, like, cross-referenced a photo from a relative's Facebook page that had half a street sign in it with some photo shoot you did at home that showed a certain tree or flower bush in your yard. That's the kind of shit they pull. They look for clues *everywhere*. Stans could solve murders if they used their powers for good. They could straight up find the Black Dahlia killer."

I threw in this last bit hoping it might make Cass crack a smile. Instead he just looked freaked. My phone lit up with a text. I exhaled with relief as I read it.

"Joe can be here in forty. When does your mom get home?"

"Ten-ish," Jade answered.

Cass stood and just stared at me, shaking his head. "Kee . . . no. You were so hype to not need him tonight."

It was true—I'd made an embarrassingly big deal of leaving home without an armed bodyguard for once. I wanted to be like any other girl going to her boyfriend's house, rolling my window down and letting my hand dance in the dusk.

But I should've known better. Cass wasn't a normal teenager, and neither was I. There was always going to be someone watching us, wanting something from us.

"Joe won't be here for me," I insisted. Cass was still shaking his head, resisting it, so I kept going. "He was on call anyway. I'll buy him something pretty."

Cass hesitated, but something did relax in the set of his shoulders. His eyes were wide and grateful—and then he was hugging me. Suddenly all I could see or smell was the dark nook where his shoulder met his neck.

I breathed in deep. He was just so *Cass:* orange blossom, shea butter, warm skin, and the faintest hint of forest from the rosemary oil he used in his hair. I could stay right there forever and forget all those other people. I could lie to myself that we were all that existed in the world. That lie would be a good one. That lie felt good.

"All right," Jade interjected, holding up both hands. "Be disgusting *after* the crisis has passed. Also: *Who the hell is Joe?*"

Cass let me go, but he didn't look away.

Joe fulfilled the promise of Joe. He arrived promptly and talked to the gathered fans with kindness, a firm hand, and the subtle implication that he was armed. The families scattered, some angry but most sheepish. Cass invited Joe to stay for the movie, but Joe opted instead to take the Wi-Fi password and a few slices of pizza to a rocking chair on the porch. Within a minute of his departure, we could hear the opening theme of *The Golden Girls* emanating from his iPad.

"Good taste," Jade said, still mildly bewildered by the whole experience.

The Campbell sibs and I settled into the family room. I tried not to be obvious as I gaped at every family photo: Anita and Violet in matching silk suits at their wedding, elementary-age Cass and Jade beside them. Cass onstage in *Guys and Dolls*. Jade in knee-high white socks and a soccer uniform, holding a ball and squinting into the sun. My favorite was of the four of them in a redwood forest, arms reaching upward, the whole family dwarfed by giant, ancient trees.

"That was a good trip," Jade said, plopping onto the other end of their plush yellow sectional. I wrenched my gaze away from the mantel. "About five minutes after that photo, Cass threw a screaming, crying *fit* because he found a tick in his butt crack."

"That is *not* what happened," Cass griped, sounding annoyed. He'd just rescued our abandoned popcorn from his room, and he placed the bowl on the coffee table as he settled in next to me.

"I would scream and cry, too," I offered. "And throw myself into the nearest ocean, or set myself on fire."

"*Thank you.*" He glared jokingly at Jade. But over the past hour the set of his shoulders had become inelastic, the easy slope of his mouth rigid. His whole demeanor was off.

"I know my truth. Anyway. You're picking the movie, Kiara." There was a dangerous glint in Jade's eyes as she said this. "Campbell rules. Guest picks."

She'd relaxed a bit now that a dozen strangers were no longer waiting to pounce on her family. While Cass had fielded the pizza delivery, Jade had changed into plaid pajama pants and a sweatshirt that hung to her knees. It read: BULLY A THEATER KID TODAY.

"We will love whatever you choose." He smiled at me like he always did, but it was a tired smile. It hurt my heart, seeing someone with such natural presence looking like he wanted to disappear. That feeling should've been reserved for people like me, the ones who didn't light up every room they entered.

"Speak for yourself," Jade scoffed. She turned to me. "If you don't pick right, I *will* lose all respect for you."

"You have respect for me?" I held my hand to my chest and widened my eyes in faux appreciation.

"I have a little," Jade said. "And it's at stake, so get to choosin'.'"

"Don't listen to her," Cass said softly. "Just put on one of your faves."

He pecked me on the cheek. Instinctively my hand reached up to the spot he'd kissed, and I got this shock of a reminder that my jaw was different now. Not wholly—but the filler had made it more defined, tracing clearer angles and lines around the bottom of my face.

I wondered if they'd noticed. Jade would judge me for it, but right now she was curled into a ball on the couch, disappeared into her phone. When I looked back his way, Cass was lost in the middle distance, gaze trained in the direction of that front foyer window. He was probably thinking of his mom, Violet, still at work at the hospital. Or of the people, proclaimed fans of his, who'd invaded his family's space.

I didn't know how to help him except to do what he wanted. So I queued up my favorite movie of all time.

"Isn't *Roman Holiday* also the name of the drink you ordered the night we met?" Cass said as the rental page loaded and a photo of Audrey Hepburn and Gregory Peck on a Vespa filled the screen.

"How could you possibly remember that?"

He tapped the side of his head. "Steel trap, this thing."

A bit of the Cass I recognized was creeping back in. I smiled, then pressed play. Swirling wind instruments filled the air as the Campbell living room was plunged into 1950s Rome. I sank deep into the couch. Cass's hand reached for mine, and as I slid my fingers between his, the movie faded out of focus.

That was fine, though. When I watched *Roman Holiday*, I tended to skip the beginning altogether. The movie opens with an announcement to the international press in Rome that Princess Ann, played by Audrey Hepburn, is on tour representing her country. They show her completing royal duties with perfect posture and poise, but the whole time you can see the boredom creeping in around the edges. It's clear to the viewer she's itching for something more.

Ann is absurdly beautiful and funny and sad, but I skipped these parts because this was not a pretty little princess story. At least not to me.

"These *clothes*," Jade muttered, in awe.

"I know, right?" I replied.

"I am going to copy every single one of these outfits for the play," she said.

I was right that a movie would be a good distraction. It was like when you're all eating a really good meal; we were just in it, watching in comfortable silence. The weight of Cass's shoulder deepened against mine as he slowly started to unclench.

My favorite parts of the movie start when Ann, high on sleeping pills and seeing her opening, sneaks out of the palace and into the Roman night. She falls asleep on some ancient ruins (as you do) and is found by a kind but deceitful reporter named Joe, played by the incredibly hot Gregory Peck. From there the two are intertwined, gallivanting around the city and having a grand ol' black-and-white time—doomed lovers connecting with parts of themselves they didn't know were there. Ann sinks deeper into a life she knows she can't keep, and for a while they get to ignore the pressures of the outside world. They have *fun*, despite being irrevocably star-crossed.

I loved how charming Audrey Hepburn and Gregory Peck were. I loved the costumes and the acting and how it was basically a movie about two people surprised to like each other so much, even though they know they only have a small slice of time together.

When they danced at the Castel Sant'Angelo, Cass whispered in my ear, "Let's go there."

"Only if we can jump in the water, too," I whispered back. We smiled at each other through the dark.

"Shh," Jade said. "This other guy's trying to take her away!"

My dad's favorite thing is watching other people watch his favorite movies, and now I could see why. I knew every move of this one, but Cass and Jade didn't, which meant I got to experience it with them as if it were my first time, too. When Ann went back to the palace and saw Joe one last time at a press conference, Jade sat all the way up for the first time all night.

"What the hell! They don't end up together?!"

"Sorry," I said. "Should I have warned you? It's this famously bittersweet ending."

"That's such bullshit!" Jade exclaimed. "She doesn't even like it there! She can't live the rest of her life in this box they're trying to shove her into."

"She's got duties! If she didn't go back, she'd cause some international incident—she can't do that to her family."

"Seems accurate to me," Cass said, yawning. "Most people do just go through the motions assigned to them, the versions of themselves other people think they should be. They give up these big pieces of themselves over time, living for the small days or weeks they get to escape the drudgery."

"But I hate that," Jade said. "I don't need reality in my movies."

"She's got a lot to worry about," I argued. "It's bigger than just her."

"I think I love it," Cass said. "Those two had such a beautiful time together."

⌒

Violet Campbell was kept at the ER late that night, tending to injuries from a pileup on the 101. The trauma came through right as she was packing up. So I said goodbye to the Campbell siblings and promised to come back as soon as I could. When I stepped out onto the front porch, Citronia Street was quiet for real this time, and Joe was zipping up his backpack.

"Thanks for tonight, Joe. You're a real pinch hitter."

"Anytime, kid. Sorry those creeps ruined your night. Entitled idiots."

"I don't think they did," I said. "Not this time."

I started walking down the driveway, then turned back. "Why *The Golden Girls*?" I asked.

"Reminds me of my mom," he said simply.

I thought about that as I got into the car. There was so much about Joe I didn't know. Then again, there was so much about myself I didn't know. So many ways I was surprising myself. It was happening almost every day now that I'd started my metaphorical tiptoe past the gates.

I hit the highway and put on my favorite Whitney Houston song. Whitney had a song for every mood, and I needed one that would bring me back to the good parts of the night.

I pumped the volume as high as my ears could bear. I sang along, very badly, and let the music drown out everything unsteady or nervous inside me.

I howled along. *"When the night falls, my lonely heart caaaaaalls."*

The song became me and Cass, dancing through an empty white room in my head. I'd lost *my* senses tonight. I hadn't had space to process what was happening before Jade knocked on that door, but here it was, now that I was alone again: Cass pressed close to me, lips swollen, eyes glazed, our very beings reaching for each other, ready to leap.

Whitney sang, her voice a driving force forward, a clarion bell.

"Oh, I wanna dance with somebody. I wanna feel the heat *with somebody."*

She let out a high, clear giggle. Her laugh was always my favorite part of this song. Only now it sounded different. Something inside me felt absolutely hysterical.

Because Cass gave me something new every time I saw him. The me of a few weeks ago had never felt anything like what I had tonight. Who cared if mobs formed when we were in public? I could bear the uncomfortable, so long as it led me back to moments like that. Something in me had unspooled in the privacy of that room.

I was cycling into a new version of myself, and I didn't know who she was yet. This Kia was unpredictable. Maybe even a little wild. I liked what she felt. This me was a curious explorer. She'd barely even broached all the new things she could feel. The world was vast, and so was I. I didn't even know yet how far I could go.

"*Dance,*" Whitney ordered. And I knew I would.

CHAPTER TWELVE

I was wired when I got home. I lay in bed scrolling TikTok, trying to get sleepy but instead replaying the night in my head. The feel of Cass's body against mine, his room, the invasive fans, Jade's sweatshirt, the movie, the minutiae of the Campbell house.

My family had always been a scattered one. At that very moment my dad was filming in Atlanta; Mom was with Sola, overseeing a commercial shoot in Paris; Lark had been out late making the rounds at red carpets and after-parties; Destiny was at some boot camp in Temecula training for her action movie. The Campbells grew up seeing each other every day like it was nothing. I wondered what that was like.

TikTok was my go-to method for drowning out the noise in my head. My algo served up the usual videos of cute animals on farms, rundowns about how people really lived in the Tudor era, and *The Summer I Turned Pretty* edits.

Then my face came up. A woman's head hovered over a picture of me and Cass at the Lakers game. In the photo we were leaning in close to each other, giggling. I couldn't remember what we'd been laughing about.

"Melora Greer is our generation's Mrs. Bennet from *Pride and Prejudice,* and she's moving up through the world by pairing her daughters with music's hottest stars," the disembodied woman said in rapid-fire monologue. I clicked to tell the app not to show that kind of video in my algo anymore, but I wasn't fast enough. My stomach dropped.

"Now, it's not that Kiara is ugly," the woman continued. "She's cute, even. But c'mon—she's not as stunningly beautiful as her sisters. So Melora's strategy here is pretty interesting—"

I usually tried to ignore my own press. But being with Cass had only made me more famous. With every date I became more unavoidable, even to myself.

I watched the whole thing. This woman basically thought my sisters and I were all puppets, which made me laugh—try calling Destiny Greer a puppet to her face, I dare you. The woman's thesis revolved around the fact that the least attractive Greer (me, apparently) had made a "culturally favorable match," and that this would secure the future of the Greer empire for years to come. She made us sound like *Bridgerton* characters.

The woman looked Sola's age, maybe early thirties. She was white, with straight brown hair tied in a messy bun. Her bio said she had a law degree. I wondered what led people with real lives to comment on who teenagers were dating. I thought about leaving a comment saying as much, but I knew that would only spawn one of those Comments by Celebs posts, more headlines, more TikTok reactions dissecting why "Kia Greer got salty."

But now I was curious. I broke my own rule: I searched my name. I gave up on sleep altogether and scrolled through every video under the #KiaraGreer and #KiaGreer tags on TikTok. My skin prickled as I realized just how *many* opinions of me were out there. I'd known it, of course, but only on an intellectual level.

Now I looked in its face. I wasn't hated, but plenty of people called me boring and not worth their time—a sentiment I found painfully ironic considering they were taking the time to make videos about me. They'd clearly found something interesting in my dating Cass. To them, his interest in me validated the place I already occupied rent-free in their minds. I'd trapped them, and now they couldn't help but lean in.

A number of others posted long rants about how my family represented everything wrong with late-stage capitalism. Those I couldn't exactly disagree with.

There was a small but vitriolic horde of Cassius Campbell fans who absolutely hated that he was with a Greer—but there were others who were grateful he was with "someone like her" instead of, say, a bombshell like Sola. Apparently the fact that I wasn't searingly hot made them feel like they stood a chance with him themselves.

A whole subsection of people thought I was a beard for Cass. Based on the flamboyance of his wardrobe and the fact that he wore obvious makeup, they figured he must be gay and closeted. Some of these people thought he'd signed a contract with my mother so the Greer fam could help him hide it.

The theory pricked at the tender corner of my heart that was still afraid Cass was too good to be true. There was always the possibility that this person I'd come to trust was lying to my face, just like Levi had. I had to work actively to push those thoughts away. I had to believe he was just as into us as I was. I *did* believe that. I'd been there tonight, on his bed. I'd felt the way he'd wanted me.

I reminded myself what I'd learned every time Lark would pull me into a Gaylor rabbit hole: Most conspiracy theories were less about truth and more about whatever their creators needed, subconsciously or otherwise. I kept scrolling.

A few videos were just slideshows of me and my sisters with Joe in the background. Apparently a lot of people thought he was hot. These ones made me smile. I made a mental note to roast him about it in the morning.

Then there were the videos from plastic surgeons, dermatologists, and other aesthetic professionals tracking every flaw on my face. Several dentists pointed out the off-kilter slant of my top right incisor, and how it was probably a sign I wasn't using my retainer enough (guilty). One woman got particularly prescriptive, walking through every procedure she would suggest to "make Kiara Greer look her absolute best." According to her, I needed masseter Botox and chin filler to slim and chisel my jawline, a brow lift to make me look more alert, lipo at my midsection, a boob job to balance my frame after the lipo, and either nose filler or a full-on nose job to "refine" my features.

I watched that video three times. To illustrate my flaws, this woman had used a photo in which I'd already had chin filler done.

I scrolled until the prickling under my skin traveled to my bloodstream, and then my lungs, until I felt tears streaming out of my aching eyes, my chest tight, rising and falling with heavy, labored breaths.

I did a breathing exercise Miss Carol had taught me. I breathed *in, in, in, in* for four seconds, held my breath for seven, and exhaled *out, out, out, out, out, out, out, out* for eight. *Out, out, out, damned spot, get out of my brain.* I repeated the process until I'd calmed enough to wash my face. *This is your life,* I told myself. *This isn't going to go away.*

I needed to grow thicker skin. People were only going to have *more* opinions from here on out, feel *more* entitled to me. I had to remind myself that Cass was worth it. I'd never felt as alive as I did with him.

I'd leveraged my name to help Sola's and I'd willingly attached myself to Cass. Now I couldn't imagine letting him go.

I walked down the hall and into Lark's room. She mumbled in her sleep but didn't protest when I slid into bed next to her. I pulled her stuffed orca, Rosie, into my chest.

I'd left my phone in my room. I stared at her wall until sleep finally pulled me under, away from my own racing thoughts.

CHAPTER THIRTEEN

"Kia, you've got to make a decision about your future, and soon," Mr. Hillis said. "You've got to choose."

"I knooooow," I whined. "But it's hard! I want to show them my best self—but, uuhhh, who is that? I don't know her."

Mr. Hillis gave me that look he always did, the *You're exhausting me* one. The look had grown more potent since Lark had graduated early. She'd always sweep into morning sessions with a serene smile and a kind word, even when she was tired after night shoots. Lark had a way of balancing out the neuroses Mr. Hillis and I both brought to the table. Without her, my long-suffering teacher had to do more of the heavy lifting.

"You have plenty of best selves, Kiara," he insisted now.

We'd set up shop for the day's tutoring session in the solarium, a room with three glass walls and a glass ceiling with plants growing across it. Mr. Hillis was a pale redhead, and over the last hour the tips of his ears had turned a painful-looking bright pink. I tsked. He always ignored my warnings to apply sunscreen. That was definitely going to peel.

"You already have great options," Mr. Hillis said. "You keep sending me drafts that we could absolutely hone into incredible college essays. I'm especially partial to the one about your grandmother."

"That was just some delusional ramble I wrote on the plane, though," I said. "Do you really think it could be good enough?"

"Yes, I do. I really do."

I sucked in a breath. It was so nice of him to say, but I didn't believe him.

"It's so purple prose-y, though," I argued. "All that stuff about how home *smells*? Who talks like that?"

"You do," he said, an amused smile twisting his lips.

"I just don't think I've written anything strong enough yet."

Mr. Hillis sighed deep. I could tell he was growing more annoyed with me.

"All right," he said. "Well, if you're not willing to use that one—even though I think you should—then let's talk alternatives. Your Cleopatra essay could be a starting point. The way you wrote about Schiff cutting past the myth of Cleopatra to the real, human woman underneath really got me. For your apps you could expand on how by reading her as Black, you may have willfully participated in the distortion of her life, but how doing so allowed you, as the audience, to engage in your own power. It's *good*, Kiara. And you know you're a shoo-in."

I didn't want to tell him why I was pressing the issue. Sure, my nepo baby status all but guaranteed admission to some of the colleges I was looking at. But the whole world already thought I was talentless. My TikTok rabbit hole had confirmed that, but it was nothing new. Last year's Emmys host had even made a joke about it. I was the "ugly" duckling, the useless spare. It didn't exactly make me look forward to putting my writing out there.

My phone was faceup on the table, and it lit up with a text from Cass. We were in constant communication. It was still wild to me. Here was this person interested in what I had to say. This person who loved the way my lips felt against his. I couldn't stop thinking about him.

I did not, however, particularly need Mr. Hillis knowing the details of my texts with Cass. I turned my phone over.

"You only have a few months until the Common App is due, Miss Greer." Oop. I knew I was in trouble when he pulled out the *Miss*. "I know you take this seriously."

"I do, I really do," I insisted, straightening my face to look like the Serious, Academic-Minded Lady I was. "It's just . . . I don't think I can get away with comparing myself to one of the coolest women in history. Can you imagine if that leaked?"

"You really think someone's going to leak your college essay?"

I sighed. He could be so naive sometimes.

"When Destiny had my niece, Deja, she went through a really bad bout of postpartum depression," I said. Mr. Hillis looked confused as to how this connected to anything. "She went to this therapist. Poured her heart out. Three sessions in, the therapist leaked everything. *The Daily Find* posted the details of my sister's psyche for the whole world to see."

There was abject horror on Mr. Hillis's face. That look came up from time to time, whenever bits of outside Greer life filtered into our sessions. A few years back he'd traveled to Rome with us, since legally Lark and I needed to go to school while we filmed the vacation storyline we were doing there. We were studying in the hotel room, and I got up to close the blinds.

"What's that about?" Mr. Hillis asked. "You hate natural light? Or did you get super into one of those vampire books?"

"People shoot through the blinds with long-lens cameras," I'd replied. "I don't want there to be some story accusing you of grooming us just because you're sitting in a room with two girls. It's easiest if they never even see you."

He looked sick to his stomach that whole day. Since then I hadn't talked to him much about the family biz.

"I can't imagine what that was like for her," he said now. His face had somehow grown even paler than usual. "And from someone she was supposed to be able to trust."

"It was bad," I said. "A college essay leak would be less bad, but you know what they say—stay ready and you don't gotta get ready."

Mr. Hillis took off his glasses and sighed.

"Well. Regardless . . . you don't have to compare yourself to Cleopatra, though there is *something* enticing in the parallels. Two famous young women with the world on their shoulders, being defined by forces bigger than themselves."

I scrunched my nose. "She had to stop empires from invading and stuff. I've got nothing on my shoulders compared to that."

Mr. Hillis's smile was small. "Just don't sell yourself short. You can write, Kiara."

He tapped the sheet of paper sitting between us on the table. It was a printout of the year's Common App essay prompts. I had to write a compelling personal essay based on one of them—and actually send it in—if I didn't want to embarrass myself to the colleges on my list. Currently the most practical choices were NYU, UCLA, and USC, since they were in cities my family frequented and I could attend part-time while I honored my Ignite contract for *Growin' Up*.

"They just want to hear your story," Mr. Hillis said. "It's up to you how you tell it."

There were five essay prompts. Hypothetically this was good.

I had choices. But so much about my life was public knowledge. The admissions officers probably already had opinions about who I was.

I'd never had to tell my own story before. It was too much pressure. What even *was* my story? There was nothing remarkable about me. I was just Kia, the least interesting Greer. Nothing had happened to me yet. The whole point of going to college was to change that.

"I know I have to figure this out," I told Mr. Hillis. "It's just . . ."

"A lot," he completed the sentence. "I know."

Mr. Hillis had spent so many hours with me over the past three and a half years that he could spot when I was getting overwhelmed. Just like I could tell when his baby had kept him up all night and he was moving slower than usual. He leaned back and sighed.

"You can have time, kid. But I want this essay on my desk no later than November first, okay? That way we'll have time to revise it before the deadline."

"Deal," I said, sticking my hand out for him to shake, which he did. "November first."

"All right. And we'll get you in front of Amanda Roth. She should be back in town sometime next month." He must have seen the doubt cross my face. "I really do think it's worthwhile for you to talk to her. You may be surprised what your options are."

"You're the expert," I said. And I meant it. Mr. Hillis was one person I knew would always look out for me. But he looked disappointed by my muted response.

"Have you given any more thought to potentially living at school? You could really immerse yourself somewhere like Vassar, Wesleyan, Spelman . . ."

"Honestly?" I sighed. "Not as something that could actually happen. Did you know that when Emma Watson went to Brown, she got called Hermione in all her classes? I can't avoid *Growin' Up* following me, but do you think I could have a real life in some tiny fishbowl?"

"I don't know," Mr. Hillis said. "I hope you could."

"What if I got stared at every day?"

"I wish I knew how to navigate that," Mr. Hillis said. "I can't imagine what that's like."

The college experience Mr. Hillis talked about sounded beautiful. It also sounded impossible. Still, against my better judgment, a dream was forming. The smallest crack in my resolve.

"It's not gonna happen," I said, "but it would be nice. To get away from all this. I'm kinda terrible at being famous, even though I'm trying to get better."

"Have you at least told your parents you're applying?"

I winced. Mr. Hillis sighed bigger this time.

"I told my dad! He thinks it's great," I said. "I just haven't found my moment with my mom. Yet!" He rubbed his eyes, exasperated. "It's just—to her, college would mean, like, brand partnerships and logistics, and a whole season set on campus. She wants me to be the next big thing on the show, and—I don't even know what college would look like for me, so why bring her into it yet? I just need to wrap my own mind around it a bit more, you know?"

Mr. Hillis looked like he was pondering how many years this job would take off his life.

"Just . . . tell her, okay? Soon. Perhaps this is unprofessional to say, but your mother scares me, and we're not in lying territory yet, but I do not want to know what happens if we get there."

I dropped my head to the table. I couldn't argue with that.

There was a knock at the door, and Max pushed her way in.

"Sorry to interrupt," she said. "Your mama wants you. I've been sent to tell you something moved in the schedule, and that your call with the producers is now in fifteen."

"She's always doing this," I protested. "We haven't even started on calc."

"I can tell her that you'd rather do math," Max offered, and she looked genuinely sympathetic. "But you know if I do, she'll just come in here herself."

Mr. Hillis closed his notebook. "Kia, just read the next two chapters in the textbook and complete the worksheets. We can go over convergence series next session."

"Fiiine," I relented, and Max left to deliver this update to my mother. "I have to go hear about my storyline," I explained to Mr. Hillis.

"How dreadful," he deadpanned.

I watched him for a moment, stalling. A question tugged at the back of my brain.

"Mr. Hillis, do you follow the news around my family?"

"Honestly? I try not to." Mr. Hillis zipped his bag shut. "I have several keyword blockers going at all times. It's just easier to do this without all the noise. No offense."

"Absolutely *none* taken," I said, relaxing back in my seat. Something about Mr. Hillis seeing my face pop up in his news alerts freaked me out.

He swung his bag over one shoulder and made for the door. When he reached it, though, he turned back to me.

"But . . . Cassius Campbell, huh?" he said, a mischievous smile on his face. "My wife's a big fan. Is that whose texts had you all twitterpated?"

I blushed bright and hard.

"No comment," I said with a groan, sinking into my seat.

Mr. Hillis smirked and walked away, and I heard his laugh ringing through the halls and all the way to the driveway.

THE GROUP CHAT

 SISTA SISTA: Szn 3 Theme Song 👀

DEST: [Link: RollingStone.com: With "Maneater," the Levi Ellis Effect Has Soured]

DEST: "With his eighth studio album, Ellis's usual folk-pop melancholy no longer reads endearing. Instead, songs like 'Cheater' feel smarmy. By album's end I was left wondering: Is Ellis actually music's biggest misogynist?"

SOL: May he burn in hell :)

KEE: THANK FUCKING GOD

LALA: Glory be hallelujah

KEE: WAIT I FOUND ANOTHER ONE

KEE: [Link: NYMag.com: Levi Ellis's "Maneater" Fails to Crack the Billboard Hot 100, May Be the Cringiest Album of the Year]

KEE: "Remember when Justin Timberlake made a whole music video about Britney Spears, and it took 20 years for everyone to admit maybe that actually sucked? Well, Levi Ellis just dropped a whole album that reeks of the same entitled bullshit. I don't know what Sola Greer did to this man, but the least he could do was make the songs about it sound good."

DEST: He's not even trending on The Daily Find. But you know what is?

DEST: [Link: TheDailyFind.com: Cassius Campbell Just Commented on One of Kiara Greer's Posts, and We're Screaming]

KEE: Oh jfc.

CHAPTER FOURTEEN

"You know that picture of Nicole Kidman leaving her lawyer's office the day her divorce from Tom Cruise was finalized?" Sola asked this as she shimmied out of a peplumed Christopher John Rogers look. When I shook my head, she pulled up the image and shoved her phone into my hands. "That's the vibe I'm going for: *freedom*. It's the word of the year, boo."

In the photo a younger Nicole Kidman was practically skipping down the sidewalk, arms wide and mouth open in what looked like pure ecstasy. I laughed and handed the phone back.

"You're, like, *so* my hero," I said.

"I don't know why they haven't made a Sola Greer superhero yet," said Noémie Cadieux, my new stylist, the words curling around her heavy French accent. "They should put you in one of those Marvel movies, but as yourself. Then I would go see them."

"I don't think that's how Marvel works, Nono," Sola said, giggling.

Noémie shrugged. I'd only met her twice before, but I'd heard plenty from Sola and Dest, who'd befriended her when she was modeling in Paris—and more recently from Lark, who'd started working with her a few months back. She was the kind of person who looked put together even in the baggiest sweats.

There was something *sharp* about Noémie: a precision-cut blunt bob that fell just below her ears, cheekbones that could cut glass. But she was ethereal, too. She didn't even have eyebrows. I'd never seen anyone look so cool without eyebrows. I wondered if still having hair on my face made me look like a hopeless dweeb.

The Greers had given Noémie her big break when she'd career-jumped to styling the year before last. Now she'd be appearing on the show, which was practically guaranteed to land her millions of followers and millions of dollars in brand deals and celebrity clients.

Growin' Up Greer was back. My first day as a lead was taking place at Noémie's modern cottage in the West Hollywood hills. It was all white walls, tall wood-beamed ceilings, and plush geometric furniture. An entire wall of sliding doors opened up to a patio and views of the city, and I kept glancing down, searching for the jutting spire of Mel's Drive-In.

Sola and I had been paired for filming for the day. Our assignment: for each of us to come of age on camera, albeit in different ways. Sola's storyline was about reestablishing her style postdivorce, so it overlapped perfectly with my need to find a style in the first place. If it got the style critics off my back, then all the better.

"I've been playing sad ex-wife too long," Sola said, grabbing the next 'fit, which on the hanger looked like a confusing tangle of conflicting materials. "It worked while everyone thought I was the devil. But we're changing the narrative."

"Hell yeah, we are," I said. Levi had gotten some low blows in, but Sola's goal was made easier now that the worst of the divorce press seemed to have passed. The album was getting resoundingly bad reviews. We were almost out of the woods.

Sola shimmied into the dress and gave us a twirl. Black pearls dripped across the low neckline, dancing across the bodice with teasing glimpses of the bare skin underneath. The rest looked to be leather and silk, so thin and delicate that it skimmed her body like a whisper.

"You look like a Vegas showgirl about to murder her ex," I said in awe. "I mean that in the best way possible."

"Our inspiration is Cher in Bob Mackie," Noémie said, stepping back to admire her work.

Sola stripped and grabbed the next look, not bothering to use the velvet room divider that had been set up for a changing area.

"I just realized why this family's always talking about each other's boobs," I said, laughing. "It's 'cause you're always showing us yours."

"This body's a Bentley, baby," she quipped. "It was made to be *seen*."

For the next hour the crew and I were regaled with every look that would define the new Sola. It was my job to provide reactions that would help pad the eventual montage. But today none of it felt fake. I'd missed seeing her like this. As she was meant to be: confident, unbeatable. The big sister who'd thrown me into the deep end of the pool because she knew I would never try to swim on my own—the only way forward was to have someone push me.

Sola had never needed pushing in her life. She made her own fate, every time.

My turn to jump in was a bit trickier than hers.

"So, Kia, who do you want to be?" Noémie asked when Sola's session was over. I laughed in her face. It was an intimidating question on any day, let alone with three cameras aimed to capture every angle of our conversation.

They'd primed me on where the scene needed to go. I was

supposed to be who I always was, but more so: more funny, more interesting, more charming, more glamorous. No pressure. I'd also try not to open my mouth too wide, lest there be TikToks about my wayward incisor.

"That's a big question," I answered honestly. "I don't know, I—"

"Hold for plane," barked Rob, one of our audio guys. We all paused and listened to the 747 beelining toward LAX. I took the opportunity to shake out my shoulders.

Growin' Up wasn't as heavily scripted as some other reality shows. The producers knew what was going on in our lives and what general arcs we could expect for a season, and they put us in scenarios that helped bring those to life. The "scripting" came from some scenes being outlined ahead of time, so we knew the rough shape certain conversations needed to take if they were going to cut together neatly.

On *Growin' Up* Sola delivered big emotion, big dreams, big drama. Mom was epic, sultry, Machiavellian. Destiny was boisterous, loud, and not afraid of a fight. Until a few years ago, Lark had been like me, mostly in the background, there to deliver reactions to the spectacle of everyone else. We'd been "friends of the show," which, in the world of reality TV, meant we didn't get paid.

Once Lark got cast on *Nick of Time,* though, she'd become our show's sweetheart. Audiences could tell she was on her way to becoming a superstar in her own right. They ate it up, and to keep things equal, our mom negotiated six-year deals for both of us. Now I had to sing for my supper.

What the producers didn't know was I'd spent every night this week awake till the wee hours, staring at the blank page that should've been my college essay. Noémie's question was just another reminder: I had no idea how to tell anyone who Kia Greer was.

"Still holding," Rob intoned. Then: "'Kay, we're good."

"This year is about growth, for all of us," Sola announced, taking my hands. I had the sense she was trying to soothe my nerves as the focus shifted to me. I was grateful for it.

"Oui. Well, my method works in two parts," Noémie said. "First: Personal style should revolve around the three E's. Guess them." She held up three fingers.

My eyes widened. "Uhhh. Excellence? Elevation? Em . . . bellishment? Please tell me I'm close—suddenly my whole vocabulary's been erased."

"Excellent guesses," Noémie assured me. She signaled to her assistant, an eager redhead (was *eager* one of the E words?), who wheeled a long rack of clothes into the center of the room.

"Pretty," I breathed, hands hovering over sequins, leathers, pearls, linens, and tulles.

"The E's are *exploration, expression, and elation,"* Noémie said. "You should feel free to explore, to adventure through different styles until you find what fits. Like one must with lovers. Don't succumb to pressure to stop at just one."

"Amen to that," Sola chirped. Her eyes darted toward me, and there was something behind them in that moment, something I couldn't name. But then she looked away.

"Expression is the goal," Noémie continued. She circled me, gently prodding my shoulders and waist, tugging at the simple black tank and midi skirt I'd chosen at random from my closet. "This is where I steal a bit from Marie Kondo's joy method: At a certain point, everything in your closet should bring an elation to your life."

"That's a lot of pressure on a T-shirt," I said. "Especially when you're not a size zero."

"Think about the smaller things you want. To be comfortable? Noticed? To have it skim from your chest to your waistline just so, creating a silhouette that will leave you comfortable and elated throughout the day? Feeling at home in our clothes helps us feel at home in our bodies, which in turn helps us feel at one with ourselves." Noémie picked through the clothes on the rack, examining each one with me in mind. "The next part of the method is about getting to know you."

"Kia's a history nerd, like our dad," Sola offered, beaming. "Maybe there's something there." I turned to her, confused. "What? You love that stuff, you dork."

"But how's that relevant? She gonna dress me for a Ren Faire?"

"That's not off the table," Sola said, one brow raised.

"Don't you dare," I said. Then: "Maybe next season."

Noémie stepped away from the rack and crossed her arms. "Whose style do you respond to, in a way that makes you want to have it for yourself?"

I gulped, glancing between Sola and Noémie. They each looked so encouraging.

"I can say anybody?"

"Anybody."

"My first thought's so embarrassing, though."

"*Embarrassment* is not one of the E's."

"Say it," Sola prodded. "I dare you."

"Nick Miller was the first to come to mind," I said, bringing a hand to my forehead to cover my shame. Noémie cocked her head to the right.

"He's from *New Girl,* this old show she likes." Sola chuckled.

She pulled up a photo on her phone and showed Noémie. I didn't even have to look at it to know he was wearing a plaid shirt and a scowl.

"We can work with that," Noémie said, inspecting the photo with judicious eyes. She looked back up at me expectantly. "Who else?"

I went blank, buffering again.

Sola jumped in with the save. "It's all about key words and vibes. Lark's a mix of pretty-pretty princess and hot-ass early-eighties pop star. One of my inspo points was Rihanna. Dest likes things that are textured, structural, with something exaggerated or odd about them. I like sexy, tailored—sometimes classic, sometimes looking like I'm the queen in *Star Wars*."

The encouragement to choose less-than-traditional inspo egged me on. I told Noémie about my deep love of *Buffy the Vampire Slayer* and, more specifically, the nerdy, chaotic bisexual witch character, Willow.

"She's this cool mix of slouchy, casual schoolgirl and, like, power witch?" I said, feeling out if I was going in the right direction. I threw in Janelle Monáe, Zoë Kravitz, and *Roman Holiday*, and as I talked, she pulled piece after piece from the rack, piling them into her assistant's arms. The assistant arranged her selections beside the velvet room divider Sola had blatantly ignored during her session. Finally, Noémie turned to me, a satisfied look on her face.

"My pitch to you is that in your day-to-day wardrobe we follow your desire for comfort, building out loose but playful silhouettes and making use of pattern and color to add some life to your days," she said, rearranging some of her choices, pairing different pieces. I got the sense I was watching an artist at work. She gestured to the left part of the rack, which seemed to be the more casual side. I was surprised she had flannels on hand. There were also various plaids, both on tops and pants, as well as several graphic tees and a variety of sweaters taking all kinds of shapes.

"For your public appearances and whatever photo shoots I style you for, I propose we follow your inclination toward whimsy and combine that with classic styles and silhouettes inspired by *Roman Holiday*. We'll make sure nothing we put you in makes you feel claustrophobic. I'd also love to throw in a bit of a schoolgirl vibe, because we can use the colors and iconography of letterman jackets—as well as, for example, pleats in your skirts, and blazers—to bring in the inspiration of Janelle Monáe's signature suits, but younger and more *you*. And if you are into it—but only then—I would love to explore a loose floral theme. It will counter the edge of some of the looks, while also paying homage to the era of growth and exploration you are in on this cusp of adulthood."

I tried on ball gowns both classic (fifties Dior) and utterly bonkers (made out of cotton balls to resemble a cloud); a pair of tan cargo pants with sharp black zigzags cut all the way down the sides that I was kind of obsessed with; a pair of overalls with Winnie the Pooh embroidered on the bib; a striped brown sweater that was the coziest thing to ever grace my body; a minidress covered entirely with fake monarch butterflies. Sola looked so proud as I changed into look after look, twirling for the cameras.

"My little girl is growing up," Sola gushed, fanning herself around the eyes.

"Sola, are you crying?" I asked, surprised.

"Don't mind me! It's a weird year."

Sola drove me home that night. She was quiet on the drive, and I figured after a long day of being "on," she just needed to decompress like I did. But when we pulled into the driveway, I said goodbye and got out—and Sola held her arm out so the car door wouldn't shut behind me.

"Hey," she said, tentative, but also a little startled, as if she'd surprised herself by speaking. I turned back to her. "Mom told me something . . . about, uh, how you and Cass got started? And I just—"

My eyebrows shot up. That was the last thing I expected to come out of her mouth. There was so much I wanted to say, but Sola was pulling at me—clearly still sorting out what she wanted to say. I didn't want to interrupt her processing.

"Please, if this is all for me," she finally said, "or for *Mom*—Kia, please don't do all this for us. It's not worth it."

"I thought you knew."

She shook her head the tiniest amount. She looked *worried*.

"I didn't. But, Kee—"

"It's real now!" I interjected. I couldn't stand that look on her face, not when everything was going so well. "Me and Cass. It's been real since the beginning, really—it just took me a second to see it. So it's not just for you or Mom or anything; kicking Levi's butt into irrelevance is just an added bonus. I really like him— *Cass*, not Levi. Duh."

She sat back, visibly relieved. I was about to say good night again and go when I saw she was picking at her cuticles. Ruining a manicure was a telltale sign of anxiety in Solaland.

"Are you not convinced?" I asked. "Because I can show you

my text chain with Cass—it is *extensive*." I was pulling out my phone when she held up a hand to stop me.

"I believe you," she said with a huff of a laugh. But she still didn't look satisfied.

"Then *what's up*?"

"It's nothing. It's your life, just . . ."

"Spit it out," I dared her.

She cut her eyes up to mine. "Just don't let them take any more from you than you're willing to give."

Now it was my turn to fall silent. I didn't quite understand what she was saying, but her eyes were wide with worry, her mouth set and determined. So I gave her what she seemed to need most from me in that moment.

"I won't. Of course. I promise."

CHAPTER FIFTEEN

It was our first red carpet as a couple, photographers yelling from the photo line and publicists hurrying us along. But Cass was looking at me like I was the only person there.

"LOOK OVER HERE!"

"TO THE FRONT!"

"GIVE US A KISS!"

We were at the Stork Gala, an annual charity event to raise money for children living in poverty. This thing was always star-studded, an opportunity for the rich and famous to give back and remind themselves—and the public—that they cared. This year it would also be the night Cass would meet my parents.

He planted a kiss on my cheek, sending the hired photographers roaring.

"KIA, YOU LOOK GREAT!"

"KIA, TELL US ABOUT YOUR LOOK!"

For once I was happy to gush about it. Noémie and I had chosen a crisp white shirtdress that fell in an A line to my ankles, pairing it with a thin black tie and a long black leather corset that cinched my waist into an hourglass and looked like a work of art. My hair was in jumbo box braids with white bows scattered throughout, and the vibe was *Roman Holiday* by way of Solange. Mom's only request was that Noémie lace the corset as tight as it would go. "You have the rest of your life to breathe!" she'd said. "The pictures will look gorgeous."

I giggled along, but a knot of doubt twisted in my chest. I hadn't stopped thinking about what Sola'd said: *Don't let them take any more from you than you're willing to give.* I didn't know where that line was, especially now. Cass and I were so close to succeeding at the goal that had brought us together in the first place. It was unclear to me if we were on this red carpet to levy one more strike against Levi . . . or simply because we were a public couple, and this was what public couples were expected to do.

We stepped off the carpet and Greta materialized in front of me, handing back my clutch. She gave me a tight nod of approval.

"Wanna go in?" I asked Cass, gesturing awkwardly to the doors of the ballroom.

"Woof, yeah," he said, shaking out his shoulders. "I get so nervous on red carpets."

"You do?!" My voice rose an octave in disbelief. Cass cocked an eyebrow.

"Yes, Kia. I'm not just swag twenty-four seven. I'm a *person*."

He said it teasing, hand to his chest. But then he snaked his hand around my waist and pulled me close again. My heart pounded at the proximity as he leaned to whisper in my ear.

"What're our chances of finding a good make-out spot in this place?"

"Um, zero?" I said with a laugh. "My parents are here."

I glanced back to the carpet, where my mother and father were still posing. My family were such big donors that my mom was the night's guest of honor, and Dad had flown in for the occasion. I looked back at Cass. He looked so genuinely deflated, it made me laugh again.

"If you can find somewhere private, I'm down," I said. "I just don't want anyone to see."

A shock of mischievous energy shot across his eyes.

"Bet," he said, walking backward away from me and looking sneakily around the lobby. "Don't let them trap you at a table yet!"

A few minutes later I pretended to go to the bathroom and joined Cass in a stairwell tucked into the back of the building. Cass's lips were warm, his hands roaming my body with purpose. Red carpets weren't so bad, really, not when Cass was a walking thirst trap who moaned when I pulled his bottom lip between my teeth.

I only lasted a few minutes before I pulled away. I couldn't tell if the culprit was my corset or the kissing, but I was winded.

"My mom's gonna kill me if you mess up my new look," I laughed, my lips numb.

"You're the one biting and shit," he breathed into my ear.

I rolled my eyes, but Cass stepped back and, smiling, took my hand and raised it above our heads, making me twirl.

"You do look beautiful," Cass said, his eyes flicking up and down my body in a way that made my skin prickle. "You always do, but this 'fit looks like *you*."

"Me but fancy," I corrected.

"You but fancy," he obliged. I didn't tell him why my breath was shallow. I just pulled him in for one last kiss.

I made a pit stop in the bathroom to reapply the lipstick Cass had done such a meticulous job smearing off my face. I was still replaying our kisses in my head when I exited, which is why I didn't notice the couple talking just outside the door. I crashed right into them, dropping the contents of my clutch all over the floor and stumbling back in abject mortification before crouching to retrieve the makeup I'd scattered everywhere.

"Shoot—I'm so sorry—*oh*—"

The man in the couple was crouched in front of me, holding my lip liner. It was Levi. Ex-brother-in-law and recent mortal enemy, wearing the same boyish smile I'd seen on him a million times before. My heart fell into my stomach.

He pulled me up and into a hug. I was too shocked to stop him.

"Kee! It's so good to see you! How you been?!"

Everything moved in slow motion. I removed myself from his grasp, my jaw slack.

It was only then that I saw who he was with.

Reina.

Reina Hila, series regular on *Nick of Time*, the wannabe songstress with the brittle voice but seventy million followers on TikTok. Reina was one of Lark's best friends.

Reina was eighteen. If we were in regular school, she would be in my year. But from the way she was looking at Levi, there was no doubt they were here as a couple.

I also couldn't help but notice her chest. It had tripled in size since I'd last seen her.

"Excuse me," Reina said, not meeting my eyes, her lips pursed. "I was going in there."

She nodded to the bathroom, and I moved to the side. I stared after her as she left.

"You're dating Reina?" I asked Levi when she was gone.

"She's gorgeous, right?" he said, squaring his shoulders in

pride. My horror must have been clear; Levi's demeanor changed fast. He buttoned his suit jacket and leveled a sour look my way. "Don't be like that. We're still family, right?"

I felt sick to my stomach. We *had* been family. Now I didn't even recognize him.

I couldn't help thinking back to when Sola and Levi had first gotten together; it hadn't been long afterward that Sola'd gotten her breasts done. Did that mean something?

"I don't think so, actually," I said quietly. I focused on rebuckling my clutch so I wouldn't have to look at him.

"I really thought better of you," Levi said, his hands in the mop of loose curls he kept meticulously coiffed. "We had a good thing going, you and I. A bond."

I flashed back to Sola in that club bathroom, wiping tears because of the lies Levi'd gleefully spread through the press. My top lip curled into a sneer.

"I really thought better of you, too. A lot's changed, hasn't it?"

Levi scoffed. "I'll say. Out of all y'all, I thought you'd be the one to think for yourself. But Cassius Campbell? Come on, Kee, that's got Melora written all over it."

"You don't know what you're talking about," I said. "Goodbye, Levi." I walked away, pressing my clutch to my roiling stomach and resisting the impulse to look back.

"Nice filler, by the way," he called after me. "I know Dr. Bogosian's work when I see it. You're gonna be plastic in no time."

⌒

"You knew?!"

Lark sucked in a tired breath and looked away. "You seen her at the house recently? I knew as soon as it happened. I was hoping it wouldn't last. It sucks, okay?"

After the Levi incident I'd walked, stunned, into the gala's main ballroom and pulled Lark to our assigned table. Our parents were still doing their regular rounds of schmoozing. Cass was, too; I saw him across the room with Simms, talking to what looked like a group of businessmen.

Lark kept her expression willfully unreadable, her eyes tracking the hired Getty photographers who were circling the event. She'd clearly been taking notes from Sola's handbook of public strength. But I knew her well enough to see the pain and anger in her eyes.

"Lala, I'm so sorry," I said. "This is so messed up."

"I told her he's a creep, but she thinks she's in love with him. She even turned down a really cool movie so she could follow him on tour." Lark shook her head. "Whatever. If she's gonna ignore what she actually wants for some dude, that's her choice. Idiot."

Lark covered her disgust to upnod an actor acquaintance passing by the table.

"It's so gross," I said when the actor was safely out of hearing distance. "Reina's, like, *our* age. Was Levi always like this? How did we miss it?"

Lark pursed her lips and blinked. "Look, can we talk about this later?" she asked, and her voice cracked the tiniest bit. "I really don't wanna cry here."

I chewed my lips, makeup be damned. I knew exactly what would happen: We'd talk later, and we'd both rant and scream, and the next day Lark would shut it all away and pretend it hadn't happened. She'd done this since she was a little girl. It was like if she didn't have to look at the bad feeling, she didn't have to deal with it. I nodded anyway. I didn't want to make her feel worse than she already did.

"Of course," I said. "Later."

"Later for what?" said a cheerful voice. We looked up as Mom sat down across from us, adjusting the train of her silky white column gown under her feet. She looked at us expectantly.

Lark and I exchanged a glance. Her eyes were pleading.

"It's not important tonight," I told Mom with a fake smile. There was a good chance she'd find out with her own eyes, if Reina and Levi brought their PDA into the ballroom. But we didn't need to be the ones to tell her, at least not yet. So I followed Lark's lead and buried it. "When's your speech?"

$$\backsim$$

Mom's speech brought the house down. She'd grown up the kind of kid the Stork Foundation had been founded to aid, and she had the audience hanging on her every word as she recalled being the seventh grader who'd always fallen asleep in school because there hadn't been enough food at home.

"No child should go without the things they need," she said. "Every person in this world deserves the chance to survive and succeed on their own terms, and I am so proud of the Stork Foundation for helping make that a reality, one kid at a time."

Lark, Dad, Cass, and I stood to applaud, and the rest of the audience joined our standing ovation. She held up her award and everyone cheered louder. When she got back to our table, she melted into her seat, chest rising and falling rapidly. She rubbed her temples, overwhelmed.

"Aw, Mom, I've never seen you nervous!" Lark said, looking a little moved.

"You killed it!" I exclaimed. Dad sloped an arm around her shoulders, and she relaxed into him. I smiled, watching them. Affection between my parents wasn't unheard of; they were just so rarely in the same place that I didn't get to see it often.

"That was incredible, Mrs. Greer," Cass said from the seat next to me. "I never knew that part of your story. You've lived quite an impressive life."

"Yes, well, I don't love to relive it," Mom said, fanning herself with her program. "For a good cause, though? Anything."

I scanned my mother's face. I'd expected her to spend the night falling all over Cass, given how instrumental he'd been in distracting from the Levi scandal. Her reaction to his praise was polite but muted—almost curt, if you really knew her.

My dad separated himself from my mom and leaned both arms on the table. "Well, now that we're all here together . . ."

"We don't have to do this," I said. My dad was the quiet one of my two parents—he was where I got it from. He didn't like being out on the town, preferring to spend his nights immersed in a good book or an incredibly boring documentary. But Dad also had what Cass did: that inner electricity that crackled wherever he went. He'd always channeled this intensity into his work, but when the full force of his charm was focused on you? You had no choice but to play along. And right now, apparently, Raymond Greer wanted to play.

"I'm talking to Cassius, not you, darling," he chided.

"Yes, sir, hello," Cass said, straightening in his chair.

"My Kia doesn't bring a lot of guys around—"

"Dad, leave them alone!" Lark said with a roll of the eyes.

"She's told me about you on our FaceTimes, and you seem

like a good guy," he said. "But what exactly are your *intentions* with our sweet, precious Kia? Please tell me you're not another musician fuckboy—we have had enough of those in this family."

"He's not!" Lark protested.

Our mom shushed her. "I'd like to hear this."

Cass took my hand.

"Definitely not a fuckboy," he assured them, voice wavering slightly with nerves. "We like each other. And we're young. This would be both of our senior year of high school under more normal circumstances."

"What does that have to do with anything?" my mom asked, shifting in her seat.

Cass cleared his throat. "I just mean that . . . Kia never got to have a high school sweetheart. I'd love to be that for her. My intention is to treat your daughter with kindness and respect. I'm all in, personally."

I squeezed his hand, unable to control the corny grin on my face.

Lark giggled and kicked her feet like a schoolgirl. I was glad that, at the very least, this could distract her from the atrocity that was Levi and Reina. My dad was beaming, but my mom's expression was unreadable.

"Nice to meet you, Cassius," Dad said. He extended a hand across the table, and Cass shook it. "You better keep that attitude, 'cause our girl's going places. Just know that if you beef it, she'll be on some college campus this time next year, breaking hearts and taking names, and she'll barely remember who that Cass guy even was."

Lark's mouth hung open, and Cass let out a bemused, uncomfortable laugh. I was so busy wondering why my dad was cursing my relationship that it took a moment for the rest of what he'd said to sink in. Then Lark caught my gaze, her eyes wide, and it hit me.

He just told my mom about college. That's not in the plan.

I shot a panicked glance to my mother, but she was just sitting back in her chair, sipping her champagne, her lips curled ever so slightly at their edges, an inscrutable expression on her face. The knot in my chest danced the tango.

CHAPTER SIXTEEN

She didn't bring up the college thing, not the next day or the day after that. I wondered if I should mention it first, but I was too busy. Or too chicken, if you asked Lark. But then all of a sudden Mom was gone anyway—off to a round of meetings in Berlin, plotting to bring her line of home goods to one of the chains there. Filming continued and I spiraled between takes, imagining every version of what she might say.

I hoped her not bringing it up meant she just didn't care. I dared to hope maybe she'd even encourage it.

Then I got an email.

SOMETHING TO THINK ABOUT
FROM: Mom <melora.greer@greer.com>
TO: Kia <keekee@greer.com>

10/14/24 1:32 a.m.

Hi baby,

Do you know the story of Jodie Foster and John Hinckley Jr.? I've been thinking about it a lot these past few days. It's such a fascinating piece of history.

John Hinckley Jr. was obsessed with the movie *Taxi Driver*. Have you ever seen that one by Marty? Hinckley watched it over a dozen times, and he developed a fixation on a barely teenage Jodie Foster. He became her stalker.

Fast-forward a few years, to when Jodie started college at Yale. Hinckley followed her there. This man quite literally enrolled in a Yale writing course just so he'd be closer to her. He hoped one day she'd fall in love with him. He called her on the phone constantly and delivered notes to her dorm room, all these delusional love letters and poems. Hinckley eventually became so desperate to impress her, he shot President Reagan to get her attention. That's a true story; you can look it up.

I know that's a lot to process, but I worry about you girls, out there in the big bad world. That man who snuck into our house won't be locked up forever, and there are so many others like him. You should see the letters we get. I keep them from you kids so you'll still be able to sleep at night.

I want you to think long and hard about this college thing. Your life is simply not like other girls' your age, and that means sometimes hard choices must be made. I never, ever want you to be in danger.

Anyway! How's shooting been going? Production says you've been doing great. I miss you babies, but I'll be home soon to hug you.

Love you,
Mom

I must've reread it fifty times. I'd thought her issue would be about scheduling—how classes would cut into my contractual obligations.

This was so much worse. This was a response I couldn't argue with.

How stupid had I been, dreaming of gallivanting around some campus doing whatever I wanted? To even entertain the idea of living at school?

I'd known it all along, but it was different seeing it laid out like this: This was my life. And the man who'd slept in our beds hadn't been our only stalker over the years—far from it. That was why every Greer residence had twenty-four seven security camped out at the gate. Dating Cass only made it worse, because on top of the usual roster of Greer stalkers, I was also now getting death threats from Cassius Campbell stans who wanted him for themselves.

She was right; school would be dangerous. Anything outside the usual Greer playbook would be. Maybe I wasn't always comfortable operating under the Greer rules, but they'd been built to keep us safe.

Mom had technically left the choice up to me. But her message was loud and clear: Stay within bounds. Keep your head down, do your work. Bloom where you were planted.

Above all: Respect the gates, because what lies beyond them could hurt.

How Kia Greer Became the It Girl of the Year

Bustle November 2024 cover story

By Erin Penn King

Kiara "Kia" Greer is either very bored or very tired. It's an autumn afternoon in Manhattan, and Greer can't stop yawning. We're taking a walk in Central Park before she's scheduled for her *Bustle* cover shoot, and Greer arrives looking like a modern-day Cher Horowitz—or Dionne Davenport—in a Thom Browne skirt suit and towering Nodaletos. Her septum is recently pierced, and her features have matured since her early days as the wallflower kid sister in her family's hit reality show, *Growin' Up Greer.*

It's safe to say Greer is in the middle of the sort of glow-up every teen girl dreams of. "My head is spinning," Greer says. "This is my third outfit change of the day."

Greer was born to be an It Girl. It's in her blood—what with her Oscar-winner dad, reality-star-mogul mom, and three multitalented sisters, all of whom have captured the hearts and minds of the world in different ways. Now Greer, who'll turn 18 this May, has taken the world by storm. And no, it's not just because she happens to be dating pop darling Cassius Campbell.

There's an alchemy to the creation of a new It Girl, and it goes far beyond the workings of any algorithm. Greer is the first to admit she's had some help. In fact, her upbringing has allowed for little alone time. On the day we meet, there are three intimidating cameras pointed at both of us, filming for *Growin' Up*'s forthcoming 12th season. Greer is also flanked by Greta Shaw, chief marketing officer of the Greer Group, and Maxine McDonald, longtime friend of the family.

"I've always been more comfortable as a supporting player," Greer says. "It's been an adjustment, being the center of attention. I don't know if I like it."

She laughs nervously at this last part. Shaw, who walks a few yards behind us, clears her throat loudly. "I'm very lucky," Greer rushes to add. "I have to make the best of the very privileged life I was born into. So I try to focus on how I can represent Black girls all over the world on our show. I just hope that my being out there and recognizable helps a few more people feel seen."

Greer seems to be seeing herself more clearly these days as well. She's had a style evolution of late, thanks in part to a recent collaboration with stylist Noémie Cadieux.

"Noémie's a genius," Greer says. "Now instead of just throwing something on, I'm actually thinking of what I wear as a form of expression. Kind of an extension of myself, I guess? I'm going through a lot of changes in my life this year, and I'm realizing how fun clothes can be, as a reflection of that."

The shifts in Greer's style have amassed her 60 million followers on TikTok, where she regularly shows off her outfits. Fans have meticulously chronicled her every date with Campbell, dubbing her new look "funky schoolgirlcore."

"I'm just trying to feel better in my own body," Greer

says. "My life may not be normal, but I'd guess that's something every 17-year-old girl experiences."

Among the many changes in Greer's life has been sister Sola Greer's messy divorce from Levi Ellis. Greer grows visibly uncomfortable when I bring up the split, and again when I ask if she has thoughts on Ellis's new album, *Maneater,* which so far has failed to break onto the Billboard 100.

"It's not my place to speak on someone else's relationship," Greer says, fidgeting with the stacks of bracelets on her wrists. "I'll just say . . . this year has been a reminder of how powerful family can be. It's our job to protect each other through anything. I'm very grateful for my sisters."

I ask next about Ellis's rumored relationship with actor and singer Reina Hila, close friend of Greer's 16-year-old sister, Lark. Ellis, 35, is 17 years older than Hila, 18. "I don't think I should comment on that," Greer says, avoiding eye contact. When asked if she misses her longtime brother-in-law, Greer purses her plump lips and says something I think about for the rest of the day: "I used to."

I change the subject to her own romance with Campbell, which started in early September, when sparks flew at Lark Greer's birthday party.

"This may be hypocritical, because we've been so public," Greer says, playing with her new septum ring, "but I'd love to keep as much of our relationship to ourselves as possible. It means something to me, and I don't want anything to jeopardize it."

She's gotta give us something, I tell her. The whole world is salivating for more news about this coupling— there was literally an *SNL* sketch about them.

"I'll say this," she says, a shy smile on her baby-fat cheeks, "I'm really happy he likes me back."

CHAPTER SEVENTEEN

There were so many bright spots that fall. I was getting the hang of filming. People were calling me an "It Girl." It felt nice to be seen as someone worth admiring. And hey, if this was my lot in life, I might as well make the best of it. I was grateful. Grateful, grateful, grateful, every day.

After the charity gala, my mom called around to *People, Page Six,* and *TMZ* to inform them that Levi was dating Reina. A "source close to the Greer family" confirmed that Sola was disgusted with Levi dating someone her sisters' age. "She doesn't know who she married," the story said. It was a field day on social media—memes upon memes. My favorite one had Levi's head photoshopped on Steve Buscemi's body from his episode of *30 Rock.* The caption read, "How do you do, fellow kids?"

Cass and I had served as handy distractions from the divorce album, and the Melorager had helped the cause along. In the end, though, Levi sank his own battleship.

Technically everything was just fine. Filming the show was, it turned out, much more time-consuming when you had actual storylines to carry. This time I ended up canceling on that Vassar lady Amanda Roth. I told Mr. Hillis there simply weren't enough hours in the day to sneak off to meet her. He wasn't surprised, then, when I told him I wouldn't have my college essay done by the agreed date—but he looked disappointed enough that it gnawed at me for the rest of the week. I didn't want to tell him it was a lost cause anyway.

College and I weren't the only star-crossed pair that autumn. Cass and I were, too. He was working on his second album and planning his first world tour as a headliner. Meanwhile, Mom was determined to leverage my "moment" into the future she imagined for me—the kind I now knew was inevitable.

As a minor, I was only allowed to film *Growin' Up* forty-eight hours a week—but there were no laws against putting me on a plane to do interviews, red carpets, editorial spreads, and appearances. I'd done all these things before, but now the invites came in so fast and furious, they made my head spin. There were no more water tanks, but I did so many profiles and shoots that more than once I caught myself posing for photos in my sleep.

Most days I barely remembered if I'd brushed my teeth. So I was grateful. I *was*. But all I really wanted to do was sleep.

I waded through the autumn with a cloud in my head. No amount of caffeine or workout-induced endorphins helped. The cloud took up residence a few inches above the knot in my chest, and I wondered constantly what was wrong with me. Hadn't Cass made me happier than ever? Why was I having so much trouble waking up to live my wonderful life?

I was no stranger to the cloud. It was this *thing* I'd had before, maybe always. It was this tiredness I couldn't shake, this nagging certainty that I couldn't do anything right. A defect in my programming.

Whenever it had taken over in the past, I'd escaped into some fantasyland: a TV show, a book, a game with Lark. I'd picture myself in a dorm room or a lecture hall, surrounded by friends. But in recent weeks the cloud was heavier than ever and unnervingly unshakable. The cloud made me question the very point of me.

Then, suddenly, there was something new in my life. There was Jade.

Jade here, she wrote one afternoon in late October, shocking me from my stupor.

Oh! Hi, Jade. What's up?

I wrote back from my perch on the edge of a tub in a hotel bathroom. I was hyping myself up to film an episode of "Beauty Secrets" for *Vogue.* I'd been freaking out because, well, I had no beauty secrets except my family's liberal use of filler and facials. Jade replied right away.

Cass didn't tell you? God damnit.

I got a sheepish voice note from Cass, and by the time it came, I'd moved on to freaking out over a lunch interview with some journalist. It was next on my schedule, and I didn't know what to say if they asked me about Cass. Now that Levi was out of the picture, it was hard to calibrate when we could stop living for the public.

I pressed play on the voice note as I speed-changed into a green plaid skirt. Noémie had suggested I pair the piece with my natural hair and big round glasses. She'd even found me this fake septum ring encrusted with blue gems that I loved. I'd never felt so cool in my life. I didn't even feel like I was cosplaying someone else. The look felt like me, even if she was a new me I was still getting used to.

"Hey, uh," Cass started. "Hope it's okay, I might've mentioned to Jade that you're feeling a bit stuck with your college essays—*Yes, I'm telling her! No, I will not drive you! Yo, if you don't leave this room right now! Byeee*—uh, so, she might have offered to help out. I promise I'm not out here spillin' everything you tell me. Jade's just, like, weirdly good at this stuff. And I know you don't even think you can do college anymore, but I really don't want you to give up on it! So I sicced my sister on you. Ditch her if she gets too annoying—*I said what I said! Go away!*—but yeah. I really don't think you should give up. Anywaaaay. I hope New York is good. I'm thinking about you every second. Lov— See you soon."

I didn't know hearts actually skipped beats, but mine sure did at the end of that message. Had Cass been about to say *Love you*?

There wasn't time to obsess about this last part, because Max was already ushering me to the car. That week I was in New York on Monday, back to film in LA on Tuesday, and then back again in New York, where we'd film Sola house-hunting for a place there.

I didn't have the heart to tell Cass that college was a lost cause, so I started texting Jade. I wanted her to be my friend. I hadn't had a lot of those, not since Mom took Lark and me out of school. Cass had become one of my best friends, sure, but I didn't want to be one of those girls who exclusively talked to her boyfriend. It was lonely, pulling seven-day workweeks, especially now that Lark and I were officially doing our own things.

So I let Jade help me, even though I knew it wasn't going anywhere. I sent her the very first Common App essay I'd written. The one about home and Grandma Millie; the one that was way too long, because I'd spent page after page wishing I had the kind of clarity about life that she did. For someone who'd all but written off college, I sure was anxious to hear what Jade thought of my writing.

It was midterms, so Jade took a few days to read it. Then one day my phone rang in the middle of filming a scene, and I walked out to answer it.

"IS CASS DEAD?" I whisper-screamed into the phone, very aware of how many producers were staring at me. "WHAT'S HAPPENING?"

"Is it weird to say I think your grandma and I woulda been best friends?" Jade said casually. " 'Cause I feel confident she would have *loved* me."

I exhaled, relieved this wasn't an emergency. "She would've," I admitted. "She loved women with strong opinions. Listen, Jade, I'm kinda filming right now—I can't—"

"*Pfft*, fiiine," she said. I could picture her rolling her eyes, wherever she was. "Just thought you'd wanna know you got a winner."

"Really?" I asked, turning down another hallway for more privacy. "Isn't it way too long? And, like, navel-gazey?"

"Trim the stuff about your new house; focus on your grandma and what she taught you. It's actually a great way to show admissions people you're not just some reality TV robot."

"Thanks?"

"You know what I mean."

"I do," I sighed. They'd sent one of the production assistants after me. A nervous twenty-year-old, walkie-talkie in hand, waiting at the end of the hall and poised to pounce.

"I gotta go," I said. "But thank you—for real."

"Anytime," Jade said. "Don't tell Cass I had fun."

After that, Jade started texting me about other things, too. My mission was accomplished. And it wasn't like the cloud lifted— but Jade did help bring more bright spots to my days.

Drama club had a meltdown today trying to pick out the spring play, and now there's literal crying and blood feuds going on??? Pray for me. This is Lord of the Flies.

Then she did it again.

Question, Jade texted once in what must have been the middle of her school day. I need valuable intel only you can provide. CAN Lea Michele read, y or n?

Incredible question, I responded as I pretended to listen to my mom recap her lunch with a trio of Real Housewives. I am blessed enough to say I've never met her.

Dang. Woulda been so much more exciting if you said she'd shit in your wig. How dare you not have trauma I can exploit for my own entertainment? You couldn't even lie?

I'll do better next time, I promise.

Pls do.

I was about to tuck my phone away, but then she double-texted.

What are you even doing right now? What does a 17yo who doesn't go to school do on a Tuesday? Are you filming? Drinking the blood of proletariat youth?

The blood of the youth is later, I wrote back. I am actually right this minute butterfly-legged on a table while a very kind woman rips out my pubic hair.

Is that even legal?!

> Parental consent goes a long way with
> these things.

Girl what is in your CONTRACT?!

This isn't for the show, I explained. I've been asked to take part
in a campaign for my sister's swimwear line. Apparently pubes are
a no-go for the billboards:/
. . . Jade wrote. I don't know what to do with this information.

> Me neither TBH. Tell me about your day?

Soon we were texting almost every day. It had been so long since
I'd had a real friend. It made the cloud seem just a little less heavy.

One night she sent me a HistoryTok about a group of archae-
ologists closer than ever to finding Cleopatra's tomb.

You're infecting my algo, she wrote.

Is there any truer sign of a blooming friendship? I wrote back.

Calm down.

Don't lie:), I wrote. You like me.

Notable Famous Teen Kiara Greer Supposedly Doesn't Like Being the Center of Attention

Litty.com | Top Stories | Celebrity Vertical

By Alexis Borges

A recent interview with Kia Greer has been receiving backlash, with many on social media accusing the reality star of being tone-deaf and privileged.

"I've always been more comfortable as a supporting player," Greer told *Bustle* in their November cover story. "It's been an adjustment, being the center of attention. I don't know if I like it."

The comments didn't go over well on social media, where many pointed out that Greer recently signed a five-year deal with Ignite Network. "For someone who doesn't want to be famous, you sure are starring in a reality show," TikTok user TheoKingOfTwinks quipped on Wednesday.

"Bold statement from someone whose face is on my TL so often I literally never want to see it again," journalist Caitlin Troy tweeted. Comedian Farrah Richards tweeted as well, writing: "Just shut up, stand there, and sell us Smartwater and bad eye shadow palettes like you always have." Reps for Kia Greer did not respond to requests for comment.

CHAPTER EIGHTEEN

The cloud twisted, foul and stinking, around every hour, even into my sleep. Like in the recurring dream I kept having that fall, over and over again.

I was on the beach with Lark the day of my sixteenth birthday. We hurled ourselves into the waves, tumbling through salty water, taking great gulps of it, until eventually the waves always delivered us back to shore. We dove back in. We'd fight the current, pushing deeper, desperate to make headway, to feel the water in our throats and let it make us something new. But each time, it was still just us, delivered by the waves back to where we'd started.

One night the dream twisted. Lark pushed out of my grasp, disappearing below the waves, the salt water overtaking her. I dove toward her, searching, but she was nowhere to be found. I woke up screaming in the present tense, alone in my bedroom on the mountain, and Lark came running in, startled and still half asleep herself.

"Are you okay?!" she asked, genuine worry on her face.

"I'm fine," I said, getting my bearings in the corporeal world. "We have a busy morning—go back to sleep."

CHAPTER NINETEEN

Is Cassius Campbell Queerbaiting Us All?

Rolling Stone | Celebrity | Opinion

By Mateo Piccino

"Hi, Greta," I coughed through a mouthful of breakfast. "Nice to see you, too."

I closed my laptop. Before Greta's rude interruption, I'd been shoving granola and Greek yogurt into my mouth in my dad's study, hoping his collection of books and Serious Black Art would inspire me to finish an assignment from Mr. Hillis. I was still determined to complete my credits, even if college was no longer a real possibility.

Then Greta had swooped in, a stiletto-clad bat out of hell. I looked at her over the iPad she'd just unceremoniously shoved under my nose. Not a strand of hair, a pore, or a piece of lint was out of place. It was a severity that expected you—your life, your very being—to be as put together as she was.

I'd bet money every single item on her body was from the Row, a minimalist brand that women like her loved because it let them feel expensive while hiding the maximalism that—whether they liked it or not—was inherent to hoarding wealth.

Greta pointed to the headline blaring from the *Rolling Stone* website.

"Is it true?" she demanded.

"I'm gonna need you to clarify," I said slowly, licking a wayward crumb from my lip. How embarrassing to be crumby in front of Greta.

I glanced again at the screen. The lead photo of the article was a high-def concert shot of Cass. He was dancing in a glittery jumpsuit and waving a pride flag. It was a bit on the nose.

"If you and Cassius have some arrangement, it's best if your mother and I know now," Greta said, her nose literally in the air. "That way we can decide how to play it before they get too far ahead of us."

"*They?*" I frowned, still confused. "Who's *they*?" She gestured to the iPad, matching my frown with an impatient glower. I sighed. It appeared I would have to start reading.

> Since even before the release of his debut album, *Passions,* Cassius Campbell has made waves with his fashion choices, often shirking the bounds of traditional masculinity. Last year, in the music video for his hit single "Luxury," Campbell wore a foot-high Afro and a beaded one-shoulder dress embroidered with watermelons, a clear reference to Diana Ross, specifically her 1976 appearance on *The Midnight Special.* He's been known to wear high heels on red carpets and to rock a Bowie-esque full face of makeup onstage.
>
> "I like clothes," the pop star explained in an interview with *GQ* last year. "I don't like the idea of being confined to what I'm 'supposed' to wear. We all have different ways of expressing ourselves."

Campbell was raised by two mothers and has also been an advocate for LGBTQ+ rights, speaking out frequently against drag bans and other anti-LGBTQ+ legislation sweeping the U.S. That, combined with the subtle lack of gendered pronouns in the love songs on his first album, has led quite a few of his fans to theorize Campbell may fall under the queer umbrella himself. Plenty have embraced this possibility. Now, though, a vocal contingent is accusing the artist of queerbaiting.

The singer has mostly remained tight-lipped about his personal life. "I'd like to keep things to the music for now," Campbell said in an early interview with *Teen Vogue.* "I'm not one to hide, so I'm sure I'll share more as time goes on. But this is my first album, and a very personal one. I do have some people I'd rather protect."

Campbell's policy on sharing changed in September, once rumors started circulating that he's dating *Growin' Up Greer* star Kiara Greer. The pair have been spotted out and about in Los Angeles on numerous occasions. Campbell seemed to confirm the relationship in mid-September, when he took to Instagram and posted a screen grab of Jasmine taking Aladdin's hand in the Disney film *Aladdin.* The caption read, "I can show you the world, princess." The post racked up a record-breaking number of likes in a matter of minutes. Greer herself left a cheeky comment under the post, telling Campbell to "calm down."

Not everyone is pleased by the relationship. "Super sad to see Cassius Campbell's just another straight queerbaiter," wrote X user @jacques4me, to which another user, @trashysquidward, replied: "Or a liar. Poor Kiara's gettin used."

"Just because someone loves bell-bottoms doesn't mean they're queer," argued @heavenisforgaypeople farther down the thread. "I have unfortunately fallen into that trap before."

"Either that girl's a beard or yet again a straight celebrity figured out the fastest way to the top is to appeal to gay audiences," X user @LouisRenaldi wrote. "I'm so tired of this cynical money-grabbing exploitation of my community."

We cannot, of course, know anything concrete about Campbell's sexuality—or his gender—until he deigns to tell us himself. Is he just a straight guy who loves to push the boundaries of fashion? A gay guy using a fellow famous as a beard? Perhaps the truth is none of the above. Regardless of what's going on here, it certainly opens up a fascinating conversation: Who gets to benefit from performing queerness? And when it comes to fashion, self-expression, and allyship, where are the boundaries, if there are any at all?

I placed my spoon in the bowl, careful not to splatter any yogurt on my dad's prized desk. Knowing Raymond Greer, it had probably belonged to James Baldwin or something.

Greta leaned against the desk, watching me. I handed the iPad back to her.

"Well?" she asked, expectant. Annoyance bubbled in my chest.

"I don't know what you want me to say," I said honestly. I

couldn't figure out her game here. Was she expecting me to come out and say, *Hey, yeah, my boyfriend's gay! Good kisser, though!*? But she kept looking at me, all imploring. I sighed.

"We don't have an arrangement," I told her. "But we are dating, at least as far as I know."

Her gaze softened exactly one iota, as if she'd just remembered I had an emotional investment here. "And you're sure he's not . . . ?"

"Not what?" I asked, lilting my voice up with faux innocence. I wanted her to come out and say what she was tiptoeing around. It wasn't so much a tiptoe, anyway, as a stiletto jab to the eye. Still, at least she had some shame about it. She glanced uncomfortably around the room. I gasped and brought my hand to my chest as if I'd just had an epiphany.

"Have you never heard of bisexual people? Greta," I asked with mock concern, "are you homophobic?"

I didn't get out much, but the twice a year I could make this woman squirm did provide some solid entertainment. Her glower returned.

"I'm telling Wen you said that," Greta said, bopping me on the nose with the iPad like it was an old-timey newspaper and I was a bad dog. Wen was Wendy. Her wife.

"I'm just looking out for you, Kiara." Greta was all business again. "Are you sure Cassius is in this for the right reasons?"

I scoffed and looked away. There was something ghoulish in watching her pretend this was protective when it was so clearly about *what people might think.* Public reaction ruled everything we did; it's what sold Greer products, from *Growin' Up* to Sola's skincare line and the eye shadow palettes they'd slapped my name on.

Moments like this were a reminder that I was one of those products. To Greta, I was something to be packaged, managed, and sold. If the public turned on my relationship with Cass, that could jeopardize her plans for the Greer empire.

My mouth tasted sour. Things between Cass and me had been going so well. I'd been trying hard not to worry about the other shoe dropping, to block out the noise of TikToks and Instagram comments. But there seemed to be shoes everywhere, and none of them belonged to us.

"Did my mom send you to talk to me?"

Mom was out of town on yet another business trip. My stomach churned, Greta's silence telling me everything I needed to know. I closed my laptop and stood, balancing the computer and my bowl as I kicked the chair back under the desk.

"Just be careful!" Greta called after me. "We don't need another messy breakup."

I pretended not to hear her, stomping out of the room and slamming the door.

I couldn't think of where to go, so I went to the gym. I got on the treadmill, barefoot, set the speed high, and ran.

If I'd learned anything from all those early mornings working away my "baby fat," it was that getting my blood moving did tend to clear my head. I needed that now. It was *crowded* in my brain. My skin burned when I thought about all these people talking about my relationship.

What did any of them know?

I knew perfectly well Cass broke conventions. It was part of why I liked him. Where I was timid, Cass was bold. Where I burrowed inside myself for comfort, Cass lived with arms spread wide-open, not only ready but *excited* to face the world. By his side I'd felt better about facing it, too.

This was how the world repaid him? With gossip and bad-faith arguments?

Certain things I was certain of. Like the fact that Cass liked kissing me just as much as I did him. The public, the press, the publicists—they'd never know Cass the way I did, and even I had so much left to learn. Maybe they knew that, deep down. Maybe it made them angry, all the parts of him they couldn't have.

I stewed, replaying my conversation with Greta. Sexuality and gender identity were way more complicated than "Is he gay or not?" You couldn't tell those things just by looking at a person. I wanted to tell Greta that even if Cass did happen to be hetero and cis, that didn't mean he couldn't wear a skirt or a dress or paint his damn nails if he wanted to—it was the 2020s, for god's sake! I wanted to tell her that my boyfriend didn't have to be straight for us to be real.

I turned the speed up to eight. I was in a sprint now.

Maybe Cass and I had egged them on by parading our relationship through the gossip pages, but that didn't entitle anyone to our every thought and feeling. To the shape of our souls, the complicated crooks of minds that held our attractions, our fears, and our hopes for ourselves.

I slowed the treadmill, then stopped it, slumping over the console, heaving.

I was used to the boxes they shoved me into.

Spoiled.

Fake.

Not gorgeous.

Not skinny enough.

Not interesting enough.

Only worth our time with a boy on her arm.

No matter what I said or did, it was never quite right. I'd been too much of a wallflower, so I'd changed it up and gone out more. Then I was around *too* much and saying all the wrong things.

But this time it wasn't me they were coming for. It was Cass. Cass, who had earned his fame because his talent was so undeniable people couldn't help but love him. Did they know they also had the power to tear him apart? Had he known, when he'd jumped up and down in excitement about his first record deal, what would come with it?

He couldn't have.

I wished I could protect him from the lessons he'd soon learn.

BLIND ITEM: This A-list singer may have a new girlfriend, but someone from his past has decided to come out of the woodwork: an ex-boyfriend who claims the A-lister's entire first album was about him, and that this new "relationship" is nothing but a farce. Said ex-boyfriend is convinced it's all a ploy to get him back.

CHAPTER TWENTY

FaceTimes, voice notes, and endless texts started blurring together. I hadn't seen Cass in far too long. I missed the bright
shock of energy he brought to my life. I missed his eyes and the
way he smiled with his whole body. And . . . we needed to talk.
I wasn't sure yet whether to bring up what Greta had said. But
I needed a day with my new favorite person, away from prying
eyes and publicity hounds.

Los Angeles had finally decided to take autumn seriously. The
air was properly November cool, palm trees silhouetted against
gray skies. Cass picked me up in his mom's Prius, a car the press
wouldn't automatically recognize as his own. He sped down the
101 as I DJed a playlist to get us in the right headspace. I teed up
songs by Jazmine Sullivan, Alanis Morissette, Paramore, Cardi B,
and the like.

"I'm sensing a theme," he said as Taylor Swift's "Who's Afraid
of Little Old Me?" cycled into Beyoncé's "Don't Hurt Yourself."
"There's an, uh, *angry* vibe to these songs."

I kept my smile coy.

"Yes," I said. "Yes there is." I left it at that. Instead of telling
Cass where we were going, I was feeding him the directions one
at a time.

He hadn't brought up the blind items and think pieces, and neither had I. If the roles had been reversed, I wouldn't have liked him giving space to baseless rumors. It wasn't necessary.

Besides, today seemed to be bringing the life out in Cass again—even though his so-called fans had been showing up on his street in waves, undeterred by repeated warnings. He'd hired his part-time security to guard the place, so he couldn't hide the truth from his mom any longer. They'd been fighting. Cass wanted her to consider moving, but Violet refused to leave.

Still, he seemed determined to have a good time. This wasn't the Cassius Campbell with the stalking fans and the constant radio airplay. This Cass knew every word to every song I threw at him.

He also did a freaky good Alanis impression, getting the twang and melodic screeches *juuuust* right. Cass was pure energy, through the good and the bad. I was just riding the wave. No clouds could follow me here.

Cass's jaw dropped as he took in the sign on the warehouse in front of us.

"A rage room?!" He turned to me. "You brought me to a rage room."

"Yeah," I said, grinning. "Let's smash stuff."

The look on his face was pure joy, pure wonder, pure excitement. I took a breath. *Good,* I thought to myself, *I did it right.*

I'd chosen strategically. Rage LA was hardly a hot spot, and it was deep enough into the Valley that no one would look for us here. Still, we took selfies in the coveralls, helmets, and face shields the staff had given us to ensure we didn't get jabbed in the eye by shrapnel of our own making. Maybe we'd post them later. Maybe we wouldn't.

"*This,*" Cass said, tapping the plastic shield dividing us, "was a *great* idea."

A nice young woman with sleeves of skull tattoos led us to a private room stocked with crates of mugs, plates, and old printers, computers, and flat-screen TVs. She armed us with crowbars, bats, and mallets so heavy I doubted I could lift them.

But we managed. Skull Tattoo Lady closed the door, and Cass and I looked at each other with wide eyes. He gave me the first turn up. He tossed a porcelain *Don't talk till I've had my coffee* mug into the air, and my heart beat hard against my chest.

I breathed out, swung, and—*CRRRTTTCKKKK*—the mug fractured into a hundred pieces that flew across the room in every direction.

"AHHHHHH!" I screamed. "HOLY SHIT." It was half delight and half terror.

"*OHOHOHOHOHO,*" Cass yelled, running in circles around the room. "ME NEXT, ME NEXT, ME NEXT."

We took turns from there, one of us throwing mugs into the air while the other swung a bat as hard as they could, sending shattered bits in every direction.

CRRRRTCKK—

CRASH—

CRACK—

TRRKK—

There was something incandescently freeing about destroying objects with all your might. We knew no one would get hurt, and so for forty-five minutes we gave in to our basest urges. I took pleasure in the way hard plastic splintered under my force. Our mouths twisted in oblong glee, alarm, and satisfaction at every strike, pull, smash, and wallop.

I pictured mugs bearing Levi's face. Mugs embodying *the public*. I pictured Greta's face on a plate as I smashed it into dust. Then I felt bad about it.

Rage is *exhausting*, it turns out. It wears you out fast. The cost of destroying something is that it leaves your own body in ruins, too.

Cass and I sank down against the wall, panting, the last of the printers torn to pieces at our feet. We sat on the floor, porcelain dust and shards of plastic, metal, and LCD around us, chests heaving as we took in the might of our destruction. We stayed that way, leaning into each other's sides for support, and eventually our breathing calmed to a steady rhythm.

I was ragged around every edge. Cass's eyelids had gone heavy. He looked as if he could fall asleep right then and there. I smiled to myself; at least *this* was a good kind of tired. Cass leaned against the wall and closed his eyes, and for a moment I was free to stare. I studied his beautiful, expressive face and wondered how I could help him. This person, this beautiful kid, had already helped me in ways he'd never comprehend. But here, alone and away, having bashed every bad feeling out of our bodies, and even with a small, languid smile playing across his lips . . . there was still something haunted in his face.

The knot in my chest tightened and I looked away, a little bit shattered. There was no easy fix to the *thing* in Cass that was being stolen away: the sense that his life was his own.

"We really goddamn needed this," Cass breathed. I turned back toward him and saw that now he was the one studying me.

"You can say that again."

"*We really fucking goddamn needed this,*" he breathed, this time with so much emotion it made me laugh. His smile spread wider.

"You have the best smile."

Cass took my hand in his and kissed my palm.

"Thank you," he said. "I know the past few weeks haven't exactly been the easiest. I've actually been wanting to, well . . ."

"Camp out on your front lawn and egg every car that slows down to gape?" I finished for him. "Because I am IN."

Cass's eyes crinkled with silent laughter. But that thing behind his eyes was back.

"Actually . . ." he said. He cleared his throat in what I now recognized as one of Cassius Campbell's rare nervous tics. "I've been wanting to talk to you about some rumors that have been going around."

I shook my head. "We don't need to, not if you don't—"

"I really want to talk to you," he insisted.

I stilled, terrified. Was I about to be dumped? I'd convinced myself that all the internet talk was false and stupid, baseless reaches for clicks that disregarded not only the existence of sexual fluidity but the way my skin felt suddenly alive when Cass touched me.

"Okay." My breath came out unsteady. What was that saying? *'Tis better to have loved and lost than never to have loved at all?* Did that apply to situations where you were maybe accidentally or on purpose being used as a beard?

Cass turned my hand over, slid his fingers in between mine, and squeezed.

"Kia, I'm *so sorry.* I should have talked to you about this from the beginning, before any of those stupid blind items started showing up." His eyes were fixed on our intertwined hands.

"I'm not exactly good at being, uh, straight-presenting," Cass continued. "I don't really have it in me to try. Never have. I should have known this would come up, but for some reason I didn't think about it. This might sound weird, but I'm so comfortable with you that it felt like you already knew? There's so much I haven't felt the need to say out loud with you, because you've kinda just *gotten* me, right from the start. But then those stories started showing up, and I didn't want to bring them up until we saw each other in person."

I commanded my brain to stay still. This was not a time to draw conclusions or have big feelings. Still, I was sure he could feel my heart pounding through the pulse in my hand.

"Because . . . you're not straight?" I asked. Then I cringed, buried my face in my free hand. "Wait. Sorry. You *don't* have to come out to me—it's none of my business. I just want to know where I stand."

Cass tapped my chin, pointing my face back toward him.

"You're my girlfriend," he said. "It very much *is* your business."

Cass leaned back against the wall. I joined him in this stance. If the roles had been reversed, I wouldn't have wanted him staring at me while I talked.

"I like girls," he said. He spoke slowly, deliberately. The soft silk of his voice didn't belong in this destroyed mess of a room. "I'm sure of that. But I do also like guys. And people who don't buy into the binary."

My exhale was long and deep. I nodded.

"That's good to know," I said. But Cass wasn't done.

"And for the record . . . I'm not sure if I do, either," he continued. He glanced at me and away, nervous. "Conform to the binary, I mean."

"Okay," I said. "What does that mean to you?"

"I'm still figuring that out. I *do* feel like a boy, or a man, but not *just* like a boy, or a man. Like, I'm still defaulting to 'he,' but I don't know if I always will. I'm having fun, exploring it all. Giving myself permission to be whoever I am on any day, in any *moment*. I like the idea of being everything at once. It makes me feel *full*. Does that make sense?"

"It does," I said. I looked straight into his eyes now. Cass wasn't me—I had to remember that. He wasn't shy when it came to people looking at him. It was special, being invited into who this person was. Into who he was in the process of becoming. "I'll call you whatever you want. Thank you for telling me. I'm *here*— for whoever you are."

Cass looked so vulnerable and so *hopeful* in that moment that I felt salt pool behind my eyes. I blinked it away. Crying would make this about me, and I didn't want that. Not when a weight had lifted between us.

"I didn't mean to hide it from you. Most people in my life know—at least the sexuality part. The gender part is still really new, and I don't even have all the words for it yet." He drew a big breath inward. "My big ex, the one some songs on *Passions* were about? That was this guy Noah. We went to school together. It was a messy breakup, which is a long story I'll tell you soon. Most people who know me know about him, but I didn't want anyone to go after him when the album came out, so I kept things vague in interviews."

"That makes sense," I said. The press would have hounded Noah if they'd known his name from the jump.

"But I was being naive," Cass said, "because now Noah's doing this thing where he subposts about me on Insta, and since gossip accounts follow everyone I've ever interacted with, that's turned into rumors, which are turning into think pieces . . . I can't seem to get him to stop. The first time he posted, it felt like an accident. Now not so much."

A corner of Cass's mouth tweaked in resignation.

"I was serious about egging those cars," I said. "Point me toward this guy's and I'll get the job done."

Cass just smiled, his eyes searching mine. "Have you ever dealt with anything like this?"

I nodded. "Practically everyone I went to grade school with participated in this story about 'what the Greers were like before they were famous.'"

"That really fucking sucks."

"I'd imagine it sucks more when it includes part of yourself you haven't yet chosen to share with the world. My leaks were all like, 'She cried at my slumber party!' and 'Once we got in a fight over tetherball!'"

Cass chuckled, sinking down so his head rested on my shoulder. "Listen, tetherball can get *real*."

"I was a beast at it," I bragged. "I *killed* at recess."

Cass smiled wide, and I smiled, too. Suddenly I was that talkative little nerd girl once more, the whole world stretched out in front of her. She'd been so unafraid of the disappointment that inevitably came after wanting something with all your heart. When had I lost that? Was it too late to get it back?

I couldn't remember the last time I'd felt this close to someone. The silence between us was light, airy. Comfortable—but *full*.

"People do this annoying thing where they assume everyone is straight until proven otherwise," Cass said after a while.

"I don't even care if the world knows about Noah. He was my first love—he can claim those songs. It's just, the *way* he's doing it is . . ."

"Shady as hell?"

"*Yeah.* And then with the gender stuff, there's still a lot *I'm* figuring out there, y'know?"

"Of course."

"And it's complicated enough being Black in this industry. Which I don't have to tell you—you've dealt with it longer than I have." Cass looked at me for confirmation, and I raised my eyebrows like, *Duh.*

He huffed a laugh. "I'm sure being a Black girl or woman in this place is its own mindfuck. Me . . . I'm someone they read as a 'man.' And that comes with all these specific expectations, all this *history.* Aalll this complicated shit that has nothing to do with me but also everything to do with me." Cass stared at the wall across from us. "It's already happening and I haven't even come out yet. The first time I wore visible lipstick on the red carpet, there were people saying I represented the 'emasculation' of Black men. I even saw a thread blaming it on me having two moms."

I let out a low whistle. "More cars to egg," I said. Then: "I'm sorry."

"It helped that my ma was a professor. I didn't have her for very long, but she made sure I knew *my* history, on all sides. Queer, Black, everything. Jade too. She made it clear *no one* gets to own us." Tears shone in Cass's eyes. I wiped one away as it fell down his cheek. "So more and more I'm thinking about the gender stuff, and how there's not just one word or way of being that can hold me. I don't intend to hide who I am, but if I ever go public, it'll only be once I've figured it out for myself. Because when

I say it out loud, it'll mean something that's a lot bigger than me. It'll affect other people. So I have to be good—like, *really* good— with the me part first. Am I making sense?"

Something calm and steady moved through me. "It makes every bit of sense to me," I said. "As much as I can know . . . I get it."

"You know what? I know you do," Cass said, and he pecked me on my forehead.

Full. What a beautiful way to move through the world. I hoped I could feel that one day. I mirrored Cass's smile with a big one of my own. "I like this journey for you."

Somehow his grin got even wider. "You do?"

I laughed, and it was joy, and it was relief, and it was so much more than I could name.

"I do," I said. "Also . . . not to make it about me, but I like girls, too. I've never said that to anyone. But I definitely had crushes, back in school. On a bunch of different types of kids."

Cass took my shoulders in his hands and shook. "KIA!!!"

I laughed again, and it radiated through my whole body.

Cass pulled me into a hug. It was tight and strong. Safe. I felt safe with Cassius Campbell, who had just shared so much with me, and who I couldn't wait to share even more with. My head rested on his chest.

"I love you," I said, so quiet and muffled I wasn't sure if he heard. It was the first time I'd said those words, and I felt so far away from the Kia I'd been in that bowling alley, the one so freaked out about kissing a person. I wasn't scared, somehow. I was standing at the edge of a cliff, but the view was beautiful, and I knew Cass would catch me if I fell. So I said it again—louder this time. "I love every bit of the you that you are, and the you that you're making."

And he did catch me. Because Cass's face broke open, and he pulled me upward.

"*I love you—every bit of you,*" Cass said back, and then he hauled me into a kiss that was all-engrossing. I closed my eyes and all of the wreckage around us disappeared. There were no sharp edges here—only soft, silken-warm skin and the way Cassius Campbell's lips and hands moved across the rounded edges of Kia Greer. We didn't have the answers. We didn't need them. We had space, and we had so much adventure in front of us. Everyone could be as loud and wrong as they wanted. We would lock in and face it together, just as we were now.

CHAPTER TWENTY-ONE

He didn't drive me home. Instead we cruised down Mulholland Drive, past guarded community gates, and up a tree-lined driveway. We were both quiet, coming down from the adrenaline rush of the rage room and everything it had unearthed in us.

More gates swung open before us—gates to a home. I looked over at Cass, confused.

"Are we visiting someone?"

"So . . ." he said, not answering my question, "I may have done something rash."

"Okaaaay . . ."

We pulled up to what looked like a multimillion-dollar tree house. Warm wood paneling and huge plate glass windows and sloping branches exploding with green. Cass parked in a drive shaded by bamboo and oak trees and opened my door for me. Then he pulled a new set of keys out of his pocket and let us in.

"Cass . . . did you buy a house?!" I said it in a whisper-scream, as if speaking at full volume would get us caught by unseen adults. My stomach dropped as I took it all in.

The front door opened into an empty step-down living room. The interior of this home was the same warm wood and glass as the outside, and inside I realized how much they softened the sharp angles and long lines of the midcentury architecture. What could have been sterile instead felt inviting and *alive*. I stared agog as Cass stepped into the center of the room, hands in his pockets and shoulders hitched up around his ears.

"I didn't buy it," Cass said. "But I did rent it."

"WHAT?! WHEN?! WHY DIDN'T YOU TELL ME?!"

Cass laughed and took my hands in his. This was another thing I was learning about Cass: Sometimes he hid things until what felt to him like the perfect moment. I wondered if this was the performer in him—or if maybe it had to do with a fear of rejection. Maybe it was both.

"A real estate agent sent me the listing this week." Cass leaned his forehead against mine. I closed my eyes, trying to calm my sinking heart and actually listen. "I've been beating myself up so much about the fans showing up. My mom's downplaying it. She won't move—so I have to. I'll tell the stans they won't find me there anymore. It's the only way to keep my people safe."

I looked around. Our voices echoed through the place. It was so empty. I didn't like the idea of Cass alone there. My heart hurt. *He'd been pushed out of his own home.*

"Cass, are you sure?" I asked. "There must be something else we can—"

"I'm getting in their way," Cass said gruffly. There it was—that haunted look from earlier. All the times on FaceTime that Cass's voice would stiffen, his focus drift, because he was so worried about what his fame had wrought. "My mom's mad, but she'll see it's for the best. You know that Swift music video where she's all giant, interrupting everyone's good time? That's how I feel."

Cass sighed and walked backward through the room. He spread his arms wide, pivoting from grim existentialist to proud host.

"But this place is great, right? Things'll be good here. It's behind not one but *two* gates. If anything does go sideways in Northridge, the fam will always be safe here."

"It really is pretty," I said, and I hated myself, because my voice cracked, and Cass didn't need to hear my heart break for him. He deserved so much more than a life locked away.

At least I wasn't lying. It was a gorgeous house. If he was making the best of a bad situation, I should, too. So I walked across the room to Cass, then past him to the tall glass doors that opened to the backyard. There was a small pool and lounge furniture. The outdoor space was dotted with a dozen different kinds of fruit trees.

"They've got orange trees," I said. "That's perfect. You always smell like those."

Cass came up behind me and wrapped his arms around my waist.

"This was the dream one day anyway, right?" Cass said into the crook of my neck. "Use the fame and the money to get a really cool house, then make really cool music in it."

I had to force the smile onto my face, but at least it was there.

I took a picture of Cass standing in his new backyard and looking up at the sky. The sun shone through the leaves and fell on the angles of his face, lighting him up like a Kehinde Wiley painting. He posted it to Instagram, choosing the caption "My house is a very, very, very fine house." It was a reference to a song Graham Nash wrote about the home he once shared with Joni Mitchell. Joni and Graham didn't last forever, but that song did.

The picture was a strategy, an announcement. *I don't live in that old place any longer,* it said to the hordes of stans who pored over his every word. *You chased me away, so here I am behind the gates, protecting the ones I love.*

You won, it said. Or, perhaps more accurately, *You lost. We all did.*

I tried to comfort him the only way I could think of.

"Let's order Chinese food tonight and eat it in the living room," I said.

"Okay," he said.

All Cass had was a few boxes from his bedroom, so we unpacked his comforter and spread it across the floor, climbing into its downy middle. Cass set up his turntable and put an Aretha Franklin record on and we talked and talked, gorging ourselves on noodles, pointing to every corner and debating what kind of furniture he should get.

Eventually, inevitably, the conversation moved to how Cass should "come out" to the public. I told him not to rush. It wasn't anyone's business. But Cass didn't want to feel like he was hiding something. He hoped telling his own story would neutralize the blind items Noah kept posting and take some of the heat off our relationship.

The knot in my chest twisted and I realized I was *mad.* That I'd *been* mad since the morning Greta shoved her iPad in my face. I was furious, really, so angry for this person I'd come to love.

Cass was famous because he loved music, and he was good at it, and he was beautiful and captivating and special. Somehow that meant it was open season on the contours of his soul.

I riffled through the box of records until I found the right one, and I put it on the turntable. As the music started up, I sang along. I wasn't very good, so I did an exaggerated expression of Graham Nash's singing—more Kristen Wiig than folk-rock star. Cass laughed mercilessly.

"Rude!" I said, but I kept going.

Cass sprang up, and much to my surprise, he dashed right out the door. A second later, the lights strung through the backyard twinkled to life, and then Cass was back with me, firmly pressing one hand against the small of my back and weaving the fingers of his other through mine. We swayed through the living room, bodies nestled close. The garden lights played over his face like a picture show only I had tickets to.

The song was holding us so tightly, I wasn't ready to drop the bit.

"Thank you," he whispered.

"For what?" I asked, pulling back to look him in the face.

"For getting it."

I tugged him back closer to me.

I hated this house, but I'd never tell Cass that. I missed his old bedroom, how lived in and storied it felt. Every inch of that place held a story of him. I'd loved, in the diner, at the bowling alley, in his bedroom, how *normal* Cass helped me feel. But we weren't normal. He never would be again. Maybe he needed someone who'd also been through that loss. Most people didn't want to hear people like us complain about our lucky lives.

Cass was making the best of a great situation. Sure, he'd been pushed from his home—but he'd found a silver lining in walls of fallen redwood.

I understood that. I'd found mine in him.

⌐⌐

We lay shoulder to shoulder, so close to the open patio door that our view was half beamed ceilings and half trees and stars and endless sky.

"Did I ever tell you the full story of what happened when my ma died?"

I turned to look at him, flabbergasted.

"Cassius Campbell," I intoned, "you literally never even told me she died."

Cass hoisted himself onto his elbows. "I definitely did. Didn't I?"

It took a moment, but something clicked behind his eyes. He dropped back down with a thump, rolled over, and rubbed the heels of his hands into his eyes.

"I didn't tell you she was *dead*?"

"You didn't," I confirmed. "You really did not."

"You didn't know my *mother* was *dead*?"

"I picked some stuff up from context clues, but not offi-cially, no."

"I guess . . . I assumed you'd Googled me and . . . seen that?"

Perhaps it was inappropriate to giggle while talking about your boyfriend's dead mother. I couldn't help it; I laughed. Cass did, too. He clapped his hand over his mouth, but the laugh just turned into a demented giggle.

"Jeez, Cass," I teased, "just because you're famous doesn't mean everyone's Googling you all the time."

His shoulders shook next to me, laughter bursting through clasped fingers.

"Jesus Christ," Cass said. "Okay, well, then this conversation is *way* overdue."

"Wanna tell me about it?" I studied the side of his face. Cass was staring up at the ceiling or the sky, mouth still twisted with mirth. He let out a concerted exhale.

"It's . . . kind of why I'm so protective of Jade and my mom,"

Cass said. "This life is my dream, but it was pretty complicated to get here. My other mother, Anita, was always pushing me to finish college before I went after music professionally. She was a professor. She took school *so* seriously—which I get, but . . . my ma's life just wasn't the life for me, y'know? I mean, I know *you* know.

"She'd take me on these tours to Berklee, Oberlin, all the conservatories, even when I was just a baby freshman, because she thought if I studied music, that'd be enough. But it wasn't. I don't know if you've noticed, but I've got a lot of energy . . ."

I smiled. I'd realized that first night I met him that Cass was a supernova. Insatiable, but in entirely his own way. Boxing that up would always be a fool's errand.

"I was trying to do what she wanted. I played in the school orchestra, in bands. But I was also putting songs online, and . . . someone noticed me. When Simms got me an offer for a record deal, it was like a bomb went off in the house. I've never seen my moms fight like that. Jade didn't talk to me for months because she blamed me for all of it."

"That's pretty harsh," I said.

"I get it. We both thought they were gonna split up."

Cass cleared his throat and closed his eyes. I played with one of the twists at the base of his neck, waiting till he was ready to continue.

"Eventually Violet won out. She saw how claustrophobic the prospect of college made me feel. I didn't want to get graded performing other people's stuff for four years—I wanted to make my own, and I'd already started. So they let me sign. I recorded the album. I was sixteen, so every day I was racing between school and the studio, and I didn't even have my license yet, so my moms were always trading off who drove me. I loved being in the studio. Then the album wrapped, and . . . my ma had a heart attack. And she died."

"Oh, Cass," I breathed. "Holy crap, I'm so sorry."

I took in the person next to me. Cass's eyes were still closed, but as pain flickered across his face, I realized I'd never seen him look so *young* before.

"I blamed myself for a long time," Cass said. "I still do sometimes. I know I caused her a lot of stress."

"It's not your fault," I said, as if my feeble insistence could alter years of guilt. I shook my head. "That is not a thing that could be your fault. That's so much bigger than you."

I placed a hand to his chest. Cass opened his eyes and looked into mine. He held my gaze—steady and full. He nodded, just a little.

"I know this is where I'm supposed to be," he said. "But I brought it up because I wanted you to know . . . you're not the only one who feels broken sometimes."

I let out a long exhale. Cass's hand circled my waist and tugged me into him. I traced the perimeter of that naturally perfect jaw, placed a finger against irresistibly full lips. Sensations crashed through me: need, desire, grief. *Gratitude.* Maybe I had no choice but to bloom where I was planted, but at least Cass and I were fertile ground. We could build something here, together, nursing our wounds and tilting our heads toward the light. Maybe I could be a happy person someday. He made that feel possible.

His lips curled up at the corners as they found mine. Cass smelled like orange blossoms and shea butter and home.

I wrapped my arms around Cass's neck and leaned my forehead against his. Something was alive in me, aching not for what was lost but for the inexorable, inevitable thing that was exactly here, alive between us.

"Thank you for being here," Cass whispered. "You make everything better."

"So do you," I whispered back. "How do you do that?"

Cass pressed his lips into mine, and every bit of bad in the world felt so, so far away.

⌒⌒

Cass and I were well and truly alone for the first time ever. There was no Joe waiting on the other side of the door, no threat of Jade knocking at any moment. It was just the house in the trees and us. We pulled more pillows and blankets from their boxes and built ourselves a nest. I changed into a pair of Cass's flannel pj pants and an oversized Cabot High School Band tee. I'd spend the night here tonight. Lark would make excuses for me back home.

There was not a drop of alcohol in my system—just orange chicken, duck sauce, Aretha, and *Cass*. I may not have liked how this house came to be, but I loved what it gave us: a sprawling sense of *space*. I was high on it, all this air. Dizzy. Cass put on a new album, and Prince's cover of "A Case of U" drifted through the empty rooms. Then Cass's hand was in mine, pulling me closer as we swayed to the beat, hips pressed flush against each other. Unlike our last dance, this one wasn't a desperate escape from bad feeling. This was slow, deliberate, and all-enveloping.

"You've never been to a high school dance, have you?" Cass asked. I murmured in confirmation.

I'd never go to prom, never attend a high school dance at all.

But I could slow-dance with my first love, his hands drawing worlds across my back. We could christen this space as something new.

I was so in love, my lungs so *full.* It was hard to imagine anyone had ever felt this way but us. Except I knew they had. I was in any love song, any movie. I'd never felt so connected to something bigger than myself. Falling in love, I was learning, was at once wholly exceptional and utterly ordinary, a shared experience that tied us to people across centuries and continents. It sent a shiver up my spine.

This, I saw clearly now, was what those scientists at Yale had meant. I was trimming away my child self. Whoever was taking shape now was malleable and *ready,* even as fear still drummed in her baby heart.

"What are you thinking about?" Cass asked next. For all his good qualities, Cass never could stand extended silence. In answer I took his hand and guided us to the center of the nest we'd made. I sank down to sitting, and Cass joined me, his legs entwined with mine and our hands clasped together as if we couldn't stand to not be touching for even a millisecond.

"I was thinking of how jealous I've been of you, ever since we met," I told him honestly. He cocked his head, skeptical.

"You've been jealous of *me*?"

I lay back and stared at the ceiling again, my hand never leaving his. I drew words across his palm as I talked.

"You know who you are, and where you're going, and you know that the people standing in the way are wrong," I said. "I think that's really rare."

He nodded slowly, seeming to now get where I was coming from.

"Well, for what it's worth?" he said. "Anyone standing in your way is dead wrong, too."

There was nothing standing in the way here. Cass lowered himself to lie beside me, a curious look on his face. I turned to my side, inching closer until my body was pressed fully against his. I wrapped my hand around his neck and pulled Cass's mouth to mine.

Cass's mouth was a home, warm and welcoming, and I made it my own. I traveled down to his neck, my breath hot against his skin as I bit and sucked, dragging teeth against tendon and tasting the traces of salt left over from our sweaty, raving efforts in the rage room.

"Kee," Cass moaned, neck arching toward me.

"Do you want me to stop?" I whispered.

Cass hauled my mouth back up to his, rolling us both until he was on top of me, his weight gloriously heavy on mine. He kissed me like he might die if he didn't, and I kissed him back just the same, hips reaching to grind against his until every sensation in my body went wild, our mouths swollen and tender, and my field of vision spun.

Cass was exploration, freedom, air, *joy.* Pathways stretched before us, here in his tree house. For once I was exactly where I wanted to be.

"Let's have sex." It came out a creak, eked out in between kisses. Cass's eyes widened.

"Tonight? Are you sure?"

I nodded. "Only if you wan—"

"I want to," Cass interjected. "Kia, of course I do."

My heart thrummed so hard he had to feel it. Relief was flooding through me—and the very best kind of terror.

"Me too," I said. Then, because it felt like a moment for the truth: "I'm really happy here with you."

Cass brushed a braid behind my ear, his eyes soft and bright in the amber glow of his living room. But then his face dropped, and my heart lurched.

"Shit. I don't have a condom."

"I have an IUD," I said. "Got one for cramps. Without a condom's not ideal, but . . . I've never been with anyone. Have you been tested?"

He had, at his annual physical. He was STI-free, and so was I. We held each other's gaze, breath still ragged from everything we'd already done, all the touches and raw nerves. I kept my eyes locked to his as I stood. I pulled off the Cabot High Band tee, then the sports bra I'd been wearing underneath. I hooked my thumbs into the pajama pants, sliding them to the floor and kicking them away.

It was only when I'd stepped out of my cotton boy shorts and the air hit my naked skin that I brought my gaze to Cass again. I was suddenly all too aware that since puberty no one but my doctors had seen these parts of me.

The realization threatened to jar me out of the moment, but Cass was looking at me with such awe that he grounded me right back where I was.

"*Kia . . .*" Cass breathed. "*You are so beautiful.*"

Happy tears filled my eyes, and I blinked them away. I took a step forward, my breath hitching as I lowered myself to straddle him. I pulled his shirt off, and he pressed us skin to skin. I felt drunk, inhaling his heady scent of shea butter and citrus. Then he kissed my neck and I was in a new dimension.

I kissed him again, and there was a grace to the way our lips fit together, the way they played and challenged and asked and answered. There was triumph in the way Cass's hands held my hips, firm and hungry—and in the way I touched him without fear, even as I had no idea what I was doing. I could be that person here: the one who wanted, and tried, and *had*.

That night I met the version of me who had sex. She was gentle and determined. It hurt a little, but not as badly as I'd expected, because Cass was gentle and determined, too.

Afterward Cass curled against the side of me, warm and spent, his head on my chest and our heartbeats slowed, united and steady. We talked through the dark until our voices faded away, and Cass's breath slowed, too, into a rhythmic chant. It was bottled magic, hearing the exact moment he fell asleep. He was in my care, like I'd just been in his.

It wasn't quite dawn, but we were deep enough into the night that the dark could break open at any moment, bringing the color and light of a new day.

I'd read once that sleep is a time of repair, when our bodies work to give us strength for whatever lies ahead. It's when new memories are written into the fabric of our brains. I relished knowing that as I slept, this night would become part of me forever.

Tell me, what is it you plan to do with your one wild and precious life?

PART THREE

Can You Drown in a Cloud?

(November–March)

TikTok Transcript

@CassiusCampbell | 60.0M followers

Bi guys, I'm hi! Nope, let's try that again: Hi guys! Happy Sunday. I'm Cassius Campbell, and I'm bi. Bisexual. Also chill with being called pan, queer—anything but straight, really. Been out to everyone in my life since I was fifteen, but here we are—people are making it weird again! If that's you, kindly cut it out!

My first album, Passions, *was written after a meaningful relationship I had with a guy. I didn't mention him during interviews not because I was hiding who I was but because I wanted to respect his privacy. It turns out he did not want that! He wanted people to know those songs were about him, so he has . . . been talking. Been sayin' some stuff. And he has every right to claim those songs were written about him, because they were! Or some of them were. Just—here I am now, with a whole lot of people thinking I've betrayed the queer community by not coming out to the public "in time" for . . . for what, I dunno. The next queer agenda meeting? Because trust, I been pushin' it!*

I've also seen comments going after my girlfriend, calling her a beard—and we're gonna cut that the eff out. If you don't believe people can love others of all sexes and/or gender expressions, then just say that. Say what's in your soul so we know who you really are, but don't project your issues onto me or my loved ones.

There are interviews from the 1970s featuring David Bowie answering questions about being bi. He's up front about it, and the talk show hosts can't seem to wrap their silly little minds around it. Let's not do this now, okay? And let's not turn this into a conversation about Black masculinity. I'm just gonna make my music and have a meaningful relationship with my girlfriend and be my bi-ass self in whatever ways I see fit. Cool?

The Daily Find **Trending Topics**

1. Cassius Campbell Just Came Out as Bisexual via TikTok Rant—Everything We Know, Including the Tea on That High School Sweetheart!

2. Is Bisexuality Real? The Internet's Bi-Furious Debate After Cassius Campbell's Bombshell Coming-Out

3. Sola Greer's Post-Divorce Style Is to Die For—20 Looks We've Loved, and Where You Can Buy Them

4. Lark Greer Stuns on First Solo Cover, Teases Debut Album

5. Everything We Know About Cassius Campbell's Swanky Mulholland Estates Bachelor Pad—Including That Time Paps Snapped Kia Greer Leaving Very Early in the Morning

6. 20 Times Levi Ellis Was Actually Kinda Gross

CHAPTER TWENTY-TWO

The holidays were my favorite time behind the gates. Cameras stopped rolling and family filtered back in from their various gigs around the world, pockets heavy with stories to tell at the dinner table. These were the rare times when business shut down, when phones were left in the other room. The weirdest part had been Miss Carol and Merv's absence; they had, understandably, opted to spend Thanksgiving with their bio family in Ohio. In their absence Lark and I invaded Merv's kitchen and spent a full day teaching Deja how to make Grandma Millie's peanut butter cookies. It went as well as you can expect a baking lesson with a three-year-old to go—we all ended up with peanut butter in our hair. We cleaned up as best we could, but when Miss Carol and Merv returned, he still found peanut butter streaked on cabinets and stuck in corners of his silverware drawers.

He could scowl our way all he wanted; the house wasn't the same without Miss Carol and Merv. I was just happy they were back.

"Cass got you beaming like that again?" Miss Carol asked a few days after her return, catching me cheesing at my phone. "Kid's good."

I tucked it into my pocket. I hadn't told her all the ways Cass and I had *shifted*.

Tonight wasn't about that, though. We had this tradition: Every once in a while, ever since Lark hit high school, she, Miss Carol, and I would wait for Merv to finish his meal service and then take over the kitchen, where Miss Carol would teach us basic cooking skills our actual parents were too otherwise occupied to pass on. We also had laundry training, sewing and mending, Car 101, and days when Miss Carol would make us sit and watch as she did her budgets. That last one was not our favorite, but Miss Carol was determined that we know how to be "functional people in the world," even if, as she put it, "your parents assume you'll spend the rest of your lives being catered to."

Lark was supposed to be here, but she'd broken the unspoken holiday rules by taking a job. Tonight she'd perform at iHeartRadio's Jingle Ball, so we'd been whittled down to two. I focused on the chicken carcass we were preparing to roast while I answered Miss Carol's question.

"It's not Cass, actually," I said, mixing rosemary and thyme into a little bowl of softened butter. "Cass's sister, Jade, made some joke. We're all in a group chat together now. I don't wanna jinx anything, but I think we might be actual friends?"

Miss Carol's face, which had been smirked and teasing when she'd asked about Cass, softened now, settling into a satisfied smile. She patted me on the shoulder.

"Now that is something to celebrate," she said, handing me a basting brush. "Is this the one who was rude to you that first night?"

"Oh, she real rude," I admitted. Miss Carol held the chicken while I painted it with butter. "She says, like, her every thought aloud. But she's also really smart, and funny. I think we might have a lot in common. More than I thought possible considering I'm an alien and I live on Mars."

Miss Carol didn't say anything for a long moment. She just watched me. Her eyes were so knowing, they made my skin feel prickly.

I put the basting brush down and pulled a face.

"I just realized it sounded like I was calling myself smart and funny," I said. "That's not how I meant it."

"You can call yourself smart and funny," she said, gathering onions, a lemon, and herb twigs. "That's what you are. You're allowed to like yourself out loud. Saying the things you like can help them sink in deeper when you're alone. You gotta get some swag, Kee."

I didn't know what to say to that, so I just started shoving twigs of rosemary and thyme up the chicken's butt. Miss Carol smiled one of her secret smiles. She had a lot of those. Miss Carol wasn't a person who spoke her every though, but I could always tell when something was bubbling beneath the surface.

This person had known so many versions of me. She'd seen my devastation when I'd been pulled out of school and when, in the months afterward, my few friends slowly slipped away. Not many people knew how lonely I'd been these last few years, but she did. She was one of the only people I'd told about the cloud, or the knot in my chest—all these ways I felt suffocated, day by day, and how confused it made me, not being able to find air in this castle of a house.

It's uncomfortable, being known. It's like parts of you live not in yourself but in those who have borne witness to you. You can't get those pieces back, even as you become a new version of yourself. Miss Carol was a living archive, a walking reminder of the best and worst of me. I only wished I could be the same for her. Maybe I could, now that she wasn't technically my nanny anymore. I hoped she'd let me. Miss Carol was one of the only people I was certain wanted me happy on my own terms.

"This is good," Miss Carol said after a long while. "This is very good."

"The chicken, or the friend?" I asked.

"I think they'll both cook up rather nicely," she said. "Let's get this in the oven. It's late, and your mother will kill me if I give you eye bags."

It was nice of her to pretend the bags under my eyes hadn't been obvious for weeks. What with the travel, the work, the not sleeping, and that constant knot of worry and nerves twisting in my chest.

It was past midnight when we took the chicken out of the oven. The last step was to cover it with aluminum foil and leave it to soak in its own juices for twenty minutes. As I pinched the aluminum foil into place around the roasting pan, I felt Miss Carol's eyes on me.

"Miss Carol?" I said, staying focused on my task. "You're staring. Like real bad."

She huffed a laugh. "Sorry, hun. I was just thinking. I'm proud of you, Tater Tot. You've made real strides. New friends are so good for you."

I smiled to myself.

"You said that already," I said. "The more 'Kia doesn't have friends!' comes up, the more pathetic it feels that I haven't had any."

"Oh, baby," Miss Carol said, crossing to me. "That's not what I meant *at all*."

"I know," I assured her. I laughed so she'd see I wasn't mad—

and that she had a point. "It is weird, though. I haven't had a regular friend since Zoe and Wynn and those girls ditched me."

Miss Carol busied herself clearing the dirty dishes we'd made, and I knew it was so I wouldn't see the frustration on her face. She always grew tense whenever this topic came up.

I placed myself next to her with a kitchen towel in my hand, ready to dry.

"Well," she said, "you know how I feel about your mama taking you from school in the first place. It's not what I woulda done."

I raised my eyebrows. Miss Carol didn't usually share thoughts on my parents so forthrightly. Usually I was left to intuit her opinions from body language.

"I want to know what you actually think. I'm almost an adult—I can take it."

"What I think is, I'm real glad these Campbells see your shine. And if you're making these kinds of friends now, just think how many more you'll make at college."

It was my turn to busy myself with the dishes. I spent a conspicuously long time drying every square centimeter of the small butter ramekin.

I hadn't known how to tell Miss Carol, but I'd taken Mom's Jodie Foster story to heart. My vision of the college experience was a pipe dream, and I had no interest in the celebrified version of remote learning and occasionally showing up to a class at NYU Gallatin. For better or worse, I really had wanted all or nothing. Maybe it was time to set the dream aside and make the most of the life I'd been given. It was a great one—ask anyone. It was just up to me to make something of it.

My mom always talked about the businesses I could create— book clubs, literary imprints, CBD wellness supplements. I could be a spokesperson raising and donating money to fight climate change. I could make a difference for other girls who looked like me.

"You could be a philanthropist like Angelina Jolie—without the vials of blood," Mom had said to me after a recent strategy meeting. "Or Meghan Markle, with a lifestyle brand, a podcast. You're so curious about people, you'd be *great* at going deep with A-listers—we could do an introvert's twist on *Call Her Daddy.* We could even get you a docuseries—people see you as the classy one now, and docuseries are the classy way to go . . . Don't forget, though, we'd have to keep your profile up for all of these. You should be posting every day, being seen in street-style roundups, doing talk shows, starting trends. It takes work to keep people caring about you."

Some of those options didn't even make me nauseous. I could do it, I thought; I could finally make my mother proud. Maybe it had been my loneliness holding me back all this time. But that was fixed now, and I was gaining confidence every day. Who was I to turn my back on the silver spoon my mother had worked so hard to shove into my mouth?

I took a deep breath before turning back to Miss Carol.

"I've been wondering, aactuuaallyy . . ." I stretched every syllable as if it would buy me time before I disappointed her. "Maybe college isn't in the cards for me? I just don't know where it would fit, between the show and . . . everything else. Mom signed a five-year contract for me. Maybe now's not the time for the kind of change college would bring."

Miss Carol stiffened. She pulled her hands out of the dish gloves and turned to me, leaning one arm on the counter and the other on her hip. I cleared my throat, braced for backlash.

"What are you saying right now?" She said it in almost a whisper. "You wrote such a beautiful essay. You're so close! You can't quit."

"I can still use that one down the line! If I decide to apply next year or something."

Miss Carol blinked rapidly, rubbing her forehead. She opened her mouth and then closed it again. The knot in my chest tightened like a vise. Miss Carol and I never fought.

"I'm gonna need you to explain what changed," she said.

I could've sworn there were tears in her eyes. I gulped.

"I mean . . . things are going pretty well—better than they have in a long time. Shouldn't I just accept that I was born into a really great life? I have the opportunity to start any business I want, travel the world, buy a *house*, when most people in this country aren't even close to that point. Why am I rushing to leave all this? I have a good job, a great boyfriend—maybe Lark and I could buy a place near Cass's house, or we could even all move in together. And they'll be traveling, and sooner or later they'll both be touring. I could go with, and take my time figuring out what I really wanna do with my life. I just . . . I don't think it's the time to run away from the people who make my life good, you know?"

I was overexplaining, but I couldn't stop, especially because Miss Carol looked as if I'd punched her in the face. I wanted her to know I'd thought this through.

"Also, more people know who I am than ever," I continued, hoping she'd at least understand this part. "How can I expect to walk onto any college campus and not have a thousand eyes on me, taking pictures of me in class? I'd feel like such a circus freak."

A single tear slid down Miss Carol's face. She wiped it away and locked her eyes on mine.

"*This* is not your life, Kiara," she said. I wasn't ready for her to sound *mad.*

"But . . . it is," I said weakly. "And I can't change it. Things are already getting better, so what's the big deal?"

I put my hands on both her shoulders, smiling with intent.

"Give me a little credit," I said, shaking her shoulders soft as I could. "I've already changed so much this year. That's not gonna stop just 'cause I don't enroll in classes."

"You're not hearing me," Miss Carol warned. She took my hands from her shoulders and squeezed them in her own. "This is your *time.* I see what you're doing. You can't just get one friend and a boyfriend and think that's enough to really make you happy here."

"I'm not—" I started to protest, but she raised a palm in the air.

"I'm scared for you, baby."

That stopped me in my tracks. Now I was the mad one.

"You're *scared* for me?"

"I am," she said, blunt as I'd ever heard her. "You're going to wither away here. You have a window, and you need to get out while you still can."

"That's a bit much," I scoffed. "Are you scared for Lark, too?" Miss Carol looked away, and that answered the question. Tears pricked at my eyes. "Oh, so just me. Cool."

Miss Carol took a big breath in and exhaled slowly, as if choosing her words carefully.

"I certainly wouldn't have raised either of you girls in this world," she said slowly. "But you and your sister are very different— you know that. It's not about which way is better—but Lark is *comfortable* in the spotlight. Thrives there, even. She knows how to use it to get what she wants, and she has an acceptance of the bad parts that you have never had. It helps that she has passions and talents that might make this sort of life worthwhile."

"So because I'm not talented, I should just give up a dream life and run away?"

"You have just as much to offer as any of your sisters," Miss Carol snapped. "But *this* world isn't built to get *your* type of greatness. It goes against your every sensibility, and it will suck the life from you if you let it."

There it was: I'd always known there was something wrong with me for not being able to thrive or even function like my sisters, but it was different hearing it from Miss Carol. She'd never lie to me. I blinked, and tears broke free against my will, streaming down my face. Miss Carol moved to wipe them away with a paper towel, but I stepped out of her reach, and she flinched, her face an open wound. When I spoke, my voice was as broken as I felt.

"You think I'm gonna *wither away*?"

Miss Carol's face crumpled. I'd never felt such resentment toward her.

"I'm just worried," she pleaded. "Kiara, I just want you to be happy. I don't think that's in the cards for you here. And when this all goes wrong, I won't be around to pick up the pieces."

"Everyone thinks I'm weak," I said, so quiet I was surprised she heard it. "Even you."

"*No.* That is not—"

My eyes snapped up to hers then, sharp and scared in a whole new way.

"Wait—what did you say? Before? 'I won't be around to pick up the pieces.' Why wouldn't you be here?"

The set of her mouth told me everything. I stepped back, the air sucked from my lungs, as she pushed forward, her arms wide, pulling me in tight, her mouth pressed to the top of my head.

"I'm so sorry, baby, I didn't want you to find out this way."

Everything that had been building—the cloud, the knot, the sinking feeling in my gut, the fear of another shoe dropping, that intuition that I would never be enough—it all imploded within me. Every gut feeling turned to bile, climbing up, up—until I pulled out of her grasp and lurched forward, my vomit splattering all over the expensive Calacatta tile.

Miss Carol wouldn't be around.

There's that saying that when one door closes, a window opens. That year it applied to people. Levi left us ragged and raw, and Cass arrived just in time to fill me back up again. Then there was the flip side: Jade came into my life, a snarky balm. And Miss Carol—my center of gravity—somehow, impossibly, was gone.

She'd been meaning to tell me that whole night. She told Lark the next morning, on their favorite hike through Solstice Canyon. Lark returned teary-eyed but smiling, quite a contrast to the wet scowl I couldn't wipe from my face.

"I'm happy for her," Lark told me. "Merv and Miss Carol are finally doing what's right for them."

I knew the beginning of the story: Tavia, Miss Carol and Merv's elder daughter, had given birth to a healthy baby boy in July. Their younger daughter, Yvonne, had driven in from Chicago to help deliver the baby, and Miss Carol and Merv had flown in. Ever since then they'd been traveling every few weekends to see their grandkid.

I knew they were good parents—of course I did. Miss Carol had been one of mine, after all. She'd been the very best of 'em. Still, I hadn't seen it coming. How had I not seen it coming?

Tavia was going back to law school. Day-care costs were a strain, and she had a mother who was professionally good with kids. Lark and I were somehow, impossibly, grown enough to leave. So she and Merv put in their notice and packed their bags.

Their last day at the house was December tenth. My mother handed them each healthy bonuses; my dad took Merv to a Browns game. Lark and I donned baseball caps and sunglasses to take Miss Carol for an early-morning stroll through the Huntington Botanical Gardens. We had tea. I lifted finger sandwiches to my mouth with a smile, but I felt like I was moving through molasses. It wasn't enough. Nothing we could give her would equal what she'd given us.

Our parents said their goodbyes and left Lark and me alone with Miss Carol. We stood in the driveway, wrapped around her like we were still scared kindergartners burying our faces in the folds of her skirt, as if it would keep us safe.

"C'mon, now, I'm not dying," she said, resolute. Lark had been crying all day, but this was when I broke again. A version of her *was* dying: the one who lived every day with us. The way we knew each other was terminal. Distance changes things, and so each of us was losing our core witnesses. Soon the daily details would fade away, replaced by vague *So-how've-you-been*s. A version of all of us was dying, and I couldn't stand it.

"We'll come visit you," Lark promised.

"I'm holding you to that," Miss Carol said, squeezing us both.

"I did not time this correctly," Merv said, and we all swiveled to see the front door closing behind him, his baseball hat in his hands.

"Get over here, Unc," I sobbed, and Lark and I pulled him into the pile.

"You still have me," Miss Carol said, pinching our cheeks as she settled into her seat in the back of the Escalade. "For *whatever* you need. You're mine, okay? And I'm yours."

Lark and I nodded, wordless and tear-drenched. We held each other as they drove away.

"What do we do now?" Lark asked. I sniffed. All I wanted to do was crawl into a hole and die. But today Lark needed me. She'd lost someone, too.

An image came to mind: Joe on the Campbell family's porch, watching *The Golden Girls* because it reminded him of his mom. My smile was sad, for him and for us.

"I think we go inside and watch her favorite movie."

"And after that?"

"I wish I knew."

CHAPTER TWENTY-THREE

The cloud transformed. It grew heavier, harder to carry around, more difficult to conceal.

Miss Carol called every day, but I didn't tell her. I didn't want her to think she was right. I had to prove I could handle this life. Only the weak wouldn't be happy in paradise.

I wasn't going to apply. It was decided. It was done.

I told myself grief was the reason for the cloud, that a childish inability to let go of my nanny was why I was sleeping worse than ever. I'd lost my favorite person, and it was okay to be sad. It was even okay to desperately want to disappear into a void. I didn't want to die, after all—just to stop existing for a while. If I could do that, I'd come back happy and ready to take on the world. I was sure of it.

My eye bags were worse than ever, though. I was informed that under-eye filler was the solution.

"All the girls do it eventually," Mom said casually, sprawled out on the living room floor in head-to-toe cashmere lounge-wear. We'd taken family photos in our Christmas jammies under the tree that morning, and Mom was picking which to post. She zoomed in on my tired eyes.

"It's the big-four initiation package—all the starlets do it:

jawline, nose job, under eyes, bleph. At this point surgeons should offer discounts for bundling them."

I shifted in my seat on the couch. "You think I need a nose job, too?"

My mom sighed and patted my knee. "All I'm saying is there are more effective solutions than those wimpy eye masks."

I got the injections two days after Christmas. They felt strange going in, like there was a layer of jelly right under my skin. I had to stay inside for a few days while the swelling went down, but I didn't mind that one bit; I snuck contraband Halo Top and binged *New Girl.*

Cass wouldn't stop calling and texting, checking in, but after a while I couldn't take it anymore. There was no need to be worried; I was exactly where I needed to be. I settled deeper into the couch, wrapping the blanket around myself like a straitjacket. I could disappear here, at least for a while. I could become *New Girl.*

Then the doorbell rang. No one was home but me. If someone was ringing the bell, that meant their name was on our list of accepted guests. I groaned, pausing the season two finale and hauling myself up.

"Oh—" I balked as I pulled the front door open.

Jade. Jade Campbell was at my door. How was Jade Campbell at my door?

"What's up?" she said, a smile sloping across her face. She'd taken her braids out and styled her hair in a short lavender twist-out.

"Hi," I said, nonplussed. I was in ratty sweats and a massively oversized tee advertising some competition show Sola'd hosted. I'd been in the same clothes for three days.

"Hi," Jade repeated, faux cheery. "You stink a little."

"You're at my house," I said.

"I can leave, if you want." But Jade swept past me, and I cringed. Our foyer opened into an airy white sitting room with high ceilings and a fifteen-foot Nacho Carbonell sculpture shaped like a tree. "It's beautiful. Reminds me why they beheaded Marie Antoinette."

There it was.

"I'll pass that on to the parents."

"Thanks. That's cool, though." Jade pointed at a small photograph. It was black and white, *Van and Vera with Kids in the Kitchen* by Carrie Mae Weems. I knew its name and origin because it was my favorite in the house, a photo of two Black women talking, a flurry of Black kids in hectic, everyday movement around them. It reminded me of Grandma Millie, my dad, Miss Carol, my sisters, and myself—especially on the rare occasion all of us were in the same space.

"My parents are collectors. I love that one." I chewed my lip. "But, uh—how'd you even get through the gates?"

From behind her came the sound of panting, and hurried footsteps, and suddenly my boyfriend skidded to a stop in front of me.

"Is she being nice to you?" Cass huffed, out of breath. "I told her to be nice to you."

My heart flipped at the sight of him. We hadn't seen each other in person since Christmas Eve, when we'd exchanged gifts at his place and done a lot of other things that took my mind off the cloud—if only temporarily.

I should've answered my phone. Cass looked incredible, as usual. He was in white sequined trousers and a crisp white shirt unbuttoned all the way down to his waist. Shocks of white makeup lined his eyes, curves and dots that made up a constellation. *Full.*

It was only then that I noticed Jade was dressed up, too: Her lavender hair was set off by white platform boots and a purple velvet minidress with seventies bell sleeves.

"We're here to kidnap you," Jade explained.

Cass stuck his hands into his pockets and shrugged, a sheepish smile on that perfect face. "Rapunzel, Rapunzel, let down your hair," he said. His eyes literally twinkled, and my treacherous stomach flipped, joining my heart.

"You're clearly depressed," Jade said.

"No I'm not!"

Jade's face scrunched up as she looked me up and down.

"What?" I said. "The week between Christmas and New Year's doesn't even count—everyone knows that."

"It does on New Year's Eve," Jade said. "That's when we get off the couch and become pretty again to go dance with our friends."

"It's New Year's Eve already?"

I only realized how out of it that sounded as it was leaving my mouth. My hand moved self-consciously up to my eyes; at least the swelling had gone down.

Now it made sense why no one else was here. I wondered what swanky New Year's party Lark had flitted off to; I felt a twinge that she hadn't invited me.

"This is worse than I thought," Jade said.

"I'm not really up for going out," I said. I looked down at myself. "I'm not exactly . . ." I trailed off.

Jade filled in the blanks. "Clean? Presentable?"

"A person," I corrected, not bothering to act offended.

"We'll fix that," Jade said at the same time as Cass said, "You're beautiful."

I looked between them. Cass's eyes were wide and nervous, as if I might bolt. Jade looked like she might pout if I tried any such thing. I sucked in a breath. They were here. For me. They were worried, and they'd shown up to help. My house was empty, but here they were.

"Where are we going?" I asked. Cass let out a relieved sigh.

"Well . . ." Jade said, "you're gonna need to shower."

CHAPTER TWENTY-FOUR

Ava Rackham lived at the end of a cul-de-sac in Studio City, a street that was half cozy-looking ranch houses and half tall, blocky apartment buildings. Her home was modest and cute, two stories with a vegetable garden out front. In the daytime, I imagined, it looked peacefully nondescript. Tonight, though, it was overflowing with teens from the Valley's Cabot High.

Ava, apparently, was treasurer of the drama club Jade presided over. Ava's parents spent every New Year's on a sound-healing retreat in Ojai, so it had become tradition that she host the drama club's annual New Year's Eve bash. My friends had kidnapped me to a real-life high school party. My heart was practically beating out of my chest.

"Hurry up and park," Jade barked from the back seat. "Cass, since when do you drive like an elderly woman with cataracts? Since when do you drive like Aunt Patrice?"

Cass ignored this heckling and focused on parallel parking behind an old Jeep.

"You good?" Cass asked me instead. His eyes searched the crowd in front of the house. "Is this too much? 'Cause we can just eff off and go see a movie."

"It's the perfect amount of much," I said. I was beaming—

weirdly not terrified of going inside. *My actual friends were taking me to an actual place where real teenagers hung out.*

"All right, Cinderella, try not to puke at the ball," Jade intoned.

I glanced in the rearview mirror and laughed. My eyes were wide as dinner plates. I did look like someone who might joy-vomit.

"I make no guarantees," I said.

Inside the party it was wall-to-wall bodies—a mayhem of kids our age laughing, yelling over each other, lying on top of one another, dancing, grinding, smoking, drinking, making out.

They were dressed to the New Year's nines: lots of sparkles, silver, and gold. Vintage tux jackets, jumpsuits, and velvet dresses and miniskirts made appearances on people of all gender presentations. Personally, I'd opted for a black minidress with a white button-up shirt beneath it. I'd nicked one of my dad's ties and completed the look with a pair of knee-high flat boots I was embarrassed not to know the price of. At least they didn't have a visible logo.

A few people looked our way, and instinctively the knot in my chest tightened. But then Cass squeezed my hand, and I was back Earthside. *I can do this*, I told myself. *Who cares if they recognize me? Just roll with it and act normal.*

"KITCHEN!" Jade ordered. The authority of her voice carried over the Reneé Rapp song shaking the floors. She grabbed my hand and I grabbed Cass's, and we formed a human chain as Jade pushed her way through the crowd, stepping over piles of friends and stray Solo cups. "Scuse me! That, what you're doing? Unsanitary! Scuse—thank you *very* much!"

It wasn't too long before we turned a corner and let out a collective exhale.

"The kitchen's always got air," Jade said, satisfied. "Y'all freaks stay here, I gotta deal with something."

It *was* more breathable in here. The kitchen was so narrow it was practically a repurposed hallway, with dark wood cabinets that made it feel right out of the seventies, but its size worked perfectly for us. Only a few people could fit inside, which meant peace (though not exactly quiet) as we got our bearings. The only other person here was a small girl with shaggy blond hair and a truly impressive number of freckles. She was fretting over the food spread, organizing hash browns on a large paper plate.

"Ava!" Cass cried. He'd looked tense since we'd piled into the car, but now his face broke open into a smile. The girl turned, and her eyes went wide with surprise before she broke into a matching grin. She rocketed forward and wrapped her arms around Cass, who laughed and picked her up in a spin. Ava was wearing silver lamé overalls, so the move made her look like a disco ball.

"Cassie! I didn't know you'd be here!"

"Thought I'd surprise you," Cass said. "How ya been? I miss you!"

"I got into Oberlin! Early decision!"

Cass yelled and grabbed her shoulders. Something shifted in my gut, and I realized for the first time that tonight was about so much more than me. Cass was returning to a group of people who used to be his, and I was lucky enough to witness it.

"Yooo! Ava! You been talkin' bout that place forever!"

"I know!" she squeaked. "Ugh, I can't wait—everyone there's so *queer*."

"I'm so happy for you," Cass said. His face was alight with meaning it. I suddenly felt like I was an intruder on an intimate moment. Then I felt Cass's hand on mine.

"Ava, this is my girlfriend, Kia," Cass said. "Kia, this is Ava, a buddy I'm realizing I *do not* talk to enough. Wow, am I a dick now?"

"Hey! No! You are just liiiiterally flying all over the planet living your dream. It's kinda super understandable. I promise you, when I hit med school, you are not hearing from me for many years." Cass's shoulders relaxed a little, and in that moment I knew I liked Ava. She was tiny, coming up to maybe my shoulder, and I was learning that her exclamatory greetings were the exception and not the rule. Ava had this deep but quiet voice that sounded like ASMR. Already she'd set Cass at ease; it was clear he trusted her opinion.

"Thanks for having me!" I said. "This is your party, right?"

"Oof," she said, holding her hands up. "I take no responsibility for what you may see out there. I just donate the house and hope for the best, but these people are gremlins."

I smiled, and Ava smiled back, bright, charming, and sweet. I noticed that her lower teeth were crooked. Her smile wasn't blindingly white, but more ivory or cream—not yellowed but also not the "perfect" shock of white I'd been taught was the only acceptable way. I preferred hers, I realized; her smile looked more human. It occurred to me then: If I was so charmed by Ava's teeth, maybe I didn't have to mind my own crooked incisor.

It wasn't until Ava's expression morphed from joyful to self-conscious that I realized I was staring at her with a goofy smile on my face. I blinked it off, mortified.

"You gotta forgive me," I said. I figured I should get ahead of my own awkwardness. "This is my first high school party. As a dorky homeschooled kid, I kinda have no idea what to do—I'm just happy to be here."

Ava's smile widened at this, and I hoped that meant she was as charmed by me as I was by her. Her eyes flickered between Cass and me, as if assessing the situation.

"I'm honored I could facilitate the occasion," she said. "Help yourself to the food! Someone ordered a Denny's spread that could feed an army."

"Ah, the law of nature: If theater kids can't go to Denny's, the Denny's must come to the theater kids," Cass said, tearing a shred off a pancake and tossing it into his mouth.

"Amen," Ava said. "And may the Uber driver forgive us."

I'd just grabbed a paper plate when Jade popped back in.

"Bet," Jade said to the room, as if finishing a conversation none of us had been part of. "Let's do this."

"Where were you?" I asked, my mouth already stuffed full of hash browns.

"Let's do what?" Cass added. "That sounded ominous."

"I can't help if I'm an ominous person," Jade said, impatient. "Come along, my sweet, innocent Kia."

"Now *that's* ominous," I said, swallowing the potatoes. But I followed her to the kitchen door, where Jade peered at the party beyond with an eagle eye. She pointed toward an impressive cuddle puddle of humans that started on the couch and pooled around the coffee table. Its members all massaged each other's shoulders.

"Lanky guy with the wispy beard? That's Simon. Up until last semester, he was one of the token straights who can be found in every drama club. Then last summer he had a pansexual glow-up, as you can see from the variety of beautiful sluts draped over him at this moment. The one on his left leg is Kenzie, one of my besties—also our valedictorian and lead in the musical. Ugh, it's insufferable. Oh, also: Ava's got the kinda crush on Kenzie that could fuel an exquisite but quickly canceled Netflix show."

"Hey!" Ava protested, her face turning a deep maroon. "Don't tell."

Jade lowered her voice, her expression softening. "I won't tell her. But you should. You wanna be all moony next year, you in Ohio, her taking allll that rizz to New Haven? She could come back cuffed to the next Lupita Nyong'o, and then where will you be?"

"Don't let her bully you," Cass said, patting Ava's shoulder. "Do it on your own time."

Cass had occupied himself with a perilously tall heap of Denny's scrambled eggs. Crushing his daily protein goals with party snacks. You can take the celebrity out of the glitzy Hollywood parties, but you can't stop their wonky diets.

"No," Ava said in a small voice. "She's right. I gotta do it sooner or later."

"Good," Jade said. "That's settled. Now, Kia, if I can direct your attention to the fireplace."

"To the pyros?" I asked. Gathered around the hearth was a quartet of kids in artfully torn fishnets. They were gleefully tearing bits of paper and sprinkling them into the fire with foreboding cackles.

Jade sighed. "My stagehands. It's their New Year's tradition to burn every piece of homework from the semester before. I don't scare easy, but . . . they're freaky. Then there's that guy." Jade pointed to a stocky, ripped dude with a short fade who laughed raucously in conversation with a bemused person with heavy blue eyeliner and lots of piercings. "Miles. Big ol' jock, auditioned for the fall musical after watching too much *High School Musical: The Musical: The Series*. I think at first it was an ironic thing, but then he got super into it. Now we can't shake him."

"I didn't know people actually wore letterman jackets in real life," I said in awe. "I thought that was only in teen movies."

"He *is* a teen movie," Jade intoned. She didn't make it sound like a compliment. "Let's see, who else we got . . . ?"

As Jade kept scanning the party, I felt a rush of gratitude.

"Jade, this is really nice, but you don't have to do this," I said. "Go enjoy your party, I can fend for myself."

"Aw," Jade said, pinching my cheek. "We do love character growth. Whatever you say, girl, just—get out there." She pushed the small of my back, forcing me to stumble out from the safety of the kitchen and into the chaos.

"She really lives for the drama," Cass said from beside me. "But I'm right here, boo." His hands were buried deep in his pockets, shoulders stiff and pointing toward his ears. Those eyes were on alert, scanning the room in a very different way than Jade had. I realized with a start that Cass was nervous.

"Wait . . ." I said. I pulled Cass to an unoccupied square of wall a few feet down from the kitchen. People were still leaving us alone, somehow, but we could be mobbed at any moment, so I had to get this out fast. "I've been so selfish. This is weird for you, isn't it? Being back here?"

"You're not selfish, you're *excited*," he insisted. "Which, by the way, is my favorite thing. Excited Kia could light up a whole city block."

I rolled my eyes but smiled sheepishly.

"But I want you to have a good time, too," I said, burying my head in his shoulder and tugging at one of his belt loops. He cocked a jaw and looked around the room.

"I will. I just . . ." Cass shook out his shoulders. He took a big breath in, then let it out in a sloooow exhale, like he was banishing something. "What if they don't like me anymore?"

"Who?" I asked, confused. It felt so impossible for anyone to dislike Cass. "Noah?"

"No," he said, mouth sloping with just a hint of distaste. "Noah is . . . not who I thought he was. He's not worth my time anymore." But Cass's foot was tapping nervously. I stilled it with the toe of my boot, a silent *Hey, I'm here* or *Hey, I see you.* I wanted so badly to calm him the way he so often had calmed me.

When Cass spoke again, it was barely above a whisper. I leaned in.

"I'm starting to get why so many celebs become hermits. Some days I don't want to leave my house, just in case there's a guy at freakin' In-N-Out with a long lens who makes me feel like an animal. But I don't wanna be like that here. These people knew me—but, like, what if they don't like who I am now, or think I don't like who I was when I knew them? . . . What if they don't get that there are reasons I'm nervous now, even though I never used to be?"

I studied Cass's face before I answered, taking in every curve, every angle, every crinkle of worry. I traced them with my hands. Then I kissed him.

"Listen up: We might be the biggest clowns in the Valley, but we're gonna have the time of our lives, okay? They're gonna love you. They already do."

Cass laughed. "I promise you, we are not the biggest clowns in the Valley."

"Then there ya go!" I said, fist pumping the air. "Already winnin'."

Cass took my head in his hands and kissed me. I kissed right back, not even bothering to care that our public display was drawing attention to the famous teens huddled in the corner.

"Awww, I told you," a deep voice said a few feet away. "Cass wouldn't go for that PR trash. They're in looooooove."

"YO, BRYCE!" Jade barked, suddenly right beside us. "WHAT. DID. I. SAY?"

Cass and I looked on as Jade stormed up to some six-foot-five kid whose eyes I couldn't even see because his bangs were so long. Jade grabbed Bryce by the collar and dragged him down to her eye level. The height difference was so comical that Bryce was at a ninety-degree angle. A stunned laugh escaped me.

"Tell me," Jade ordered. "What did I say?"

"Wegh—" Bryce coughed. Jade released her grip. Bryce rubbed at his windpipe. "You said to leave them alone, but—"

"That's right, *Tuba Boy*," Jade said. "And what did you do instead?"

"I play trumpet," Bryce said pitifully. Jade pulled at his collar again. "I was just defending them! They were cute!"

Cass stepped forward, planting himself between Jade and Bryce. Bryce, who, if I had to guess, was a member of the pit band.

"Jesus, Jade, leave him alone," Cass said. "Nice to see ya, Bryce."

"Whassup, Cass? Missed ya, bro," Bryce said, his eyes still wide. "And, uh, sorry."

"No apologies necessary, man." Cass clapped Bryce on the back, and the color slowly returned to the poor boy's face. "You were just pointing out the obvious."

"Whatever." Jade rolled her eyes and walked away.

I figured it was now or never to start being social. This kid was too scared of Jade to do any damage, so he seemed a safe place to start. I stuck out my hand.

"Hi! I'm Kia."

The corners of Bryce's mouth tweaked in what looked like baffled fear, but he shook my hand. I'd take it.

"Nice to meet ya," Bryce said. He nodded in the direction of the TV area. "We were just 'bout to tear up some *Mario Kart.* Wanna play?"

"Heck yeah!" I said. Cass snickered.

Bryce's long legs had already carried him across the room to a couch. Cass snaked an arm around my shoulder and steered me that way.

"What were you laughing at?" I asked.

Cass smiled. "Are you gonna shake everyone's hand?"

"Should I not?" I asked, confused. Cass laughed again, those eyes sparkling brighter than ever. Then he hauled me in for another kiss, deep and perfect.

"Ignore me," he said. "I love you."

"YES! YES! YES! GOGOGO! AAAAHHHHHHHH!!!!"

I threw down my controller and stood, still screaming, my arms in the air. I had sailed over the finish line to victory yet again, a boastful Wario with Mr. Scooty as my steed. Bryce dropped his controller with a frustrated "Oh, come on!"

"YOU CRUSHED THAT, FAMOUS!" Miles yelled. The jock Jade had pointed out before had gravitated our way shortly after Bryce, the pyros, and I started playing. He'd fast grown into my biggest fan. It had nothing to do with my family and everything to do with the fact that I happened to be freakishly good at *Mario Kart.*

"That's very kind, Miles," I said, giving him a bow. "Thank you for your sportsmanship."

"I know talent when I see it," he said, a look of genuine awe on his face. "You da king, Greer. Respect."

I was out of breath. I plopped back next to Cass, who was lounging with his legs slung over the arms of the couch. He handed back my second canned cocktail of the night.

"I may suck at bowling, but I have played a *lot* of *Mario* in my day." I shot an apologetic look at Bryce and the pyros. "Sorry if I got intense."

"Nah, it was cool," said one of the pyros, a goth-looking girl named Nina. "I didn't even know some of those tricks existed."

"Yeah, can you show me how to do that thing with the glider?" asked another, a girl named Sheridan, who had slicked-back hair and a septum piercing.

I smiled and picked up my controller again. Finally I could make use of the many, many hours Lark and I had spent playing every single *Mario* game—on the plane, in between lighting set-ups, visiting Dad on set.

Bodies swayed around us, dancing and chatting, and though I felt the occasional glance my way, I didn't feel like a spectacle. From what I'd gleaned, Jade had threatened everyone with death if they dared single us out or snap a nonconsensual photo. Even so, I was surprised everyone seemed to be taking our presence in stride.

After a while I noticed a stream of bodies heading out the front door. The air in the room had shifted—the chatter growing faster, more urgent.

"Where are they going?" I asked. Miles's head whipped around.

"YO, YES!" he yelled, jumping up and promptly abandoning us.

I looked toward Nina, who rolled her eyes, and Sheridan, who had this chaotic look of excitement on her face.

"It happens every year," Sheridan said. "Especially when people are drinking."

"They do cartwheels in the street," Nina said. She looked long-suffering but resigned. "At least until someone takes out a car window. It was mine last year."

Cass stood, towering above my seat on the floor.

"Coming?" he asked, extending his hand. "What's more high school than this?"

I chugged a White Claw on the way out. I was definitely drunk for real now. I felt *flowy*—relaxed, but buzzing and wobbly. I held on to Cass's biceps for stability.

Teens filled every square foot of Ava's front yard. I craned my head to see if they were steering clear of my favorite part, but there were indeed people treading on heads of lettuce.

"Hey!" I yelled. "Don't mess up the garden!"

"Thanks for looking out," said a voice behind me. Ava was there. "I worked hard on those snap peas."

"So *who* all's doing cartwheels?" I asked. In answer Cass just nodded in the direction of the road, where a variety of shoes were flying through the air.

I peered around the tall person blocking my view. The first legs I ID'd were Miles's. Instead of doing cartwheels, he was doing full front flips down the street. I yelled out, genuinely impressed. Simon, Kenzie, and some kids I didn't recognize were also out there. Then my eyes caught on a purple dress and a pair of white platform boots I recognized. I *gasped.*

"Ohmygod! JADE!" I clapped my hand to my mouth.

"Ten years of gymnastics," Cass said, a gleam of pride in his eyes.

Jade twisted and turned through the air, graceful and surprising. After one such turn she righted herself, straightening her dress, and my drunk recognized her drunk. She had a wide crooked grin and a haze in her eyes that helped me understand how such an ordered, stern person wound up in such a place. Still, I couldn't help but let out a bewildered laugh.

"YES, JADE! KILLING IT!"

Jade and Kenzie hopped back into action at the same time, delivering a set of five perfect synchronized cartwheels landed seamlessly. The crowd roared in approval. I laughed so hard, I fell back into Cass. His arm crossed over to hold me, chest rising and falling with the frenetic rhythm of his own laughter.

"I can't believe this is happening," I blurted to no one. I'd been to Hollywood parties way more wild than this, but New Year's Eve at Ava Rackham's was different. These were people who went to school together, who bore witness to each other's most embarrassing moments. They'd graduate together, some in only a few months, and they'd always have those four years.

I let myself wonder, just for a second, where the friends I'd made in school were on a night like this. I didn't follow them on socials anymore; the reminders of the life I was missing were too painful. I wondered who they'd become when I wasn't looking.

"That was so hot," Ava squeaked next to me. She was looking at Kenzie with the most obvious heart eyes I'd ever seen. "I'm losing my mind. Am I still here? Or did I evaporate?"

"You're still here, technically," I said. "How long have you had a crush on her?"

"Three years," Ava breathed. "Now I'm running out of time."

I reached out and squeezed her shoulder, sympathetic.

"You've got this, Ave," Cass said. "You've just gotta nut up and do it."

"You think so? 'Cause if I ask her out and she says no, I will officially dissolve into a puddle of broken dreams."

"Being a puddle wouldn't be too bad," I offered. "You could be a home to, like, tadpoles and other creatures. So if that's how you're thinking about it, the worst-case scenario's not awful."

Ava looked at me, brows furrowed, and for a second I worried I'd messed up. But then she laughed. And kept laughing.

"Thank you, Kia. That's a delightful way of looking at it."

I wanted to ask her more—about life, her classes, her college plans—but Cass stiffened next to me. I followed his gaze across the cul-de-sac—to where Noah stood in the orangey glow of a streetlight.

Cass's first love, his big betrayer, the guy with floppy green hair whose eyes had followed Cass around Mel's Drive-In that first night. Noah, whose loose lips had forced Cass to come out to the public before he'd planned. My stomach lurched, and not from the alcohol. I squeezed Cass's hand to stop myself from storming over.

Tonight I could finally see just how beautiful Noah was. With those impossibly long eyelashes and high cheekbones, he might as well have been a teen dream, too.

"You okay?" Ava asked. Cass swallowed, lips pursed. Jade strode toward us and pulled us back into the living room. It was quieter now, with most of the party still outside.

"That bitch," she said. "I was hoping he wouldn't come tonight."

"It's fine, you guys," Cass said. "It was bound to happen. I can't avoid him forever."

"Sure you can." Jade's tone had become threatening. Out the window we could see Noah growing closer. I grabbed a handful of Jade's dress to pull her back.

"Did you just scruff me like a cat?!" She turned to me, disarmed.

I didn't have time to respond before Noah was there, right in front of us. He gave me a dismissive once-over before turning to Cass and Jade.

"Jade, you're not gonna attack me," Noah said. "You're a nonviolent softy—I know you."

"Wanna bet?" she asked, teeth bared.

"Noah." Cass's voice was measured, careful. "It's good to see you."

"You too," Noah said. "Maybe now we can finally talk."

Cass's jaw clenched. He blinked rapidly—angry, no doubt, at the refusal to acknowledge that he had been reaching out for *months*, desperate to make amends and stop the gossip.

"*Finally*? I've—I've been . . ."

"Don't get riled." Noah stepped into Cass's space and placed a hand on his biceps, squeezing the same spot I'd held for stability only a few minutes prior. "Let's just talk. It's time."

A protective fire lit inside me. Jade shot me a look: *Are you gonna tackle him, or am I?*

Cass dropped my hand as Noah steered him deeper into the house.

"I'll be right back," he assured me. I smiled so he'd know I wasn't worried.

Cass and Noah fell in love playing Sky and Nathan in the school production of *Guys and Dolls*. They'd been each other's first time—first love, and then first heartbreak. You could see it now, even across the room, in their body language: taut, brittle, but overflowing with backstory.

I was a little worried. It wasn't jealousy, at least I didn't think. But my head was spinning, and I was embarrassed, suddenly, to be so drunk and out of sorts.

"So, Kia, you thinkin' 'bout college?"

I whipped my head around. Jade had gone to intimidate Noah's friends, but Ava and Kenzie stuck near me. They'd been talking about . . . well, I hadn't been paying attention. But now they were looking at me, expecting an answer.

"Sorry, what?"

Ava shot me a sympathetic smile. Kenzie leaned in and patted my shoulder.

"We're not gonna focus on that mess over there," Kenzie declared. "Cass has got this—Noah's always been a hothead."

I sighed, forcing myself not to look to where Noah and Cass were huddled. There was nothing I could do right now that would help him.

"You're right," I said, and shook my shoulders as if to shake the nerves away. "What did you ask about? College? You're going where again, Ava?"

"Oberlin!" She beamed. "It's in the middle of, like, cornfield Ohio, but the school's super famous for its social activism and being a safe haven for queer kids."

Kenzie watched Ava talk with the same heart eyes Ava'd been using on her outside. If these two didn't kiss by the end of the night, there was something seriously wrong with the universe.

"Sounds rad," I said. "And, Kenzie, did I hear someone say you're going to Yale?"

Kenzie did a smooth-as-hell dance spin, a cocky smirk on her face. "That I am."

Then her demeanor changed to something closer to the gentle nerdiness Ava and I seemed to share. She plopped onto the couch, pulling her legs underneath her.

"Ugh, those *libraries*," she gushed. "I picture myself in a cardigan with elbow patches, glasses sliding down my nose—even though I don't wear glasses—standing in the rare books section, carefully turning parchment pages and learning from ye great thespians of old."

"This might not be the fun fact to share right now," Ava said, "but—did you know parchment wasn't paper? It was made out of skin."

"You're kidding me," Kenzie deadpanned.

"What?" I breathed, awestruck. "I didn't know that!"

Ava's face dropped, looking between us. "It's animal skin, if that helps! Sorry. I spend way too much time in Wikipedia k-holes."

"So do I!" I said, breaking into the widest, goofiest smile. "That and TikTok."

"Prove it," Kenzie said, an ironic smirk sloping across her face. "Let's play a game. Everyone give me your best fun facts."

"Oh god, *best*? I'd have to think about that," I said, wide-eyed from feeling *seen*.

"Then first one that comes to mind," Kenzie countered. "Go. Off the top of your head."

"Do you know the origin of the ice cream cone?" It was all I could think of.

"Please enlighten us," Kenzie said, leaning in.

"Well," I started, "back in the day, ice cream vendors would sell homemade ice cream all over the place—at fairs, on the streets—and they'd serve it in these shot-glass-lookin' glass cups called penny licks. People would slurp down the ice cream and give the cup back, and the vendor would just fill it with more ice cream and hand it to the next guy."

"Oh no . . ." Ava groaned, her face contorting into a grimace. "I know where this is going."

"Yeaaaah, I might just know depressing facts," I admitted, embarrassed. "I'll stop there."

"Don't you dare," Kenzie laughed.

"Let's just say a lot of ice-cream-loving Victorian children died," I said. "Cholera, tuberculosis—y'know, stuff like that. They even found sewage bits in the cups because people were rinsing them in river water to clean them. Anyway, penny licks were outlawed. Some guy invented crispy wafer cones to eat ice cream in instead, and that's what we use to this day."

I was worried I had indeed gone too gross with my offering. But then Kenzie laughed again.

"This century may be an unrelenting garbage fire," she wheezed between laughs, "but hey, at least *that's* not one of our problems."

"A lot less diarrhea these days," Ava said, chuckling. "I, for one, am grateful."

"Do I wanna know what I just walked into?" Jade asked, coming to perch on the couch. I opened my mouth to explain, but raised voices across the room pulled our attention.

"If you were serious about any of this, you wouldn'ta brought your sorry excuse for a PR 'girlfriend'!"

I whipped around in time to see Noah's less-than-kind use of air quotes.

"Don't talk about her like that," Cass warned, voice serious. "She has nothing to do with what happened between you and me. I'm just trying to apologize for my part in it."

"You can't go anywhere these days without swingin' your fame around the room, can you?" Noah's mouth twisted, sour. "Boy, you picked wrong. She'll keep your name in the press for a few more days, tops. You shoulda fucked her little sister instead."

Jade jumped to her feet, but I wrapped an arm around her waist to hold her back. She squirmed in my grasp. Cass took a step toward Noah, his voice low and severe.

"Sober up, sit down, and shut your mouth right now."

Noah's smile was mocking. Then my vision was overtaken by a blur of space buns, and suddenly Kenzie was between them, getting right up in Noah's face.

"Bitch, you do not know that girl over there, so why is her name in your mouth?" Kenzie spat. "You've had a pretty hard time minding your own business this year, so let me not mind mine: You've been nothing but jealous and manipulative since Cass blew up. It's *gross*. You know he wasn't hiding you—he was *protecting* you."

I let the alcohol urge my feet forward, and then I stood in front of Noah, too. My voice shook, but I was doing it.

"And instead of protecting Cass, you did what? Oh yeah! You told borderline lies that forced someone to come out before they'd planned to. That's pretty shitty, if you ask me. But who am I?" I shrugged and took a step back. "Just a sorry excuse for a PR girlfriend."

Cass pulled away from Noah, grasping my hand like a lifeline.

"Our conversation is over," Cass said. "If you ever want to talk for real, you know where to find me. If you post even a single lie, though, you will be hearing from my lawyers."

"They wouldn't let me beat you up," Jade said from behind me. "But just know I still gladly would."

"Y'all need to chill," Noah sneered. "It's just ex mess—it's no big deal."

I heard a sigh behind me and saw that Ava had joined us, arms crossed.

"I think it's time you leave, Noah," she said.

"Ave, you serious?" Noah protested. "Come on!"

"There's a strict no-bully clause in the bylaws," she said. "You broke it tonight. We can talk it out when school's back."

"That is so hot," I heard Kenzie whisper next to me.

With Noah gone, Cass hugged me from behind, burying his face in my shoulder.

"You're my hero," he said. He shot a sad smile at Ava. "You too."

"This house suffers no dicks," Ava said.

We filtered back into the kitchen. My vision was swimming—apparently getting undrunk wasn't as simple as taking a stand. I chugged water while Ava distracted Cass with questions about his world tour. It worked; Cass always got excited talking about the stops he got to make in places like Amsterdam, Paris, and Dublin. I listened as he downloaded Ava on the grueling rehearsal schedule that would kick into gear next week.

My head was so *full*—of *Mario Kart*, cartwheels, Denny's, the sound of a crowd cheering, the sight of Miles tumbling through the air. The room swayed.

"I don't know how much time we'll have during the days to sneak around, but I've got lists of things I wanna see," Cass said. There was a pause, then: "Kia? You okay?"

I hadn't noticed they were both looking my way.

"Nooo," I said. "You shouldn't be asking me that. I should be asking you!"

"Then we'll ask each other," Cass said. "It can be both."

"Are *you* okay?" I pressed.

Cass sighed. "I'm . . ." he started, tugging at his earlobe. "I think I'm discombobulated."

His smile seemed genuine now.

"Well, then you've come to an expert," I said.

"Two experts," Ava said.

"Ava!" I exclaimed. "You shouldn't worry about Kenzie. She *simps* for you."

"Don't lie to me," Ava breathed, her eyes wide.

"Would never," I promised. I was relieved to be done talking about Noah, if only because anger had clouded my vision. We'd been having such a dream night until he showed up.

Cass pulled me closer, reading something on my face.

"The night still young," he said. "What next?"

It was at that moment that the music cut off suddenly. Bad Bunny was replaced with a much more . . . twinkly melody. It sounded floaty—and then it was joined by vocals that were very much live. Cass's mouth fell open. I looked between Ava and Cass, confused.

"One day more . . . Another day, another destiny . . ."

"It's that time already?" Cass asked, a hushed awe to his voice.

"It always comes sooner than expected," Ava said as Cass tugged me to the edge of the kitchen, where kids had come back in from the outside. It wasn't just one person singing: It was everyone.

"I did not live until todaaaaay—"

"It's drama club tradition going into a new year," Ava explained. Cass was practically buzzing next to me, and such raw, real excitement brought a goofy grin to my face.

"I know it's corny," he said, "but . . ."

A beautiful alto voice rang out: *"One more day all on my owwwwn."* I found the singer in the crowd—it was Kenzie.

"I mean, yeah, but I'm kinda obsessed," I said. The crowd was moving, this time to the back of the house—and then out the back door. "People are leaving again?"

"Pool," Cass said in explanation. He held both his hands behind his back, and I grabbed on for dear life, holding tight as we streamed through and with the bodies on their way to the backyard. People kept clapping Cass on the shoulders, urging him to join in.

"What are you doing?!" I yelled. "You said you didn't want to hide!"

Cass bit his lip, and for a second I thought he wouldn't do it—that fame had made him too afraid. But as we pushed through the sliding back door, Cass stepped forward and let that gorgeous voice fly over the gathered bodies.

"ONE MORE DAY BEFORE THE STORM!"

The crowd went wild. Kenzie, Simon, Miles, and several kids I didn't know all joined in, their voices layering and trading with Cass's: *"Do I follow where she goes?"*

"AT THE BARRICADES OF FREEDOM—" *"Shall I join my*

*brothers there?" "WHEN OUR RANKS BEGIN TO FORM—" "Do
I stay, and do I daaare?" "WILL YOU TAKE YOUR PLACE WITH
ME-EE-EEEE?" "THE TIME! IS NOW! THE DAY! IS HEEERE!"*

It was the most gloriously corny, intensely nerdy thing I'd ever
seen, and also one of the most baldly beautiful. I didn't know the
song well enough to sing along, but even just being there felt like
I was part of some organism larger than myself.

Everyone had a part. Mine was to cheer, yell, and laugh with
every ounce of raucous joy coursing through my body. My every
cell felt alive.

The song was reaching its climax as Cass turned back and
found me in the crowd.

"Put your phone on that chair," he said.

"What?!"

"Trust me!"

So I did it, and so did he, and it was good that we did, because
as the final notes rang out, someone screamed "MIDNIIIIGHT!"
I looked over just in time to see it was Bryce, but then the living
organism of the crowd surged, and Cass was beaming ear to ear,
guiding me, and everybody in the crowd started jumping into the
pool. I let out a high-pitched scream to the stars as I catapulted
forward. Cool and quick, the water felt like a baptism—into what,
I had no idea. A new moment? A new year? A new life?

Run toward this, I dared to think.

This should be your life, too, I dared to dream.

Jade was splashing Miles, who was riding Simon's shoulders. And Ava and Kenzie were making out in the shallows!
Hands in hair, arms around waists, enveloped so fully in each
other. I laughed, triumphant—and then I swam for the deep
end. I plunged under, my flailing limbs losing my grip on Cass,

but I kicked up, up, up. And it was all okay, because I broke through the water's surface and gasped in the cold night air, and I looked over and Cass was right there with me. At the sight of each other, we laughed and we screamed into the brand-new night.

CHAPTER TWENTY-FIVE

I spent the rest of the night screaming show tunes with Jade and Cass in Cass's tree house. We housed leftover pizza and Face-Timed Ava to strategize a perfect first date with Kenzie. I fought the racing thrum of my heart, the part of me reaching blind panic. I hadn't submitted my college applications. Maybe it had all been a pipe dream, but why had I been so quick to give it up? I caved at the first sign of resistance. And now I would always be a stranger to nights like these.

I fell asleep in the crook of Cass's chest as he whispered in my ear: *"You were in your element tonight. The world is yours to take."* I let myself believe the lie, knowing that by morning it would all have disappeared like so much smoke.

New Year's Day was bright on my little mountain. The gates shut behind me, and a flood of shame hit me square in the ankles.

Don't be delusional, the intrusive thought whispered. *This is your life. Be grateful.*

My heart beat fast again as I pushed through the front door. I took a deliberate breath *in, in, in, in.* I held it for seven seconds, then exhaled *out, out, out, out, out, out, out, out.*

Voices echoed from the direction of the gym. Lark, it sounded like, and Mom. I tucked myself around a corner. Mom was less than strict about curfews, but I didn't need her seeing me in my current state.

"*Please* just talk to him about it?" Lark pleaded. Her voice was high, tight, and desperate. "Explain the market data Simms showed me—and that I *want* it, it's not just them pushing me—"

"Baby," our mom interrupted, "I'll try. But *I'm* still not fully convinced, and your father will definitely think you're too young."

"Sola started when she was eighteen!" Lark argued. "I can't wait till then. Do you have any idea how much it'll help the album launch? I can't compete with these other pop girls, Mommy—I'm a twig compared to them."

I inched closer, my heart hammering for a different reason now.

"Honey . . ." Even without seeing my mom, I could picture her: eyes closed, rubbing her temples, running this through the algorithm in her head that determined what was best for the Greer empire. Lark must have seen a crack in her resolve, because she kept going.

"Sola booked Victoria's Secret the second she had curves! You know it's just as crucial in music—they want you to look innocent, but if you look *too* innocent, you're dead. I have to show them I can be sexy, too—it'll give me staying power."

The knot in my chest was malignant, radiating nausea through me.

"I'll talk to him," Mom said. "I make no guarantees. But I get it. Okay?"

"*Ohmygodohmygodthankyou!*" Lark gushed. Her voice was muffled; I could perfectly picture her launching herself into our mother's arms.

"I'm running late," Mom said. "I've got breakfast with Gwynnie in thirty. Talk later, 'kay?"

And she was gone: out the front door with no idea I'd over-heard her devil's bargain with Lark. I stepped out from the hall-way, into Lark's view. She was texting, but when she saw me. the triumphant grin wilted off her face.

"What was all that about?" I asked.

"Where have you been?!" she countered, ignoring the ques-tion. She looked mad. "You totally ditched me last night!"

I blinked. That was the last thing I'd expected out of her mouth.

"Uh, *you* ditched *me*. You left first, remember?"

"Yeah, but just to Nobu with Jonny and Austin and some of the guys." She had the nerve to be indignant. "It was an early din-ner! I brought back dessert! I thought we were gonna ring in the new year with a *New Girl* binge!"

I didn't have room in my head for whatever she was saying, so I waved it away. "You didn't tell me that! There was no one here, so I went out with Jade and Cass."

"Out where?" Lark asked, pouting now.

I shrugged. "Some high school New Year's party. It was nerdy, mostly *Mario Kart* and show tunes—you wouldn't have liked it."

"*What?!*" Lark whined. "I can't believe you didn't invite me—that's so mean."

"*I. Thought. You'd. Ditched. Me,*" I said, emphasizing every word. "Wouldn't be the first time."

"What's that supposed to mean?"

"I barely see you anymore! Ever since you got your big fancy record deal, it's like you're too busy and important for me."

"That is not true," Lark said, stepping back like I'd slapped her.

"I still tell you everything about my life!" I said. "You don't tell me anything!"

"THAT'S NOT TRUE!"

"Then what was that convo with Mom about?"

That shut her up. Lark looked anywhere but at me. I crossed my arms.

"C'mon," I said, "you wanna stay close—tell me."

"It's not a big deal," she said, shrugging, her hands in the air. "I've been talking to Mom about getting some work done."

My blood ran cold.

"What kinda surgery?" I asked.

"A BBL, if you must know." She cleared her throat. "And my boobs. I think Mom's close to saying yes—she just needs to convince Dad."

I recoiled. "Dad's not gonna say yes to that."

I said it more as manifestation than belief. Historically Dad followed Mom's lead. I had to hope there was a line.

"Well, he should," Lark said. I recognized the look on her face from when she was little and decided we were done playing video games because she wasn't winning anymore. She'd definitely inherited the Melora Greer stubbornness. "It's my body, my choice."

"That phrase doesn't apply to sixteen-year-olds who want plastic surgery," I spat.

"As if you didn't get new filler *last week*."

"Maybe I shouldn't have! Maybe I looked fine before!" I stopped yelling and took a breath. I needed her to hear me. "You know it's different, Lala. This is *surgery. Painful* surgery."

Lark cocked her jaw and looked past me.

"Some of us have jobs we love, okay? I'm trying to be the best. That takes *work* and, yes, sometimes *pain.* You won't find a pop star worth her salt who hasn't gone under the knife, especially a girl one. It's been hard enough to get anyone to see past me being the *Growin' Up Greer* girl. I'm not gonna blow my one shot. I won't."

The knot in my chest twisted. My little sister, my beautiful, talented, undeniable little sister. I wasn't the only one in the family who spent her days afraid.

I took a step forward, but Lark held up her hands to stop me.

"It's not my fault you hate your life," she snapped. "I don't hate mine."

I flinched. "What are you talking about?"

"I have a dream, and I'm going after it—there's *nothing* stopping you from doing the same. Except all you do is sit here, rotting and resenting us, half-assing the show and feeling sorry for yourself because your life in this *castle* isn't *exactly* how you want it. Who does that help?! *No one!* You're weak as hell for that, Kia. And no one can fix it but you."

I blinked, stunned tears filling my eyes. I pulled in a deliberate gulp of air—*in, in, in, in.* Then I took a step to the side and walked around my sister and out of the room.

CHAPTER TWENTY-SIX

More often than not that winter, I woke with a groan in my throat, the knot twisting at the thought of another day. The cloud would descend. I was too small, weak, and worthless to have much fight in me. Lark and I were barely talking. I wasn't returning Miss Carol's calls.

I grew well and truly tired of myself. So I did the only thing I could think of: I finally met Amanda Roth. Because maybe Lark was right; maybe it was up to me to fix whatever I had broken inside.

It turned out Amanda was from Pasadena. She'd spent the holidays with her family and was staying with them as she got ready to write her next novel. She was a bit confused as to why I was asking for a college interview after the Vassar deadline had passed, but she still agreed to it.

She suggested we meet at a coffee shop in Hollywood. I countered by offering to treat her to breakfast at the Chateau Marmont. It was mortifyingly ostentatious, but the hotel restaurant had a no-photos policy, and everyone there would just assume I was taking a business meeting. And so it happened, at last, on a Friday in February. I'd carved out the slot in my schedule by going behind my mother's back to cancel an eyebrow appointment. Melora would just have to deal with a couple stray hairs.

I'd brought Joe, though. More and more I was practicing being out in the world without a tether—the New Year's party, dates with Cass, runs to the grocery store, drives down the hill to CVS. But Joe was a comfort, especially since I didn't know this Amanda woman at all.

She arrived four minutes late with her curly red hair still wet from the shower, her *All Things Considered* tote bag overflowing. She looked to be in her midthirties, and she had a no-nonsense attitude that intimidated and inspired me in equal measure.

"So, Kiara, what is this very unconventional meeting about?"

I laughed, nervous. "Can I be honest?" I asked. "And can I trust that nothing said here will be passed on to the press or Deuxmoi, or even put on Instagram?"

"I have the NDA," Joe grunted from the next table over, moving to pull something from his inside pocket.

Amanda's eyebrows shot up. "That's still a thing?" She chuckled. "I thought the Me Too movement killed those."

"It won't be necessary," I told Joe before turning back to Amanda. "People have leaked so many sensitive things about my family. I'm just asking you to keep our convo to yourself."

"I can do that," Amanda said, her eyebrows curving downward in sympathy now. "My lips are zipped unless you do something that literally puts me in danger. Sound fair?"

I nodded. "I promise not to stab you. Not that that was on the table before, or anything!"

That made Amanda laugh. I let out a relieved breath I hadn't realized I'd been holding in.

We talked over coffee and French toast. I explained that because of the idiosyncrasies of my life in Hollywood, I'd chickened out of submitting my college apps and was now regretting it. I'd talked to Mr. Hillis about his own college experiences a lot, but he'd gone to a busy city college. I was curious what it was like going to school somewhere that felt like its own bubble. It sounded appealing to me, but it also made me wary.

"I was hoping I could pick your brain about what college might look like for someone like me," I explained. Amanda took a sip of her latte before answering.

"Kia . . . as you know, I can't speak to the specifics of your situation," she said. "There aren't many out there who can. But from what Tom—Mr. Hillis—told me in his first email about you, you and I share some interests. History, anthropology, creative writing, gender studies . . ." I nodded along, encouraging and eager. "So why don't I tell you about my college experience, and from there we'll branch off and try to imagine yours?"

Amanda Roth had been a student in the Vassar class of 2011. She'd started as a sociology major but switched to women's, feminist, and queer studies by the end of her sophomore year because she clicked more with the classes and professors. She worked a job making smoothies at an on-campus café, joined an a cappella group, and eventually became an editor at the school's newspaper. Her social life included dorm parties with friends and house parties hosted by strangers, late nights studying at the campus library, and piles of people who'd gather to watch every new episode of *Sherlock*.

"That might be a little dated." She chuckled. "I was also a member of a Harry Potter club, and I made a number of my current best friends through that. Consider that a lesson in the connections that can be made from student activities."

I ate up every detail. My head swam listening to her talk.

"I don't know if any of this was helpful, Kia, but just know that I loved college," Amanda said after we'd been talking for a while. "Some people aren't ready for it right after high school, and that's okay; there's this big pressure to go, but I had a few buddies who really needed to take time to figure themselves out."

"You didn't, though?" I asked. "Why was that, do you think?"

She pulled a face and looked into the middle distance, contemplating the question.

"I was the kind of kid who really benefited from being pushed out of the nest," she finally answered. "I was shy in high school, but my first week at Vassar I had real, interesting conversations with every single girl on my hall. We didn't all stay close, but we watched out for each other freshman year. Being on a small campus made it feel like we were a part of something together. We got to create our own universe. For me . . . I think that helped me find my path."

Tears filled my eyes, and I turned my head to hide it.

"Sorry," I said, wiping my face. "This is so embarrassing."

"That's okay," she said softly. "This stays here, remember? So tell me: What's up?"

"I just—" I had to stop to gather myself. I took a breath, steadying my voice. "Everything you said sounds really great. But . . ."

"But?" she egged me on.

"But stalkers? Most of the time I travel with a literal armed guard." I pointed over my shoulder at Joe, who was at the next table pretending to read a book. "I think I could live with people looking at me weird in class, asking me weird questions—that's my life anyway. But how do I build a different kind of life without quite literally putting myself in danger?"

Amanda sat back in her seat, her head tilted slightly to the side. She looked stumped.

"I—dude, I really wish I had an answer for you there," she said. "I can't imagine what it's like dealing with something like that, especially at your age."

I rushed to add: "Don't get me wrong—I know how privileged my life is. I just . . ."

Amanda placed a hand on top of mine.

"You just told me you're afraid you'll get *stalked and die* at school. You don't have to caveat that with the privilege thing—that's pretty universally sucky."

Behind me Joe cleared his throat. I ignored it at first, not thinking it was aimed at us—but then he did it again. I turned.

"What's up, Joe?"

I got the impression he was weighing what he was allowed to say.

"There are ways," Joe said with his usual gruff simplicity. I cocked my head.

"Ways to what?" I asked, confused.

"Why don't you join us?" Amanda offered, gesturing to an empty seat between me and her. "I'm sorry, I didn't catch your name before."

"Joe," he said. He held out his hand, and Amanda shook it. "Joseph D'Amiano, Greer security since 2017."

"Nice to meet you, Joseph," Amanda said. She didn't immediately let go of Joe's hand, and for a moment I felt like the third wheel at the table.

Joe looked back at me as if waiting for permission. I nodded, and he sat in the empty chair between us.

"I am trained not to interfere," Joe said, "but there are things you should know, if you want what you're talking about. You have options."

Joe looked between me and Amanda. Amanda smiled and held up two hands.

"Don't mind me, I'm just curious," she said.

Joe smiled shyly. "Kia, it's important that you remember how many celebrities aren't walking around with security twenty-four seven," he said evenly. "Taylor Swift, Beyoncé? Yeah, they probably have 'em all the time, or close to it, because the threat level against them is beyond what even ninety-nine percent of A-listers have to deal with. But they're the exception, not the rule."

"But our family does have security on retainer always," I pointed out. "So doesn't that mean we need it?"

Joe nodded, conceding the point. "Your mother had good reason for putting that into place. She was scared after the incident when you were a kid. And there have been a few threats since, as you know." I nodded. Nothing quite so bad as the man who'd broken in and slept in our empty beds, but I'd assumed that was thanks to our security.

"Security is a game of risk and reward," Joe continued. He leaned forward with his elbows on the table, talking with his hands as if planning the moves in a football game. "Plenty of clients only use teams like mine for specific events. A lot of celebs don't want to lose the autonomy they feel being out in the world alone."

"So you don't think Kia would be in danger, say, walking around a college campus?" Amanda asked, vocalizing the question racing through my mind.

"There's always a risk," Joe said carefully. He held my gaze as he continued. "But there's a risk when you're *anyone*. We should teach every kid, especially every girl, the basics of street smarts and self-awareness as they go off to school. Anyone can pick up a stalker."

"But what about my situation?" I asked, impatient. "It's not exactly normal—is there any way for me to be safe out there?"

"The public's awareness of you has definitely increased this year, which certainly doesn't help things," Joe said, and the knot tightened. I looked at my hands, thinking of the public dates, cover stories, brand collabs. I'd plastered my face across the world, and now I wanted to turn around and ask everyone to pretend they didn't know who I was. They'd crucify me. "*But* there are ways to minimize your risk," Joe continued. My eyes snapped back to his, an irrational hope kindling in my heart.

"Tell me." Amanda leaned in. The corner of Joe's lips turned up.

"Well, first off, as a celebrity, your risk decreases exponentially when you're not on social media," he said. "I ain't blaming the ones who post all the time, but socials can make crazy fans think you're sending coded messages, and posting your routines or location in real time can tell them exactly where to find you."

"*Creepy.*" Amanda cringed.

"I don't care about social media," I said. "I'll get off it tomorrow if I have to. But what are you saying? Are you saying I'd be fine at school?"

"*Everything* is a risk," Joe repeated. "JFK was always sneaking out of the White House to meet Marilyn Monroe—*that* was a risk. But it was one he thought was worth it."

I laughed at the analogy. "Joe!" I exclaimed. "Can I go to college or not?!"

Joe raised his hands in surrender. "All I can do is explain your options. You can keep us on through school, but we'd cramp your style at parties. One of us also costs about twenty thousand dollars a month."

Amanda and I gasped in unison. I'd never known the numbers.

"But if you really wanna know, Kia? I don't think you need it."

"You don't?" I breathed.

"You can be smart about your safety without giving up your life," he said. "I can work with you to build protocols, habits, that can keep you safe out there. I can help you, for free, whenever you want. You deserve a life."

My heart swelled uncontainably. I lunged a hug on him and squeezed tight. He patted me on the back. When I pulled away, I saw Amanda's eyes were shiny with tears.

"What a man," she breathed. Joe blushed bright pink.

Oh, It's On: Destiny Greer to Host *SNL* for the First Time

Litty.com | Top Stories | Celebrity Vertical

By Alexis Borges

Remember when Destiny Aaliyah Greer was just some girl on TV who was pretty likely to get a DUI or try to hit you over the head with her purse? Those days are long gone, and it's about time we accepted it. The former rabble-rouser is a serious actress these days, haven't you heard? As we type this, she's off in Nova Scotia shooting the adaptation of Charles DeGrunnig's epic blockbuster spy novel *Frost Nine-Sixty*.

But that doesn't mean the fun is over: The *Growin' Up Greer* star will be hosting her own episode of *SNL*. The ep is scheduled to air March 8 and will also feature musical guest SZA. This may be just what we need to tide us over until season 12 of *Growin' Up* premieres in August.

CHAPTER TWENTY-SEVEN

The Ignite offices were in a New York high-rise, so high up that the elevator ride made your ears pop. I'd never actually been inside them. Today, though, my presence had been requested. When the elevators opened, the first thing I saw was my own face. All of ours, really—the path to the lobby was lined with floor-to-ceiling "character" posters of every main player of *Growin' Up Greer*.

"Holy . . ." I breathed.

"Spooky, right?" Greta said next to me.

"But also kinda great," Mom corrected. "We built this place."

We were greeted at reception by two suited white men and one woman I vaguely recognized from our mandatory exec dinners over the years. They shook each of our hands while piling on the kind of generically complimentary small talk that went in one ear and right out the other.

"Kia, your dailies this season are *fire*—"

"Are you sure we can't talk you into getting Cassius on the show? Becaaaauusee . . ."

"People are going to FLIP for you this year! Huge! You're gonna be huge!"

I wondered if now was the time to tell these people I wanted out. I hadn't yet gotten up the nerve to tell Mom I'd reversed course on college. I was too busy being mad at her, honestly—

I still couldn't believe she was considering signing off on Lark's BBL.

Now didn't seem like the time to fight about the contracts or the surgery. We were in New York to see Destiny on *SNL,* and in this building so the Ignite execs could pitch me on some new opportunity I was pretty sure I'd have no interest in.

"You've taken the world by storm, Kia," one exec said. "It's a glow-up for the ages."

For once I actually said exactly what I was thinking, out loud, exactly when I thought it.

"I don't know that I did much, really," I said. "I just dated someone cute and got some filler, did some press . . ."

There was a half beat of awkward silence until the suits broke into what could only be described as Raucous Fake Corporate Laughter.

"Let's get to it, shall we?" Mom said, smiling tight.

They had it all laid out—the next two years of my life.

It was remarkable, actually, the details they'd hashed out. They knew the cameras that could follow me to international stops on Cass's tour, the stars from Ignite's luxury real estate reality shows who could help me shop for my very first home. *Kickin' It Kia* was the name of my proposed podcast, and it would be a masterpiece of network synergy and branding opportunities. Reality show spin-offs were over, apparently—podcast empires were the new *thing.*

"It'll be *Call Her Daddy* for the eighteen-to-twenty-five set," promised the exec with too much hair gel. "*Armchair Expert,* but with Kiara Greer's own brand of empathy and insight."

The plan was for my sisters to cycle through as guests, promoting their various businesses but "baring it all" in their interviews. Greta'd also come prepared with a list of potential businesses I could launch through the seasons: skincare, makeup, shapewear.

"This is our chance to *really* let the world know Kia Greer," Greta said.

"Look, we're ready to hit the ground running on this," said the exec with dye-damaged blond hair. "We think this next generation of Greers can mean big things for Ignite."

I had no idea what to say, so I glanced down the table at my mother. She had a look of pride on her face I'd never seen directed at me. I'd waited so long for exactly this: proof that I could be what she needed me to be. With an opportunity like this, I could make a lot of money, and maybe a few more shy Black girls would listen to me on the way to school and feel validated in who they were. I could donate money that could help heal the world a little at a time. I could have power, resources, and opportunities for the rest of my life. And maybe my mom would keep looking at me like that—like I was fulfilling her every dream. Did I have it in me to say no to a look like that?

"Can I have time to think about it?" I asked.

"Of course!" said the exec with the smarmy smile. "We'll be in touch."

But my mother's mouth had already settled into a dissatisfied line.

Sola Greer's fresh start was well under way, and New York City was officially her new home. She'd rushed escrow and the interior design process so her new penthouse's grand debut could be filmed for the show. Sola was still the most dutiful, business-minded daughter Melora could ask for, even after the year she'd had.

The building at 333 Greenwich Street was not your regular apartment complex. This was the best of the best, designed specifically for the constantly hounded A-list celebrity. The building claimed to be "paparazzi-proof," thanks to a secure underground garage and a specific style of window that made it hard to see in from the outside.

"The three words here are elegance, vintage but minimalist vibes, and *peace,*" Sola said, walking backward through the space like this was her *Architectural Digest* tour.

"Sis, that was way more than three words," Destiny said.

"Let her have this," Lark lectured sweetly. "She's excited."

Deja was already running around the place. She clambered onto a giant love-seat swing that hung from the ceiling, swinging from one of its support chains.

"Is that thing secured?!" Destiny exclaimed, alarmed. She rushed over, sweeping her kid into her arms and biting at her little shoulder. "Stop that—you're scaring Mommy."

Deja obliged by instead sprinting around the room and launching herself into the conversation pit that sat in the center of the space.

"Dej, I love you, but if you scuff Auntie's new stuff, I *will* cry," Sola said.

The space was open concept, a massive loft with high beams and streaming light, filled with lush, plush couches in creams, light blues, and muted purples. There were three terraces, and the kitchen was all bright white marble tile, with a large breakfast nook that looked comfy enough to sleep in. That wouldn't be necessary, however: The place had guest rooms designed with each of us in mind.

"Sol, it's beautiful," Mom gushed. She had the same look I'd seen on her face earlier, and the knot in my chest twisted at the thought that I might never again see it aimed my way.

Sola glowed under the compliment.

"I didn't do it on my own," Sola said. "We're all in this together, remember? Ride or die. This is the house Greers built."

⌐⌐

We had dinner as a family. Even Dad joined us, sitting at the far end of Sola's grand kitchen table so the producers could cut around him. We ate a catered dinner of Italian food from Via Carota. I went all in on the single serving of risotto Mom let me have, but a while into the meal I noticed Destiny's plate had only a pile of sad spinach and a tiny slice of chicken breast.

"You still on that diet?" I asked when the cameras were focused elsewhere. "I thought it'd be better once you were filming."

"Ha! If I gain an ounce, the whole production has a fit. As if letting my costume out an inch is the end of the world." She waved it away. "Whatever. At least I'll look snatched on *SNL*."

If I was the face of Ignite's podcast empire, I might not be on TV, but I'd still be filmed. I'd spend every day worried about how I looked. There'd be even more upkeep appointments and endless early-morning workouts, because the entire show would center on me. The very thought of that made me queasy.

I'd been feeling nauseous since the meeting, actually. I rubbed at my stomach.

"Auntie, can I sit wit you?" a little voice said. Deja had abandoned her seat and was now standing next to me, the beads on her twists *tink-tink*ing, her big brown eyes looking up at mine. "Auntie Sola's seat's uncomfy."

"Auntie Sola's seats are *custom Claudio Silvestrin*," Sola protested, laughing. She shook her head at Dest. "Don't worry, one day your child will understand the meaning of fine things."

I pulled Dej into my lap. It always freaked me out how small her three-year-old body was. She had so much growing left to do, this tiny person who was just getting started on this planet. She was only three, but she already had so many opinions. It was nice—even when she was hand-feeding me prosciutto like I was some interactive doll.

I let her do it, wondering all the while what she'd think of this life she'd been born into. The paparazzi already stalked her ballet classes. She was afraid of them now, but maybe as she grew, their impact on her would lessen. Maybe she'd be stronger than all of us and have it all figured out by the time she was my age.

I hoped she would. I also hoped she wouldn't have to.

PART FOUR

Spin Off into Oblivion—I Dare You

(March and Onward)

CHAPTER TWENTY-EIGHT

Most nights I tossed and turned, my mind swirling with everything and nothing. Sleeplessness was my norm. That night, though, sleep took me fast. But when it left, just a few hours later, it was sudden and violent. An attack.

I crawled to the bathroom and stayed there. Every cell in my body fought to sleep, but there was no point in trying. One by one every single thing I'd eaten was ejected from my body.

This went on for a small eternity before a bewildered Lark opened the door connecting her room to the guest bathroom. She looked down at me, scrubbing sleep from her eyes.

"What is going *on*?"

"Something bad," I croaked. Then I hauled my face up to the toilet for another round.

I felt her kneel beside me. She tucked the long bonnet that covered my braids out of the way. Then she got up and tiptoed out of the room. When she came back, she had a wet washcloth and a big bottle of electrolyte water.

"You didn't have to . . ."

"You look *rough*, dude," she said. "Drink this."

Just like that, everything between us was forgotten. She pressed the cloth onto my temples while I sipped gingerly at the water. Too much too fast and I'd hurl again.

"I must have caught some stomach bug or something," I said.

"Yeah, maybe," Lark said. She sounded doubtful for some reason.

"Uggghhhh," I whined. "My mouth tastes like *booty.*"

I lay on the bathroom floor. The tiles felt cool against my skin. Lark went into her room and came back with her phone. She had that serious look on her face she got when she was thinking something through.

"Do you have other symptoms? Fever or anything?" She pressed the backs of her hands to my forehead and arms. "You don't feel warm."

"My symptom is I feel *bad,*" I groaned.

"But how specifically?"

"Just let me puke in peace."

She tapped at her phone, and I could tell from the way her nails click-clacked all aggro against her screen that she was pissy. Then all of a sudden she stopped.

"Kee . . . do your titties hurt?"

I knocked the phone out of her hand with my foot. I admit I was not at my best, but Lark's WebMD habit was pissing me off. She sucked her teeth.

"Bitch, do they hurt or not?"

"I dunno!" I felt myself up. "Sure! Whole middle section not doin' great right now!"

"I'm just saying . . . Kee, what if you're—"

"*Stop!*" I said, knowing exactly what she was about to say. "Don't curse me with that!"

There were absolutely no brain cells left to think about that option. Lark picked her phone up from where I'd kicked it and read from the screen.

"Tender, swollen breasts, nausea—I'm just *saying*!"

"I have an IUD! They're ninety-nine percent effective!"

"That ain't a hundred!"

My head was throbbing, and my mouth tasted like the continent of garbage in the middle of the ocean. I had nothing left to give, to her or myself.

"Just go to bed, Lala," I said, my voice tiny and taut. "I think that was the last wave. I'm gonna brush my teeth and try to sleep."

"But don't you think—"

"Can you tell Jay Dub I won't be able to do our morning session?"

"Sure," she said, finally relenting. "Of course. I'll tell him you aren't feeling well."

"Thank you."

Lark went back to the kitchen and returned with a bottle of ibuprofen and another bottle of electrolytes she made me down. I crawled back under the covers an empty husk, my baby sister curled up next to me, my head spinning into oblivion.

When I woke, the sun was still low in the sky, Lark was gone, and my dad was perched on the edge of the bed, gently shaking my shoulder.

"Hhrm?" I murmured.

"I wanted to let you sleep longer," he said softly. "But we gotta go."

His expression was strained; his eyes were red and sad. I sat up, startled.

"Daddy? What happened?"

"Everyone's okay," he rushed to assure me. We both knew there was a *but* coming. "I don't want you to worry too much . . . but Destiny collapsed this morning during her workout. They took her to the hospital."

"And you don't want me to *worry too much*?!"

I'd already thrown the covers back and was tearing through the mess of clothes spilling out of my suitcase. I placed a hand on the wall so I wouldn't faint while I pulled baggy jeans over my sleep shorts.

"She's okay," he said. "They've got her hooked up to IVs, she's getting fluids, and she's awake and talking. Your mother and sisters are there with her."

I froze. "Why are they there and I'm not?!"

Dad crossed to envelop me in a hug. He spoke into the top of my head.

"They were with her in the gym when it happened," he said, his words muffled by my bonnet. "It was early. Lark didn't want to wake you—she said you weren't feeling great."

"Well, let's go," I said, my wide, terrified eyes staring up into his.

"Let's go," he agreed.

Sola had bought a new Porsche for her life in New York, so we took that. We sped along the edge of Manhattan toward Lenox Hill, and I alternated between furiously texting my sister group chat and staring blanky at the passing city.

Neither of us spoke for a long time. I felt like I might vibrate out of my skin. This was too much time with my own thoughts. I had to get some of them out or I'd start vomiting again.

"She's pushing herself too hard," I whispered. "She's barely been eating."

I didn't look my father's way, but in my peripheral vision I saw him nod.

"Sometimes I wonder if it was right, letting all you girls get into the business," he said. His voice was choked with emotion. "But then I think: Would y'all even be better off out there? Far as I can see, everyone in the world is killing themselves to be beautiful, and if not that, then to be perfect in some other way. At least you have money, and a certain amount of protections."

I stared hard out the window. We were silent for another block before I found my words.

"The thing is," I said, screwing my face up to the morning light, "part of the perfect all those people in the world are trying to be . . . it's us. We try to make ourselves perfect, because if we don't, we'll get torn apart. And then we're everywhere—on TV screens, in movie theaters, on billboards, in commercials and headlines—and I just . . . We're all anyone sees. It's us and a bunch of other people also killing themselves to look and sound and act perfect and beautiful to even be considered *acceptable*. I feel bad about that all the time. Don't you? Because it's *us*. It's our fault. And it's not just hurting them, it's hurting us, too."

"You think about this a lot," Dad said. Not a question but a realization. I finally looked at his face, and it cracked something inside me.

"Yeah." I gulped. I stared at my hands, willing away the tears I knew were coming. It didn't work—they streamed down my face, and I was helpless against my own emotions. I gasped for air. "I'm *exhausted*. Mom doesn't know how different it is for us than it was for her, because how could she? It's so much worse for Black girls—it's *impossible* to please everyone, and so many people are determined to hate us no matter what we do. I wish I could sleep for a thousand fucking years, but I can't, because then who'd help Lark through it?"

I gasped for air, breathless. Dad put on his turn signal. He took the next exit and we pulled off the FDR, onto a quiet side street lined with apartment buildings. I crossed my arms on the dashboard and leaned my head against them. I curled up like that and just breathed. My dad rubbed my back until I calmed down.

At the time I took it as grace that he didn't immediately jump in and try to fix me. I didn't need platitudes right now—I needed to *scream.* He let me, and then he let me breathe. After a minute I sat up. I leaned my head against the seat headrest and sniffed.

"How are any of us supposed to *live* like this?"

He studied the side of my face for a while before he spoke. "I really don't know," he said. "I really wish I knew how to answer that."

I felt so helpless, and so alone, even with him right there next to me.

Destiny was fine. Or rather, Destiny was determined to be fine.

"Hell no," Destiny said as soon as she saw my face. "We ain't doin' pity today. Pity can go down to the cafeteria and cheer the hell up before coming back to *this* room."

She was draped across her hospital bed like it was a chaise longue, still in her impeccable Sola-designed workout set, Deja and her coloring books spread out next to her. The only signs my sister had suffered a health scare were the IV in her arm and the slight unfocus of her gaze.

"I'm fine!" Destiny said cheerfully. She tickled Deja's sides, and the little girl squealed in delight. "Isn't Mommy fine?"

Deja growled in her dinosaur voice. She stood on the bed and stomped like Godzilla. Then she dive-bombed her mother. "MOMMY IS A WARRIOR QUEEEEEN."

Dad rubbed my back. I looked at his face and saw he was trying just as hard as I was to believe this. But he looked shell-shocked—by what I'd said or by Destiny, I didn't know.

Dest threw Deja two feet in the air and managed to catch her without messing up the IV. She hugged her kid to her chest, and Deja wrapped her tiny arms and legs tight around her.

"I am," Dest said, looking first at my face and then at our dad's. "I promise."

I smiled and pretended I believed her.

Mom, Sola, and Lark entered with bags of food from a nearby café, Mom and Sola chattering about some hot barista. Lark sat down next to me in the room's little seating area.

"I'm sorry I didn't wake you," she said. She looked so scared and tired.

"It's okay. You kinda had some stuff to deal with."

She nodded, staring at her hands. Deja stormed up to us, and her dinosaur voice was back in full force.

"AUNTIES! PLAY DINOSAUR WITH MEEEE."

"Bossy!" Lark laughed.

"What are you gonna do if we don't?" I asked.

Then Deja tackled me.

We had breakfast together in the hospital room. I had a bagel to settle my stomach and ignored the looks my mom kept throwing me. Destiny was released by noon and at 30 Rockefeller Plaza by one-thirty. In her *SNL* monologue she joked about her weight loss.

"You know I've always been down for a fight," she said. The crowd went wild. "Now look at me: I'm in the best shape of my life. I've got superhero in my genes, so if you've got [bleep] to talk—say it. Let's see what happens."

Lark pulled me to a quiet corner an hour into the after-party. Max was with her.

"Don't be mad," Lark said. "I had Max do us a favor."

Max moved close, speaking in a whisper only we could hear.

"It was no problem," she said. "Neither of y'all shoulda been seen buying this."

We went back to Sola's place before the rest of the family so I could take the pregnancy test in peace. That second pink line showed up within a minute.

CHAPTER TWENTY-NINE

I'd always known Cassius Campbell was a supernova onstage, but it was different seeing it in person. The world tour for *Passions* would kick off on June 6, 2025, at the Strawberry Arena in Stockholm. In the meantime, Cass was rehearsing in an airplane hangar in Long Beach, California, 5,500 miles from Sweden.

Cass lit up the stage even in sweats. The band was running through "Flux," a bombastic glam-rock jam about being caught between stages of life and choosing to stay young and free.

I hadn't slept the night before, and in an effort to keep the nausea at bay, I'd barely eaten. I felt brittle from the inside out, as if someone looking at me wrong could crack me down the middle like a sheet of glass. It was the opposite of how Cass looked, sidling and sliding across the stage, feet tapping and hips swaying, so *alive.*

His voice soared and sliced as a hundred people watched and worked around him, dancing, arranging rigs and lights, and taking frantic notes.

I was about to ruin Cass's day. There was also the possibility I'd be ruining his whole life.

"Whew!" Cass hollered into the mic as the song ended. "That one felt good. Can we get that purple light to pulse a little more?

I want it to feel like a heartbeat or *somethin' else* is pulsing, y'know? How'd it sound to you, Simmsie?"

I turned, for the first time noticing Simms manspreading across a folding chair to the side of the stage. I turned away, not wanting him to notice me. I was not in the mood to fake pleasantries with the guy who'd suggested my teenage sister needed to surgically alter herself.

Cass jumped down from the stage and crossed to him, dapping him up. I hung back as they talked, tucking myself behind a stack of amps. Soon enough, Cass finished with Simms and gratefully accepted a bottle of water from an assistant. He was walking toward his stage manager when I stepped out from my hiding place.

Cass's face split open in joy, and my heart cracked in half. A smile spread on my face, too, and for that one second we weren't two kids who should've doubled up on birth control.

"Whaaaat?! Keeeeeee!" Cass screamed, sprinting over to me. He picked me up and spun me, planting kisses all over my face.

"How are you here?!" he gushed, searching my face. "Aren't you filming?"

"Lark's covering for me. She and Mom are going to a petting zoo or something—they don't need me for that."

"Did she tell you the news?" Cass asked. He was smiling from ear to ear, and when I didn't immediately respond, he rushed on. "Lark's gonna open for me on tour after her album's out!"

"Holy— That's so cool!" I threw my arms around Cass's neck. "She must be so excited! I can't believe she didn't say anything."

But as soon as I said it, I knew why. Lark hadn't wanted to drop good news while I was dealing with . . . well, all of this.

"This tour is gonna *HIT*!" Cass yelled, throwing his head back. A few people around us clapped their agreement.

"I'm so happy for you," I said. "Listen . . . can we take a walk?"

Something shifted in Cass's face—a realization, for the first time, that maybe all was not well. I took his hand and led him outside.

⁓

Cass canceled the rest of rehearsals that day. We drove past Carbon, past Zuma, until I directed him to pull over. We parked along a nondescript stretch of highway and tiptoed down a rickety staircase that was most definitely not up to code. We rounded a corner and there it was: a stretch of sand, dune, and rolling rock that had, one morning two years prior, belonged to me, Lark, and an old man fishing for halibut. My heart expanded seeing it again, even under the circumstances.

No one was here now, not even the fisherman. Cass and I were alone.

"But you have an IUD . . ." Cass repeated for the thousandth time as we spread out a blanket he kept in the van.

He was in a daze. We both were, but Cass's was more frantic, desperate, reaching out for every possible explanation or solution. At this point I just felt numb.

"Maybe it moved out of place," I recited without emotion. I'd Googled the issue exhaustively since that night in New York. IUDs were ninety-nine percent effective, and I was in the unlucky one percent.

"So . . ." Cass continued. This is the part we kept circling around, distracting ourselves and each other from reaching. "What do we . . . do?"

I sucked in a great big gust of breath. The air was salty and sandy, fresh and crisp with a hint of brine and sea creature. I closed my eyes and tried to blot out every other sense.

This was the hard part, and I didn't want to face it. I didn't want to see the look in those eyes I loved so much when I told him what I needed.

Cass dreamed of being a dad one day. He'd told me that, way back on one of our first dates, when I'd pointed out a cute baby riding on her dad's shoulders at a Lakers game. Part of me thought a baby might fix everything. Unconditional love was an attractive proposition. Maybe a kid could give my life the meaning I'd been struggling to find . . .

"Do you want kids?" Cass asked quietly. We were both looking out toward the ocean. "I don't even mean right now—for a sec let's take that out of the equation. In general, is that something you want one day? Let's just start there."

I cast around my soul for an answer. I stared at the spot where two years before I'd watched the old man collect fish and soak up the early-morning sun. It was mid-March now, still winter in so many places, but the sun was too hot here. It bore down on our faces.

"When I've pictured having kids, it's always in this, like, blurry future, y'know? I could picture some kid and me having fun, but nothing else really existed around it. I didn't know what job I wanted, or who my partner would be, or even where I'd want to live. Now it's so hard to picture any of it, because I don't even know what September looks like."

Cass nodded, understanding.

I turned to him. "Do you want kids now?" I asked. "With a world tour coming up, a new album?"

Through the obvious anxiety on Cass's face formed a faint, almost playful smirk.

"I don't know how much my answer matters. It's your body." I rolled my eyes, and he pulled me closer. "Really, though—I didn't picture it being now, but if that's what you want, we can figure it out. *Is* it what you want?"

I let out a long, loud, deep-in-my-body groan of frustration. I stood up and started pacing in circles. Cass stood, too, his arms folded, patiently waiting.

"I hate that it's on *me*. I don't have the best track record of making my own decisions!"

"Well, then, I'm here!" Cass insisted. He looked so helpless. "We can make the decision together, but at the end of the day it is yours—more than it is mine."

"Thanks," I shot back, and it sounded way more biting than I meant it to. I sighed. "The thing is, we wouldn't just be teen parents. We'd be"—I held a hand up and counted the descriptors on my fingers—"Black, queer, famous teen parents who somehow with aaaallll their wealth and privilege still couldn't avoid becoming a statistic."

"I take offense at that," Cass said, "for both of us."

"You have to admit it would be a circus if people found out. Like an I-shouldn't-leave-my-house-for-nine-months atomic bomb of a shitshow. It was bad enough when Destiny had Deja—there were literally *helicopters* circling her house trying to get pictures, paparazzi screaming at her to reveal the dad's name. And she was twenty-seven! We're barely eighteen."

"I don't think we should let the public make this kind of decision for us," Cass said.

"I'm not!" I yelled. Now I was the one offended.

Cass closed the distance between us and took both my hands in his.

"Then we won't," he said softly. "I don't wanna fight, okay?"

I kicked at the sand.

"We'd have the cutest babies," I said. "Just objectively."

"Those apple cheeks!" he said, pinching mine. "Big brown eyes? They'd be so good."

I looked into Cass's big brown eyes. They weren't pushing me; they were reading me.

"But is that what you want?" Cass asked again, his fingers gently tracing my chin. His voice was so low, it was almost drowned out by the sound of the waves.

I looked out at the ocean again, the tide, the endless in-and-out of it.

There were so many reasons the answer was no. Destiny was such a good mom to Deja, but my heart hurt every time that little girl had to walk from the car to dance class with grown men pointing cameras in her face. I didn't want to raise a kid like that.

Cass was about to embark on a two-year tour. He'd throw it all away if I asked. But this could change everything for him. The tour could cement Cassius Campbell as an icon. It was this Northridge kid's chance to really see the world like he'd always dreamed.

We had the resources to do it. Between us there was more than enough money to afford the bedrooms, the nannies, the schools. That was more than most people could say. We could each have careers and still give a kid the silver-spoon life.

But this wasn't about the logistics.

Did I want a baby?

Did I want a baby *now*?

Did I want a baby *here*?

Did I want my future decided? At least eighteen more years of having to think about someone else's life before my own?

Right this moment there was a bundle of cells inside me, and if I didn't do something, they would change my life forever.

I didn't know what I wanted for my future, but this wasn't it. *I* wanted to be the one to change my life.

"No," I said. "I don't want this at all."

CHAPTER THIRTY

And so on a sunny day in early April, a little more than a month before my eighteenth birthday, I had to sneak in through the back door of my doctor's office at six a.m. Yet another grace note of my lucky life was that I lived in California, where abortion was readily accessible. I could even have picked up the pills from a specially certified pharmacy, but that felt too risky; I didn't know the pharmacists. They could see my name on a prescription and seize an opportunity.

This intel was a special kind of radioactive. Kia Greer pregnant by Cassius Campbell and having an abortion could rake in quite a bit of cash from the tabloids. Whoever discovered our secret could sell out someone else's kids to put their own through a semester or two of college. I'd hardly even blame them.

My family doctor's office had held strong to HIPAA all these years. It was the safest bet. They had celebrity clientele, so the place would be crawling with paps stalking Pap smears by noon, but they could do it. I just had to be in the office before their first appointments of the day.

That morning had the audacity to be eighty-five degrees in Los Angeles, with a sun so glaring it felt like a personal attack. I threw on a sweatsuit regardless; I'd be inside all day. I planned to be wrapped in blankets for the duration of this experience.

Sola arrived promptly at five a.m., her hair slicked back in a sleek and straight pony. Dark sunglasses and a faux cheer covered tired eyes, and she carried a steaming hot cocoa that somehow hadn't spilled on her crisp white athleisure set. She held the drink out to me.

"Baby!" Mom's voice rang from the hall. "I didn't expect to see you today."

Of course Mom was already up. She sashayed into the foyer, still glistening from her workout. I focused on clutching the cup of cocoa close to my chest, feeling its warmth soak through to my hands. I didn't want to spend today mad at her. My chest was already in a vise, all the air squeezed outta me.

Sola seemed to sense this. She swanned over to peck our mother on the cheek.

"Mama! You look glorious. Those abs! We gotta get you on *Sports Illustrated* this year."

"Oh, please, I'm not even to my goal weight."

"No, I mean it," Sola said, positioning our mom away from me and making a show of looking her up and down. "I think we should get Greta on the phone with them today."

Sola snuck a glance at me over Mom's shoulder and winked. I slunk out the door, breathing a sigh of relief as I crossed the threshold.

Cass was waiting in the Volvo that Sola'd rented as a precaution. We didn't want to risk a paparazzi tail today; they'd long since caught on to our usual decoy cars.

I slid into the back seat next to Cass, and he pulled me into his arms. I buried my head in the crook where his shoulder met his neck.

"Even at five a.m., you still smell like orange blossoms," I said. "You're a marvel."

"I put it on for you," he murmured into the top of my head.

The doctor's office was eerily quiet this early in the morning. It smelled like cleaning solution and too-purified air. I could barely look at Dr. Gail as she moved an ultrasound wand over my belly. She'd been the Greer family doctor for years, and she'd been the one to help me get an IUD in the first place. Then I'd gone and messed it up.

I pushed back the wave of shame welling up within me. Something had happened, and now we were dealing with it. That was all that mattered.

"Now, Kiara," Dr. Gail said, setting the ultrasound wand aside and handing me a wet wipe to clean myself. "How are we feeling? You still sure about this? 'Cause we can discuss options again, if you want."

I cleared my throat because I needed my answer to come out strong and true.

"I'm sure," I said. *I'm sure,* I repeated in my head. *I really am.*

"I, um . . . is there any danger?" Cass asked. His face was drawn. I looked at him, startled by the thought of any danger at all. He looked at me, his eyes so apologetic it hurt my heart. "I think I know the answer. I just wanna know everything I can."

"Both medical and surgical abortions are remarkably safe," Dr. Gail assured us. "With these pills, the bleeding and discomfort you feel should resolve on its own within a day or two. In rare cases—and I mean *rare*—there could be excess bleeding, or there's a small chance you won't pass all the pregnancy tissue. This happens to an exceptionally small percentage of people, but before you leave here today, I'll instruct you on what to look out for."

"Thank you," Cass said, visibly relieved. "Sorry to interrupt."

"It's okay," I said. "I wanted to know, too."

Dr. Gail explained that I would take one pill in the office and four at home. She prescribed me anti-nausea meds, in case my morning sickness interacted with the abortion meds and I felt like I might throw up. The pill I'd take in the office was mifepristone, a hormone blocker that would stop the pregnancy from growing and help the embryo detach. The round of four pills at home would be misoprostol, which would cause contractions in the muscular lining of the uterus and push the pregnancy out of the body. When I got home, I had the choice of inserting the medication vaginally or holding the four pills in my cheeks for thirty minutes. And then I'd bleed. I might cramp. And then this nightmare would be over.

I listened as Dr. Gail explained every detail. I felt like the world's most boring science experiment.

When I took the first pill, a wave of anger cascaded through me. It wasn't even for myself. There were just so many lucky coincidences about where and how I'd been born into this life—in that moment, living in a state where I could have an anticlimactic abortion skyrocketed to the top of the list.

"How you feelin'?" Cass asked. His hand hovered over the small of my back, as if worried that if he touched me I'd break.

"This isn't gonna work if you ask me that five hundred times," I snapped. I regretted it immediately. I opened my mouth to apologize, but Cass wouldn't let me.

"You're good," he said. "I'll stop asking. Or at least come up with new and uniquely interesting phrasings."

Shame rushed through me. Good Cass, sweet Cass. I had to remind myself I wasn't alone.

I put my hood back over my head and reached over and did

the same to Cass's hoodie. It was still early, but we couldn't chance anyone getting a picture of CassioKia leaving this office together. Today was ours, and ours only. I'd never let them own it.

Sola rose from her seat in the waiting area and I took Cass's hand. I laughed for their sake more than my own. So they'd know I was okay.

"Just no one pull out your guitar like Justin Timberlake did with Britney," I joked. "We're not doing that."

It was a long day. We set up camp at the tree house, where Cass arranged his bed into a nest of every pillow and soft blanket he owned. He'd ordered every variety of heating pad he could find online, and my heart grew three sizes seeing them arranged for my picking. I ate a huge pile of pancakes Sola ordered in, and then I put on a pad as big as a diaper and crawled under the covers to await my fate.

Sola had to leave for a meeting she couldn't move. Cass left us alone for a minute; I could hear him making me tea in the other room. Sola perched at the end of the bed, her hand holding my right foot through the blankets. She cleared her throat.

I remembered how Dad had woken me up when Destiny was in the hospital—how worried he'd been. I was glad he didn't know about today. There was nothing he could do.

"Listen," Sola said, her eyes glued to her own hand on the duvet. "It can take anywhere from an hour to a full day for the bleeding to kick in. It might feel like any old period. For a lot of people it's like that. For some people it can feel like a flu. Mine was some of the worst pain of my life. I spent the day in the bathroom, letting the blood drain into the toilet. I did a lot of screaming. I got really scared. And I don't say that to scare you—just to prepare you. This day will end, all right?" She gave me a significant look to make sure I was getting it, so I nodded. "I want you to know that no matter what happens today, you're going to be okay. This experience is temporary, and then you are going to have whatever beautiful life you decide for yourself."

I lurched forward, pulling Sola into the tightest hug.

"I never want you to feel ashamed of this, okay?" Sola said, her voice choked with emotion. "Don't let anyone make you feel ashamed of this."

My face crumpled. I hugged her tighter as sobs heaved out of me. Sola had just broken something open in me, something she didn't even know was there.

I did feel such shame, not for the act itself but for everything that preceded it. For not making college happen. It all welled up in me: months and years of indecision, my own wrenching passivity and sadness, my fear that I wasn't doing enough, being enough—but for who? It had taken so long to even admit to myself I wasn't happy. I'd felt worthless for so long.

Today was different. I wasn't ashamed of the abortion. It was a commitment to do better—a commitment to myself. Taking these pills was a promise. *You're going somewhere*, it said. *You deserve the chance to get there in your own way, on your own time.*

Had I wanted needles to change the shape of my face, or was that just what I thought I should feel, should look like, should do? I think I'd done it because it would make things easier for everyone else if I looked the way they thought I should. But I was seventeen; my face hadn't even reached its final shape yet. I deserved the time, space, and grace to become who I was going to be. I was furious with myself for the ways I'd bent and broken and compromised myself. The shiny, twisted world I'd been born into wasn't the problem here—I was.

But maybe Sola was right: This would end. Today would, and maybe this feeling could, too. Maybe I could do something to change the shape of my own life.

But I didn't know how to say all that. Not yet, at least.

"*Thank you,*" I said instead. "I love you."

We hugged more, and cried more, and then Sola left. I asked Cass to show me the first season of *Grey's Anatomy,* since the Campbells loved it so much.

Eventually the bleeding started. My temperature spiked, and I got the chills. I took 800mg of ibuprofen and hugged the covers to my chin while I watched a bunch of hot TV doctors get tested for syphilis. This show was *juicy,* it turned out. A good distraction.

Cass didn't leave my side except to scurry around the house looking for ways to make me more comfortable. I learned that day that blood made him queasy—and there was a lot of it. What Cass lacked in an iron stomach, though, he made up for with a steady devotion.

I wondered how it was possible for this person to love me unconditionally. I wondered if we'd survive if I left the world that had brought us together.

I slid in and out of sleep. Destiny was in the final stretches of filming that action movie, and she FaceTimed right when the cramps got brutal. She was in her trailer on set and cracked jokes about my "scrambled eggs" as I wrapped multiple heating pads around my midsection.

I fell into a deep sleep around seven. I had nightmares:

cameras flashing, blinding me, a stranger on the street grabbing my arm *so tight,* yelling in my face. I couldn't understand what they were saying, it might not even have been real words, but they were foaming at the mouth. Bits of spittle drenched me—they were so angry and I didn't know *why.* I tried to run but my feet wouldn't move. I tried to scream but I didn't have a voice.

I startled awake, and Lark was in bed next to me, her back turned, scrolling TikTok on mute. Cass was snoring on my other side, one arm snaked protectively around my waist.

"When did you get here?" I whispered.

She turned toward me, a sad smile on her face. "Couple hours ago," she whispered back. "Cassie and I baked you about a thousand batches of cookies."

"You did?"

"He really, really loves you, Kee," Lark whispered. "It's really beautiful."

"Yeah," I whispered. "I really, really love him, too."

"I ate like five of those cookies," she whispered. She pulled a face. "Don't tell Mom."

I smiled into the dark. Lark must have seen that it didn't reach my eyes.

"Are you gonna be mad at her forever?" Lark asked.

"I don't know," I answered honestly. I changed the subject. "Will you eat ten more cookies with me in the morning?"

"Abortion Kia is bossy," Lark said. "I like it."

"So we've got a deal? More cookies in the morning?"

"We've got a deal."

CHAPTER THIRTY-ONE

I spent three days at Cass's house, bleeding, cramping, and recovering. I missed one day of filming and responded as little as I could to my mom's constant calls and texts about it. I knew I'd be in trouble, but I couldn't bring myself to tell her about the abortion. I'd gotten what I needed from Cass and my sisters, and the last thing I needed was a lecture about what would have happened if anyone had found out. So I played a role close to what I was: a teenage girl so madly in love she couldn't be bothered to show up for work. When I got home, my mother was in a state I hadn't seen since years before, when Destiny had gotten her DUI.

"KIARA IMANI, I RAISED YOU BETTER THAN THIS," she railed, pacing back and forth in the sitting room.

When I'd arrived home, she'd sat me on our deeply uncomfortable sculpture of a couch for a talking-to. Now her voice was stuck at that register that technically counted as yelling but hadn't yet crossed over to screaming.

"WHAT HAS GOTTEN INTO YOU? YOU CAN'T JUST GO GALLIVANTING WITH YOUR BOYFRIEND WHENEVER YOU WANT—YOU HAVE RESPONSIBILITIES."

"We weren't gallivanting," I said calmly. "I just needed some time away."

"THERE ARE CREWS WAITING ON YOU! YOU CAN'T BE UNRELIABLE IN THIS BUSINESS—IT GETS AROUND. DO YOU WANT THAT? DO YOU WANT PEOPLE TO THINK YOU'RE A SPOILED BRAT WHO CAN'T HANDLE THE *MANY* GIFTS SHE WAS HANDED IN THIS WORLD?"

I kept my eyes trained on a flower arrangement perched upon the marbled stone coffee table. It was a great, grand burst of lilies, blazing orange and covered in dark spots. They reminded me of characters from *Alice in Wonderland*.

I did feel bad for leaving the crew hanging. Maybe she was right. Maybe I was as ungrateful, irresponsible, and spoiled as she'd always made me feel.

"Are you listening to me, Kiara?"

"Didn't Sola step in for me?" I asked. "On the day I missed? She said she would."

"You can't just sub in sisters whenever you want a day off! The audience is going to want to see you this year!"

I didn't know how to tell her that the last thing I cared about was an audience of strangers.

"I'm sorry I wasted people's time," I said carefully. "I just needed a break."

"A break from *what*?!" she asked, bewildered. She gestured to the palatial room with a sweep of her arm. "You've got a pretty cush life here, kid! What else do you need?!"

I chewed my lip, deciding on my next words. I needed her to understand what I was about to say.

"I've been, um . . . I've been experiencing some depression this year," I said, finally meeting her eyes. "A lot of anxiety, too?"

It wasn't meant to come out a question, but it was the best I could do. My mother pursed her lips, unsure where this was going.

Her eyes flew back and forth like they were reading something in a language she didn't speak. I took it as a sign to keep going.

"It's gotten pretty bad." Potential tears tickled the backs of my eyes. I blinked a few times to banish them. I was so tired of crying. "I can feel it in my *skin*, every day—and in my heart. I feel like I can't breathe. I feel worthless all the time, like I'm disappointing you no matter what I do. So I needed some time. I still . . . need some time."

Melora Greer let out a long exhale and sank into a chair. She put her head in her hands. When she straightened again, there were tears in her eyes.

She reached over and rubbed my earlobe. There was something base-level comforting in that small touch. She'd been doing it since I was a baby. This little motion had carried us from diapers to bedtime stories through now.

"Honey . . . there's always help for you," she said. "My daughters will never be alone in this world like I was. I just wish you'd told me sooner."

Hope shot through my heart.

"I didn't know how to name it at first," I explained. "And I didn't want to be a spoiled brat, or jeopardize anything. I know how hard you and Dad have worked to get us here."

She scanned me up and down. I could practically see the thoughts racing through her mind. When she spoke again, her voice was softer.

"You didn't sleep through the night until you were ten. Never ate what we put in front of you. You've been so quiet. You weren't always, as a kid, but then you were."

I wondered where she was going with this. Then I wondered how she didn't know I still didn't sleep through the night.

"Our family is full of strong personalities," she continued, and I huffed a low laugh to match hers. It was the most obvious statement a person could make; it was practically the tagline of the show. "Daddy's focused, sometimes to a fault. He can get so bullheaded about his work that he forgets about everything else. Sola shines, aggressively so. She'll fight for her shine. Destiny . . . she'll fight for what she believes in, for better or worse, and Lark will fight for her craft, to do things her way. You all take after me in some way. And you're all stubborn as hell because of it."

"I am not stubborn!" I protested. Mom gave me a look.

"Girl, you're my kid. You're stubborn, and you're loyal. You ride hard for the people you love. It's a great strength, and one this family needs."

She squeezed my knee, and something in me warmed at the affirmation. Loosened. She sighed. That ever-present knot twisted again. I waited for the *but.* And then it came.

"But with my other kids, I know what makes them *happy.* I've been able to pinpoint that, then help them achieve it. With you . . ."

Melora Greer's eyes don't crinkle. A team of doctors and aestheticians has made sure of that. Still, my mom looked sad as she said this.

"You've given me a run for my money, kid."

"I haven't meant to."

I racked my brain for what I'd done, before this week, that had made me so hard to deal with. I'd tried so relentlessly, my whole life, to never be in anyone's way.

But I realized that wasn't her point right now. I recognized that look in her eye. She was formulating a plan.

"We'll get you back in fighting shape," she said. "The season ends in May, so we'll get you checked into a facility in June. I know the woman who runs Meadows—I'll give her a call."

"But that's a rehab," I pointed out. "I don't need to be sent away."

"Yes, but they handle exhaustion, depression, anxiety, all of that. They're very discreet. This will be our best shot to get you better before *Kickin' It Kia.*"

I didn't understand how the conversation had slipped away from me so fast.

"Mom . . ." I said carefully, "I . . . I don't want to do the podcast."

"Well . . ." I could see the mom and the momager fighting in her head. "Why don't we revisit that in a few days, after you've taken more time to think?"

"I've had plenty of time," I said. "I don't want to do it. I don't want to do *Growin' Up* anymore, either. I don't want to be on TV."

My mom froze in place again, her eyes lost in the middle distance.

"I need my mom right now, okay?" *Please, please, please let her listen.* "Not Melora."

She was silent for a long moment. Even sitting right next to each other, we felt miles apart. I looked down at her hands, the only part of her body that showed her age. I knew it killed her not to be able to "fix" them like she'd always fixed everything else.

"Hun, Ignite's already moved forward with *Kickin' It.* They've already hired a producer."

"But I never said yes," I said, confused.

"We were all under the impression that was a foregone conclusion."

I stood suddenly, frustrated. Now I was pacing the room like she had before, my hand to my forehead, casting around in search of where this had all gone so wrong.

"But—I never said yes!" I repeated helplessly.

My mother leaned forward, her arm slung over the back of

the couch, and rested her perfectly molded cheekbone against the back of her hand. She wore a practiced look of serenity, but I could see she was angry. After everything I'd just shared, she was still mad because I wasn't enough.

I took a step toward her, desperation bubbling up.

"Can I talk to my *mom*?" I asked again, my voice choked. "Not Melora. I need Mom."

"Kiara, you are taking that old joke far too literally. Your mother is getting you into that facility so you can have the 'time' you're asking for." Her voice was clipped, frustrated. She made the word "time" sound like a frivolous indulgence only some silly little girl would ask for. "Melora's the one keeping a roof over our heads. Your father would've spent all our money on old cars and vacations, but I built us an *empire*. I am the one who gave you your wonderful, blessed life, and I am the one telling you now: We have a contract. Multiple, actually. There are dozens of crew members counting on us, and we've managed to deliver twelve seasons of excellent TV—through grief, illness, recessions, pandemics, and scandals. You have to work hard in this world, and sometimes that means pushing through your own weaknesses. This doesn't all come grinding to a halt because you need a *nap*."

I stared at her hands again, blinking back tears. I felt smaller than I ever had, the smallest girl in the whole wide world.

"That was harsh, I'm sorry. I promise, we'll get you your time," she said. "And I hear you about the podcast. I'm not happy about it, but I can accept it."

I felt another *but* coming.

"We'll talk more about all the rest. We'll get you the help you need." It was coming—and it was right there. "But we need you to finish the season. Can you stand a few more weeks?"

CHAPTER THIRTY-TWO

Teyana Price was an up-and-coming Black designer, a wunderkind in the couture world, and the woman dressing Lark and me for our very first Met Gala.

The Met Gala was a rare event I was actually looking forward to. Lark, Miss Carol, and I always used spring trips to New York as an excuse to sneak off to the Met. We'd spend hours in the annual costume exhibit and getting lost in the American Wing. I loved the history of it all.

And so I'd decided I could stand a few weeks. I'd finish the season, and then I'd beg my mom to help me get out of my five-year contract with Ignite. I'd wrap up whatever else I was still beholden to—an Alo Yoga collab here, a Smartwater ad there—and then I could decide for myself what to do next. Cass would be down with me following him on a few tour dates. I could apply to those colleges Mr. Hillis had mentioned, schools like Wesleyan, Spelman, and Vassar, or other ones I liked the sound of, like Bennington, Howard, UC Berkeley, and Reed. Or maybe I'd use my savings and take a gap year or two, find a therapist I could trust, before I dove into school. Maybe I'd get a house with Lark or something. One with a cat.

This year was the first time every Greer was invited to the

ball that opened the exhibit. But the Met Gala wasn't as simple as just scoring an invite: Most celebs attended at the behest of a fashion house. A designer would dress you, and you'd walk the red carpet as a showcase of their work. The theme of this year's ball was Notes on Regeneration. The exhibit highlighted how three major fashion houses evolved through different eras, shifting with the pressures and trends of the times.

Mom and Dad were attending with Prada. Sola was with Versace, Destiny with Schiaparelli. For months Noémie had been working closely with Teyana Price & Company to ensure that whatever looks they designed fit what Lark and I were each most comfortable in.

"For you two I went with a theme within a theme," Teyana explained at our last fitting. "You're announcing a whole new era with this debut album, Lark. And, Kiara, happy early birthday—turning eighteen is a huge milestone, a thrust forward into being the woman you're meant to be. Without further ado, meet your personal theme: In Bloom."

We'd been doing fittings in muslin until this point, so it was our first time seeing the full vision for our looks in person. Teyana gave a nod to a waiting attendant, who wheeled away a partition. Behind it were two dresses—two pieces of art, really.

"Oh my *god*," Lark gushed. "Tey, they're *beautiful*."

"Aren't they?" Noémie said, standing back with her hands on her hips.

The two dresses were different but so perfectly in tune with each other, two pieces of a larger story, just like Lark and me.

Lark's was inspired by the ballet: a black tutu that fell just below her knees, and a bodice embroidered with faux monarch butterflies. It had a plunging back—a little skimpy, but not too much, which fit perfectly with the "innocent but sexy" image her record label wanted. But I couldn't be cynical about this dress, because it also felt like *her*. This was my little sister, just more grown, a bit bolder, but still elegant, still herself.

Mine was an explosion of life and color, a full floor-length ball gown with hundreds of the most realistic-looking flowers stitched into cascading layers of green tulle. I would be a walking garden, not an ethereal fairy princess but a formidable *queen*. Somehow, though, it felt less like a costume and more like what I'd always *wanted* to feel inside. I reached out to touch it.

"What do you think?" Teyana asked me, her hand hovering nervously under her chin.

"This is the most incredible thing I've ever seen," I whispered.

"Oh, thank god," she breathed.

"If you are into it," Noémie added, coming up next to us, "we have concept art for your accessories as well. Flowers in your natural hair, I think, Kia, and for you, Lark, slicked-back hair leading to a braid down your bare back."

"You're geniuses," Lark said, "geniuses, the both of you."

"What the *hell*," I laughed. "How did you even learn how to *do this*?!"

For one night I would get to be art. After that I could be anything.

The Met Gala was always the first Monday in May. This year that meant it would fall on the fifth—the day before I turned eighteen. Cameras weren't allowed inside the gala, but preparations for the ball would serve as the penultimate episode of *Growin'*

Up Greer's twelfth season. The finale would be my eighteenth birthday, a massive after-after-party my parents were throwing in the Plaza's Grand Ballroom. Cass would be performing at the latter.

It wasn't a bad way to go out, really.

That Sunday, Lark, Cass, and I gathered in Cass's hotel room at the Mark. I was officially hooked on *Grey's Anatomy* now, so Cass and I were forcing the show on Lark. She was easy to win over: a softy who lived for high drama.

"Wait, this is *good*," she said after the fourth episode, the one where Katherine Heigl's Izzie Stevens gives a powerful striptease monologue to her fellow doctors, who'd been judging her for modeling in med school. "She kicked those misogynists' *ass*."

"I *been* told you," Cass complained. "Didn't I say this to you, like, last July?"

"I'm here now, okay?!" Lark said. She adjusted her pillow and plopped back onto it. "How many more eps can we get away with?"

It was a perfect night, even with carrot sticks instead of popcorn.

Met Monday was a marathon into a sprint. The whole family was staying at the Carlyle since it was so close to the museum, and Sola treated us all to lymphatic drainage massages in our room. Then came facials: microcurrents to subtly shape our faces and oxygen infusions so our skin looked hydrated and nourished to the gods.

Once my face was beat to the high heavens, my hairstylist got to work teasing my natural hair into a giant Afro. He spent three hours meticulously pinning real live flora of every color into my hair: roses, daisies, sunflowers, eucalyptus leaves, baby's breath—you name it, and it was on my head. The effect was rather breathtaking. I looked how I wanted to feel: overflowing with life, a living monument to growth and constant change. Beauty in the truest sense of the word.

Getting into my dress was a three-person job: me, Teyana, and an assistant she'd brought along for this very purpose. I changed into the shapewear and corset they'd provided, which Teyana laced up herself. Then it got tricky. My dress was such a structural marvel that the best way to get into it without damaging the flower appliqués was to stand on the hotel room desk and be lowered into it from above. It took a few minutes of game-planning and some basic geometry, but eventually Teyana buttoned me in.

With the dress on I felt transformed. I was me but bigger—me but *mythical.* This was a dress that could conquer nations, lift souls. This was a dress that could guide you to the afterlife.

What surprised me most was how graceful it was. This thing didn't feel bulky; it felt powerful. Like if I really wanted to, it would help me fly away.

Lark was getting ready in the adjoining room, and I couldn't wait to show her. I posed in the doorway like a supermodel, but her back was to me. She'd just finished glam, and Teyana was showing her how to wriggle into her corsetry.

"We were able to work in the padding you requested," Teyana said, pointing to places on the hips and breast area where some kind of specialty shapewear added volume.

"It'll look natural, right?" Lark asked, examining the piece.

"I'm trying to head off any before-and-after photos that could come later."

"Yes, yes, we worked with the best—no one will notice."

Lark's look was relatively simple to get into, so Teyana left her to it. Lark shimmied into her shapewear and presented her back to me.

"Can you lace me up?" she asked, not meeting my eye.

I obliged, but the knot in my chest was back, and it was tight.

"What was that about?" I asked. "Why d'you need a custom corset?"

"No reason," she said, moving her head in such a way that I couldn't see her face. "We just thought the silhouette of the dress would fall better if I had more hips."

I didn't say anything for a moment. I just watched the back of Lark's head. Her lighter skin betrayed her feelings: Her ears were bright red.

"You know you're a terrible liar, right? You always have been."

Lark sighed and stepped away from me.

"Look, don't be mad, okay?"

"Okay," I said. "Mad about what?"

CHAPTER THIRTY-THREE

"DID YOU SAY YES?!"

I'd burst into my parents' hotel room, and everyone was looking my way: a cameraman, a sound guy, two makeup artists, two hairstylists, two designers, four assistants. And the two people I was looking for: the people who'd made me. People who increasingly felt like strangers.

No one was answering me. Everyone just stared like I was crazy, even though I wasn't. I knew I wasn't.

"Did you say yes?" I asked again, more forcefully this time. Lark caught up to me then, her expression torn between panic and mortification.

"Kia, stop—it's not your business," she said.

"Baby girl, you're gonna have to be a bit more specific," my dad said. He looked sharp in a three-piece black suit with a floor-length spin on a tuxedo jacket that trailed behind him.

"Yes, what on earth is going on?" my mom asked, adjusting her opera gloves.

I was suddenly *so* aware of all the other people in the room. It occurred to me this wasn't information Lark or my parents would want them to know.

"Can we get the cameras out of here, please? I'd really like to talk without the cameras."

My parents exchanged a troubled look. I was not usually one to make a scene.

"Clear the room," my father ordered. "Family only."

Everyone but the cameraman left. I glared daggers at my mom.

"Chris, you too," she said finally.

"We don't have to do this at all," Lark said. "The decision's made."

"THEN UNMAKE IT!" I turned to our parents, my eyes pleading. I was desperate for it not to be true. "Did you tell Lark she could get plastic surgery?"

"I hate that phrase," Mom said, fiddling with the fascinator clipped to her hair. "It's just a few small tweaks."

It hit me like a punch to the gut. I reeled back.

"A few small tweaks? It's *surgery* on a *sixteen-year-old*." I rounded on my father, who avoided me by checking his phone. I wanted to knock it right out of his hand. "Daddy, I can't understand why you'd agree to this."

He wouldn't look at me.

"Your mother and I discussed it," he said. "I hesitated for a long time, but ultimately we decided that if Lark is really passionate about this, we wouldn't stand in her way."

"What your father and I decide as parents is not open to notes," Mom added.

"It's my body, Kia! Not yours!"

I stumbled back, overwhelmed. I felt like I was suffocating— like if someone in that room didn't see reason, I was going to explode.

"Does no one else see this is OUT OF CONTROL? Her body's not even done growing yet! This is spitting in the face of SCIENCE—she could get boobs next year on her own! She could do more damn squats, or gain weight and it could go to her hips—ANYTHING BUT THIS! WHY DID YOU SAY YES TO *THIS*?"

My mom puffed her chest up, indignant, and she'd just opened her mouth to say something when the door opened, and everybody fell silent.

"*What* is going on in here?" Destiny said, sliding into the room.

"Y'all are loud as hell," Sola said, looking over her shoulder as she closed the door behind them.

"*We* are not loud as hell," Mom said calmly. "Your sister, however, is out of line."

I threw up my hands—and pure frustration burst from my eyes in the form of hot, devastated tears. Destiny rushed to me.

"What is *happening*?"

"Oh, honey," Sola said, "you're gonna ruin your makeup."

My chest heaved so hard, I literally thought it might burst. All eyes were on me, so I tried my best to get my words out.

"Mom and Dad"—*gasp*—"are letting"—*gasp*—"Lark"—*gasp*—"get *surgery*"—*gasp*—"a whole-ass *BBL* and freakin' *BOOB JOB*!"

"Well, when she turns eighteen, they can't really control that, sweetie," Sola said, digging through the detritus of the room's glam materials for a tissue.

Destiny, though, got it immediately. She turned to our parents with betrayal in her eyes.

"Not in a year," I told Sola, finding my breath. "*Now.* Before the album comes out."

"And like I've been saying," Lark said from where she'd sunk, resigned, onto a bed, "it is none of anyone else's business."

Sola handed me a tissue and sank onto the bed next to Lark.

She wrapped an arm around her shoulder, and Lark slumped into her.

"You're going to drop this, Kiara," my mother said sternly. "I said yes to my strong, capable daughter making her own choice to benefit her self-esteem."

"You didn't make a parenting decision," I spat. "You made a *business* decision. That's all we are to you, isn't it? I didn't want chin filler, *you* wanted to make *your* life easier. I didn't want eye filler, *you* didn't want the world to see you were running me into the ground!"

She tsked. "It got you a boyfriend, so I don't see why you're complaining."

"*Ma, that is out of line,*" Dest growled. "Kee, you know that's not true, right?"

"What the hell, Mom?" Sola protested. "That's a low blow."

"Cass met me before either of those things," I said. "Stop twisting this around. This is about not letting your daughter hurt herself on the off chance it'll help her 'succeed.'"

"You don't think I'll succeed?" Lark asked. She sounded so wounded.

"NO! No, that's not what I meant." I rushed to her, realizing in that moment that I was making her feel small with all of this, too. "I'm just trying to protect you. If you still want the surgery when you're past eighteen, go for it—you know I've never judged that before."

She looked into my eyes, and I saw something click in hers— some understanding, I hoped. I looked at Destiny next—but her gaze was fixed on Dad.

"Dad," Dest intoned, "you're being way too quiet in all this."

He raised his hands in surrender. "I said my piece."

"Let me guess: You're letting Mom make the decisions? Ain't that always the way."

"Destiny Aaliyah," Mom warned. "Now is the time to check yourself."

But Destiny didn't take her eyes off our father. Sola, Lark, and I watched in silence.

"You've always hidden behind her," Dest said. "She makes all the choices, while you go off and be a movie star. But someone's gotta protect us, Dad. There are things she'll never understand. We need *both* of you—because clearly sometimes she makes the wrong damn call."

I flashed back to the morning Dest was in the hospital, when I was wounded and railing against the pain. I'd felt so abandoned in that moment, aware for the first time of my father's insufficiencies. But maybe it wasn't just a moment. Maybe the four of us had, in actuality, been given a father who had no idea how to protect us—and who'd never bothered to try.

"We still need *parents*," I said, the tears flowing freely down my face. I was so damn tired of crying. "We shouldn't be getting hospitalized because we're not eating, or pimped out to solve each other's problems, and we sure as hell shouldn't be *getting major elective surgery at sixteen fucking years old!*"

"Oh, please." Mom waved her off dismissively. "You pimped your damn self out. Why can't you just admit you wanted what your sisters have?"

"I WANTED YOU TO BE PROUD OF ME!" I screamed with every bit of breath I had left. "AND I WANTED TO HELP MY SISTER! I didn't need the profiles and the red carpets and the inane-as-hell podcast—I just wanted us all to be okay! I wanted you to love me!"

My mom let out a deep sigh. "Is the vent session over, girls? We have work to do."

My blood ran cold, her words ringing in my ears. Was that all this was to her?

There was a knock at the door just then. I opened it, and Greta went very still as she took in the energy of the room. More than one person had makeup running down their faces.

"I was going to say we should leave in ten," Greta said slowly. "Let's make it forty-five to be safe. I'll get the glam teams back in here."

There was so much left to say and also nothing at all. We were, every one of us, deflated—and then, just like that, people filtered back into the room and we were back to business as usual. The show must go on. Right?

We were silent in the Sprinter van on the way to the Met, standing awkwardly so we wouldn't wrinkle our dresses. The air in that van was so brittle, I thought it might crack. When the doors opened, though, the six of us transformed from a group of broken shells back into the Legendary Greers, America's favorite family to love, hate, and binge.

This is only temporary, I told myself. *It has to be.*

Every bit of my training kicked into gear: smile wide and bright, making sure it reaches the eyes; chin up, but also down, but also forward; drop the smile when you hit the carpet; replace it with the sleek 'n' slack, eyes vivid but the rest of your face relaxed.

We posed as one big happy family. I was numb. I felt like I'd just witnessed a murder-suicide. Who was our protector now? Had we ever even had one?

Lark and I met up with Teyana on the carpet and walked it with her. I would fake it for her, this brilliant young Black woman whose work we were helping to launch in a whole new way. *This* was someone who deserved a platform.

Lark and I gushed to every interviewer on the line how incredible it was to work with Teyana Price. The first jolt of real feeling I regained came when Lark took my hand during one of the interviews and squeezed. It told me she wasn't mad at me. It told me we, at least, would be okay.

"It's people like Teyana who should be lifted up in this business," I said to a young woman reporting from the carpet. "Honest, hardworking people who just want to make good art that lifts instead of damages."

"Hey, are we good?" Lark asked when we were out of earshot. "I want us to be good."

I nodded, relief flooding me. "You and I are good," I said.

"Fam might be a toxic trash fire, though," she intoned. I let out a tragic bleat of a laugh.

"CASSIUS! CASSIUS, OVER HERE! CASSIUS, GIVE US A TWIRL!"

Lark and I looked to our left, and sure enough, there he was: Cassius Campbell in his full glory, diaphanous Stevie Nicks sleeves flowing all the way to the ground. There was a celestial crown of stars atop his head.

"You look perfect," I said.

"And *this*!" Cass boomed. "Incredible." He made each of us do the twirls the photographers were demanding of him. We must have shown our hands, though, still stiff from the recent brawl, because Cass whispered in my ear as we entered the building.

"Is it just me, or is the vibe there . . . weird?" Cass asked. "Something go down during glam? 'Cause that *would* support my theory that glam is the most dangerous time of the day."

"I'll tell you about it later," I promised. My voice shook over even those words. "But it was . . . bad. Like, really, really bad. I-dunno-how-to-look-at-my-mom-anymore bad."

He pulled me closer, alarmed now. "Is there anything I can do?"

I shook my head. "You've got deals to make, people to meet," I said. "Go be a rock star."

"Ugh, I do have to mingle."

I playfully shoved his shoulder. "Don't act like you don't love it."

Cass smiled and was off to hobnob Anna Wintour, who greeted him with a rare smile.

I was alone for the first time since the fight. It was only then that I realized my heart was still in my throat, my pulse racing. I glanced over to the Prada table, where my parents were talking and laughing with some billionaire as if nothing had happened. Shouldn't they be serious, their heads pressed together, trying to figure out how they'd hurt their children so deeply?

I thought about that facility my mom had mentioned—Meadows, the rehab in Malibu. She might actually make me go soon. She'd brought it up when I'd told her I was struggling. And after my latest "outburst," it would be the easiest way to get me out of her hair and back under control. She'd write me off as too anxious, her hysterically neurotic troubled daughter—but *Oh, don't worry,* she'd tell the execs, *she'll be ready to work again in three to six weeks.*

"You okay, sweets?" Teyana asked, coming up behind me.

"Yeah, I'm fine," I lied, my vision blurring. "I'm gonna go get another drink."

"Okay, baby," she said. "I'm hitting the dance floor. Tell your sis I *love* this song."

The event DJ started playing "Sweet," and I smiled to myself, remembering all of us jumping up and down on the dance floor at Lark's birthday party.

My hands were tingling, my face hot. I was in one of the most glamorous rooms in the world, yet somehow I was still in that hotel room, screaming at my parents. I couldn't escape.

In a few weeks they'd ask me to relive this day all over again, dressing me up and sitting me down in a warehouse to recap the whole thing when we filmed "confessionals."

Then what? Meadows? More fights with Mom, more resigned silence from Dad?

I braced both my hands against the nearby bar for stability. I felt dizzy. I felt like the room might cave in.

It got you a boyfriend, so I don't see why you're complaining.

You pimped your damn self out.

Why can't you just admit you wanted what your sisters have?

I said my piece.

We have work to do.

I gasped for air, but it didn't come. I couldn't breathe.

I made a beeline for the bathroom. I was suffocating here, and I had to get out.

Joe moved to follow me, but I put a hand to my heaving chest.

"Please," I said. "Thank you, but I just need a moment."

He nodded, seeming to understand. I smiled, grateful—and ran.

The bathroom was no relief. That was a party of its own,

slammed wall to wall with a who's who of the most famous women on the planet, taking selfies and sharing contraband cigarettes. I counted to five and then peeked back outside the door; Joe had moved to where Lark, Sola, and Destiny talked up Cardi B at the bar. Our other guard, Oscar, was with my parents, who were still schmoozing the billionaire.

Something inside me crystalized, fast and true and terrifying: I didn't have to stay. I had to get out of there, and that was a choice I had the power to make. I had the ability to bring the breath back into my lungs.

I don't have to be here.

So I ran. Or rather, I strode, my steps steady and my head held high, weaving in and out between bodies and towering set pieces until I tasted air.

Outside were paparazzi, of course. I smiled and waved, more genial than I'd ever been, and trod along Fifth Avenue until I found our Sprinter van. The driver's eyebrows rose when she saw me, but she opened the doors.

"Wasn't expecting you so early," she said. "What they do to you in there?"

"Not feeling well," I said. "Would you mind taking me back to the hotel? Would that mess up your night?"

"Not at all, honey," the woman said. "I'll be back in time for the rest of 'em."

I climbed in.

Cass. Cass, Cass, Cass. I couldn't leave him with no explanation. He'd be occupied all night, but he might still look for me in the crowd.

I love you, I wrote in a text. I'm not feeling well, so I ducked out. I'm sorry. See you tomorrow?

I reread the text, then deleted See you tomorrow?

Talk tomorrow? I wrote instead. It was less of a lie.

I added another I love you because it was the truth. I love you, I love you.

⌒

Everything collided in the elevator up to my hotel room: My breath rushed back in too fast, heaving through me in great waves. I grasped for the buttoned backing of my dress, desperate to get out of it. I didn't want to ruin Teyana's art when I exploded.

I burst into the blissfully empty hotel room. I gasped, popping one button, then another. It was easier to shimmy out of the dress from the bottom, so I lowered myself into the skirt and crawled out from under it. It stood there like a statue, perfect and beautiful even without me in it.

I tore the corset off, and tears came fast and wild, jerking from me in violent spasms. I sank to the floor, now in nothing but a thong, a hand to my mouth so the noise wouldn't stir Max, who was in the suite next door getting ready for the after-parties.

I could take fuller breaths without the corset crushing my lungs, but now I was shaking, from my toes to my fingers, terrified.

My phone lit up—a call from Mom, no doubt wondering where I was. That just made me sob harder. I sobbed until there were no thoughts, good or bad, until my whole body ached, until my insides felt like they had that day in April when I'd taken the abortion pills. I cried until my shoulders, arms, chest, and hands were heavy in salt and smeared with foundation.

I have no idea how long this lasted. I just know that after a long, long time I stilled. My lungs steadied and filled. I wiped my nose and crawled to the bathroom, where I sat in the corner of the shower and let the water wash me clean. After a few minutes I pulled myself up and scrubbed the rest of my makeup off. I turned off the shower and wiped the fog from the mirror; my eyes were bright red. Swollen. I looked like I'd been in a fight.

I looked back at the bed—and my phone lit up again, this time with a call from Lark.

I couldn't ignore the calls; she'd send someone after me. So I sat wrapped in a towel at the end of the bed and stared at my phone. Then I started typing.

I'm fine, I wrote. Don't worry about me—go have a good night!

No, that wouldn't work. Too vague; it'd invite questions. I deleted it and started again.

Don't worry about me. I just need some time to think. More honest, but nope—they'd spend the night worried about me. I sighed. Then I decided to lie through my teeth.

IDK what was in those canapés, I typed, but I've got the bubble guts from hell. Gonna curl up in bed with some Tums before I ruin any priceless couture.

As soon as I hit send, I realized the clock was ticking. The gala itself would end at eight, at which point everyone would head to the after-parties. They'd change over their hair, makeup, and outfits in Sprinter vans and be on their way downtown to Chanel's event at the Mercer. Eventually, though, they'd come back uptown to the party at the Carlyle. Someone might even reroute to check on me first. But I couldn't face them yet. I didn't even know what there was to say. They wouldn't understand that

I wasn't just throwing a fit. But I wasn't mad—or at least I wasn't just mad. This was something bigger.

The most logical move would be to go to Cass's suite at the Mark. It was just one block over. Instead, I found myself Googling flights from New York to LA. I didn't even know what my plan was—go home? Go to Cass's house, or Destiny's? Rent my own place and fight my contract, get out of the show?

It's no use, my brain mocked. *This will always be your life.*

My heart started hammering again.

"Breathe," I said, hoping that speaking it aloud would override my brain. I took a measured breath in, counting the seconds, one, two, three, four—*hold*—and then out, one, two, three, four, five, six, seven, eight.

Then I had an impossible thought. It was the first one all night that didn't scare me. There was somewhere I could go, somewhere safe.

I didn't let myself believe I'd actually do it. I went back to the bathroom and lotioned my body. I did my skincare and slicked my hair into a low bun. I put on my trusted sweats and a hoodie I'd stolen from Cass's house. I sat back on the bed and turned on the hotel TV. *The King of Queens* was playing.

But I couldn't fight the itch. I hadn't felt it this strong since my sixteenth birthday, when Lark and I stole Mom's T-Bird and spent a salty, sun-drenched day at the beach. That day I'd woken with this undefinable, immovable need to be anywhere but where I was.

I put the remote aside. For the first time all night, my breath was mine. I felt awake and alive. I knew what I needed—and exactly how to get it.

I walked into the adjoining room and found the bag Sola'd left when she'd come over from her suite to get ready. I rummaged through it until I had what I was looking for.

I didn't want to take my suitcase, so I packed my travel backpack with the very basics. I looked up my route on Google Maps: If I wanted to avoid Times Square, the straightest shot downtown was to take the 6 train and then walk twelve minutes. My hands shook as I slung the backpack over my shoulder and took one last look at the room.

Should I leave a note?

No. The longer lead time I had, the better. I'd make sure they knew I was okay; I just had to get out first. I picked up the hotel landline and called the concierge. Legend had it Marilyn Monroe and JFK used a secret tunnel under the Carlyle to evade paparazzi. In more recent years Meghan Markle had frequented this hotel; if she could get in and out unscathed, so could I. You got what you paid for in places like this.

"Hi!" I said, my voice high and cheerful. "This is Kiara Greer; I'm staying in the Royal Suite. I need to get out of the building without any pictures being taken—can you help me?"

Somehow, the tunnels were real. I had assumed it was urban legend, that I'd be escorted through the kitchens to a backstreet or something. Instead there I was, under Manhattan, and an elderly concierge in a three-piece suit was escorting me through dimly lit caverns. We walked for a surprisingly long time before we came to a padlocked metal door.

"These stairs will lead to Seventy-Eighth Street between Park and Lexington," the man said as he unlocked the door and held it open for me. "Can I help you with anything else, miss?"

He had kind eyes and the same type of aged face Grandma Millie used to have—the kind that felt like a badge of honor. I wondered what he saw in my face that night. I was scared, but strangely steady. Could he tell? Did he see a scared little girl before him, or a tired but determined woman?

I smiled, grateful. "No, that will be it. Thank you so much, again."

I handed him a tip and ascended the stone stairs. The tunnel had spit me out in a narrow walkway between apartment buildings on a residential street. The sun was just starting to turn, the sky still blue but the light on the buildings a brilliant gold. Seventy-Eighth between Park and Lex showed no signs that the Met Gala was even happening. Three men exchanged neighborhood gossip on the sidewalk, but they didn't look my way. I breathed, *out, out, out.*

Before leaving the hotel, I'd pulled my hood low over my forehead and put on a pair of oversized sunglasses, and now I jumped at every sudden noise as I made my way to the Seventy-Seventh Street subway station. I fumbled through figuring out how to pay for subway fare, but I got it eventually, and when the train came, I thought I might vibrate out of my skin. The train car was packed. I was sure I'd be recognized. I sucked on my lips, hoping if fewer of my features were visible, I'd be less recognizable.

A girl my age got on the train at Fifty-Ninth Street. She had a backpack just like mine, and she was scrolling Met Gala looks next to me. She paused on a picture of me in my flower dress, and I held my breath. She must have sensed my eyes on her, because she glanced up. I looked away, and she looked back at her phone. I stayed as still as I possibly could. But she just let out an approving "Hmm" and kept scrolling. She never looked my way again. By the time we passed Grand Central, my shoulders began to relax. I sent a silent thank-you to the city of New York for minding its business.

I got off at Canal Street and my heart started pounding again. Never in my life had I walked through a big city alone. Dusk had fallen, and every variety of person streamed past me as I tried to orient myself. No one paid me much attention, though; every glance fell away. That emboldened me enough to keep going.

These were streets I'd seen by car so many times but never really walked. My every nerve was still on alert, but I let myself enjoy actually being in the city, streaming along the sidewalk with all the people getting off work, doing some shopping, or meeting friends for dinner. It felt like we were all part of one giant organism.

When I turned onto Greenwich Street, I had to be extra cautious. But there was no one milling outside the grand redbrick building—the paparazzi knew Sola and the other big-fish celebs who lived there were otherwise occupied.

I removed my hood and stowed my glasses before approaching the doorman on duty. This time I needed them to know who I was. I smiled and they let me through. I walked up to the black-lacquered front desk, where a sleek woman in a sleek dress smiled politely at me. I pulled Sola's keys out of my pocket and placed them between us on the desk.

"Hi," I said. "My name's Kiara. My sister Sola Greer is lending me her car. How do I get it from the garage, please?"

Hardly my most mature effort. I smiled, tight and nervous, while the woman looked me up and down and tapped away at her computer. The last thing I wanted was for her to spot me as the repeat-offender car thief I was.

"I see your name here on the list of authorized users, so we can arrange that for you," the woman said instead. Her voice was impossibly serene. She picked up the landline phone in front of her. "I'll just call down to the valet—they'll have it ready for you."

By the time the elevator opened on the building's stately underground garage, Sola's Porsche was already prepped and ready, a uniformed valet holding the door open. I handed him a hundred-dollar bill and slid into the leather driver's seat.

As soon as the valet closed the car door, a hysterical laugh bubbled up from my chest.

"Holy shit," I blurted to no one. *"This is happening."*

A Porsche was hardly the most inconspicuous car to run away in, but I didn't have much of a choice: I was too young to rent a car, and I'd be seen by far fewer people if I avoided the airport. Sola would forgive me for borrowing it.

Besides, this would give me the next eight hours to think. So I headed west.

The sun set on the first Monday in May as I descended into the Holland Tunnel. I turned eighteen halfway through Pennsylvania, flying down the interstate ten miles above the speed limit and screaming Whitney Houston's "I Wanna Dance with Somebody" at the top of my lungs.

CHAPTER THIRTY-FOUR

Tptptp—I startled awake. It was early morning, and *there was a man tapping on my window.* I gasped, and before I was even fully aware of what I was doing, I'd shoved myself as far as I could into the farthest corner, my heart pounding in my chest.

Then the tapping hand curled into a fist. I braced myself for broken glass, a very different end to my story—but the hand rubbed the dew from the window, and a face came fast into focus. I exhaled in deep relief: Mervyn Binion was in a tracksuit with a large dog at his heel, and his whole face was wide with shock.

"*TATER TOT,*" Merv shouted through the window. "*ARE YOU KIDDIN' ME?*"

Just a few hours before, I'd exited the highway in Elyria, Ohio, and wound through hushed suburban streets until I finally landed at the two-story house with the blue-thatched roof Miss Carol had told me all about. It was four a.m., far too late to knock, so I'd double-checked the locks on the car and crawled into the back seat. I'd curled into a ball, my hood lowered tight over my eyes. I'd sent one last text to Cass before sleep pulled me under: I'm safe, I promise. I'll be able to tell you more soon. I love you, I love you, I love you.

Now I was at Tavia Binion-Burkhart's kitchen table, still

blinking sleep from my eyes. Miss Carol was in her robe across from me, tearing me a new one.

"You can't just do this! Your parents must be beside themselves. What if you'd been *seen*? Eight years traveling with a bodyguard and you decide an *eight-hour solo road trip's* the way to go? What if the car had broken down? You'd have been at the mercy of whatever sicko happened across you. The complete disregard for your own safety—what were you thinking?"

I had my answer ready; I'd had eight hours to think about what I wanted to say.

"I couldn't breathe there," I said, locking my eyes onto hers. That shut her up fast. "I know it seems rash, but you were right: That's not my life."

I didn't stare at the table this time or wish I'd said something different. I kept looking right into Miss Carol's eyes.

"Oh, baby," she whispered. She took two strides around the table to where I sat and wrapped me up tight. After the night before, I was fresh out of tears, but I hugged her hard. I buried my face in the blissfully soft folds of her stomach. She felt like coming home.

"Ma!" called a voice from upstairs. I pulled away, bracing myself. Stairs creaked with the sound of rushing feet, and Merv and Miss Carol's daughter Tavia appeared from around the corner. She had a toothbrush dangling from her mouth and an impossibly round ten-month-old on her hip. "Quentin went to work early, Malcolm needs a change, and I got five minutes—"

She saw me and ground to a halt. The toothbrush dropped, splattering white bits of toothpaste all over the floor.

"Wow. I thought Dad was joking."

I rushed to wet a paper towel and clean up the toothpaste.

"He wasn't," I said, scrubbing the floor around Tavia's feet. "I'm so sorry to drop in on you. I just needed somewhere to go, and—and—"

I was humiliated. I didn't want Tavia to think I was just some sad rich girl trying to appeal to her pity, even though I was exactly that. I sniffed, still on all fours. Tavia handed baby Malcolm to her mom and gently pulled me up by my arm.

"You're always welcome in my house," she said, guiding me back to my seat at the table. "God has perfect timing—my parents have been missing the hell outta you and your sister. Lookin' at you, I'd say you felt the same."

"Missed her every day," I said, looking to Miss Carol, who was nibbling at the rolls on her grandson's arms. She winked at me.

"Pants," Tavia exclaimed suddenly. "I still need pants. Listen, I got class, but my husband and I'll both be home around six. I assume you're staying the night?"

"I can find a hotel—"

"Girl, chill," Tavia said, Merv's sly smile echoing on her face. "I got you. We'll do dinner, I'll bore you with my day at law school, and you'll tell me all about the Met Ball and that cute li'l boo of yours."

I huffed a laugh, so relieved I could burst.

"Thank you so much, Tavia. You have no idea how much this means to me."

She waved this away and was around the corner once more, footsteps clattering back up the stairs. I stared after her, stunned this had gone my way.

"I'm not gonna subject you to this one's diaper," Miss Carol said, moving in the direction Tavia'd just gone. "But while I'm upstairs, you're calling your parents. Deal?"

It wasn't my best day. The conversation with my parents was long and circular, comprising phone call after phone call. They all seemed to go the same way: heartfelt concern that inevitably warped into frustration and anger that I was messing up my mother's plans.

"*Oh my god,* we've been so worried—where have you been?" she said during our first call.

"Are you safe?" my dad asked. "What do you need?"

They listened as I gave the explanation I'd rehearsed: I was safe, I was with the Binions. I told them I'd broken down the night before and needed space—from the family, but mostly from the whole Hollywood machine, because it had proven to be an unhealthy environment for me.

I talked for a good five minutes. At the end of it my mother just sighed. My dad was the first to reply.

"I'm so sorry about yesterday," he said. "We all said things we didn't mean. It got so heated—of course you needed space. But, Kia, Ohio? That's a little extreme."

"A little?!" My mom scoffed. "We'll have the jet there in three hours. This hissy fit's lost us the day, but we can salvage tomorrow."

"*Hissy fit?*" I repeated. "Are you serious?"

"I have all the sympathy in the world for needing some space," Mom said. "Trust me, I'd love to take a break now and then—but we've got contracts. If you're not back filming by tomorrow, Ignite will be up our asses. We already lost—ugh, that party, everything—"

I sat there, stunned. The knot twisted in my chest, tight and painful.

But this wasn't last night. I could still breathe—because I could say no.

"You can send all the jets you want," I finally said. "I'm not coming home. And I'm eighteen now, so you can't make me."

You can't make me is objectively one of the most childish things a person can say, but it felt like freedom. I heard a shocked huff on the other end of the line.

"I've never known you to overreact like this," my mother said. "Kiara, this is unreasonable, unstable behavior."

My laugh was pained. "Then I wish I'd let myself be unreasonable years ago."

"KIARA IMANI GREER, IF YOU DON'T GET YOUR ASS BACK HERE—"

"MEL," my dad pleaded. "Please. Let me talk to her."

My mom put up a small fight, but eventually she handed the phone to my father.

"I know I didn't handle this in the best way," I said. "But I'm not coming home. Not until I can figure some things out for myself. I really need this, Dad."

"I hear you . . ." he said carefully. "We all need time to ourselves sometimes. But to steal your sister's car and cross multiple state lines, all because you were mad at us?"

"This is so much bigger than me being mad at you guys," I said. "This is something I really, really had to do. For myself."

"But did you have to worry everyone sick? We could have organized a vacation for you, gotten you away from everything for a while."

"Mom was trying to send me away," I told him. "She's more worried about the business than about me."

"Kee . . . you know your mother gets tunnel vision about these things. But when she realized you weren't with Cass this morning, she just about lost her mind. She loves you so much. Can you come back, please? For me?"

I'd started pacing between Tavia's kitchen and living room, afraid that if I stopped moving, the full brunt of my grief and anger would catch up to me. It was the kind of house where every wall was decorated with family photos and every couch or chair had the coziest throw blankets draped over them. I stared out the front window, onto the suburban street dotted with trees, kids' bicycles strewn on practically every lawn.

"This is bigger than a vacation," I said. "Dad, I can't live in that world anymore."

"We've given you *everything*!" my mother protested, bursting back onto the call—she'd clearly been listening the whole time. "What do you mean, you 'can't live in that world'?!"

The knot in my chest twisted.

"If you come here, I'll just move somewhere you won't find me," I said as evenly as I could. "I love you, but I've got some other calls to make. Talk to you later."

I hung up and sank into the soft, worn sofa.

A few minutes later Miss Carol came back downstairs with the baby, who was sucking his fist. I was still in the same position, just sitting and staring ahead, stunned. She sighed, unsurprised.

"I take it that didn't go so well?"

⌣

"So are you gonna live in Ohio now?" Lark asked over FaceTime, confused and wounded. "All because I wanted surgery? I won't get the BBL, okay? I heard you loud and clear."

"It's not because of you," I told her. "It's not even about Mom or Dad at the end of the day. That just pushed me over the edge, but I wasn't happy there. I love you, and I love Sola and Dest and Deja, and being with Cass and being friends with Jade made me happier than I'd been in forever . . . but it couldn't change what was fundamentally wrong. I was never meant to be famous, Lala, you know that."

She let that sink in, her eyes focused past the phone. Without my eighteenth-birthday party keeping her in New York, she'd flown home, and now she was in our gardens. I could picture her view: freshly bloomed jacaranda trees. Their purple leaves fell everywhere, dotting every surface of our mountaintop. From where Lark was sitting, she could see where the mountain dropped off. The view stretched all the way to the ocean.

"Yeah," she said finally. "I think I did know that."

"I have to start making my own choices, for myself, not anybody else," I said. "Otherwise I'll never be happy for more than a moment at a time."

"That makes sense," she said. Then she smirked. "But you didn't answer the question about Ohio."

I laughed. "I dunno," I said. "I'll stay as long as they'll have me."

Her eyes grew a different kinda sad than they'd been at the beginning of the call.

"You're not gonna be down the hall anymore."

"I'm sorry," I said. "But I'm gonna be just as annoying and up your butt from here, I promise. You're not getting rid of me. And you can visit whenever you want."

"I've got a weekend in July, when the show's not filming and there's no promo on my schedule. How 'bout then?"

"It's a date. We'll get an Airbnb by the lake and sleep till noon."

"Okay, but I've gotta get some Malcolm time," she said. "That kid looks *chonky.*"

⌒

Sola was more amused than angry that I'd taken her car. She hadn't even been worried.

"Mom's in a tizzy about the *Growin' Up* production schedule," I complained.

"Screw all that," she scoffed. "I'll talk her down. We can find other storylines. Hell, I've been sleeping with a former K-pop star—I'll let that slip and we're off to the races."

"Sola," I said, "I mean this with every fiber of my being: I love you so much."

"Right back atcha, kid." I could hear her beaming on the other end of the line.

"You don't think I'm crazy for this?"

"Bitch, you remember what I was like at your age! I almost got married in Vegas three separate times. *Three.* I was on molly more often than I wasn't. There were whole *months* none of y'all saw me."

"How were our parents about that?"

"Dad was vaguely worried but mostly inept, as always. Mom was livid but couldn't really do anything about it."

"Sounds familiar," I said. "Any advice?"

"Just do *you*, boo. I mean, be safe, but—you're supposed to be a mess at eighteen."

⌒

I hadn't expected Destiny to be the one to cry.

"I didn't know you were this unhappy," she said. "How did I not see it?"

"I tried really hard to hide it," I said to soothe her. "It didn't occur to me until recently that I didn't have to live like that."

"I should have seen it."

"I should have said it."

"You're my little sister," she sobbed. "It's my job to protect you."

"That's how I was feeling about Lark," I said. "That's why I started that fight in the first place. But you know—we can talk to her, and we can guide her, but she's gonna make mistakes no matter what we do. Maybe they won't even be mistakes to her."

"There's no way I'm letting her get that fucking surgery," Dest growled.

"I hope not," I said. "But soon she's gonna be a grown-up, too."

"Kia, I love you, but you are not a grown-up just because you turned eighteen today."

I laughed. "You know what? I agree."

The longest day ended with soul food night at the Binion-Burkhart house. Tavia's nerdy-cute husband, Quentin, came home, patted me on the back, and then spent the next hour playing peekaboo with Malcolm. He treated me like I'd always been there. It was a quiet gesture that made me feel more at home than anything else.

Merv made his famous oxtail, though he complained while serving it that Elyria produce wasn't up to his usual standards.

"I didn't take you for such a snob, Unc," I teased.

"Thank you!" Tavia exclaimed. "I been tellin' him we're literally in farm country."

"Tell the asparagus that," Merv grumbled. "There's just somethin' missin'."

I liked being at their kitchen table. I learned that Merv was working on starting a restaurant in Cleveland, with this oxtail as part of the menu. Quentin told me all about his work at the air traffic control center (I didn't understand a single word), and Tavia told me she'd recently begun studying environmental law. I learned that night that her laugh sounded exactly like her mom's, and that Miss Carol's eyes lit with pride every time her daughter smiled. I ached knowing I might never have that relationship with my own mother. I mourned what might've been if my father had been the kind of person who could've stood up to her—or if I'd become that person sooner.

Miss Carol kept looking my way, and I knew she was checking in on me, gauging how broken I felt at any given moment. I waited until everyone else at the table was distracted by Malcolm, then squeezed her hand.

"I'm okay," I assured her.

"It's okay if you're not," she said back. I nodded to let her know I heard.

At the end of the meal, I tried to help clean up, but Miss Carol and Merv shooed me away. Miss Carol did the dishes while Merv put Malcolm to sleep, and Tavia and Quentin led me to the living room. They sat me down on their couch, each of them taking one of the two armchairs that flanked the fireplace. It was time. I braced myself to be booted back to California.

"We've given this a lot of thought, and you are welcome to

stay with us for as long as you need," Tavia said. "You will not be rushing out of here, okay?"

"Wait, what?!" I looked between them. "You don't have to do that. I don't want to be an imposition. I can find a hotel, or . . ."

I trailed off. I didn't know where else I could go that would feel half as good as here.

"It's no trouble," Quentin said. He took his glasses off and polished them on his sweater. He reminded me so much of Mr. Hillis. "There's a pullout couch. It's ancient, but it's all yours. I'm going in to work more and more these days anyway."

"Mom's starting her PhD in the fall," Tavia said. "So we were already about to be in a bind. We could use a babysitter, if you're down. Malcolm already loves you."

I nodded, speechless. "I'm so down. That is one cute kid."

I was overwhelmed. *Why were these people being so nice to me?!*

Tavia must have read my expression like a book, because she kept going.

"I know we haven't spent a lot of time together," she said, leaning forward. "But my mama loves you and Lark like you're her own. She wouldn't have stayed workin' for *your* mama so long if she didn't. So I know you've got a whole mess of other sisters, but you can count us as family, too. Always."

My breath came quick and raspy now, and I knew it was only a matter of seconds before I was bawling.

"This could get complicated, though," I explained, my voice cracking. "You should know what you're signing up for. It might be that no one cares I'm here—or there might be paparazzi at your door tomorrow, getting up in your business, digging through the trash . . ."

"We'll cross that bridge if we come to it," Quentin said.

"But—"

"Stop trying to fight it—damn," Tavia laughed. "Actin' like you don't wanna live here."

I laughed. "I would *love* to live here. Thank you. *Thank you.*"

CHAPTER THIRTY-FIVE

Cassius Campbell and I walked together along the edge of the world. Or at least that's what it felt like, looking out as the sun set over Lake Erie. Quentin had directed us to a spot of rocky beach that was mostly deserted in the offseason.

I'd never grasped how big the Great Lakes were, but Erie stretched out so far, it looked as if it would never end. There was a bowling ball in my gut, realizing Cass and I were about to.

We walked in silence until everything we weren't saying came crashing down around us.

Cass stopped in his tracks, his head low and his voice tight. I knew him well enough by now to see that he was mad.

"I know you're breaking up with me," Cass said. "Can we just get to the bad part, please? I can't take the waiting."

I was unsure of where to start. So I just said what I felt.

"I don't want to," I said. "But I have to."

"You *don't* have to," he said, firm in his conviction. "Isn't that the point of all this? You did the brave thing, Kee—you burned your life down! You're gonna stay here; that's great! But didn't you do all this so you'd have the freedom to live *your* way?"

"Yes, but—"

"So why are you running away from *this*?"

"I'm not running!" I insisted. I needed him to understand. "But I refuse to burn your life down alongside mine."

He sucked his teeth, shaking his head. "It doesn't have to burn my life down."

"Your tour is going to be *amazing*," I said. "Eight legs, *two hundred* shows—you'll get to go to almost every major city in the world."

"*And you can come with me,*" Cass pleaded. His voice and my heart both broke.

I breathed *in, in, in, in,* then *out, out, out, out, out, out, out, out.* I needed to keep my wits about me. I needed to make him get this.

I bent to pick up a small, smooth rock. I turned it over in my hand.

"It's two years." I practically whispered it. "You can't be tethered to some girl in Ohio for that long. Or at least you shouldn't be."

I skipped the rock across the water. It sank on the second bounce. I picked up another.

"I could be tethered to you forever," Cass said. It hit me in the gut; I blinked back tears.

"Right back atcha." I choked on the words. "But that's not where we are right now."

I skipped the second rock, and it went a bit farther before disappearing with a *plunk* into the water. I picked up another, and when I straightened, I saw Cass was right beside me again.

"Why can't it be?" he asked. "You can do your thing here, and then come with me to whatever dates you want! You can explore Vienna or Madrid, Bangkok, Mexico City, all while you apply to schools. How is here better than *everywhere*?"

Cass sounded so adamant, like this would solve everything.

"I can't," I said, barely audible.

"Lark's on the second leg! You'd get to spend so much time with her."

In, in, in, out, out, out. Out. Out was the key.

I'd pictured myself in those places every night since I'd gotten to Ohio. I'd tried to work it out in my head, even making lists of things to see in each city. While Cass and Lark were in sound check, I could research schools and brave new places. We could eat every kind of food the world had to offer, and after shows we'd stay up late dancing, talking, watching movies, and plotting out newfound dreams.

It could be a good life. It could be a dream.

But there was no way around the flashing lights. The photographers would follow that tour wherever it went, hungry for snapshots that could make headlines and pad their pockets. Once news broke that I'd quit *Growin' Up,* there'd only be more interest in pictures of me. The only way around it was to not be seen at all.

On tour I'd be in constant motion, dashing between hotels and jets, just like I'd always been. There would be headlines, just like there'd always been. Life would be a constant invasion that I'd spend my days trying to dodge and deflect.

Tears filled my eyes, and this time I didn't try to banish them.

"I can't come with you," I said, my voice full and wet.

Cass broke away, storming down the beach. I didn't follow. I understood what it meant to need space. I understood that his anger was also grief. My heart was breaking, too.

I skipped another rock, and another, and another. Then I took a few steps toward him, and he took a few steps toward me.

Those eyes I loved so much were bloodshot, but when I opened my arms, Cass placed himself in them, tucking his face right into the crook of my neck.

"I want you to have your dream," I said into his hair. "You'll be an *icon*, and you're going to make a difference in so many people's lives, and for you the bad parts are never going to outweigh how much *good* you'll do and feel."

His shoulders shook with sobs. He pulled away, wiping the tears from his face.

"I can't take back who I am." His voice was thick and rough, so far from the silken hello I'd gotten at Lark's birthday eight months before. "Fame's not some reversible thing, not for me *and* not for you, Kia. You can't just disappear."

"Maybe not," I said, shrugging, "but I can't fuel it anymore."

Cass's hands tugged at his hair. He turned away from me again, and I felt helpless against everything that had brought us here.

But that was the opposite of the point. I *could* help this. I could be all the way honest—something it had taken me so long to be, even with myself.

"You have no idea how much you mean to me," I told him, my eyes clouding with tears. "But I've been living my whole life for other people, and I'm afraid if I keep doing that, I won't ever figure out who I'm supposed to be."

He didn't turn back right away. He raised his head to the sky and sniffed.

"What did your mom say when you told her you weren't coming back?"

"She made me feel like I was some problem that needed solving. She's made me feel that way most of my life, actually."

Cass turned back to me now, eyebrows drawn together.

"Fuck that," he said. He pulled me in, and I found a temporary home in the way we held tight to each other, breathing together and memorizing every bit of curve, muscle, and smell.

We found a boulder on the shore big enough to sit on for hours. We stared at the water coming in, in, out, out. The waves here followed the same patterns as the ocean: Created by friction, they'd travel as far as they could manage until they reached shore. Then they'd become something else.

Cass was right: I'd burned my life to the ground and run away. I doubted I'd've ever gotten the guts to do that if I hadn't met Cassius Campbell. He'd brought me back to a part of the world I'd lost.

Now I had to do the rest myself.

"I don't want to drag you back into a world you hate," Cass said quietly after a long silence. "I just . . . I always want to know you."

I smiled to myself.

"We'll always know each other, okay? I promise." I wrapped his pinky finger in mine. "We'll grow, and change, and maybe one day we won't recognize each other anymore—"

"Don't say that."

"Let me finish," I whispered, insistent. "Maybe in a few years we'll be completely different people. That's allowed. But if that happens, we're just going to have to reintroduce ourselves, okay? Because we are *always* going to know each other."

Cass drove me back to my new home, and we buried ourselves in each other's arms one last time. We'd be preserved in each other as exactly who we were in that moment, inseparable and *full*. Something calm and steady moved through me, just like it had that day in the rage room when we'd poured ourselves out to each other. I was certain, with every fiber of my being, that I would carry this with me wherever I went. I'd stitch Cassius Campbell into the lining of my heart, and I would never, ever forget.

CHAPTER THIRTY-SIX

June was the hardest month. May was all logistics—phone calls, shipped boxes from home, Cass and the aftermath of Cass. May was me in the house most days, and then it was an email from the lawyers at Ignite telling me I was in breach of contract. When I refused to come back, May was "a source close to the family" insinuating to *Page Six* that I was in rehab after a mental breakdown.

Then May was a court date: me on a plane back to California, standing in front of a judge with my new lawyer, asking to be released from every single contract my mother had signed for me. It turned out there were child labor laws to protect people like me, ones I hadn't looked into when I thought my mom would eventually see my side. The laws ensured that since I was entered into business deals as a minor, I could no longer be held to them as an adult with her own free will.

My mom didn't show up to court. She didn't even return my calls telling her that I was in town.

June was when I realized I'd left my bedroom for the last time without even knowing it. I didn't know if I'd ever see it again, at least not as it was. I wondered how long my parents would keep the clouds Miss Carol and I had painted on the ceiling.

"Mom really misses you," Lark insisted whenever we talked, which was often. "I think she's just using being mad as a cover."

June was when I realized I might not have a mother anymore. June was when that sucked the breath from me. It knocked me off my feet. Was my mother not a part of me? Wasn't she in my bones, and my blood, and my heart, irrevocably and forever? How could she leave me behind when I needed her the most?

June was when the *Passions* tour started. I'd chosen not to follow the person I loved around the world, and I wondered constantly if I'd made the biggest mistake of my life. Every morning I'd watch all the videos I could find from his show the night before. Cass lit up the stage every single night.

One night he pulled out his acoustic guitar and sang a new song. It was called "Rage." Despite its title, the song was lilting, insistent, and romantic, a neo-soul anthem of lost love.

We can rage against the world, dear
But I'll hold you close
Here, I'll take your weary heart
Your ready soul, eighteen
Is the time to get lost, unclean
We'll wash the world,
A new me, a new you

Summers in Ohio were mercurial. Every day the air was thick with humidity. There wouldn't be a cloud in sight, and then suddenly, somehow, the sky would open, releasing torrents of thunder and rain. I learned this the hard way, again and again: I'd take baby Malcolm to the park down the street. He liked it when I chased him around and made up stories for us to act out on the jungle gym. Then the sky would change and we'd be caught in a real-life epic, drenched through and running for cover, Malcolm's baby laugh ringing in my ears all the way home.

I kept busy babysitting Malcolm and forcibly hiring myself as Merv's unpaid intern. I followed him around various spots in Cleveland as he searched for the perfect location for his new restaurant. When he landed on a place in the Ohio City neighborhood, I was his first big investor. I made a few phone calls, and soon my sisters and father were his second, third, fourth, and fifth.

By July, Malcolm had started calling me Auntie Kee, which made me happy. I'd be his full-time nanny when Miss Carol started her PhD schedule in the fall. I wasn't letting Tavia and Quentin pay me, considering I was still sleeping on the pullout couch in their office. But it felt good to have a job of sorts— a little guy to watch over as he grew into himself, while I tried to do the same; someone who soaked up everything he saw like a sponge for knowledge. Malcolm saw me as exactly who I was to him, nothing more and nothing less. To him, I wasn't the sad girl, the lost Greer, the one who'd run away from her problems. To Malcolm, I was the girl who played.

In August, Destiny showed up at our doorstep, a sleepy Deja on her hip. A driver unloaded suitcase after suitcase from the Escalade behind her.

"Hi," she said, bouncing the fussy toddler. "I rented the house up the street. That cool or nah?"

It was only for a while, she said—but after me, she'd been the most affected by that fight the day of the Met Gala. She'd fired Mom as her manager and backed out of every project shooting in the next few months. She was still contracted for *Growin' Up,* but in between seasons she was taking a beat. So she'd rented the house at the end of the block, a three-bedroom with a porch and a yard Deja could run around in. She invited me to move in, and I took the opportunity to unclog the arteries of the Binion-Burkhart house. Miss Carol could use the office to study.

"I can't believe I didn't see it," she said her first night in Ohio. She was so mad at herself, she was shaking. "I can't raise my kid there. She's not even four and she's already afraid of photographers. What kind of start is that to a life? If she wants to be part of the family circus later, fine—but I want her to be able to *choose* that for herself. You didn't get that choice, did you? Not really."

I'd never seen my otherwise impenetrable older sister cry like she did that night. She cried hardest when we got to the body stuff. Her beautiful daughter had inherited Destiny's old nose, her old chin. She'd never regretted the work she'd had done, but now she worried: Would Deja grow up seeing that Destiny had gotten rid of features she now had on her own body and think she should get rid of them, too?

Destiny needed time to gather and think and heal. The good people of Elyria, Ohio, had no idea what was coming to 'em with Destiny Greer in town.

She'd be okay. So would Deja, and so would I. The sky opened up almost every day here, but I was getting used to it. As quickly as it had started, the rain would stop, and for a time the air would feel fresh and new and *clean.*

CHAPTER THIRTY-SEVEN

That fall Ava Rackham started college just a short drive from the Binion-Burkharts and their new neighbor. I texted Ava in September.

> Hey!!! It's Kia—we met at NYE at
> your house??? I hope it's not weird,
> PLS feel free to block me if it is, but I
> remembered you were going to Oberlin! I
> asked Cass for your number. I'm staying
> in Elyria, which is like 10 minutes away!
> Anyway this is my incredibly awkward
> way of begging you to be my friend. NO
> PRESSURE AT ALL THO!

She texted back right away.

!!!!! KIA! THIS IS THE BEST TEXT EVER. I could really
use a familiar face from back home. Can we hang out
literally this week??? Is that too soon?!

Oberlin is a liberal arts college tucked away in a tiny town of the same name. I'd used some of my savings to buy a car of my own, a sensible hybrid that would give me plenty of mileage for road trips back east to visit Sola. On the day Ava and I set to meet, I drove the nine miles between home and campus and parked on a sleepy side road ironically called Hollywood Street. I couldn't have been farther from my old world, but for the first time since moving to Ohio, I was branching out, testing the vast perimeters of my new life. I was just beginning to touch its endless possibilities.

I walked across campus to a small quad surrounded by tan-stoned castles. It was the kind of crisp fall day you don't get in Los Angeles, and the leaves had just started to turn. This world was Technicolor.

I pulled the brim of my hat lower on my forehead. I'd gone with no makeup and big glasses in hopes that would throw people off the scent of wayward celebrity.

I did have an advantage here, though, in this town of fewer than nine thousand people: No one expected me. I caught a few stray glances from passersby, but my eyes would meet theirs and they'd look away, probably dismissing me as someone who just happened to look kinda like that one girl. Because why would Kiara Greer be here?

I stood in the center of the quad and let myself look around. I breathed through the fear of reprisal or sudden attack I'd come to accept was innate in me after years of stalker stories and mobbed crowds. I could try to train myself out of it, but that would take time. So meanwhile, I let myself hope that the likelihood of disaster was slim to none here. There were no paparazzi for five hundred miles. *Of course you're afraid,* I told myself, *but you're going to be okay.*

Even if someone did recognize me, I could handle it. I'd been through too much not to own who I was. My life was mine now; I was making choices for myself. Maybe someday I'd be able to stop living life on the defensive.

It was eleven a.m., and I was standing in the middle of the campus's beating heart. Some students lay on the grass, sunning themselves in the autumn light, books and laptops open in front of them. Others hustled to class, flying by on bikes or walking with groups of friends. One person in a maxi skirt and glasses just like mine strode past with purpose on their face and a Lark Greer song blasting from their headphones. I smiled to myself and texted my little sister right then and there.

Something tugged at my chest. Was it regret? Longing? I couldn't tell, but it was welling up inside me, pooling behind my eyes. This was the world I'd dreamed of, the one my own fear—and my mother's—had stolen from me. Could I get back to it one day?

"You made it!"

I recognized the calming timbre of her voice instantly. I turned and was greeted by Ava's perfectly imperfect grin. She'd chopped her blond hair into a shaggy pixie cut, and just like the first time I'd met her, she was wearing overalls. This time they were denim patchwork instead of silver lamé. She swept me into her arms just like Cass had done to her on New Year's, and relief flooded my bones.

"It's so good to see you!" I exclaimed in sloppy exuberance. When the hug was over, she took my face in both her hands.

"Are you kidding?! It's so good to see *you*! Being a freshman is so weird—it's like 'Here's this whole new universe and a thousand new people, have fun, don't drown!' I'm so happy to see someone I even kind of knew before, y'know?"

"I really do." I nodded.

"I got us a picnic!" she said. "Will you eat it in Tappan with me? You'll probably get less stares there."

"Sure!" I chirped, enthusiastic. "What's Tappan?"

Tappan Square, it turned out, was the park that sat between the college campus and the small T-bone of shops and restaurants Oberlin called a downtown. A big curved white stone memorial beckoned us in, and I followed Ava toward a gazebo-looking bandstand in the square's northeast corner. We'd just started up the stairs when some sort of small white mythical creature ran across my foot. I gasped and stumbled backward.

"WHATISTHAT?" I yelled, grabbing a guardrail to regain my balance.

"You saw an albino squirrel!" Ava said, holding the hem of my T-shirt so I wouldn't fall. "That's good luck. They're our mascot."

"Oh," I laughed, "okay. Cool?"

We settled into the center of the gazebo. My heartbeat calmed as Ava spread out the haul of sandwiches, chips, and smoothies she'd brought for us.

"Let me pay you back for this," I said, "because I promise you I am gonna *devour* those chips. Like, it's about to get feral."

"Pfft," she said through a massive bite of sandwich. She held up a finger and I waited with a goofy smile as she chewed and swallowed before continuing. "This was all meal swipe, baybeee. Nothing to pay back."

"Are you sure? 'Cause—"

"Pay me back in tea," Ava said with a soft chuckle. "Are you and Cassie friends yet?"

I puffed my cheeks with air and slowly blew the air out.

"We're getting there," I said. "We both needed time, especially as he got settled on tour and I acclimated to . . . all this."

"And now?" Ava asked, her mouth full again.

"He gave me your number, and ever since then we've been texting more. Updates on our lives, memes that remind us of each other—y'know, stuff like that."

"That's great! You're on track!"

"I hope so," I admitted, melting a little. "I miss him."

Ava smiled knowingly and I distracted myself with my own big bite of sandwich. Then it was my turn to talk with my mouth full.

"Whatboutyou?" I attempted to ask. I swallowed. "What happened between you and Kenzie? Last I saw, y'all were mauling each other in the pool."

A bright pink blush crawled up Ava's ears. Then she burst into the most radiant smile.

"Oop!" I chirped. "You gotta tell me."

Ava and I talked for hours, until resounding bells in one of the campus castles announced it was three p.m. This meant Ava had to head to a class she told me was called How to Win a Beauty Pageant: Race, Gender, Culture, and U.S. National Identity.

"That's a class?" I asked. "That sounds so cool."

"Yeah, it's really hard but *really* good," she said. "In a few weeks we're going on a field trip to the Miss Gay Ohio drag pageant in Columbus."

"Whaaat?! That's amazing."

Ava hugged me tight. "Please come back," she said. "I'm serious. There are some really cool people here, but I also really wanna be your friend, please."

"I really wanna be your friend, too," I replied, beaming.

I kept my promise. Ava and I made a standing weekly friend appointment that soon spiraled into more of an all-the-time hang situation. With Ava, I went to concerts—a cappella shows, opera performances, jazz recitals, and the occasional scoring of a silent film with a live metal orchestra. I met her for trivia night at Oberlin's Slow Train Cafe. Sometimes I'd go there alone and just read for hours.

By midway through her first semester, I'd treated Ava to every restaurant in town, and eventually her friends became mine, too. There was Krutika, a former color guard champion from the Pittsburgh suburbs who always had a D&D game going, and Justin, an athlete who'd traded a storied sports career for a double major in cinema studies and neuroscience. Then there was Chioma, a self-professed pop culture addict from Portland. She found it especially surreal when she suddenly started having late-night philosophical conversations with a former fixture of her favorite gossip tabloids, but the two of us never ran out of things to say.

Together my new friends snuck me into nights at the 'Sco, Oberlin's only club, and we'd dance until the wee hours of the morning, sweating till we were soaked through. We screamed extra hard when songs by Lark or Cass would come on. We'd stumble across campus, cackling and singing and talking over each other, and I'd sleep like a baby on the couch in the common room of Ava's quad suite. I even made flash cards and spent long nights with them in the campus library, helping them study, or studying myself for the online college courses Mr. Hillis had helped me sign up for.

Of course people caught on that I was me. I drew some confused and judgmental looks. A handful of people came up to tell me they loved me on the most recent season of the show, which was finally airing. By the time it happened, I found that it didn't really bother me. A few shots of me on campus or in town circulated on social media, but whenever they picked up traction, Sola would conveniently be spotted kissing someone new. I sent her flowers every time, and she'd respond with a text telling me the only payback she wanted was a visit from me soon.

Famous was just part of who I was, but here it didn't have to define me. No paparazzi showed up, maybe because there were no other celebs around to justify the cost of the plane tickets, or maybe there was just always another scandal that needed chasing. After a few weeks no one really cared. Slowly but surely that knot in my chest unraveled, and I was just another young person eating dinner at the Feve.

The first snowstorm came in November. It blanketed the whole world in white and didn't let up until the semester let out. I took a local driver's ed class to learn how to drive in the snow. I spent a lot of days making blanket forts with Malcolm, or taking over loading boxes into the empty space that would become Merv's new restaurant so he wouldn't break a hip. Lark flew in for Thanksgiving, and this strange offshoot of my family ate with Miss Carol's family, trading stories about her PhD program, Lark's newly released chart-climbing album, and my growing circle of friends.

⌒⌒⌒

"Hey," I said one night when Ava walked me to where I'd parked the car. "Would it be weird . . . I've just been thinking . . . Do you think I could apply here?"

"I've only been waiting this whole time for you to say that," Ava said.

So, about Oberlin . . . I texted Mr. Hillis as soon as I got home. Will you write me a recommendation?

He responded immediately. YES. YES. YES. I HAVE BEEN WAITING WITH BATED BREATH FOR THIS MOMENT. YES. KIARA, YOU HAVE MADE ME A VERY HAPPY MAN.

Calm down, nerd :), I told him. But I was laughing.

Oberlin didn't accept first-year students for the spring semester, so I'd have to wait till the fall to start classes. But I could do it. I was happy here. I didn't feel like a grown-up, not yet, even after everything. I was still so unfinished. I had all this money and all these bruises from who I'd been before, but who I was here was entirely mine. I was in the process of becoming, and I was excited to meet every new version of myself that would come.

Are you sure the essay's ready??? I texted Jade that fall, nervous. She was in her senior year back home, but we still FaceTimed whenever we got the chance.

BITCH IF YOU DON'T SEND THAT DAMN THING, she wrote back.

I submitted my application for early decision on November first, and I couldn't help but remember the cloud cover I'd been living under the same time the year before.

There was still a lot I missed about home. I missed the smell, the eucalyptus and pine, chaparral and night-blooming jasmine of our mountain.

I missed my family most of all. My dad hadn't skipped a beat; he'd kept FaceTiming three times a week like he always had. I was still mad at him; he hadn't had the strength to stand up for his daughters when we'd most needed him. I don't think he even realized how absent he'd been in our lives. One day I'd be able to confront him about all the ways he'd hurt me. For now, though, I kept taking the calls. We never got too deep. I'd tell him about my new life and the books I was reading, and he'd smile and nod along as if nothing had changed, regaling me with stories from his film sets. It wasn't perfect; it wasn't even enough. But I promised myself we'd get there eventually.

I still didn't talk to my mom. She didn't reach out. Whenever I needed a box of my things shipped from home, she'd reroute the issue through her new house manager. I was fast developing too much pride to be the first to bend. Maybe I really was Melora Greer's daughter.

I mourned what we could have been and what we no longer were. I knew she loved me. My new therapist had helped me realize love wasn't enough. She had to accept me, too—all of me, even the parts that didn't fit her plans.

Some days, though, I missed her so much I could barely think. She'd made me who I was, and now she wasn't there to see what I was becoming. Still, that had been her choice just as much as it had been mine.

So I could miss home. It was only natural. So, too, was moving forward, finding new places to unfurl parts of myself I hadn't even known were there. Finding new ways to breathe.

⌒

The notification came February first.

Dear Kiara Greer,

Congratulations! I am pleased to inform you that you have been accepted to Oberlin College's Class of 2030.

I GOT IN. I was making PB&Js for Deja and Malcolm when I found out, and I screamed so loud Destiny came careening down the stairs in a panic. I buckled over laughing, squeaking out half-hearted apologies through my hysteria.

"If this isn't about college—" Destiny wheezed, "I am going to kill you."

"Auntie Kee went crazy," Deja said with a shady sip of her apple juice.

"Yes she did," I agreed, still holding my side laughing.

"She get into college, though?!" Dest demanded.

"YES SHE DID!" I hollered. Destiny screamed then, with her whole chest. She threw me over her shoulder and spanked my butt in triumph. Malcolm clapped as if he was getting his own personal show.

"You're too strong!" I cackled. "Let me down!"

"My sister's going to college, my sister's going to college," she chanted, carrying me around the airy dining room of our rental house. "Smarty-pants, smarty-pants, smarty-pants—Oop!" she said, suddenly stopping. "I'm still on a call with my exec."

"Go do that!" I giggled, squirming out of her arms.

Destiny Greer was in the process of starting her own production company, Bitchcamp Co., a banner under which she could produce and star in movies on her own terms. She'd be in control of where she went and who she worked with, and the company was preparing to take a public stance against asking actors to lose weight for roles. She was also already working on a retelling of the story of Cleopatra, as interpreted through the genre tropes of Blaxploitation. She was staying in Ohio for the year as she got it off the ground, and then she and Deja would start a very *Gilmore Girls* kinda life somewhere in small-town Connecticut, away from prying eyes.

I caught my breath as Destiny bounded back upstairs. I still smiled ear to ear. *I GOT IN! I GOT IN, I GOT IN, I GOT IN.*

I was still getting used to the feeling of knowing exactly what

I wanted to do next. I was so *sure*—and then I was doing it. I was actually doing it.

That Monday I started a scholarship fund. I had money sitting in savings, some from *Growin' Up* but most from years of brand deals, collabs, and paid appearances. I didn't need all of it. I'd keep enough that I didn't have to worry, but the rest could pay for dozens of other people to attend the schools of their dreams. I'd found my way here; now hopefully they could, too.

EPILOGUE

Four days after my twentieth birthday, I woke with a groan. The early-morning sun was shining right into my eyes. I pulled the covers over my head and told myself it was okay to miss class, even if it was my favorite, Visible Bodies and the Politics of Sexuality. I could sleep another two hours and rally in time for History of Science.

I'd been so excited in my first year of real-life, in-person, actual college that I'd made the fatal mistake of signing up for eight a.m. classes every day of the week. Most often this was doable, because for the first time in my life I was actually sleeping long, well, and often. On Saturday, though, Ava and our roommates Chioma and Anna had thrown a house party in my honor. We'd planned to rest on Sunday; instead Anna'd driven us to Steak 'n Shake, and the four of us stayed up until three a.m. downing burgers and milkshakes, dyeing our hair over the sink. It was a perfect night, but now my curls were auburn and I had a sneaking suspicion I was lactose intolerant. Class was simply not in the cards.

BANGBANGBANG—there was a knock at the door. I groaned and burrowed deeper under the covers. A morning like this was the time for deep denial.

"COME ON." Chioma banged on the door. I groaned louder in response, but this did not deter her. "YOU TOLD ME TO YELL AT YOU IF YOU TRIED TO SKIP THIS CLASS. LET'S GOOOOO."

Damn it. I had said that. I groaned one final time and rolled out of bed. I stumbled over the pile of presents I had to open today, because no matter how far away I moved, I'd never be able to stop my family from spoiling me.

I managed to squeeze in a few bites of leftover birthday cake for breakfast. We were on our way by seven-forty-five. Plenty of time on a campus this small.

The end of winter in Ohio always came later than you wanted, but when spring finally broke through, it was the sweetest reward. It had been two summers, two falls, two winters, and now two springs here, and I'd transformed within this place. Maybe I'd stopped growing taller back in LA, but my cells felt all new; all of me had expanded and grown in the flatlands of the Midwest.

It wasn't like I felt so mature now. I didn't, not yet, even though I was technically an adult. But I'd thrust myself forward, into a world I didn't understand, and every day I was finding my way through. I was studying, working, and playing. I was going to parties and sometimes kissing strangers long into the night. I'd even danced one dawn on the shore of Lake Erie. There was so much more of me still to meet, and I knew now that I had what it took to let her happen.

Still, I had regrets. I had run away, and now I was worried I might have left behind parts of myself that were worth keeping. I finally understood what nostalgia really meant: It was a yearning for home, a pain for something you couldn't get back to.

Just because I'd left, it didn't mean that part of my life never mattered. I told myself I wasn't abandoning the girl I'd been; I was fulfilling her wildest dreams.

The walk to campus that day was green and aromatic. The town was still quiet. Dew sat pert on the grass. Chioma regaled me for the fifteenth time with details of a fight she'd gotten into with her cinema studies advisor, who'd disappeared to Antarctica to make a documentary and hadn't bothered to tell any of her advisees. Chioma had a way with stories; I could listen to her talk forever.

It's why I didn't notice them, at first, when I ran up the white stone steps to class.

"Hey," a silky voice said from behind, right as I was reaching for the door.

I froze. I turned, slowly, not quite believing what I'd just heard.

Cass. *Cass.* Cassius Campbell, in the middle of rural Ohio, sitting on the steps of the King Building, completely unbothered by the gaping stares of students passing by.

I don't know how I'd missed them, except I'd thought they were still on tour, off in Stockholm or Hamburg. Instead they were here, those eyes boring into me with an intensity I hadn't seen in almost two years.

"I'll meet you inside," Chioma squeaked. I'd never heard her *squeak* before. "Or not. Probably not, I'm guessing."

"I'll see you later," I told her, and she went inside, a *WTF* grin bursting from her face.

I turned to Cass and stared for a few beats too long. Then I laughed.

"Hi. Sorry. You've got me all kindsa discombobulated."

"Hi," Cass said, soft and true.

CASS IS HERE, my heart screamed. *CASS IS HERE FOR YOU.*

A warm smile spread across their face, and that thing shot through my body like a lightning bolt. A shiver went up my spine as they stood up.

"You can go to class, you know," they said. "We can talk after. I saw a good coffee shop along the main strip."

My lips cracked at the edges from smiling so hard. Cass was still standing with a certain unsure nervousness, their hands stuffed deep in the pockets of their embroidered jean jacket. An absolute clarity came over me, the kind I relished: I knew exactly what I wanted to do, and I did it. I lunged forward and wrapped my arms tight around one of my absolutely favorite people, and I didn't let go until their breath synced back up with mine, our hearts beating wildly against one another.

Orange blossoms. Cass still smelled the same.

We pulled away, laughing.

"I mauled you," I said. "I'm not sorry this time, though."

"I'm not mad about it," they said, retrieving the book bag I'd dropped in my attack.

I noticed a new piercing at their eyebrow—a little change in them that reminded me of all the changes big and small we'd missed in each other.

"That coffee shop you mentioned's called Slow Train," I said. "We're going there together, and we're going to catch up."

"You got bossy," Cass said.

"Yeah, well, part of Melora was bound to sneak in there."

Something inscrutable crossed over Cass's face, and then they were the one hugging me.

"What's this for?" I asked.

"Part of me was afraid you'd send me away again."

I took Cass's jaw in my hand and marveled once again at the

exquisite shape of it—sharp as cut glass but soft to the touch. That face, so legendary in its beauty—and yet, when they looked at me, so warm and tender, I always felt seen. Everything about Cassius Campbell was larger than life—their beauty, their talent, the legacy they were building—and somehow Cass had never, ever left me feeling small. They'd only ever helped me expand. And they were still expanding, too, breaking down barriers around gender and sexuality every time they appeared onstage.

We got looks as students passed by. Of course we did. It didn't matter here, two years in. Both of us honest, free, and wholly ourselves. I wasn't afraid of what anyone would say, or where the clandestine photos they were taking would go. *Cass was here.*

Tell me, what is it you plan to do with your one wild and precious life?

This. Everything here and now was what I planned to do.

"I've been waiting to reintroduce myself," I said. Cass closed their eyes, turning to smile into my open palm. "Are you ready for that?"

"I'm in if you are," they said. "I've missed you."

"Bet," I said, giving them my best Cassius Campbell impression. "LET'S GOOOOOO."

I grabbed their hand and tugged them toward my favorite place as Cass's laugh echoed through the quad.

ACKNOWLEDGMENTS

When I first sat down to write this book it was the summer of 2022. I was burnt-out—burnt to a crisp, really—and I needed an escape. One of the escapes I found was Kia. For the first time in a long time I allowed myself to write for fun, building out a world and a fictional family I couldn't wait to spend all my time with. I am so grateful for each and every person who has made this book possible in the days and years since.

Thank you to my agent, Julia Kardon, who I met in 2016 and who has *very* patiently been waiting for my first book ever since. Thank you to my editor, Katherine Harrison; your belief in and guidance of this book means more to me than you'll ever know. Your collaboration on this project is felt on every page in the best way. Thank you to every single person at Knopf and Penguin Random House whose eyes and work contributed to this book seeing the light of day—I don't know every single one of your names, but I am grateful to all of you. Some names I do know from those teams: Kris Kam, Stephania Villar, Spiros Halaris, Amy Schroeder, Jenna Stempel-Lobell, Lauren Klein. Thank you to Regan Aliyah, whose voice brought Kia to life for the audiobook—it has been an honor to watch you thrive from our shared land of *XO, Kitty*, and I'm still over the moon that you joined me here as well. Thank you, also, to my writers' group, my unfailing creative support group. You are all so very hot. Thank you to Eesha and Saron, whose early reads of *TEOKG* helped me make it what it is today. Thank you to Siobhan Vivian, for championing me through trying to sell this thing, and to Jenny Han, for inspiring me. Taking it way back on the inspiration track: Thank you to my English teachers throughout the years, especially Lisa Souther and David Hillis, for those first glimmers of passion for writing that ignited in your classrooms, and for the encouragement that helped me chase them.

Thank you to my mother, Linda Bennett, for aiding and abetting each and every one of my lofty dreams while I was growing up. It instilled in me a deep delusion that anything I dream of I can make happen. Without that energy this book would not exist. Thank you, also, to my fiancé and the love of my life, Justin Casselle. Cassius is called Cass because of you; Cass smells like orange blossoms because of you. Your eyes were on practically every draft of this book, and you held me through each of the breakdowns I had when I thought I couldn't do it. Thank you for being who you are.

It feels so strange to say goodbye to Kia. I will love her forever, my sweet anxious girl. I hope she thrives—and I hope we get to meet again. Above all, even if you can't relate to the extravagances of Kia's life . . . I hope that you, dear reader, were still able to find something valuable in reading the journey of a girl trying to figure out what she wants out of life. I know I did.